CW01521147

Q-Day

By

Colin Isard

LEGAL DISCLAIMER

Some names, groups, characters, products, and events—including but not limited to "Corvus", "Hammerfall", "Sang", "Tiroclaw", and "Vectraxis" in this book—are entirely fictional. They do not represent, nor do they intend any connection, direct or indirect, to any person, musical band, company, entity, event, or thing, whether living, deceased, real, fictional, past, or present.

When real elements are mentioned, such as weaponry, real places, products, or established technological entities (e.g., the FBI, MI5, NSA, SAS, Harvard, Oxford, and 'The Cloud'), their portrayal is solely a product of the author's imagination. Any associated events in relation to these elements should not be taken as factual representations of their current activities or capabilities. These depictions are based only on publicly available information and/or creative interpretation and do not reflect or imply any direct knowledge of their actual practices, internal operations, or proprietary information.

PROLOGUE

The twenty-first century dawned not with a roar but with a whisper, a misplaced confidence cloaking humanity in fragile, tragic unawareness. Beneath the surface ticked a cataclysm poised to shatter destiny itself—a reckoning far beyond the political chess games of the age.

From East to West, governments and elites alike—from shadowed halls of power to the gleaming spires of finance—stood laughably unprepared. They were blind to a profound genetic reckoning buried deep within the blueprint of life itself.

This fatal oversight sprang from a single, lethal arrogance: humanity's unchallenged faith in its own design. A minority birthed this conceit, yet the majority drank deeply from its poisoned well. What began in corridors of power soon spilled into the hearts of the willing. Humanity, drunk on its own reflection, crowned its inventions flawless and its hubris wisdom.

Not all were oblivious, but the elite mindset trickled down, fuelled by those who saw power as an end in itself. This hubris, written across the enduring struggle—the age-old human conflict spanning history, the battle for dominance, control, and survival driven by greed, ambition, and inequality—mirrored the relentless contest over land, power, and wealth.

In this new millennium, that timeless struggle had curdled into a tyrannical oligarchy, a hegemony of wealth and influence masquerading as progress. Innovation was shackled to the profit of the few, extracted at the expense of the many, and truth itself had become a commodity traded in markets of manipulation.

The most powerful elites, driven by insatiable hunger, codified their dominance through socioeconomic policies designed for self-serving gain. They wielded media and legislation not merely to control, but to psychologically subjugate, manufacturing a world where the gulf between the 'haves' and 'have-nots' became unbridgeable.

Their policies, propelled by an unquenchable thirst to monopolise every conceivable form of capital, created a fiscal inversion that impoverished the masses while enriching themselves. The subversion was quiet, slow, nearly complete: a democracy suffocated by unseen hands. Freedoms eroded, counter-narratives were silenced, and the collective conscience fractured under deliberate mistrust.

Their plan unfolded with military precision, plunging the world into financial and political anguish—'harvest time' for their greed. Their criminality knew no bounds.

Yet their rapacious pack mentality might prove their downfall. The hunters could become the hunted—not by the subjugated masses they despised, but by something far more intimate, buried deep within us all: our DNA.

Unbeknownst to them, the greatest secret lay not in banks or parliaments, but in the lab. At the millennium's turn, the Human Genome Project mapped the human genome, unveiling far more than anyone had bargained for. Vast stretches of genetic code baffled scientists and were dismissed as 'junk DNA'—a lazy, dangerous conclusion.

Persistent curiosity, however, fuelled clandestine projects probing this so-called 'genetic dark matter.' Slowly, complex message codes began to emerge, sparking rumours in classified circles that human DNA might bear a manufacturer's stamp—a revelation so profound it hinted at a countdown: an imminent, species-wide event known only as Q-Day. Whether this event would be a blessing or a catastrophe remained unknown.

If a genetic blueprint existed, was everything planned? Was every design already rendered? The answers eluded even the most brilliant minds.

The elites, convinced they alone had orchestrated society for their own gain, now questioned whether this blueprint—the Q-Day Algorithm—was the true source of their wealth and ambition. Their socio-political hegemony, their oligarchic grip on power, could unravel if the genetic outcome did not favour them.

Desperate to seize the prize, they schemed to capture research from independent university teams already harnessing supercomputers and cutting-edge technology in a frantic, secret race.

Whoever cracked the code first may hold the key to immeasurable rewards: financial might and dominion beyond even the wildest dystopian dreams. Yet whether this power would cement control or unleash unpredictable change remained uncertain.

Why settle for mere control of society when the biological keys to absolute power might lie within their grasp? The alternative—non-elites wielding the code—was too dreadful to contemplate, threatening to unravel the very foundation of their authority.

There was no time to lose. The race was on, and the clock was ticking down to Q-Day.

787-9 Overture

The silken whir of the four Rolls-Royce Trent 1000 engines effortlessly carried the 787-9 Dreamliner from Boston to Heathrow. Their hypnotic lullaby and velvety embrace lulled the weary first-class passengers into a welcome slumber.

Among the privileged few in first class was Professor Michael Adams, who had accepted the invitation with a quiet, almost desperate gratitude. An eminent geneticist at Harvard University, he carried the fatigue of a man long burdened by brilliance and unrelenting expectation.

This flight across the Atlantic was not merely travel. It was a personal pilgrimage, a long-awaited opportunity to reconnect with his close friend and fellow academic, Professor Peter Magma, who held a similarly distinguished position at Oxford University.

Michael had first met Peter during their undergraduate years at Oxford. What began as a straightforward, platonic friendship deepened over time, especially during their doctoral work. Their ideas had moved in concert, forming patterns as intricate as constellations, traced in long hours beneath the ancient, vaulted ceilings of Oxford's libraries and lecture halls.

Though their upbringings had been vastly different, their minds worked in perfect alignment. A shared devotion to scholarship bound them, and in time, they thought and moved with the quiet precision of a single intellect.

Professor Adams, unfailingly courteous but quietly determined, had emerged from a working-class household in Borehamwood, Hertfordshire. Born in 1970, he showed little academic promise in his early years. Then, around the age of twelve, something shifted. A spark of intense focus ignited within him, marking the beginning of a relentless hunger for learning.

Almost overnight, he transformed from a disengaged student into a voracious learner, driven by a need to understand that defied simple explanation. For years, the source of that drive remained a mystery. Only later, through his studies in gene function and behaviour, did he begin to suspect its origins. He came to believe that certain unique genetic interactions had hardwired him with an innate compulsion to pursue knowledge and achievement.

He often wondered how much further his progress might have reached if Tim Berners-Lee had invented the World Wide Web a decade earlier. In those days, knowledge had to be earned the hard way. Research meant long afternoons spent in crowded libraries, poring over dense volumes and outdated texts, scribbling notes by hand, and sifting through disorganized shelves where the books he needed were often missing or misfiled.

Despite the obstacles, his persistence paid off. He passed all twelve O Levels with top marks. Only then did his parents truly grasp the full force of his ambition. Their support, already unwavering, grew even stronger. His mother took on evening shifts at the local bakery, her hands aching with fatigue. His father, ever practical, adjusted the household budget with careful precision, even giving up his weekly pint at the pub to help cover the costs of his son's growing academic journey.

They poured their dreams and sacrifices into acquiring precious reference books and hiring tutors to fuel his pursuit of five science-based A Levels. As with his O Levels, he didn't merely excel—he soared, earning straight "A" grades, some reaching the very pinnacle nationally.

Oxford beckoned, drawing together his passions for biology, evolution and mathematics into a vast intellectual constellation. His degree became an exhilarating journey, a treasure hunt uncovering hidden truths. His subsequent DPhil was awarded with the rare distinction *summa cum laude*. Although this accolade is more commonly associated with American universities, it stood as a powerful testament to the exceptional calibre of his scholarly work.

Yet, in that moment, the brilliance of his past achievements faded beneath the overwhelming urge for rest aboard the 787-9 to London. Indeed, Professor Michael Adams simply craved the embrace of his seat, F4. A lie-flat bed would have been ideal, but prior commitments meant a standard booking. Now, however, the need for sleep asserted its undeniable dominion, and he silently surrendered to oblivion.

With just an hour before landing, his sleep was rudely broken by two sensations: a sharp prod, then a rough shove against his ribs. Groggily, Professor Adams's eyes snapped open, a knot of dread tightening inside him. "What's happening?" he thought, the question a sudden, unwelcome jolt.

'Wake up!' The man's voice cut through Adams's peace, raw and desperate. Sweat streamed down his flushed, unshaven face, flickering in Adams's widening gaze.

Beads of sweat traced down the man's flushed cheeks, briefly catching Adams's eye—then something stranger happened: the droplets seemed to recoil from his wild eyes, as if repelled by the boiling hate behind them. Those eyes burned with a terrifying internal fire, madness festering deep within his mind. His breath hit Adams like a physical blow—

a noxious, sewer-like stench that clawed at his throat, suffocating his awakening senses. It seemed to rise from a putrid, unseen abyss lurking within him.

Before Adams could fully process the terror gripping his mind, a sharp, blunt force slammed into his left side once again. A searing pain blossomed, serving as an instant, brutal reminder of the fragile vulnerability of his ribs. His gaze dropped, drawn by instinctual dread, to a small handgun, its cold metallic glint a promise of violence. It looked like a Glock 19, but he needed no expertise to understand its true function: the chilling termination of life.

An adrenaline surge flooded Adams's middle-aged body, untrained for combat yet desperate to fight back against the looming threat. Yet, honouring his primal instinct for survival, he did not—he was clearly outgunned.

'Stand up!' The command ripped through the air, a militant roar from the assailant. Sweat coursing down his face seemed to carve deliberate paths, mirroring the stark, unyielding order in his voice.

Even before Adams could process the intent in the attacker's demented eyes, he felt mounting pain from the pressure of a gun against his ribs. Adding to the pressure, the foul stench of the attacker overpowered and diminished any desire to retaliate.

He now felt a powerful hand on his left shoulder, its gripping force slightly softened by his Gucci suit jacket. The bruiser's right hand was remarkably strong, lifting Adams to a standing position without conscious effort.

Adams fixed his gaze on the assailant's extraordinarily large right hand. It sprawled over the top of his left shoulder, swallowing the tailored cut of the suit's collar and lapel. The crushed fold of the left lapel seemed to plead for help—a

4

silent cry Adams felt deep in his own chest. This stark display of dominance made him feel unbearably small, inadequate, and trapped within a surreal nightmare.

'You, Professor Adams, yes?' the aggressor growled, his maddening eyes boring into Adams's mind, demanding an answer.

Without hesitation, Adams nodded—an act of appeasement, knowing any other response could ignite an already volatile situation.

'Come with me!' the assailant commanded, anger burning with a ferocity Adams had never known.

'Er, yes, sure!' Adams stammered, torn from his first-class seat. He offered no resistance as the assault consumed him. His research papers—once neatly stacked in his lap—scattered to the floor. Each sheet fluttered down like fallen leaves, silent echoes of a world breaking apart.

Roughly shoved toward the half-open cockpit door, frightened and dazed, Adams's trained mind pierced through the chaos, catching sight of several alarming details.

First, the flight attendant who had served him a drink before his ill-fated slumber lay motionless on her back. Unresponsive. Her presence now eerily still amid the growing din. A chilling thought cleaved through his terror: "Was she dead?"

Then his eyes settled on five other figures—three men and two women—whom he instantly recognised as the aggressors. Heat shimmered off them like a living haze. Their shouted commands rose into a deafening crescendo, swallowing the cabin.

They brandished guns, their presence a dark, malevolent force amid the spiralling chaos.

Were explosives strapped to their chests?

5

Then something caught his eye—scribbled in unfamiliar handwriting across the top sheet of his scattered research papers: "Sophia Sterling. Oliver Parker. SASBA059." He stared at the names, confused. He hadn't written them. A chill threaded down his spine. Who had?

Consumed by terror and the burden of everyone's safety, any thought of surrender was swiftly drowned beneath a rising tide of retaliation. His self-discipline dissolved as adrenaline surged through him, unleashing a primal urge to survive. His suppressed will erupted like a volcano as he launched into a desperate fight, punching and kicking wildly. The air pulsed, charged with a violent electricity.

The chaotic drone of the armed assailants suddenly rose into a terrifying chorus: 'Kill him!' They surged forward, a tide of malevolence intent on overwhelming and silencing Adams. In the struggle that followed, their bodies crashed into seats and ricocheted off walls, a frantic and brutal dance within the confined space.

Despite his frantic struggle, Adams was swiftly overpowered, his resistance collapsing beneath the sheer weight of force. He was hurled like a ragdoll towards the cockpit door, his head slamming against the unforgiving metal with a sickening thud. Yet in that fleeting moment of impact, a strange, disorienting calm descended. He felt no pain—only the slow, inevitable pull of the dark.

- 2 -
A Royal Wake Up

'Dad, for God's sake, wake up, will you!' loudly pleaded his concerned daughter Elizabeth.

She had worriedly returned to the family mansion in West Cambridge, Massachusetts, from a cancelled dinner in Boston, where she now found her father in a profoundly deep sleep. To emphasise her displeasure, she waved her clutch bag emphatically above her head as she spoke.

'You were supposed to meet me for a leaving dinner... remember! You know, Dad, perhaps you meant a leaving dinner literally, as you missed yours and I had to leave to come back here!'

'Oh my God, that's so awful!' Adams managed, with as much energy as he could muster, as the terror from his diminishing sleepy state receded.

'Awful? You're damn right. I waited for an hour at the Royals Restaurant, and no dad, no man, no friends, no bloody anything! I phoned you, and guess what—no answer. I even phoned for company as obviously you weren't available, but they were all busy at various family restaurant gatherings. I feel so outcast at the moment; I bet if I had God on speed dial, I'd be put on voicemail! Argh! Is irony your middle name?' Elizabeth continued to remonstrate.

'The Royals' smartly-attired diners made me feel so awful. It was almost as if I could hear their collective thoughts – "Was she stood up? Ignored?" Get the picture, oh invisible father?'

The silver lining to this disdainful outpouring of emotional upset was that Adams had time to gather his thoughts into a more mechanical and linear way. This would hopefully appease the very real, and potentially explosive, situation with his unhappy daughter.

'Bambina, I just had a nightmare!' said Adams, as if pleading for clemency and a reprieve from any further vitriolic judgement from her. Moreover, addressing her as Bambina, a nickname she cherished from very early childhood, would quell her emotional stance, which was analogous to verbal warfare across two personality trenches.

Elizabeth gave little thought to her father's slow return to full consciousness as she continued her remonstrance.

'Nightmare you say?! Did it involve your daughter and Royals Restaurant by any chance?' she questioned, her folded arms and a stare that could freeze Earth's core making it clear that negotiation was not an option.

Adams had seen all this before and laughed quietly to himself before replying, 'I dreamt I was on a London flight to see Peter. Then, and without warning, I was attacked you know!'

'By me, I hope? Oh yes, do laugh, at least that would be better than just falling asleep as if you couldn't be bothered.'

At last, Adams had woken enough to assemble his thoughts and explain the situation more clearly.

'Look, I'm sorry, Bambina, but please appreciate that my mind and body sometimes want to be in two places—that's just my life. I get tired, just like you do. I just fell asleep on my return from work. In fact, my current project is fast evolving into a transformative state driven by research, impacting my life, your life, and honestly, everyone's lives. I need my rest, just as much as you do.'

Elizabeth watched him, a thoughtful resignation settling over her. She loved her father dearly, despite his flaws. He was a brilliant academic, certainly imperfect, and she often wished he possessed the ability to be in two places at once – a wish she was sure he'd shared keenly over the last few tumultuous hours.

She looked at him, and Adams knew their contretemps was as quickly over as it had begun. Her eyes, facial composure, and bodily stance now took on a more relaxed state, confirming a verbal détente had been reached across their personality trenches.

'Dad, just tell me this: you haven't eaten since this morning, have you, because that will just eat me up if so!' joked Elizabeth.

The jokey pun delivered, Adams, sensing the tension had eased, stood up. His body ached inexplicably. He moved forward tentatively, as if the floor were mined.

'Elizabeth, you have an animalistic, pugilistic, and deeply ingrained sense of being right, which, at times, can be unpleasantly abrasive at best, and bombastic at worst,' Adams confidently said.

'Did I say you were ironic? Well, add paradoxical as well,' sardonically replied Elizabeth. 'Dad, if this were true, I wonder where I inherited it from,' she rhetorically continued, ending with a laugh that resonated with both sarcasm and love in equal measure.

Adams looked on with the love that only an impassioned father could show.

'You asked about having eaten earlier? No, I haven't really eaten anything substantive since this morning. So, if you're still willing, shall we try for a "Take 2 dinner"?'

'Hmm, yes, I think I could "take two" that,' joked Elizabeth. 'Perhaps those diners will see I am not as errant as they imagined after all!' she continued.

As she spoke, Adams had walked across the drawing room that seemed to have been furnished straight out of a dream of grand living. He needed to reacquaint himself with his iPhone, which he had unceremoniously dumped on a Regency Chair in the marbled entrance hall during his earlier return. As he began to pick it up, a stinging command powered its way from daughter-central, terminating his action.

'Oh yes, you can put that phone down right now — this is my time. Of course, you can listen to my frantic voicemails of where are you… or words to that effect, if you wish?' Elizabeth cuttingly opined.

Adams quickly acceded to Bambina's command, returning the iPhone to its earlier Regency Chair dumping place.

This stinging rebuke by Elizabeth was delivered as she too left the spacious drawing room and entered the elegant entrance hall, still holding her clutch bag. She briefly stopped by the ornate curved staircase to drink in the beautiful memories of fun and joy that had been cherished over the years since childhood.

Her conscious mind was flooded with warm, embracing visual memories of love from her subconscious. Nevertheless, she quickly compartmentalised these thoughts, choosing instead to simply feel the magical warmth of love and great past times they evoked.

She walked with elegant grace and poise towards the beautiful Boca de Lobo entrance hall mirror. As a very young girl, she'd only seen her reflection in it when her parents lifted her up. She often wondered if her impatient nature, her desire for immediate gratification, had partly sprung from her yearning to grow taller, just to admire herself in its reflective surface.

10

The mirror was as expensive as it was aesthetically beautiful. Depositing her clutch bag on the hall table that was directly below the mirror, she admired herself. Her beautifully styled long bob with bangs wasn't unkempt, as if it would dare be otherwise. Nevertheless, she extracted her Mason Pearson Nylon and Boar Bristle Brush and began to brush her hair with manicured precision.

'Very nice, very nice,' remarked Adams as he walked towards her and stood a few feet to her right side.

'It is, isn't it!' Elizabeth replied as she continued to brush elegantly and daintily.

'Yes, always liked that mirror, your hair's not bad either,' teased Adams.

'Oh, ha ha, you're such a riot, Dad! At least I have more hair to brush on top! Guess that makes us even now,' she retorted.

'Don't forget the lipstick,' Adams tentatively instructed, as if Elizabeth needed a lecture on her own routine.

Elizabeth was indignant about the word "lipstick". She politely put her hairbrush down on the hall table with restrained urgency and quickly fumbled about in her clutch bag for her lipstick, as her father called it. She extracted it and held it up to the mirror with its fatherly reflection. However, it was not lost on her that in showing him her lipstick through reflection, she also made a pointed gesture by raising her right index finger to hold it.

'Dad, this isn't just any lipstick; it's a Guerlain KissKiss Gold and Diamond lipstick.'

'Of course, it is,' sounded a bewildered Adams who knew as much about lipstick as Elizabeth knew about DNA.

As if she read his mind, she suddenly asked, 'What does DNA have in common between us, Dad?'

'I'm not sure I want to know, but I'm a scientist; curiosity inspires me, so please tell me,' Adams asked perplexed.

'Not only does it mean Deoxyribonucleic Acid, but when applied to our verbal discourse, it means "Do Not Argue with me".'

'Is that not five words rather than three?' her father quizzed.

No riposte was necessary as Elizabeth just gave her dad a radiant, almost angelic smile that could cross an infinite space, let alone the few feet to him. Adams smiled back as he looked at her mirror reflection and thought how much she mirrored his own personality—minus her attitudinal predilection for raising her right index finger, of course.

'Come on, apply the lip gloss and let's be on our way.'

'Argh! Lip gloss! Men!' exclaimed an increasingly exasperated Elizabeth.

'Dad, men sweat, women shine. Men get older, women get better. Therefore, we need to look good, after all, one sex has to!' quipped Elizabeth just before lipstick application quietened her propensity for constructive argument.

'Hmm, it's suddenly very quiet. Perhaps you should apply lipstick more,' wisecracked Adams.

To the outsider this additional, albeit brief verbal exchange, may have suggested worse to come. But for Adams and his daughter, this was nothing more than familial banter.

As Elizabeth applied her expensive lipstick, Adams retrieved his Gucci suit jacket from the other Regency chair near the ornate staircase. Before putting it on, he checked the left shoulder for a strange hand mark, as if the physical force from his nightmare might linger. Of course, no mark was there, but the memory of the struggle remained vivid in his mind.

Of course, there wasn't, but it left Adams questioning why, after spending a third of his life asleep with countless dreams, only now had he remembered one so vividly. And then he remembered the writing on top of the research paper: just who did those names belong to and what was "SASBA059", if anything at all?

'Well, I'm ready, Dad; how does your daughter look?' Elizabeth enquired.

This was a tricky question with an even trickier answer; akin in difficulty to, 'Does my bum look big in this?' But Adams' lightning speed of cognition and answer was welcomed by Elizabeth: 'I couldn't wish for better.'

Suddenly, as Elizabeth basked in her father's rare approbation, her gaze snagged on something odd. It lay near where his suit jacket had been casually tossed across the Regency chair.

Beside the chair stood a beautiful French-made, 19th-century wrought iron Campora marble console table, its surface a rich tapestry of deep burgundy and grey tones. The table's attractive visual style, symmetrical design, and composition of colour drew Elizabeth's attention to their home telephone, which sat upon it.

At the best of times, it seemed (to her) an anachronistic appendage, given the beauty of the table it sat upon. Even more so now as the handset was lying several inches away from its base unit.

'Dad, I don't wish to start again, but why is the handset off the base unit?'

'Don't know, Bambina,' as Adams turned around to see the offending oddness.

'I didn't try the home number as you're never really at home, unless it's very late or the weekend.'

Adams explained it away by saying he probably knocked it off its base as he placed (or perhaps dumped) his jacket on one of the Regency Chairs when he arrived earlier.

In any case, he caught up with some valuable sleep time. Elizabeth walked over to the handset and replaced it on the base station. Turning around to her dad, she smiled apprehensively, not sure if he had or had not acted with any deliberate intention to avoid their arranged dinner reservation.

'Well, that's all sorted then. How about we now sort out our digestive rapacity!' she cheerfully extolled.

Preparing to leave their idyllic family mansion, Elizabeth knew it was silly to dwell on such a minor detail, her voracious mind usually consumed by far grander intellectual pursuits. Still, she couldn't shake the oddity of the phone, detached from its base station. It was a peculiar occurrence, one that had never happened before, even when the mansion was brimming with guests.

Noticing her distraction, Adams politely asked with a hint of underlying impatience, 'Are we ready to leave?'

'Oh yes, of course; try and stop me and my restaurant-sensing appetite!' Elizabeth quipped as she walked towards the mansion doors where Adams now stood in preparation to leave.

Adams opened one of the large Knotty Alder Estancia double mansion doors with V-groove panels to facilitate their egress. He looked at Elizabeth undemandingly; wisdom had taught him never to rush her as she walked towards him slowly with a polished, graceful look.

Elizabeth smiled warmly, elegantly moving past her father to exit the door, a movement a ballerina would envy. Her charismatic elegance was doubled as she playfully glanced

14

at her dad, pretending to adjust her hair. No doubt this was a humorous evocation of their recent conversation and how lovely it really was… her hair, that is!

Elizabeth stopped just outside the doors and was immediately struck by the freshness of the evening crisp air, borne of the woodland appurtenance that surrounded the mansion.

The woodland's mission was to propagate as nature had intended, as well as be the mansion's symbiotic, organic barrier from the outside world. This made the grounds so resplendent in a mosaic of beautiful colours, calmness, and freshness. It was akin to an umbilical cord of metaphysical purity that fed and invigorated the souls that lived there.

Some of its natural yet magical grandeur was temporarily lost in translation as Elizabeth thought how it invigorated the senses like Chanel fragrance caught on a lazy, hazy summer's breeze of infinite maternal love.

Adams followed Elizabeth out, closing the door as security beeps confirmed the mansion's watch. Descending the elegant Portland stone steps onto the sprawling gravel driveway, they continued their conversation. Adams, too, now felt invigorated by the idyllic splendour around them.

The early evening atmosphere revitalised his tired senses in ways no medicine ever could; nature's sensory elixir truly had no equal.

'Tell me all about what you're up to, Dad. I'm so intrigued. As you say, if it's going to affect us all, then perhaps I have a right to know what it is,' jocularly yet inquisitively asked Elizabeth. She locked her right arm around her dad's left arm as if to unlock his mental safe of restricted knowledge.

However, Adams seemed preoccupied as he suddenly said, 'Very nice, very nice!' as they now stood side by side next to her Mercedes-Benz AMG S63 Cabriolet. This observation took precedence over the driver's door, which Elizabeth had left open in her rush to ascertain what had happened to her dad only some 20 minutes earlier.

'Yes, lovely, isn't she! Company, of course,' she remarked. 'Come on, Dad, do tell, what is going to happen. Should I upgrade my Mercedes, spend loads of money on credit, travel the world, become hedonistically reckless, even vote Democrat?'

Elizabeth was just joking, but wanted to articulate her innate need as an information gatherer. She turned and faced her father in a very non-confrontational way, even if her facial demeanour had taken on a more concerned appearance.

'Seriously father, what's going on?'

He took a deep breath to calm himself before delivering his disquieting words. In fact, over the last several weeks and more, he had considerable practice in taking such deep breaths to calm his boyish enthusiasm. This happened whenever project data became more detailed and networked into deciphered messages.

Adams reluctantly released his daughter's right arm and raised both his arms to place them gently on Elizabeth's shoulders to emphasise his next words.

'Elizabeth, Bambina—'

Elizabeth worryingly interjected, her apprehension building, 'This sounds so bad!'

Adams nervously smiled and continued as his hands grew tentatively tighter on her shoulders.

He asked, 'What if I told you that bubbling inside you, me, all of us, is an evolutionary coded bomb that will change us all in ways I have yet to decipher?'

'Argh, stop right there, Dad!' howled Elizabeth. 'I need a full stomach for this. Park it for now, at least until I have reacquainted my stomach with some food at Royals. I need to feed my brain so that it can feed my understanding,' she tried to joke, but her underlying emotional unease at her dad's question could only be circumvented temporarily.

With this in mind, they both eased into their car seats. She made idle comments about work, a subtle ploy to prevent her mind from dwelling on what her father had just asked her.

As she drove from their mansion, she continued to chat with her dad about anything but his question. But by the end of their Royal dinner, her father had served a cocktail of research background and distressing findings that hit her like a genetic bombshell.

She had thought that whatever it was, she could rationalise and absorb it into her everyday understanding—but this was something else. Indeed, so much so that she considered this must be the finality of human existence. Unlike previous finalities, this was really it—a genetic doomsday bomb that was remorselessly ticking down to change or even end our way of life as we know it.

3

Brickman And Butt

Earlier that afternoon, around 5 p.m., a significant meeting was about to unfold. Several miles distant, two terrorists were approaching a safe house in the quiet Boston suburb of Aylgreen.

Banton Brickman, the cell leader, stood silhouetted against the grimy light of his rented apartment's first-floor window, his gaze imprisoned by the street below. He was a predator impatiently awaiting his accomplice's return from some dubious garage on the city's fringe. His phone, a rarely disturbed sentinel on the small living room table, lay silent, a testament to the shadows in which he operated.

Security surveillance, the omnipresent gaze of agencies, could easily pinpoint their voices and locations. Yet, this precision was a fickle tool; it only became a weapon if agents, by some fortunate chance, first recognised their elusive quarry amidst the endless static of intercepted signals.

Brickman was wanted by the security agencies. Whenever a job matched his ideological need, he embraced it with a menacing hunger to inspire, incite, and execute a terrorist outrage.

Across continents, Brickman had gorged himself on the perverse pleasure of orchestrating and executing brutal mission outcomes. He saw himself, chillingly, as a twisted kind of tourist, paying a heavy price to traverse the globe, not for its beauty, but to savour the grisly sights of his own villainous making.

But unlike any ordinary tourist, Brickman found his grotesque beauty in the chilling stillness of captured prey or the final, gasping breath of murder. By any measure, he was a moral void, utterly bereft of conscience for his targets or for anyone with the temerity to cross his path.

His current mission was chillingly straightforward: to seize Professor Adams and his daughter. Mere slaughter felt crude and unfulfilling. The true prize lay in their capture and delivery—a far more demanding task for the shadowy figures who pulled his strings. Money, after all, was his true god, reducing his ideological convictions to little more than shifting mist.

What was not fluid was his wickedly depraved psyche, which could be purchased by the highest bidder. This nefarious adaptability of a polluted mind made him incalculably more dangerous as an enemy, for the end truly did justify any barbaric and bloody means to achieve it.

Brickman's gaze, fixed through the tattered, pollution-streaked net curtain, followed the oblivious flow of life outside. The grime that blurred the edges of reality mirrored the moral decay he had long since embraced. Sunlight, heavy with the city's filth, cast a sickly yellow glow across the squalid room. The air hung stagnant, thick with dust, stale smoke and a nameless stench that embodied his own festering anger.

'Fuck, where's that arsehole gone to?' he muttered, wiping his nose with the back of his right hand. Rather than cleaning, the motion only smeared grime and sweat across his face. The oily residue found its final, inglorious resting place on his once-white vest, a garment that had long since accepted its fate as a permanent mosaic of multicoloured stains born of city grime and poor hygiene.

The arsehole in question was his comrade-in-arms, Wanton Butt—a brute of a man whose sheer size often sufficed to intimidate. But if it wasn't his bulk alone, his expression reinforced the threat he posed. His dark, menacing eyes had long since swallowed any glimmer of life. When you met their gaze, even briefly, they seemed to hypnotically consume your insecurities, using them as toxic currency to command your very being.

But the menace was not confined to his gaze; it was etched across his entire face. His skin, a feverish landscape of inflamed redness and angry pustules, seemed to radiate a deep, unsettling heat that was almost tangible. Its intensity never waned. One doctor who briefly examined him remarked with a visible wince that his complexion was so relentlessly and vividly red, it was profoundly unsettling to behold—a stark, unhealthy hue that laid bare the internal turmoil within.

As tall as he was broad, and with the eloquence of a brick wall, Butt inhaled orders as others drew breath. While these traits moulded him into a formidable instrument of fear and obedience, it was his honed mastery of hostage taking and brutal close-quarters combat that truly made him the ideal, devastating tool for Brickman's grim objectives.

Right now, Brickman continued to survey the varied street activity from his first-floor advantage point. Pedestrians, cars, and small shop activity collectively created a hum of societal movement. Suddenly, Brickman's waning attention span was invigorated by a dreadful vehicle, driven by a man of equally poor taste.

'What the fuck's he driving?' Brickman mumbled as Butt came into view in a red car that looked as if it was on the way to the wrecking yard.

He watched as Butt pulled up just outside the ground-floor entrance to their apartment. Brickman's thoughts flickered between which was worse—the car or Butt. Their equally dishevelled appearances seemed made for each other. Shaking off his bewilderment and still muttering in disbelief at what he'd just witnessed, he stepped away from the window and left the apartment to meet Butt.

Unbelievably, Butt hooted three times in rapid succession, thinking he'd yet to be seen by Brickman. The point of being covert and "blending in" with the community was precisely not to draw attention to oneself or others by hooting.

Such irresponsibility was nothing more nor less than an announcement, encouraging locals to see who was shattering the relatively quiet neighbourhood atmosphere. Clearly, such an unwanted display of presence was anathema to their mission's *raison d'être*.

Brickman, a tight coil of suppressed fury, propelled his weighty, athletic frame down the single flight of stairs. Each brisk step hammered his impatience into the worn treads, driven by the need to confront Butt.

Butt smiled as he watched Brickman exit the apartment building to approach him. He posed by the car, as if Brickman was a potential buyer at his own car dealership.

However, Brickman didn't keep any social distance, coming up close to whisper something. He wanted his outraged personal message to Butt to be precisely that: for him alone and not the locals.

'What the fuck's wrong with you, bro? You want attention? I tell you what, why don't you go to Fort Meade and park this, er, well, whatever it is, outside the National Security Agency? Screw our mission, screw everything?' sounded off Brickman in Butt's right ear.

If the grating sound of "burnt ear" had a scent, it would reek of burnt rubber—a nauseating aroma that perfectly matched the moment.

'OK! All right! I got it wrong. But look at the car,' Butt said apologetically.

'Where is it? Oh, you mean this?' Brickman quizzed, as Butt sarcastically waved his hands along and over the contour bodywork lines.

'You don't like the car?' Butt asked.

'I asked you for a car that can handle roads; this has got grip like shit in water,' protested Brickman before Butt interrupted him.

'It looks great, doesn't it!' said Butt. 'It's fast to get there and even faster to get away,' he added.

'I said a fast car with good road handling,' barked Brickman. 'What we have here, you solid fuck, is a coffin on wheels. If we have to travel on roads at high speed, we're burnt bread, or even fuck toast, whatever. Remember what they told you at school: be prepared, not scared,' added Brickman with a didactic intonation.

At this point, Brickman just looked at this caricature of a sentient human being and wondered if Butt would fulfil his mission objective. Unable to find an immediate answer to this conundrum, he signalled to Butt to follow him up to the unhealthy apartment where even insects chose not to reside.

The warm day in the Aylgreen neighbourhood continued unabated as they ascended the stairway to Brickman's apartment. Its warmth was swallowed by the apartment's ingrained squalor, not surprisingly, as the apartment itself had been unmolested by any cleaning agent in months.

The living room's core was dominated by two chairs, their frames sagging in a state of abject decay. Between them, a small round table bore the ghostly rings of countless spilled cigarettes and drunken nights. The mobile phone, a tiny, alien presence, rested amidst these fossilised stains. The damp walls, however, told the true story, their surfaces draped in an unhealthy grime that seemed to silently scream for absolution from countless past health hazards. It was undeniably clear: this apartment had been abandoned by far more than just love.

Brickman and Butt walked into the apartment and sat in their respective chairs of palpable decay. Each creaked under their respective body weights, but refused to capitulate to outright collapse. Under orders from Brickman, Butt reluctantly rose to get two ice-cold beers from their fridge. Its white colour seemed to dazzle against the apartment's grimy backdrop.

With two cold beers in his hand, Butt dropped back into his seat and, without a word, launched a beer bottle towards Brickman. Unaware, unannounced, and utterly unprepared, Brickman barely registered the glint of glass before the bottle slammed into his forehead with a sickening, wet impact. A deathly, hollow thud echoed from his skull, a chilling counterpoint to the sudden pain.

'What the fuck!' shouted Brickman as he caught the offending bottle before it continued its fall to the table for a second collision.

'You asked for a beer,' said the not-so-sympathetic Butt.

'For my mouth, not my head, fuckwit,' lambasted Brickman, desperately trying not to throw it back at Butt's head. Instead, Brickman tossed it back to Butt, who dropped his unopened bottle onto the table.

'Now, throw it over properly, fuckwit,' demanded Brickman.

A flicker of something akin to thought, slow and cumbersome as a rusted cog turning, finally sparked behind Butt's vacant eyes. It prompted a sluggish retraction of his right arm, poised once more to hurl the glass missile. But Brickman, his senses honed by a simmering crucible of days-long resentment towards his oafish companion, anticipated the clumsy telegraphing of the movement.

With a coiled, predatory swiftness that belied the squalor of their surroundings, Brickman lunged forward, his right fist a tightly packed knot of fury exploding into Butt's fleshy jaw, then nose.

The impact resonated with a sickening crunch, the force born not of mere physical strength, but of weeks of suppressed irritation finding violent release. Butt's massive frame recoiled, his thick legs flailing skyward in a grotesque ballet of surprise and pain as he crashed backward onto the grimy floor.

His eyes, dark dull orbs that usually held no spark of intelligence, now swivelled wildly in their sockets, reflecting the stunned incomprehension of a startled beast.

Brickman watched the brutal efficacy of his blow with a grim satisfaction, the fleeting image in his mind's eye of a divine, vengeful thunderbolt delivered with righteous fury. A vibrant bead of crimson slowly bloomed beneath Butt's brutalised nose, a visceral, scarlet exclamation mark confirming the searing punctuation of Brickman's simmering rage.

'Bastard shit, I'm fucking bleeding,' roared Butt.

'Fucking moron, that's the shit from your pores,' laughed Brickman.

His laugh didn't last long as he realised some of the volcanic pustules had left their residue on his right fist. As usual, he wiped it on his vest where all previous daily crap went to live and evolve in their own biodome of filth.

'Get up moron, that fucking chair has got more strength than you,' taunted Brickman. Butt wriggled and writhed around on the dirt-oozed floor in a pathetic attempt to get back up. His uncoordinated muscles ceased to be a collective unit. Instead, its individual components moved independently as he tried to get back up. Legs, arms, and head battled with each other in a dysfunctional and pointless bodily squabble that resulted in no success.

'Catch!' shouted a manic Brickman.

The sight of his not-so-cold beer arcing towards him spurred his bruised and battered body back into action. He just caught the airborne bottle. In stark contrast to his recent sprawl on the floor, he used his decrepit chair to heave his uncoordinated bulk back to a standing position. The effort was significant; his large chest heaved loudly and deeply as he gasped for needed oxygen.

He pulled a grime-laden tissue from his right trouser pocket and rubbed the hardening pustules from his face. Brickman just looked on with disbelief. They looked at each other with venomous stares that reflected their anger.

But Brickman quickly broke his upward stare as Butt's eyes that seemed to be trying to devour his very being. In any case, work was at hand, and so Butt moved his chair back to where it had been and sat down again, knowing he could take Brickman anytime he wished.

Because of their paranoia of being listened to or watched by the security services, Brickman's only mission intelligence was in three parts. First, there were photographs of Professor Adams and his daughter, along with her car. Second, a copy of the road network in and around The

Royals' Restaurant. Third, the knowledge in his head of the best place to intercept them and the place to deliver their soon-to-be hostages.

'Fortunately, it's quite simple, Butt. This is where we take them,' said Brickman as he jabbed his dirty right index finger on the roadmap he'd taken out of his pocket and unfurled it across the table.

'Is that it?' said a backward-looking Butt.

'What the fuck does that mean bro?' demanded an angered Brickman, who knew he was keeping several plans from Butt.

'So... we stop them there... then what?' Butt pressed.

'When we get to here, your fucking training will kick in, won't it? If not, my gun muzzle will be up your butt, Butt,' stated Brickman, leaving no room for questioning.

'That's perverted to say up my butt,' Butt muttered with embryonic concern for his future rectal health.

He indignantly stared at Brickman for what seemed like an age. Brickman, however, was not tempted to reciprocate with a long stare himself, as he knew it would make him feel nauseous again.

'Can't you tell me what you expect now?' Butt demanded anxiously, as he stopped his hideous stare, one evolved over many years to frighten and disarm.

To recapture his thoughts, as well as his superiority that was being sucked away by Butt's stare, an indignant Brickman took a rhetorical stance, 'Who's the boss on this?'

Butt was not schooled in rhetoric and chose to further Brickman's conversational irritation.

'I don't know, whoever gives you the orders,' replied Butt, oblivious to the further irritation he caused.

A vein throbbed visibly in Brickman's temple. The sheer idiocy of Butt's statement—a testament to the man's bottomless intellectual void—was an affront to Brickman's meticulously crafted command. He'd dumbed down the instructions, condescending to Butt's Neanderthal level of comprehension, and yet still, this brain-fart drivel. Diplomacy was a foreign tongue to Brickman, and attempting to illuminate Butt's dim mind with anything beyond the most primal directive was like lecturing a sedated ape on the intricacies of quantum entanglement.

There was no other option for Brickman but to lean forward in his chair of insecure purpose to angrily slap Butt, first to the left, then to the right. He was momentarily seduced by the urge to do it again, finding it cathartic. However, Butt's war-scarred facial skin looked as if it would begin to erupt red lava liquid from even more pustules, given it profusely covered his face, or "countenance landscape" as a doctor once called it.

Butt, his expression a mask of bemused incomprehension at being slapped instead of punched, merely blinked. Brickman, however, wasn't finished. 'I do,' he snarled, his voice a savagely bellowed declaration, 'I give the orders as I'm the fucking boss. Any problems with that?'

'Ok, Ok,' reservedly bemoaned an appeased Butt.

Brickman wondered how Butt ever got to be assigned to him except for his physical size. But this negative thought was fractured by his mobile ringing.

'Fuck, it's Radon... oh shit, forget I said that!' said a shocked Brickman.

'Said what?' replied a nonplussed Butt.

Brickman hesitantly picked up the mobile phone. The display said "Call Forward: No Caller ID" but he knew it was Radon, his boss. Who else could it be? 'Yes,' Brickman said, aware that breaking silence might well set the security services into a frenzy of listening and signal triangulation.

'Plan B is a go,' said a foreboding, monotonic voice.

'Yes, yes, I got it, Plan B,' replied Brickman quickly.

The surprise on Brickman's face was not lost on Butt. Unbeknownst to Butt, three plans had been discussed at a safe location between Brickman and Radon just two weeks prior. These plans had been devised to ensure they could keep one or two steps ahead of security surveillance.

'What's Plan B?' Butt asked.

'The one between "Plan A" and "Plan C" moron. You'll find out. Time to move,' ordered Brickman.

A frantic, adrenaline surge of motivation seized them as the two terrorists snatched up their meagre supplies, tossing items—including their guns—haphazardly into the mouths of drab, unassuming bags. Butt, clutching both bags like a desperate man fleeing a fire, lurched down the stairwell with a gait that suggested a drunkard wrestling with gravity.

Brickman, however, moved with a deliberate, calculated stillness, lingering in the decaying apartment for several tense minutes. He conducted a silent audit, his eyes scanning for any lingering trace of their presence, any whisper for the government dogs to sniff out.

All that remained was to collect the bag of three guns and place it in the boot. The ingrained lesson to never gift the bastards a crumb of evidence briefly but poignantly echoed in his mind. A grim satisfaction flickered across his lips as this would soon be his third apartment bombing. His fingers brushed against the cold, hard casing of the one-pound, remote-armed C4 explosive, nestled discreetly amongst the squalor.

The explosive had been moulded into a long, thin sausage and pressed into a large wall crack that ran from ceiling to floor, near the dilapidated apartment front door just days after moving in. To make sure, he had also put a small gas cylinder by the explosive for good measure.

He pushed a switch on the bomb to prime it. He closed the apartment door, walked down the stairway and out onto the pavement. He thought about arming it with his remote-control device immediately, but thought better of it, just in case it accidentally exploded.

Butt was sitting in the driver's seat with his left arm hanging lifelessly against the outside driver's door. Perspiring heavily, he tapped the steering wheel in synchrony to the engine turning over. The engine was making squealing noises that Butt had ignored when buying the car, after the seller called it a "characteristic" and he mistook it for a useful, added extra.

He looked at Brickman and silently mouthed 'come on'. Brickman briskly strode to the back of the car, opened the boot and tossed the unzipped bag of guns inside. The weapons tumbled out across the floor. He gave the mess a dismissive glance and slammed the boot shut before walking to the nearside front door and getting in.

'We go boss,' said Butt.

'Go there!' shouted Brickman, whilst raising his right arm to indicate that way, which meant straight, then first left. As they turned left, Brickman told Butt to pull over. Butt pulled to the kerb quickly, and Brickman looked at him, a cold gaze meeting his own. With a quiet click, he pushed the activation button on his bomb remote control. The explosive was now live. The next action was inevitable.

4

The Apartment Bomber Kid

'BOOM!' Brickman shouted, his arms flying up and out in a crude mockery of a blast that was yet to be. A manic laugh escaped him, the sound echoing as his gaze fixated on the remote in his hand.

'It would be a waste of C4 just to take an apartment out,' Brickman mused, a cruel glint in his eye. 'Why not take a few secret service fucks with it?'

Butt looked round at him in addictive admiration. For fifteen minutes, Brickman directed him street by street, a monotonous litany of 'next left' and 'next right'. Just as Butt's patience began to wane, Brickman announced they were nearly there.

Butt drove into an underground car park, hugging the concrete pillars so tightly it was like squeezing through a congested pavement. He descended three car park levels, navigating to a spot where reconnaissance had confirmed the cameras were long dead. There, he finally slowed down, awaiting Brickman's signal for their rendezvous point.

'Stop over there,' ordered Brickman.

'We're no way near the Royals restaurant. I don't get it,' said a bewildered Butt as he parked the car.

'We're waiting for a car,' said an anticipatory Brickman.

'We won't wait long. It's a car park,' moronically stated Butt.

As Butt demonstrated his prowess at inductive reasoning, the screeches of a car could be heard getting louder and louder. As it descended the very three levels they had just negotiated, the tyres increasingly screeched and echoed in tortuous anguish. The tyres were pushed beyond their capabilities by the speed and tightness of the steering to negotiate the corners. The screeches seemed to be everywhere as they ricocheted off the car park pillars and walls and subsequently into their ears.

This only served to make their minds race with anxiety that this might not be their cell colleagues but security services racing to make this their last stand. In automatic anticipation of the worst, their right hands caressed their Glock 19s which were in the bag Butt had carried earlier. Their gun fingers twitched with excited menace in preparedness to depart this possible security service gun fodder into the next world.

Fear of what might be often manufactures irrelevant thoughts until reality kicks in, as Brickman soon realised.

'Good, it's the other half of our cell,' said Brickman, as a red car appeared in the distance.

'How can you tell?' Butt asked.

'Not again knucklehead. I am the fucking boss, remember!' exclaimed an exasperated Brickman.

In response, Butt wore an expression of contempt as he looked away from this admonishment and continued to watch a red car approach. The sight of their brothers-in-arms made them relax their hands from their Glock 19s.

The car pulled up next to them and half-hearted smiles were exchanged between them before they all got out. Brickman moved over to speak to his two terrorist cell colleagues, Hardmeat and Cullthem. Butt, meanwhile, could not help but be mesmerised by the red Vectraxis.

'That's a red 2000 Vectraxis,' said Butt to Hardmeat, the driver.

'What the fuck is on your face, brother?' Hardmeat said in shock.

'Never seen acne before?' said a bewildered Butt at Hardmeat's stupidity.

'Not that brother, you've got a fist mark in your left cheek. I can even see a ring mark from the middle finger,' laughed Hardmeat.

Unbeknownst to Butt, Brickman's punch had been so hard, his right fist had indented its forceful signature into the volcanic topography of the cheek in question.

'It's a war accessory. Now, answer my question,' demanded Butt trying to disown his newly acquired facial dent.

'You have yourself brother, this is a red 2000 Vectraxis, courtesy of the boss two weeks ago. Its fast, agile, and great traction' finally responded Hardmeat.

Just before Butt could continue his growing affection for the car, Brickman called them together to huddle around the Vectraxis bonnet. The car was indeed courtesy of his boss, Radon, having been delivered by Brickman two weeks prior. As they huddled, Butt's eyes lingered on the Vectraxis with a look of romantic attraction. However, unbeknownst to all, Brickman was soon to reveal other plans for the car.

Brickman pulled the map out of his jean's dirty right pocket and unfurled it over the bonnet. Without realising it, they all leaned forward in synchrony to view the map as if orchestrated by some unknown force. He took his right index finger and, as before in the apartment, pointed to where they would take Professor Adams and his daughter hostage. He looked at each of his three colleagues and explained Plan B.

'Plan B is for us to exchange cars,' Brickman explained, his finger tracing a route on the map. He pointed to a quiet road about a mile from the Royals restaurant. 'You two will follow them from there and intercept them here.'

He continued, 'We know their route; they're as predictable as I am to success. It's quiet there at that time of night, so it should be all right. Once you've stopped them with speed and courage, we will step in to clean up. Your job ends and ours will continue.'

'Why are we changing cars?' asked Hardmeat, quite unaware that to question Brickman was to invite a rebuke. The ferocity of that rebuke would soon be evident.

'First, your car is faster than ours; that's why we'll have it. Second, one floor up is a complimentary, if cheap, car wash. That'll wash the cheap red veneer paint job off to reveal its original black bodywork. We will do the same but ours will be a common blue underneath. Third, they'll be looking for two red cars, won't they?' answered Brickman with a hint of self-satisfaction at the plan's simple cleverness.

But there was more from Brickman. 'In our cars are false plates and dark screen window covers; we need to fit them before we leave. Then, drive here to wait for our two victims to come out,' explained Brickman as he pointed with his right index finger to the map and their stop location near The Royals. He did this with such force that his dirty fingerprint was imprinted on it as if a small fly had been unceremoniously squashed against it.

'Why not just have a "fresh" car waiting right here rather than change all this?' probed Hardmeat with an educated intonation that really only served to be laughably idiotic to Brickman.

'Are you Butt's brother by any chance?' Brickman dug at Hardmeat.

He looked condescendingly at Butt, as if he'd just risen from a sewer with all the stinky accoutrements one would expect.

'How do we look like brothers?' Hardmeat quizzically asked.

'You both ask fucking stupid questions, that's why. Too many fucking crackheads and car thieves around here,' Brickman ballistically fired towards Hardmeat, not realising an element of local truth in his statement. Suddenly, in the distance, a loud, deathly explosion pounded their ears, causing them to temporarily duck in fear.

'Fuck, what was that?' Hardmeat exclaimed.

'More stupid fucking questions. It means the National Security Agency (NSA) didn't say "please" before entering our apartment,' manically laughed Brickman.

'You bombed your own fucking apartment?' Hardmeat shrieked.

'Oh yeah, he bombed it! He's bombed two others during the last two years as well!' laughed Butt.

'That's three apartments in three years. They should call you the apartment-bomber kid!' joyously exclaimed Hardmeat.

Brickman smiled admiringly about the last comment. More so as a wild and bizarre idea crossed his feral mind. He fleetingly saw himself as a western gunslinging kid whose very "explosive" presence shook fear through all, even the dead. As with so many others of his villainous ideas and plots to harm, this too was sucked into an abyss of mindless terror from which it empowered his everyday vile thoughts to nurture harm. Brickman was simply a bomb on legs, primed to detonate, primed to harm, and remorselessly self-reconstructing to repeat atrocities over and over again

Gunslinging thoughts over, he looked at the three men, their faces turned towards him with unquestioning loyalty. He suddenly realised that none looked particularly intelligent. He stifled a bitter, private laugh, musing that their combined waist measurements would undoubtedly dwarf their measured intellects. Yet, this was his cell, and he believed his singular intelligence would carve their path to success.

Brickman spoke, and all three leaned forward to listen intently. They seemed to almost breathe in his words of direction, hoping it would deepen their understanding and heighten their satisfaction with the outcome.

'Once I'm finished and the plans are done, I will be known for much, much more than just the "kid" who did this or that.' His reference was lost on the three men, they had forgotten as the focus was on their mission.

'The bombing is just a distraction,' Brickman explained, his gaze moving between his colleagues. 'It'll only seem insignificant until they find out it's related to this hostage action. Then both become significant.' He paused, a condescending sneer on his lips.

'Speaking of insignificant things, if we don't move, you'll be that way,' he added slyly. His infantile slur, a barbed arrow launched in their direction, simply dissolved into the intellectual void between them. Given their demonstrable IQs, this lack of comprehension was no surprise.

As they headed to their new vehicles, intent on carrying out the plan, a single thought never crossed their minds—not even Brickman's. If the NSA already knew their safe house's location, what other insidious threads had they unravelled? What darker, unseen plots might they already be meticulously plotting for them?

5

The Alpha Readiness Protocol

NSA intelligence analysts monitored communications between Professor Adams, his daughter, friends, and associates, as well as their online presence. This effort bridged knowledge gaps and provided a clearer situational awareness of potential threats from terrorists. These threats came from those who sought to harm the interests of Professor Adams' work and family specifically, and the United States generally.

If the surveillance chiefs had had their way, they would have simply moved Adams and his family to a secure place. The problem was that any secure place would detach him from the very tools he needed to continue his work and, just as importantly, his highly valued way of family life.

They couldn't move the university, his team of highly-trained specialists, and the academic networks that supported them all. To do so would severe vital collaborative links, thereby impacting the research. Moreover, the money wasn't available to even consider such a thing.

Ironically, their valuable asset also served as a homing target and bait to help them uncover the terrorists they knew intended to capture them. This was evident from messages intercepted and decoded by NSA analysts between several known terrorist cells. The terrorists' mission was to capture them and hand Adams over to their paymasters upon final payment. The daughter would be their bargaining chip to ensure completion. What the paymasters had in store for him was unclear, but using terrorists meant it wasn't for benign reasons.

NSA intelligence analysts, along with information received from the National Reconnaissance Office (NRO), became concerned. This stemmed from several red flags concerning recent terrorist cell activity. The NRO's intelligence included downlinks and other critical data.

The NSA had to balance the need to collect data to uncover networks with the safety of those they served to protect. Critically, "Sentient", an AI supercomputer that constructed a synthetic model of the real world, alerted analysts to expect a "hit" against Professor Adams and Elizabeth within hours. It also identified the likely backers for the terrorist operation.

As a result, NSA intelligence analyst Savannah Abbey initiated an "alpha readiness" protocol, phoning Natalie Colton, her boss at NSA's Signals Intelligence Directorate, on a secure communications line named Falcon.

The phone rang at her boss's home with unmistakable urgency. A party, arranged weeks before, was going beautifully and so noisily that it completely masked this urgent call.

It just so happened that Colton wasn't wearing the communications bracelet, a device she needed to wear to alert her of NSA communications. She'd taken it off (as allowed) to shower, but her two playful children had distracted her just as she was about to put it back on.

For a full hour, the vibrant current of welcoming guests and loud music had utterly swept away her attention. The communications bracelet, a constant presence on her wrist, lay forgotten; she hadn't even registered its absence.

Analyst Abbey grew more impatient by the second, knowing "Sentient" was never wrong, and neither was her own ability to unpack intelligence data for meaning. She looked across at her fellow team analyst for advice.

'She's not answering, damn it,' exclaimed Abbey.

'Perhaps she's been taken hostage by aliens,' said fellow analyst Lucas Wilson with a spooky intonation. A brilliant analyst, he nonetheless retained his childhood tendency to sometimes say the wrong thing at the wrong time.

He added conspiratorially, 'You know, I heard on the grapevine that our noble director, Dr. Denton, is at that party too.'

After a brief silence, Wilson leaned forward in his office chair and looked at Abbey in a playfully mischievous way, saying, 'You know, perhaps he's there to talk about aliens? Hell, maybe he's been taken hostage as well.'

'Aliens? Oh, ha ha... pity you weren't abducted!' Abbey retorted sarcastically, reacting to his absurdity. She pressed on, her voice rising with anxiety. 'Wilson, this is no normal situation for me. She should be there, absolutely accessible,' Abbey added, sounding increasingly fraught.

'Well, if her boss is there, this isn't going to end too well for her, is it?' Wilson implied, leaning back in his chair with a reserved air of superiority, as if he believed he was the human equivalent of their masterful AI, Sentient.

'Not sure whether to keep buzzing her, message her husband, get a local patrol there, or "go upstairs"?' Abbey muttered to herself.

'Why, what's upstairs? Another floor perhaps?' Wilson asked, looking up.

'Get real, moron, the boss, our deputy chief, you know?'

'Yes, I know what you mean. Do that, best option, safe for you, safe for us.' Without further hesitation, Abbey looked back at her phone.

With a hesitant tone, Abbey spoke into her secure voice-recognition telephone link, 'Call Bob Tinton, priority one.'

The line connected quickly. Bob Tinton, her line manager two levels up—a man always available and known for his subtle humour and patriotism—answered promptly. 'Bob Tinton, here, what's the problem, Abbey?'

'I'm trying to contact Natalie Colton, but she's not answering. Protocols indicate my next move is to contact you, as our previous line manager left last week. I've indicated an "alpha readiness" for Professor Michael Adams and his daughter.'

'You're right, that's what the protocols are for. But I'm not the next in the hierarchy; that's George Garcia now. You know, the horse owner? Those close to him affectionately call him "Gee-Gee" because of his initials.'

Tinton chuckled modestly to himself and once again reminded himself of his secretive, if pointless, aspiration to be a nightclub comedian.

'Thank you, sir, I wasn't aware. My absence last week and recent return meant I missed this change. Frankly, the demands of our work often keep us isolated in here for what feels like a whole day, with little interaction beyond the phone,' Abbey explained.

'I understand entirely, Abbey. But an electronic Level Three memo went out last week regarding changes to the chain of command, so in the future, please contact him in the first instance,' Tinton explained. He shifted gears. 'Anyway, what's this "alpha readiness" all about?'

'Intelligence and Sentient both clearly show a "hit" is imminent against Professor Michael Adams and his daughter, Elizabeth.'

Hearing this prediction, Tinton's voice revealed his disconcertment, speeding up and becoming slightly higher pitched. His anxiety was now evident.

'While we've been talking,' Tinton said, 'I've also been briefly reviewing the intelligence data. I see the suspects' safe house became active in the last hour, and they've since moved.'

'You've certainly used a variety of software to access mobile data. I can also see a satellite image from the car boot, containing three identified weapons—two semi-automatic Deagles and an AK47.

'Imagery also suggests they're carrying Glock 19s. This is a go, Abbey. Sentient has yet to be wrong, especially with a 95% probability calculation. Let's aim for arrests, not a shootout or civilian casualties. I'll get a local snatch team there in 15 minutes,' directed Tinton.

With palpable tension in her voice, Abbey replied quickly, an anxious concern in her tone: 'Probably 20 minutes given the traffic. Anyway, thank you. I'm pleased to say Colton is now uplinked. Do you wish to conference on this, sir, or should I speak to her?'

'Go ahead, already done on my separate secure link, Abbey. Good work. It's a go from me.' With that, Tinton promptly ended the communication uplink.

'Hello, Madam,' Abbey intoned.

Colton answered, 'It's not the usual protocol to call me at home, Abbey, but thank you. Before you ask, I forgot to relink my bracelet; it's now on. I trust it's urgent?' a slightly embarrassed boss responded.

'Madam, Intel suggests there's a 95% chance Professor Adams and his daughter, Elizabeth, may be "hit" in the next hour or so.'

'Yes, Bob's assessment aligns with what I'm hearing now. He never misses a thing, does he? He's a proven expert on

all things like this. If he says it's a "go", then it must be…
But still, brief me with other intel before I sanction this!'

'Madam, voice data analysis from Crossbeam confirms
two wanted suspects: Banton Brickman and Wanton Butt.'

Before Analyst Abbey could continue, Colton interrupted
loudly.

'Those two bastards! Continue,' forcibly uttered Colton.

'Madam, Agents Sterling and Parker followed them from
their "safe house" using mobile phone software, Toteghostly.
They moved from there about an hour ago after receiving an
activation command from their cell leader, Radon.'

'They've now tracked them to a car park, one mile from
Royals. They've been there for about 30 minutes. "Dropout
Jeep" software has accessed and networked all their
communications contacts; we've identified seven primary
and three secondary targets.'

'All target devices and computers are compromised and
connected to Sentient for network analysis. Meanwhile, the
FBI raided Radon's "safe house", and took Radon and two
other suspects into custody. Bomb-making equipment and a
small arsenal of weapons were also seized.

'Tragically, two other suspects were shot dead. The FBI
has also neutralised two other terrorist cells. Agents Sterling
and Parker are outside the car park exit, waiting for your "go"
once the local snatch team arrives in about 17 minutes,'
analyst Abbey concluded.

'Good work, Abbey. How many agents do we have on
scene besides Sterling and Parker?'

'Just those, Madam. However, before Colton could react
to this limited on-the-ground presence, Abbey continued
with another crucial update.

'The local Boston FBI counter-terrorism unit also raided Brickman's apartment. It was wired, but they'd disconnected it. Nothing has been found yet, except for numerous fingerprints. To keep up the illusion, the FBI and FAA ordered an F15EX to fly supersonic (at 5,000 feet) over a military airfield five miles away, creating a sonic "boom carpet" heard by the terrorists.

'How ingenious!' remarked an impressed Colton.

'Leave it with me, Abbey. Ensure you keep me up-to-date using Falcon.'

'Thank you, Madam.' Having concluded her call with Abbey, Colton immediately reopened her secure Falcon line to her deputy, Bob Tinton. "Right", she thought briefly as the line connected. "Bob needs to know... now."

'I'm back again, Bob. It's a "go" on this,' Colton insisted, her voice tight. 'Brickman and Butt are utter psychos. This is going to get messy if it isn't contained quickly.' The loud, joyful party music was in stark contrast to the urgency in her voice.

'What concerns me, Bob, is what happens if those dangerous individuals leave the car park before we get there. The snatch team may be too late. We need to send a second unit in. And another concern is what we know about his daughter's personality – employer tests indicated she was high in neuroticism, prone to recklessness, and not very conscientious.'

Because of this, Sentient predicts a strong chance she will act recklessly in any confrontation. If people provoke her too much, she might become a danger to herself and others.

'First, thanks for taking time away from your party, Natalie,' he remarked, his tone dripping with sarcasm.

He pressed, 'Yes, regarding the potential for a messy situation, such as a car chase, perhaps? Oh, blast! She drove her father to the Royals. That implies—' but his boss interjected, her concern escalating.

'Yes, yes, I know, she'll be driving back as well,' Colton said, sounding exasperated. 'Get them now, Bob! Send in Stenastor and Drum to the exit but from another strategic position. Drag in some local backup. I didn't want to use them, but we haven't any choice now,' she anxiously continued.

Tinton grew anxious as he said, 'But there are others. Although the FBI raid found nothing, we're fairly sure there's evidence to suggest at least two more high-value targets are with them as we speak.'

'Get them all! If we don't, our success will be short-lived, and our regrets prolonged. We're playing a constant catch-up, Bob. Even with this technology, we can cut as many heads off the terrorist beast, yet they still regrow. Where is the origin of all this cat-and-mouse chasing?' an exasperated Colton remonstrated. Both sighed deeply, thinking the conversation was at an end, when a secure message came through from analyst Abbey.

'Oh hell!' Colton bellowed down the line to Tinton. 'Images from closed-circuit TV inside the restaurant suggest they're preparing to pay their bill and, by implication, leave. I thought we had more time.'

'Bob, we must move fast on this now. The snatch team will take too long. Agents Stenastor and Drum will get there quicker. Plus, while it's on my mind, we'll send another two officers to the university campus in the morning to act as round-the-clock bodyguards.

'Additionally, send a surveillance unit with drones to patrol the grounds and put NSA protection on the mansion entrance. Their own university security is quite good, so this tripartite arrangement should be sufficient. One moment, Bob,' Colton added, as she scrutinised her small but intricate communications panel. She flicked a button to speak to analyst Abbey again. 'Abbey, any updates on Brickman and Butt leaving the car park?' Colton demanded.

'Nothing yet,' Abbey replied. 'The constant stream of cars leaving is hindering our surveillance, and cameras on the lower floors aren't working. Fortunately, Sterling and Parker are outside one exit, but Stenastor and Drum are still at least five minutes away because of traffic. We can't see through concrete, so satellite imagery is useless, but they're definitely still inside.'

'Natalie, you mentioned Adams' mansion security the other day. Have you followed up on that?' Tinton asked. Colton didn't hesitate. 'Already done, Bob. I authorised the Watchtower team in Cambridge to install a Kirlian surveillance interface at their mansion today. They were there for about two hours and established secure uplinks to us. Adams won't know about it, although some fool knocked his phone off its base and forgot to replace it.'

'The fewer who know about this, the better, especially for legal reasons. Anyway, no mistakes on this, Bob, or we'll both be in trouble,' Colton said, a chilling sense of blame and shame hanging in her words.

"Both be in trouble," Bob thought. "How so?" He didn't think he had done anything wrong as he was following stated protocols. As Colton cut the link, Bob, reflecting on his bemusement and implied attack on his professional abilities, knew what that really meant: just him.

- 6 -
A Bloodied Tapestry Of Death

Brickman wasn't stupid. Murderous, yes, but not stupid. He'd guessed a tracking device had been placed on the car somewhere between the dealership and their apartment building.

The security services, having failed at earlier arrests, were now determined to dismantle the entire terrorist network of the leader Radon. They knew the grim reality that 'Cut off one head, another will just take its place,' a lesson they had found difficult to act on. Now, with an edge in technology and personnel, they had seen some recent successes. Little did Brickman know that his boss, Radon, his two gunmen, and two four-man cells were either no more or already in custody, being prepped for interrogation.

He was taking no chances with his own life; he still had too many lives left to unceremoniously murder. By exchanging cars, he knew Hardmeat and Cullthem wouldn't see another sunrise, yet their deaths wouldn't be in vain. Yes, they would be tailed and probably shot, but Brickman saw an opportunity in their deaths: he would move in and capture his prize hostages, right from under the security services. What sweet joy!

Brickman announced another change of plan, as the ability to dismantle existing plans always excited his crude, primitive intellect.

'You two, forget about using our car; we've just had one delivered,' he said, nodding towards two unsuspecting shoppers who were quietly yet joyfully returning to their car.

'Forget Plan B or even Plan C, you murderous bastards. You're going to earn your money with Plan D,' Brickman said, his voice and stare brooking no argument. His three cell morons stood with mouths open in surprise, as if awaiting to be fed.

'Hardmeat, take the woman, Cullthem take the man. Go over, shake their hands and tell them you'll shoot them if they don't do what you say. Outside, you know what to do,' directed Brickman.

Such soulless, wanton disregard for these two unfortunate shoppers made it hard to believe he belonged to the human species. His plan, decided in seconds, went without a hitch, massaging his ego sweetly.

With a car newly acquired by theft, the intelligence services were blinded. Nothing appeared wrong on the cameras that were working, and the car's license plates indicated ordinary citizens inside. In fact, there were two more passengers—Hardmeat and Cullthem—crouching behind the front seats, their vicious intent soon to be realised by their hostage shoppers.

The car initially drove in the opposite direction to the Royals before parking in a side street. Hardmeat hit the driver over the head. The woman passenger screamed so delightfully that Hardmeat decided he wanted more; he delayed her fate, if only for a moment.

Cullthem pulled the dazed driver out of the car and unceremoniously pushed him in front of an oncoming truck, ensuring a fatal collision. Meanwhile, as this heinous act was in progress, Hardmeat gagged the woman with her neck scarf, pulled her out of the car and pushed her into the back, knocking her out cold.

And remarkably, amidst this unfolding barbarity, no one who witnessed it seemed to stir. Their indifference was a chilling silence until the stark, brutal finality of a man versus a truck shattered their collective apathy.

The two perpetrators slithered back to their murderous car, unnoticed and unrecognised. 'Look at that,' said Hardmeat as they both stared at the ongoing people shuffle around the lifeless body. 'Pancake time, sucker!' he muttered. 'Never liked that western food shit until now,' retorted Cullthem as he slammed the back door shut.

'You know what that is?' Hardmeat asked rhetorically. 'Death curiosity?' Cullthem answered. 'Maybe, but it's what the Germans call schadenfreude,' Hardmeat replied. 'They're thinking about his misfortune and how lucky they are that they aren't him,' he continued.

With these deathly thoughts, they drove off to do their worst again. Their psychotic minds, devoid of remorse, already considered their sleeping female passenger dead.

While Hardmeat and Cullthem indulged in their grim thoughts, Brickman was setting the next murderous stage in motion just 500 metres away. Butt, driving the now-dark Vectraxis with new plates and darkened windows, passed the NSA agents who were still focused on the car park. Although authorised by NSA boss Natalie Colton to make the arrests, the agents were delayed by traffic and had to put on their body armour before moving in.

Yet, right now, their targets were unsuspectingly driving right past them. Brickman noted they had body armour on— a clear invitation to attack. He reached over and pressed the hooter several times, attracting the agents and ensuring they stayed put. He knew they wouldn't get out; they were so dumb they'd probably think he was an undercover agent or something similar.

Brickman ordered Butt to park the car just ten yards behind them. He got out and, with his Glock 19 ready behind his back, coolly walked towards the agents' car as if needing their assistance. As he approached, he could see their concerned eyes in their car mirrors, surveying his body for any potential threat. He was too clever to betray his murderous intent.

Tapping on the driver's window, it slowly opened to reveal agents Stenastor and Drum. Pulling his Glock from behind his back, Brickman pointed it straight at Stenastor first. The only thing Stenastor had time to say was 'Fuck' before he and Drum were shot dead—two bullets, two lives ended.

'Textbook!' chillingly muttered Brickman as he surveyed his bloodied tapestry of death. His egotistical elation was such that he couldn't help but mimic the western caricature Hardmeat had mentioned earlier. He raised the gun and blew on it, a single puff of smoke a testament to his pride in being utterly ruthless. He walked back to the car without looking back, without fear of being caught.

'Wow, you really smoked those bastards. What textbook did you learn that from, bro?' Butt asked enthusiastically as Brickman leapt back into the car. Overjoyed, his heart hammered with the joyous adrenaline of a viciously ruthless killer.

'Assholes die like assholes,' Brickman laughed unemotionally. 'The other assholes will be looking everywhere but here.' Butt stared with limitless admiration. 'Bro, you're amazing, and that's coming from me after all my own shit over the years,' he claimed. With Butt's vile praises polluting the air, they drove off towards their next assignation of death: The Royals Restaurant.

During their brief journey, their conversation was a macabre mix of previous exploits, eliminating human targets, and other acts of mayhem. However, as Butt began to park the car, the topic returned to his earlier cold execution. 'More to come, bro, more to come,' Brickman said with a sinister grin, a final reprise of all things murderous.

Butt parked the Vectraxis about 100 metres from the glitzy venue. The car was not far from their comrades-in-arms, Hardmeat and Cullthem, who were already observing the entrance. The buildings beauty was strikingly visible, its grandeur dancing with the changing lights that played across the expensive façade of bricks, Corinthian columns, and glass.

For a moment, their thoughtless, callous depravity seemed to ebb. The occupants of both cars admired not only the Royals' lights but also the city's thousands of other lights. They shone brightly and seemed to dance to the vibrant very early evening's thermal undercurrents.

Some of the brightest lights lit up the Royals' entrance, revealing a cornucopia of expensive cars and common taxis that came and went, depositing and withdrawing the venue's monied clientele. Indeed, at times, it was like a who's who of Boston's well-to-do.

In contrast, the four terrorists were anything but well-to-do. Hardmeat and Cullthem sat assiduously watching the comings and goings. With the car windows shut, the summer heat only exacerbated the smell of their body odour. The stench, once overlooked, now stubbornly clung to the air, becoming overwhelmingly noticeable. This equality of stench was the only thing the two men shared.

Hardmeat had one significant advantage over Cullthem: he was using binoculars with powerful clarity to watch the minutiae of people coming and going at Royals.

'Why do you get binoculars?' Cullthem quizzed as he squinted to see distant movement.

'Because I'm the one with poor eyesight,' retorted Hardmeat.

'That makes no sense, a lookout with poor eyesight,' Cullthem scoffed.

'It makes perfect sense to me and these binoculars, so shut up and keep watching that entrance,' said an exasperated Hardmeat.

'Fuck, we need a window open. It stinks in here,' bemoaned Cullthem.

'If you shut your sewer mouth, I'd say our chances of survival are even,' laughed Hardmeat.

Just then, an ambulance rushed by, its sirens a wailing banshee tearing through the early evening. The sight and sound of the emergency vehicle, a fleeting red and blue blur, snagged a sudden, disquieting thought in Hardmeat's mind. He ripped the binoculars from his eyes, bemused by the happiness of others as his thoughts crashed together, forging a chilling, plausible scenario.

'You know, something's not right about all this?' Hardmeat questioned.

Cullthem still had his last statement in mind, so he naturally assumed this was what Hardmeat meant.

'Some blonde bitch medic once said it's just halitosis,' Cullthem drawled, utterly oblivious to Hardmeat's revulsion. 'She asked me to breathe over her, so I did. Poor doc fainted!' He cackled. 'Crazy how "halitosis" is about bad breath, and you have to deliberately exhale just to start saying it.'

'For fuck's sake, shut up about your breath. I'm not talking about that!' Hardmeat exclaimed, exasperated.

'Not that! Oh, you mean the cars. Yeah, this one is shit,' replied Cullthem.

'Not the fucking cars... okay, maybe so. No! Have you noticed something odd about the traffic?' Hardmeat probed, demanding an answer.

'More of it than usual,' responded Cullthem, trying to guess if he was on the right track.

Hardmeat simply stared ahead and inhaled, the foul stench clawing at his lungs. Perversely, the reek seemed to sharpen his mind, blowing away the dulling effect of Cullthem's vapid thoughts. It anchored him, holding back the surge of frustration at Cullthem's relentless stupidity. When a flicker of unease darkened Hardmeat's expression, Cullthem, ever the opportunist, swiftly revised his shallow guess.

'I see, there is less traffic,' Cullthem smiled. He hoped this correction would finally counter Hardmeat's persistent belief that his intelligence was genetically flawed from the start. It was perhaps a lucky guess, as Cullthem dimly realised his own name held a certain eugenic irony.

Hardmeat hastily ended Cullthem's disastrous cognitive foray into inductive thinking.

'Consider this,' Hardmeat stated, his voice a low, precise cut through the stale air. 'This road is the artery to and from the city hospital. Given the thunderclap of Brickman's apartment exploding, where are the screaming sirens? Where are the emergency vehicles?' He posed the question, a steel trap of logic clicking into place, a deduction that would have made Sherlock Holmes nod in grim appreciation.

'Sadly, perhaps, no one was slaughtered today,' Cullthem smiled, his eyes seeming to rage at the mere thought of no life being taken.

Hardmeat hideously smiled at Cullthem for his second-rate effort in trying to be evil.

'If that bomb went off with that noise, half of that block should have gone, just blown away. I don't get it,' Hardmeat puzzled.

'Well, I do. It happened, it was blown away. Yeah, just blown away,' Cullthem insisted, nodding his head along with his words. He then pursed his lips and exhaled a contemptuous puff of air, whispering, 'Gone, bye bye.' A cackle escaped his lips, and he waved a dismissive hand in a final, eerie farewell.

'Knucklehead! Don't breathe out like that. Your breath stinks as it is,' bemoaned Hardmeat.

'Then open the windows... 10 seconds?' Cullthem demanded. Cullthem, it seemed, was free to indulge his lack of clear thinking, as Hardmeat was about to demonstrate.

'Yeah, good idea. Then everyone who glances our way will wonder why two out-of-town, poorly dressed, smelly spectres are loitering. We look and dress completely out of sync with the polished clientele constantly gliding in and out of that notorious den of luxury and sophistication. We're hardly here for a reservation, are we? What's left, then? Something reeking of sinister intent judging by our very appearance.'

Had this conversation gone on, a bad outcome for both was inevitable. A tense, gnawing energy, born of nervous waiting and mounting anxiety, was slowly eroding their thought processes.

Suddenly, without so much as a tremor of warning, Hardmeat's hand clenched around his binoculars, his grip tightening with such raw, visceral disbelief that the plastic almost buckled beneath his fingers.

'Fuck, I think it's them! They're coming out. I can see them through the entrance windows,' Hardmeat said excitedly. His legs, confined for too long, ached to get out and run, to take the two targets there and then. Urgency aside, that wasn't going to happen—not like that anyway.

'Who?' asked a bemused Cullthem as if his brain had booked a holiday and left without saying goodbye or leaving a forwarding address.

'Them, pisshead! Our victims, our prey, our gruesome game to play,' Hardmeat chuckled, the words laced with such chilling undercurrents of malice that they curdled the stale air. He momentarily devoured them with his gaze, as if deciphering the final, vital clues on a blood-soaked treasure map.

He loosened his grip, letting the binoculars drop onto his dirty, grease-smeared lap. They would've bolted from the stained mess of his trousers. With the eagerness of someone about to collect a massive cheque, he picked up his quarry's photographs. He'd already scrutinised them a thousand times, but one last check was only right. Their ransom money certainly deserved that much.

After scrutinising their faces one last time, he dropped the photographs carelessly to the car floor. Picking up the binoculars, he mentally super-imposed the details onto his two targets, who resembled them perfectly.

'It's them. They're coming out. Look at them, all filled up with their foolish sanctimony,' savagely commented Hardmeat.

53

'Sanctimony, what's that? Give them to me, I want to see sanctimony close up,' demanded Cullthem as he grabbed the binoculars.

'Hello you two! You're coming out to play with us, aren't you?' Cullthem asked rhetorically, his intonation chillingly psychotic. Finally! Hardmeat and Cullthem were back in sync with their nefarious thought processes.

Spurred by Cullthem's chilling declaration, Hardmeat's voice surged with dark excitement. 'Yeah, come out to play, my foolish morsels,' he snarled. 'We're ravenous for our prey.'

He turned to Cullthem, a predatory glint in his eye. 'Ready to bag our prize, dog breath? It's game on.'

Cullthem ignored the reference to his breath. Instead, he just continued to squint in watchful anticipation as their prey moved slowly through the Royals foyer.

Car Chase

Their hunger satisfied, Professor Adams and Elizabeth drifted through the Royals' foyer, once again mesmerised by the chandeliers' shimmering, diamond-like light. They re-entered the city's vibrant embrace, waiting at the restaurant's *porte cochère*.

Moments earlier, a valet had gone to fetch Elizabeth's car. As they waited, the summer evening air, richly infused with the aromatic fragrances of the cordon bleu cuisine, almost intoxicated them. Unseen by them, however, four figures watched from the shadows, their eyes fixed with an unsettling, cold intent.

Her father, lost in thought, stared silently into the city lights beyond. Elizabeth observed the convivial flow of restaurant patrons, their chatter a vibrant hum that sharpened her perceptions. The smell of expensive perfumery, the taste of aromatic foods, and the excitement of partying the night away usually presented an invitation too tempting for Elizabeth to decline—especially after such a superlative dinner at Royals.

But the buzz in her mind from her dad's work couldn't be subdued by the sensory feast of city life. Her desire to know was as tangible as it was immediate. He'd mentioned travelling to England very soon, so she had to know now. After all, information was power.

Her usual weekend partying might have to wait as well, at least for the moment. Elizabeth knew the upcoming weekend would dissipate the stresses of another demanding week. Just then, she noticed a subtle shift in her father, a sign he was about to speak.

'The food, as always, was excellent,' said a well-fed Professor Adams.

'And the service, don't forget the service,' Elizabeth reminded her father.

'And what was best of all?' she asked.

'The atmosphere, of course,' he replied, thinking what else it could be.

'Father, isn't your bambina worth more than the atmosphere?'

'Of course! What would anything be in this world without my lovely daughter?' he replied. 'So lovely, in fact, the maître d'hôtel couldn't remember you from an earlier visit,' he teased.

'It's a busy evening, and you know faces do blur,' Elizabeth said.

'That's true,' Michael replied, 'just like everything, we eventually habituate to things if experienced regularly.'

'To think, Father, we're growing accustomed to this— agents out there, their gazes fixed on us, observing our every movement. All the while, they're supposedly ensuring our security. How comforting,' Elizabeth purred, a delicate smile playing on her lips. She clasped her hands and gazed contentedly into the middle distance, a picture of serene naiveté.

A polite cough from the valet, a sharp sound, cut through their quiet banter, signalling the car's readiness. Elizabeth's mind, adrift in soft currents of past weekend thrills, jolted back to the impending drive home with her father. The familiar comfort of their departure, that gentle certainty, was about to be brutally interrupted.

56

As their vehicle smoothly merged onto the main highway, Elizabeth's gaze snagged on a police cordon rapidly appearing ahead. This was no fleeting incident; the sheer multitude of uniformed officers and marked cruisers, their flashing red and blue lights, painted a stark tableau of chilling gravity.

Elizabeth slowed, her gaze fixed on uniformed officers expertly redirecting traffic around a dark vehicle utterly shredded, a grotesque sculpture of twisted metal and bullet holes that gaped like a macabre Swiss cheese. The scene thrummed with raw immediacy, the air heavy with the metallic tang of destruction; temporary blinds were already being unfurled, flung into place to conceal whatever fresh horror lay within.

One body partly hung from the driver's door, and an indistinct form was faintly visible in the passenger seat. The very lights that signalled the police presence starkly illuminated what was meant to be hidden.

As Elizabeth drove past, a woman, clearly disoriented and distressed, was wrapped in a blanket and attended to by medics. The shredded car held two bodies, the very individuals who had been pursuing them—a fact mercifully hidden from Elizabeth. Had she known, her eager anticipation would have shattered into immediate fear for their lives.

Elizabeth remained oblivious to the true horror, her mind still buzzing with her father's enigmatic research. To pull them back to the comfortable world of their Royals conversation, she offered up a string of startling facts.

'Consider this: on average, we have 30 to 40 trillion cells, each containing DNA. If stretched end to end, this DNA would span roughly 45 billion miles. That means you can make 240 round trips to the sun, and even at the speed of light it would take nearly 68 hours. And beyond that, the name of God is encoded into DNA. Some even call it the "God gene". The fact that you can read the genome like a binary code is profound.

'But to then suggest that names, messages, a manufacturer's encoded mark, even prophetic messages about our existence, are encoded… that's truly astonishing!' Elizabeth exclaimed, her voice buzzing with wonder.

'You know, Dad, you talk about codes, information, and secret stuff, which I appreciate right now more than ever, but what about security?' Elizabeth questioned.

As she expertly negotiated the busy city traffic, she briefly glanced at her father to emphasise her question.

'Security for both of us is uppermost in my mind right now. Bambina, just slow down to 25 mph, please. Try to express your excitement through words and not through your driving!' her father implored.

'I would, but that stupid car has been following us since we passed that wrecked car,' Elizabeth quickly retorted.

Elizabeth and her father had just crossed the well-lit Longfellow Bridge, where any pursuer would have been easily visible. Michael hastily checked his wing mirror first, before moving somewhat awkwardly in his seat to see a dark car, similar to Elizabeth's, right behind them.

However, he couldn't see it very clearly, as its headlights obscured most of its central body detail and its passenger or passengers.

He fumbled with the wing-mirror realignment buttons, but each frantic adjustment only twisted his view further, reflecting everything but the car he desperately needed to see. A flicker of panic ignited in his gut, the simple failure igniting a larger dread. Swallowing his rising anxiety, he turned to Elizabeth, his voice a forced calm.

'Perhaps he's just going the same way as us for the time being,' he said, as much to contain his own anxiety as to calm his daughter's tendency to drive even faster and ask questions later.

'Maybe. Let's just make sure though,' excitedly retorted Elizabeth.

Michael heard it in her tone, the electric snap of defiance, and saw it mirrored in the subtle, almost imperceptible press of her right foot on the accelerator. His mounting anxiety twisted, a dark counterpoint to her almost giddy excitement at the thrilling prospect of being pursued, a perilous symmetry of emotion that now filled the entire car.

At this moment, Elizabeth flicked a switch on the driver's central console, replacing the familiar satnav display with the rear camera view normally used for reversing. Suddenly, the car Michael had wanted to see more clearly was right there.

'We got him now, right in our sights!' heatedly exclaimed Elizabeth.

'Heat, sights, chase…relax, relax, please Elizabeth,' implored her increasingly anxious father. 'Red lights, Bambina, please stop!' Michael remonstrated nervously.

It was already game on for Elizabeth, who had already worked out her next several directional moves like a chess Grandmaster. She knew many small roads at right angles followed, offering options to lose her pursuer.

Ignoring the red light and without signalling, Elizabeth braked sharply and turned right without warning. She looked in her mirrors and at the rear camera to see what her pursuers' next move would be.

Almost in synchrony with her brash manoeuvre, they also braked sharply and turned right. It was undeniably a chase now, though why and for what, they didn't yet know.

'They are following us!' Elizabeth shouted. The realisation that her playful assumption was now a reality, perhaps even a deadly one, made her drive faster, hoping her intricate knowledge of the streets would outwit them.

Several sharp turns left and right in quick succession only accelerated their car's speed, their heart rates, and the risk to their lives. Such reckless driving was too good an invitation for nearby police patrol cars to miss, and they soon joined the chase. In moments, a car chase scene straight out of the movies had manifested — only this was terrifyingly real.

Typically, even as the adrenaline of fear and excitement fuelled her actions and thoughts, Elizabeth wondered who was at fault: them or the pursuers? Maybe they were undercover cops? Perhaps she should stop. 'Whoever they are,' she thought, 'it's too late for that now.'

'They call that chasing, let's see what they've got,' Elizabeth said manically, her eyes wide with a dangerous excitement. 'Buckle up, old man, a tornado of speed is about to hit.' The tension inside the car was palpable, a taut wire ready to snap. Her brain, desperate to outrun their unseen pursuers, felt close to breaking point.

The engine's roar became a terrifying extension of her frantic thoughts, and the "old man" gripped his leather seat with his fingernails. The seat belt offered little comfort, for the pursuers were gaining ground, their lights growing uncomfortably large in the rearview mirror.

Just when their bodies and their speeding car seemed to have reached a precarious balance with the road at high speed, Elizabeth went for broke—literally.

Her Mercedes seemed to shriek in raw agony, its tyres howling a tortured protest as it veered precariously, left then right, a desperate ballet of physics despite its advanced traction and comfort braking systems straining optimally. Somehow, she wrestled the powerful machine into a sharp right, into a street mercifully stripped bare of traffic and parked cars.

The pursuing car stood no chance. It couldn't handle the G-force of deceleration and maintain the traction needed to turn right as sharply as Elizabeth's car had. Needing a wider turning radius, it came to a sudden, crashing halt.

A shuttered shopfront, its quiet façade instantly annihilated, exploded inward, violently devouring a car and its two occupants. Their lives, a flickering spark against the consuming evening, were savagely snuffed out the moment their vehicle ripped through the plate glass and slammed into the unyielding side wall.

In a brutal, final lesson, the chasing occupants discovered that walls do not negotiate with speeding vehicles; they simply break them. The car's ruptured fuel tank erupted, a hungry orange blaze devoured the mangled, torn bodies within, illuminating their grim, unexpected journey to whatever lay beyond.

The raw, terrifying spectacle of the fiery wreckage exploding behind them forced Elizabeth's foot to slam the Mercedes' brakes, the car skidding to a halt in the middle of the road. She turned to her father, his face ghostly pale in the flashing lights, already wishing he was back in the surreal, safer confines of his plane dream.

'Oh my God, they've crashed. Bloody hell! They've crashed!' Elizabeth's scream tore through the evening, a raw, primal sound twisted with both terrifying elation and dawning horror. In mere heartbeats, the street behind them further ignited in light. A blinding, strobing symphony of red, white, and blue police lights painted every building and window in an infernal, pulsing secondary glow of purple and magenta — a macabre display of death.

'What do I do, Dad?' Elizabeth screamed wildly.

'Look left, left is the answer,' replied a shell-shocked father.

Elizabeth's breath hitched as a police officer suddenly appeared at her nearside, his eyes boring into her with palpable menace. 'Get out! Lie on the ground!' he commanded, each word a sharp, undeniable order. There was no mistaking his meaning; the Glock 19 he gripped was pointed with chilling intent.

Before she could even comply, a second officer approached Michael's side of the car, barking the same command at her father. Her immobile father, however, was frozen by fear. In contrast, Elizabeth was ready to comply and move, with no need to be asked twice as the Glock 19, held in a Weaver stance, ominously pointed straight at her.

As she exited the car and slowly knelt on the road, she was abruptly stopped from lying face down by someone running and shouting towards the officers from the crash scene.

'Hold back, officers,' the well-dressed female agent commanded. She arrived on the scene, her composure unruffled despite the rapid approach.

Holding an ID card in her left hand, she drew the attention of the officer who had barked at Elizabeth. The agent then flashed her ID at the other officer. Recognising her authority, the officers seemed almost imperceptibly to bow and take a step back in reverence to her status. The NSA had arrived.

- 8 -
Protective Surveillance

Watching from her kneeling position, Elizabeth looked up for acknowledgement, hoping to be told she could get up. This woman, she thought, was definitely somebody important—the officers' superior even.

The officer beside Elizabeth signalled a stand-down to his colleague, who still held his Glock 19 in a Weaver stance, pointing it at her father. Their readiness for action instantly deactivated, like machines suddenly deprived of power. Both officers slowly and dejectedly walked around to the back of the car, awaiting her next instructions.

An unspoken understanding passed between them as they stood down, so Elizabeth stood up. It made her smile. 'Evening, Miss Adams,' the senior officer said.

'How do you know me?' Elizabeth stammered, her voice a mix of astonishment and dawning curiosity. 'I mean, us? Or maybe just me?'

She looked over to her father, who had now exited the car. He was still disorientated, pointlessly leaning against it and waiting to be searched—perhaps even handcuffed. Still in shock, he hadn't noticed the two officers who had been barking commands had now withdrawn a few metres.

'Dad, over here please,' Elizabeth blurted out, breaking his almost trancelike state. He seemed to be experiencing a strange mix of anxiety and relief. A black Chevrolet Suburban, with two antennae mounted on the roof, pulled up two metres behind them. A burly male officer stepped from the SUV and began walking towards his colleague.

The two agents briefly huddled, exchanging a few words while looking suspiciously at her and her father. Once information was exchanged, they turned as one and closed in. Just before addressing them again, she ordered the watching police officers to secure the immediate area of containment. They would speak to the two car occupants in private.

'My colleague and I are government agents; this is my ID,' the female officer announced. Gesturing to their specially equipped SUV behind them, she continued, 'Please follow us.'

'Are we under arrest?' Elizabeth demanded, a tremor in her voice.

'Do you want to be?' the male agent retorted with a knowing smirk.

'Of course not,' Elizabeth shot back, a cheeky defiance in her tone, 'even if you are trying to ensnare my emotions!'

Her father's eyes shot up in disbelief. He drew a deep, steadying breath, marvelling at how his daughter could even conceive of such a flirtatious comment, let alone utter it. The situation, he thought, was dire.

As all four of them made their way to the designated SUV, the male officer inexplicably stopped and doubled back to the car. Elizabeth, though obliging and walking with her father, couldn't help but glance nervously over her shoulder. She was desperate to discern the reason for the agent's return.

Once a metre from the car, he produced a black, multi-faceted device from his pocket. A bluish beam of light washed over the vehicle, perfectly crafted to its contours. Elizabeth mumbled incoherent words of disbelief before a sudden shout shattered her thoughts.

'Stop, or there'll be a second crash this evening, Elizabeth!' the female officer exclaimed, just as Elizabeth was about to walk straight into the SUV's thick bodywork.

'Sit in those seats please,' the officer commanded as Elizabeth and her father stepped up and into the SUV, closely followed by their attentive agent. The officer sat in front of them, spinning around to address them.

'Do you know who I represent?' asked the female agent.

'Crazy question! Of course we do. You're the FBI or something close, judging by the way those officers backed off at your command,' quipped Elizabeth.

'Your levity surprises me, given only moments ago, two dead bodies back there were hoping you'd be in their position instead,' the agent said, her tone now seriously sombre. 'I am Special Agent Sterling. This is my colleague, Special Agent—'

Before she could state her colleague's last name, Elizabeth interjected with fright.

'Shit, where did you come from?'

The unintroduced agent, who had been sitting behind them all the time, quickly retorted, 'Calm down, Miss Adams. You have what we call "weapon focus". It's a natural tunnel vision on central threats, making you miss peripheral details. That explains why you didn't see me as you got in.'

Sterling smiled at her colleague, then finished her sentence. 'If I may finish, Miss Adams, this is Special Agent Parker. We work for the National Security Agency.'

'Wow, NSA! No wonder that officer backed away when you spoke to him. That also explains why no other officers have come this way. You really are somebody, aren't you!' Elizabeth rambled, like an excited child.

Sterling continued, her voice a low hum of calculated gravity. 'We have been covertly following you for many weeks. You are a prime, vulnerable target for capture (or worse) because of your father's work.'

'You were being chased by a ruthless cell of two assassins, specifically tasked to seize the both of you. Your driving, Miss Adams, a furious dance on the edge of chaos, saved you; it was exemplary, dare I say, despite its blatant illegality.'

Suddenly, a faint smile began to form on Sterling's face as she said sardonically, 'Perhaps a reflection of German engineering as much as your driving skills.'

'Indeed so,' said the agent who had scanned her car, as he got back into the SUV opposite Elizabeth.

'I think that's a compliment,' Elizabeth replied, her eyes flickering between all three agents as if further approval was required. Her face, however, was furrowed with unease that betrayed her calm statement to the watchful trio.

Agent Sterling, trained to "read" faces, confirmed it was a compliment. She continued, 'But in any case, your driving or not, the outcome would have been the same, as we were about to cut them off from that side street just behind you and to your right. We would have used deadly force if necessary.'

Elizabeth looked at the agent who had scanned her car and asked, 'What did that scanning light do to my car?'

The agent explained, 'Explosives have a "vapour pressure", meaning a tiny amount of their constituent chemicals will evaporate into the air. My device was checking for those chemicals.'

'Explosives? What do you think I am, some kind of fanatical terrorist?' Elizabeth bellowed.

'You need to know,' the agent began, but Sterling cut him off. She told him to go and supervise the clean-up down the road, and what Elizabeth needed to know would come from her. The agent, whose name was never given, left as quickly as he had entered.

At this point, her father, who had been stoically quiet, shocked the two agents with a question as profoundly as the chase had shocked him and Elizabeth.

His gaze, unwavering, fixed first on Agent Sterling. 'Sophia' he uttered, his calm voice shattering the air. Then, his eyes shifted to the other agent, the one Elizabeth hadn't seen at first. 'Oliver', he mumbled, quietly but assuredly.

The two agents seized up, statues of disbelief, their faces crumpling with shared consternation as they helplessly read the shock in each other's wide eyes.

'Who told you our first names?' Sterling asked forcefully.

'Yeah, who?' Parker echoed forcefully.

'Nobody told me; I saw your names in a dream earlier on,' stated Michael as if this were an adequate explanation for it all.

'That's bizarre,' an agitated Sterling said. 'If you were not Professor Adams, I would not so easily accept your answer, as this implies a security breach. We never, ever give first names for protocol reasons.'

Michael was clearly unmoved by her concern. He thought, "Their training could be improved if they acknowledged my point. They would do better to ignore my suggestion and just move on. That would retain their control and my deference to it."

These thoughts led Adams to a small outburst of annoyance as he chafed at his statement being questioned, especially when he knew he was right: 'Well, live with it!'

Over the next fifteen minutes, the two NSA agents addressed the Adamses' now precarious situation, explaining how their lives would be balanced with the need for protection.

Parker didn't hold back, encouraging them to recognise the sheer brutality of the evil that had pursued them. He began with a summary of the evening's events, first explaining about the two men shot dead near the Royals, then moving on to the two recently cremated just down the road.

He explained that the NSA had been watching the first two men after flagging their licence plate. The plate had been traced to a brutal murder and a female passenger abduction earlier. 'Our ANPR cameras caught them cold,' he stated gleefully yet clinically, adding that the standing order was to detain them for questioning.

But that precise instruction was abandoned the moment they opened fire on our agents. They knew the game was up, and in that desperate, final second, they chose to go out not with a whimper, but in a blaze of futile glory, much like those poor bastards back there, incinerated in their own personalised coffin. 'We know their identities too, though I'm not at liberty, at present, to confirm them,' he added. 'I can say they all knew each other.'

Elizabeth and her father sat in silence. Suddenly, what they saw earlier was not some remote event, unconnected to them. It was inextricably entwined with their lives in ways that made them shudder with anxiety and fear. Elizabeth grabbed her father's hand for reassurance. In response, he gently gripped her hand and offered a warm smile, whispering, 'We'll be all right, don't worry.'

This knowledge only spurred Elizabeth on to demand, not ask, why her dad's work was so important it had become a national security issue, and why their lives were now targets. She'd been told so much, but for people to want to chase and kill them – that was utterly beyond her comprehension. Would her dad finally tell her? She had merely tasted this knowledge earlier; now she craved the full feast.

Consequently, the ad hoc security briefing also included a surprising detail about data security. Elizabeth was shocked to learn they knew about her father's network and the security of their mansion. It dawned on her: her dad wasn't just important; he was incredibly important. And now, she had inherited a kind of de facto importance herself.

His computer data was shielded by a special device, developed by the same people who created the world's most unbreakable encryption algorithm, one that even the most sophisticated computers would struggle to decrypt. This, he'd been told, would provide more than enough time for the NSA to intervene with any hackers.

To enhance the mansion's security, they had stealthily installed two cutting-edge CCTV cameras. The first was a thermal-imaging camera designed to pinpoint any unusual body heat inside the mansion or around its extensive grounds.

The second type, which looked just like ordinary CCTV, were special Kirlian cameras placed inside the mansion itself. These covered three areas any burglar would have to pass through to gain full access.

These advanced cameras didn't just record; they interrogated. They scanned a person's subtle energy field, an invisible aura surrounding all living things from humans to plants. They were ingenious, utterly infallible. Computer algorithms unravelled intricate images, meticulously cross-referencing known signatures against the unknown. Any anomaly, any ripple in the expected, was instantly flagged as red, triggering an "appropriate" and immediate response.

Both Elizabeth and her father didn't fully grasp the technicalities, but the outcome was more easily discernible: Any mansion intruder would be treated the same as an illegal Area 51 incursion, meaning a fatal response was legally permissible.

The briefing over, Elizabeth and Michael stepped from the agents' SUV and walked the few metres back to her BMW, where a local detective kept a quiet vigil. Their impending journey back to the mansion would be under armed escort. Their car would be positioned between two armoured SUVs, one in front and one in pursuit. Parker and Sterling would ride in the lead SUV.

Just as Elizabeth prepared to start her BMW, footsteps, fast and distinct, hammered towards them. Given the secured area, they knew this swift approach was for them alone.

With every stride, the cadence grew clearer—the relentless, unmistakable rhythm of a fit, agile runner. So synchronous and rhythmic was their beat, it could have been a chilling, percussive backing track, a drumbeat of impending discovery.

Suddenly, Special Agent Parker materialised at Michael's window. Michael didn't seem particularly concerned. Elizabeth fidgeted, annoyed, as she tried to adjust her hair, but it stubbornly refused to lie properly.

'Sorry for coming back. I think you need to know something about tonight. The people after you were terrorists, paid terrorists. By "paid", I mean there are people out there who simply revel in creating mayhem, provided they're not the ones who actually bleed for it,' Parker said, with a dry, almost cynical amusement twisting his words.

'In other words, they'll pay the price for someone else to pay the ultimate, bloody price,' Parker added sardonically, a low rasp of bitter truth in his voice.

'Wow, you're so ironic!' said Elizabeth.

'We've got your backs from now. I know you want your personal space, and we'll give that willingly, within reason of course. But you must recognise there are some very dark forces out there. They want your father, and maybe even you now, as bargaining tools, or maybe even for your deaths. Tonight was just one manifestation. You must expect more to come.'

With that, Parker walked back to the SUV to join Sterling. As he moved, a piece of NSA intelligence lingered with him, a detail he just couldn't convey: the terrorists had been handsomely paid by dark forces to take them hostage, and the price included torture and death, if they weren't compliant

Parker experienced an internal conflict. He liked Michael and Elizabeth, but felt a greater need to be economical with the truth, hoping to prevent them from being unduly terrorised by their own thoughts. It was the NSA's job to counter the terrorist mindset and eliminate threats permanently.

Parker got back into the SUV with the 3.5-litre engine idling. Sterling asked about the conversation, and Parker recounted it word for word. While they spoke, another NSA SUV had joined them and would be the chase car.

With this, Sterling drove off, leading Elizabeth and Michael back to the mansion. On the way back, the NSA agents found themselves reviewing their encounters with the elite, a collection of experiences that consistently left a sour taste.

They found these powerful figures were undeniably approachable, yet their demeanour swiftly transformed from engaging to haughty, as if power and money acted as the most intoxicating of aphrodisiacs, hardening their reserve.

Any attempts at genuine conversation were frequently met with rudeness, often shading into outright patronising tones. When Parker and Sterling dared to probe their motivations, or their view of the world's billions of socioeconomically poor and illiterate populations, the elites responded with impenetrable nonchalance, remaining distant even when asked how they might improve their plight.

Ultimately, Parker and Sterling concluded that their lived experiences and compassionate perspectives were fundamentally at odds with those of the elites they encountered. Their patriotism was sacrosanct; it had no price. They worked for the country's commitment to democracy, security of the homeland, and the promise of the American dream.

Meanwhile, as Elizabeth drove, closeted by their SUV metal bodyguards, their conversation reprised what had happened and what was said, from the Royals to the briefing. Phrases like "alpha-level clearance", "DNA", and "genetic bomb" hung in the air, weighted with the gravitas of what it all meant for them and how it would play out.

For Michael, the true heart of the matter resonated deeply. If his daughter was to forfeit her freedom, he decided, it was only right to grant her access to some of the secret documents.

Elite Dark Forces

About halfway back to the mansion, the conversation between Sterling and Parker about elites concluded, but Parker's warning about dark forces reverberated with chilling certainty. While Michael was an enigma to most, Parker understood a fundamental truth: a government's unwavering interest in anyone with widespread influence invariably branded them a target for those operating in the shadows.

Sterling drove, headlights carving streaks on the road. Parker's gaze danced restlessly as oncoming headlights slashed through the twilight. The memory of his first briefing on these elites chewed at the raw edges of his awareness.

His rise through the NSA had granted him access to ever more guarded operations, unveiling the subtle currents that twisted beneath everyday society. He recalled the bone-deep, sterile chill of Sub-Level Gamma, the oppressive quiet of the briefing room at an undisclosed facility.

Senior officials ghosted into the sterile room, their identities as ephemeral as the facility's spectral presence. Then, a humanoid machine glided in, its unnerving sentience and chilling tone sending a visceral jolt of fear through Parker.

In this room, the briefing explained how a minority of power brokers spun their insidious web across the world—a toxic mixture of coldly calculated harm and relentless manipulation. No government was immune. Every government policy had their mark of approval.

Their public image was deliberately unremarkable, presenting as societal pillars, seemingly oblivious to the festering rot they cultivated in the shadows. They held high-profile positions of power, but in private, the insatiable amassment of wealth and subservience to a misplaced ideology proved a corrupting power.

The statistics screamed their stark truth. The richest 1% of the world's population owned more than double the wealth of seven billion people and a staggering 75% of global land and capital. This concentration of power meant the top 1% commanded more wealth than 95% of humanity combined, an accumulation that didn't happen by chance alone.

Such wealth brought power, often exerted through lobbying, campaign contributions, and media ownership. This power ground into dust any who dared impede. Greed and predatory gain were their sacraments; charity, anathema. They tightened their iron grip on the structures of public and private life.

Their modus operandi was chillingly encapsulated by a Latin phrase: *Divitiae, terra, potentiae; elite tantum necessitates sunt.* In English, it declared unequivocally: 'Wealth, land, power. Only elite needs exist.'

Their power, therefore, seeped into every aspect of modern society. People were slowly drained of their essence, reduced to mere tools of production, glorifying the elite's vacuous existence and bloating their wealth.

The elite's influence, a creeping vine, didn't merely spread; it systematically strangled. Its tendrils first insidiously entwined, then venomously poisoned, and finally inexorably bound employees to their will.

The non-elite, tethered to a system long unchallenged, could never grasp its true form: it was a nameless phantom, unseen yet palpable in its nefarious demands. Like ruthless farmers, the elite cultivated the minds of the many, harvesting not sustenance, but a choking, bitter obedience the labourers would never taste.

The levers of law and taxation, ostensibly necessary pillars of a functioning society, were insidiously recalibrated. Seemingly innocuous adjustments—a slight increase here, a novel levy there—disproportionately crushed those outside the elite's protected circles.

Legal complexities, deliberately convoluted, became a suffocating labyrinth only the well-resourced could navigate. They snared the unwary in webs of fines and bureaucratic quicksand, the constant pressure of financial strain gnawing relentlessly at the majority's spirit.

'Any questions?' it asked.

After such a detailed monologue, a two-word question seemed lacking in specifics.

So immersed was Parker in this memory, he accidentally blurted aloud, 'No questions.'

'I didn't ask anything,' a bemused Sterling replied, focusing on the road ahead. Exasperated, she asked, 'Parker, where's your mind?'

Parker hadn't really gone anywhere; he could absorb a scene and process complex thoughts simultaneously. Dark forces were clearly at play with Michael and Elizabeth. It seemed only a matter of time before their insidious, malicious tentacles would slither forth once more to poison their lives. The question was not if, but when and how it would happen.

- 10 -
The Synthetic Exomorph

Thirty minutes into their resumed journey, the mansion loomed into sight, its imposing, ten-foot-tall, double-swing main gates abruptly halting their progress. Each gate, anchored to impenetrably strong concrete columns, had a voice sensor on the right. The lead car gently swerved to the left to give Elizabeth's BMW room for access. Michael watched as her window whirred down. She leaned out, a smirk dancing playfully on her lips, and cried 'bra strap' at it.

The gates groaned open, a metallic lament, and Michael suppressed a chuckle, his password of 'deoxyribonucleic acid' feeling a touch excessive. As the opening widened, Elizabeth shifted into gear, eager to drink in the idyllic property's dazzling views and intoxicating fragrances.

Outside the gates, two NSA SUVs idled. On their radios, Parker and Sterling agreed all four would take the first four-hour shift; then four more would take over for the next four hours. This would be the pattern for all the teams securing Professor Adams and his daughter.

Overhead, small drones already hummed, their collective vigilance complemented by a Secret Service team covertly embedded at various points within the mansion grounds. Together, they formed a collective response to maintaining the security and welfare of their charges.

Evening moonlight draped the verdant grounds, casting a soft glow on the partially illuminated mansion as Elizabeth drove towards it. The two-minute ascent to the front doors unveiled a breathtaking panoramic view.

Trees, hedges, and flowers embraced the mansion, a symbiotic embrace of beauty. In shared awe, Elizabeth and her father fell silent, utterly absorbed by the foliage's complex artistry.

Silhouettes layered, their monochromatic shades subtly shifting and deepening with every foot of distance. To fully immerse himself, Michael lowered his window, eager to drink in the potent, invigorating air—a feeling, if bottled, that would command a king's ransom.

She parked by the mansion's Portland stone step-entrance, then turned to her father, a question poised on her lips.

'Pinch me,' she murmured, disbelief lacing her voice. 'Did that really happen tonight? The chase, the accident, the NSA... all in one hour of intense insanity?'

'It did,' her father replied, his voice a sardonic blend of anxiety and profound exhaustion. 'But only through the grace of German engineering are we still here to talk about it.'

Elizabeth offered a fleeting smile, her mind awash with a swirling maelstrom of shocking memories. Her gaze drifted past her father, to the grounds serenely bathed in moonlight, a peaceful counterpoint to the evening's terror. Lost in their wooded cradle, her anxious reflections softened, replaced by a more practical concern: immediate security was on her mind.

'Just think of the NSA agents out there,' Elizabeth mused. 'Do they ever sleep? Do they eat and drink? Would they really shoot if they had to?'

'Let's get out,' her father suggested, 'and carry our shock into the mansion to rest.'

'Alpha wisdom, as always, Dad,' Elizabeth replied, a thoughtful pause.

Stepping from the car, they climbed the Portland stone steps to the mansion's front doors. Their synchronised ascent, step by step, was a testament to shared genes and thoughts. Unlike the main gates' verbal entry, they now faced facial recognition.

Microseconds passed before welcoming beeps resonated across the front entrance. Michael pushed open the right mansion door, entering slowly, Elizabeth close behind.

'Welcome, Professor Michael Adams and Elizabeth Adams,' the AI security system announced.

'Well, that's different... why, thank you, darling,' Elizabeth shot back, unable to resist the sarcasm. 'That's a sexy voice. Do you look as good as you sound? Perhaps—'

'Extant End 999,' her father cut in, patience audibly frayed.

'Cancelling entry protocol for both of you,' the AI stated.

'Elizabeth, you know this is a computer-generated voice,' her father explained, a faint hint of amusement touching his tone. 'Though for all you know, it might generate a hologram and visit you at night.'

'How exciting,' she replied saucily. 'I wonder what proportions it might assume?'

'Haven't you had enough excitement for one night?' her father asked, his gaze drifting towards the top of the staircase and his nearby bedroom.

'There was that small matter of a document you said I could look at, remember?'

'And I will,' he promised, exhaustion now overtly shaping his posture and tone.

Elizabeth entered the drawing room as her father began climbing the curved staircase. She couldn't help but glance at the telephone handset, her eyes darting to confirm it was still on its base.

'You're sure you'll let me see the details about your project mission?' she pleaded, her voice tinged with a playful edge. 'Especially that super-secret synoptic paper that's not for the likes of me to see,' she added playfully.

'Of course, of course, I trust you implicitly,' he replied, his tired, still-shaken body slowly, deliberately ascending the stairway.

Adams showered and retired to bed, but not before granting Elizabeth access to several synoptic pages. They lay hidden in a secure safe, specially installed within the mansion and visible to covert Kirlian cameras.

Elizabeth settled into a drawing room chair and viewed the first page.

A watermark subtly emblazoned the page: large, red italic capital letters stretching from bottom left to top right. The three words – "ABOVE TOP SECRET" – collectively evoked goosebumps, chills, and a sense of foreboding within her. A sense of anxiety and fear surged through her body, as if someone was breathing down her neck. To reassure herself, she furtively scanned the empty drawing room before turning to the next page.

The Department of Defense symbol topped the page. A few lines below, her father's name appeared as the author. She smiled, seeing his name on such a super-secret document. Strange tingling sensations shivered through her, as if a brief chill wind had ghosted over her. This feeling was countered with a comment, in keeping with their earlier verbal sparring.

'Smart arse,' she jokingly mumbled to herself about her father. A few lines below, she saw an array of names from various departments. Most meant little to her: senior Air Force, military, and naval personnel, along with top-ranking banking, financial, and government officials. The only names she recognised were from the Executive Office of the President of the United States, and the President himself.

The document's importance now bestowed upon her a sense of specialness. It replaced her recent fear and anxiety with a strange elation. A quiet giggle escaped her as she recognised the document's immense secrecy and the select few—herself included—who had been privy to it. She quickly turned to the third page, hoping the substantive information began there.

Feeling thirsty, she quickly placed the document on the nearby Coco Chanel side-table, watching her hands shake with elated nervousness.

'Get a grip, girl!' she exclaimed to herself. Nothing else penetrated; the enormity of what lay before her precluded further thought or speech. Realising she needed to calm her nerves before diving into the paper's subsequent pages, she decided a good red wine was in order—a stress buster against its likely findings.

Her father's well-stocked wine cellar, a cool 15.5 degrees Celsius, beckoned. She walked off for something special but not too ostentatious.

She returned with a perfectly appropriate Château Cardinal-Villemaurine 1966. She pinged the Mina Murano wine glass selected from a nearby cabinet, its expensive tone resonating before she poured a generous amount. Back in her chair, she felt the wine, like the paper's contents, was about to impact her. Elizabeth picked up the paper to read page three. Her focus was so absolute, she read it softly to herself.

This briefing paper is for designated personnel only (pages 1 and 2). More detailed evidence regarding military implications requires Level 33 clearance, per defined protocols. Read on:

1.   From molecular biology's genesis, following the landmark discovery of DNA in 1953, its co-founder, Francis Crick, championed a profoundly audacious hypothesis: 'Directed Panspermia'.

This theory posited that life itself—and by direct implication, the intricate code of our DNA—was not indigenous to Earth but rather an extraterrestrial import, deliberately sent to our nascent world.

2.   Crick's vision suggested our DNA code was no random terrestrial occurrence. Instead, he proposed it as an inherent blueprint, a veritable 'manufacturer's stamp' meticulously implanted by an advanced, external civilisation. This radical perspective fundamentally reshaped life's genesis, transforming it from a purely Earth-bound evolutionary process into a deliberate, profound cosmic connection. Implicit in this cosmic design was the tantalising notion that humanity, upon reaching sufficient scientific and technical advancement, might one day truly decipher this embedded, inherent code.

3.   For over seventy years since Crick first articulated his theory, as DNA research has burgeoned with ever more sophisticated forensic techniques, the resonant idea of a hidden code has resurfaced on a persistent basis. Three major milestones in this ongoing quest for interpretation are:

(a)   The Human Genome Project (HGP; 1990–2003): An international scientific research project, one of the greatest feats of scientific exploration in our still adolescent history. Unpacking DNA's genetic blueprint, it successfully identified and mapped all our genes, collectively known as the genome.

This genetic blueprint, a cosmos in itself, allowed us to understand the fundamental biochemical mechanics that constitute us: physical, functional, and even psychological. Note: It only sequenced 92.1% of the human genome (the so-called euchromatic regions); heterochromatic areas remained unsequenced.

(b)   The "100,000 Genomes Project" (2013–2018): A UK-based project. Although both projects sought to understand the coding interrelationships of DNA, this one focused on the cause or aetiology of rare diseases.

This project significantly improved the knowledge of disease causes, treatment, and care. In so doing, intelligence suggests they stumbled upon further evidence to support a code.

(c)   "ENCODE X" (2003 – ?): Regarded as an HGP follow-up, this multi-phase study is being conducted by several known alpha-coded research institutions, including Harvard, the Indian Institute of Science, Oxford (England), and Tsinghua University (China).

They have separately uncovered previously hidden switches, signposts, and signals that may carry a chemical message, though its nature remains mostly presumption and speculation.

Note: Intelligence suggests their research findings (what little exists) have been designated military intelligence and are TOP SECRET, applying Level 33 and above access. NSA directorate approved.

We now possess a massive, almost unfathomable data jigsaw, its understanding vast and networked. This is unsurprising; DNA is, by design, probably the most efficient storage system, now and in the future.

Evolution has ensured this network of storage has mutated to evolve, and not just environmentally. The genetic program is beyond world-class—indeed, it's not of this world.

Within us, DNA undergoes trillions of replications, and countless mutations arise; yet, this astonishing complexity, scientists suggest, is not a product of random evolution, but the directed result of an inherent program within our DNA itself, leading to algorithmic exactitude of genetic resolution.

Elizabeth sat, utterly stunned. The wine, a small mercy, had tempered the information, its dizzying effect making the unravelling implications marginally easier to bear.

Her gaze snagged on "Findings: Turn over". Her eyes, suddenly wide, seemed to gulp the words in, desperate to absorb every detail. Sweat pricked her palms as an undeniable sensation washed over her – the thrilling, terrifying feeling of standing on the precipice of something truly remarkable.

Compelled, she turned to page four and read on. 'Findings (summary only):

- A global event is pending: "Day of Quanta" or "Q-Day"
- Only humans are affected; all other life is spared
- A biological DNA clock is ticking down to "Q-Day"
- Q-Day is close to midnight, December 31, this year
- Messages (many others awaiting decode) may share a master code, from which servant codes derive

- The past, present, and future are one—all planned—and encrypted until the right time (Einstein, Hawking, block universe theories may apply)
- All strategic defences (subterranean, surface, aerial) are useless against the "code"
- World universities are reluctant to cooperate—each vying for the first decode; the power spoils are incalculable (Oxford may collaborate; reference Dr. Peter Magma)
- Names and dates are suggested for those unpacking and producing package composites noted within DNA—intelligence confirms others' findings
- We believe we lead the decode effort
- As we decode, it bizarrely reports our progress, as if an omnipotent, omnipresent conscience watches (or judges?) our advance
- Disturbingly, we've decoded the possibility of internal specifications for an artificial lifeform genetically coded for external development—a "synthetic exomorph".

'Synthetic what?' Elizabeth muttered, grappling with the word "exomorph". "'Exo" means outside, I think, and "morph" means change. Something that changes on the outside?' She resisted the urge to grab her mobile and look it up; it was too late, too many scary details already swirling in her increasingly tired mind. She settled on it meaning a lifeform of some kind.

Elizabeth, who had devoured countless books in her young life, eagerly escaping into narratives and impossible worlds, now confronted a chillingly different reality. The document splayed open on her lap, stark against the fine fabric.

This wasn't fiction she could simply close and set aside. It bore the disquieting hallmarks of a film so bizarre it walked a tightrope between reality and pure fantasy, blurring lines until she questioned what was real.

A cold knot tightened in her stomach, an unnerving sense of impending chaos, a pervasive dread that something monumental and utterly uncontrollable was about to unravel.

The sheer, oppressive weight of its implications pressed down. Given the theoretical models' inherent, wide margins of error, the situation remained agonisingly fluid, refusing to solidify. She needed her father for comfort and explanation; this was a truth too heavy to read alone.

It was impossible, at present, to form a definitive outcome. The truth, if it existed within these pages, remained out of reach, an evasive phantom she couldn't quite grasp. She read on.

"To Professor Adams (Harvard): We are sorry to note that pages five to seven of your copy have been temporarily redacted and are for the eyes of Level 33 personnel and above only.

"We hope you understand this is due to political and military implications beyond your investigation's remit. Budgets, technology, and personnel have been redirected to your research; full disclosure will be on a need-to-know basis. We wish you every early patriotic success. Regards, Dr. Denton, NSA Director. End."

Elizabeth looked up in bewilderment, her palms glistening with anxiety. What sinister revelation lurked on pages five to seven? A ticking genetic time bomb, undefusable?

Her awareness, questioning, and unease weren't lessened by the brief reading; they merely magnified, a swirling vortex in her mind. Yet, her reason and concern soon yielded to the insistent biological need for sleep. It was time for bed. The mental energy for questioning quickly faded, especially due to the Château Cardinal-Villemaurine's velvet, mind-numbing embrace.

Slowly, as tiredness overwhelmed her and her grip on the super-secret report diminished, it became a slippery weight, inevitably falling from her fingers. It dropped to the floor with a soft rustle, a final, lonesome sound as she, too, succumbed to a deep sleep.

Just as her earlier return to the mansion had begun with her father asleep, so it ended with her doing the same, slumped, utterly spent, in the very same chair.

The Battle Of Wits

At his university office Regency Desk, Professor Adams was besieged by a fortress of paper, a sea of awaiting research and decoded material from his team. His immediate workspace was a small, beleaguered island of reading. Some conclusion papers were missing, undoubtedly swallowed by the chaos of his work-from-home sessions several days earlier. Yet he worked with his hallmark diligence, meticulously gathering key findings.

His desk, already a battleground of intellect, was consumed as research papers to his left, right, and front metamorphosed into relentless, ever-mounting citadels of information. He devoured, dissected, and distilled findings; each act of analysis, theorising, and revision adding to the overwhelming bulk.

The few telephone calls and insistent knocks at his office door were not mere breaks, but jarring intrusions that shattered his laser-like focus. Every slowly grinding minute drummed with increasing urgency, driving him to forge his scattered insights into a coherent narrative. This feverish mental intensity chained him to his desk, destroying any thought of reprieve.

What he possessed was not merely amazing, but apocalyptic in its scope. He knew that even his long-term friend, Peter Magma of Oxford, his academic counterpart, would require time to fully grapple with its staggering implications. Peter was a man of prodigious intellect and unwavering composure. It was a truth of such unfathomable magnitude that it would irrevocably reweave, or perhaps tear apart, the very fabric of human existence.

His own fabric of conscious existence fractured with a knock at his office door at midday. The first few door knocks went unaddressed; his laser focus was absolute, immersing him in a self-constructed cognitive laboratory of scientific discourse.

The third knock was louder and more insistent. It finally broke his immersion in theoretical research. His return to reality was revealed through the door window, where a silhouette stood to attention, seeking his approval for admittance.

Adams bristled, a raw fury tightening his jaw at such a breach of his cognitive indulgence. In a voice laced with acid and sharp enough to splinter wood, he snapped, 'What?' toward the offending door. The resonance of that single syllable seemed to physically compress the very air, causing the person knocking to shift uncomfortably, their brittle, arthritic knees emitting a faint crack.

The door rattled in response, as if vibrating from the shockwave that pounded its hardened exterior. Yet, even with this almost pugilistic request, his emotional bar of annoyance rose again as a softer, inexplicably fourth knock was heard.

Not only that, his self-imposed axiomatic and dialectic thought processes—a mosaic of probabilities and possibilities from colliding schools of biological thought—were finally shattered.

The cognitive fracture spurred Adams to discard his usual restraint. Responding to the fourth knock, he bellowed even louder than before, 'Just open the bloody door before I tear it off its hinges, oh for God's sake!'

Adams unleashed this emotional diatribe at the inanimate door with such feral rapacity, he felt he could shred the very wood and confront the knocking perpetrator on the other side. Indeed, such was the raw, unbridled force of his outburst that any mortal with a shred of sense would not have obliged his command. Instead, they would have fled in terror, their future wellbeing a distant second to immediate escape.

His growing militant thoughts toward the door and the knocking beyond were ready to be put into action. Just as he was about to get up, the office door's handle turned. It creaked with agonising slowness as the mysterious knocker finally revealed himself.

It was the esteemed Harvard President, Harvey Pabellon. His demeanour was at odds with his illustrious role. This unease was mirrored in Adams himself as the President stood partly hidden behind the door, awaiting a command.

'Harvey, what a surprise, I mean, what a lovely surprise!' said a startled and conciliatory Adams, who began to stand to greet the President. Owing to the President's half-hearted entrance, all thoughts of door harassment were immediately banished from Adams' mind.

As Adams stood from his opulent green leather Captain's chair, its cool leather armrests beneath his hands, a subtle disquiet, like a faint tremor in the air, settled upon him.

His sharp eyes, honed by years of meticulous observation, registered a phantom flicker of movement—the indistinct, shifting outlines of one, perhaps two more shadowy figures glimpsed through the narrow sliver of space revealed by the opening door's swing. He instantly catalogued this visual anomaly, a cold prickle of unease snaking across the periphery of his awareness.

But for now, his primary attention remained fixed on the President's undeniably troubled presence. Harvey lingered by the threshold, a static figure against the brighter hallway, reluctant to fully enter the sanctuary of Adams' office.

His posture, usually so composed, now betrayed a distinct unease, a barely contained agitation that radiated from him like a palpable tension, its source a complete mystery to the professor.

'Michael, lovely to see you too,' replied the man fondly known as "HP"—a nickname that was both an acronym of his name and position, as well as a nod to his love for a certain table sauce.

Michael joked, 'Well come in, entry charges don't start till tomorrow for people affectionately known as "HP".'

A silent plea formed in his mind, directed at the unmoving figure of the Harvard President. He hoped this inexplicable hesitation would soon break, allowing Harvey to finally cross the threshold into Adams's domain. The tableau at the doorway was unsettling; it was a stark contrast to HP's usual commanding presence.

It struck Michael as odd: who would willingly remain in that transitional space, caught between the hallway and Adams's inner sanctum? Surely, the logical course of action, even for someone facing a potentially unpleasant encounter, would be to cross the threshold, but Michael conceded, with a mental wince, that extreme caution was paramount.

Adams's legendary volatility and unpredictable nature were well-documented, a fiery inheritance that his daughter, with her own sharp edges, had undoubtedly claimed.

HP looked over his right shoulder at something just outside the office, and then back at Michael, before ominously saying, 'Professor, there are some, erh, gentlemen here to see you.'

'Well, Harvey, I'd say show them in,' Michael joked, trying to lighten the tense atmosphere. 'But you all seem to sense something nefarious about entering my noble, if humble, seat of learning!' He hoped his jocular tone would ease the ominous feelings that were building within him, and seemingly within HP too.

Just then, two men in black suits, who had been mere silhouettes moments before, followed HP into Adams' office. Adams watched their arrival with shock and a sense of bewildered awe.

Standing in the doorway, their black bespoke suits that shrieked of tailored precision, were a stark contrast to HP's common, off-the-peg attire. They wore impossibly dark glasses, obsidian discs that seemed to absorb all light, rendering their eyes unseen.

With their contrasting heights and unnervingly synchronised, hesitant demeanour, these two figures appeared less like men and more like a grotesque, living parody, mirror-images of the absurd made flesh. A chill wind of unease, invisible but palpable, seemed to coil around them, clinging to their bespoke suits.

Adams kindly requested them to fully enter his office of learning by saying, 'Harvey, please ask your two men in black to honour my hospitality by fully entering my humble yet riotous abode of connectome research.'

He added a small laugh at the end of his request to keep up his jocular pretence. Yet he was inwardly alarmed; his pretence was fatally wounded, as he suddenly realised the unintended implication of what he had just said.

He had just called his mysterious visitors, "men in black". His thoughts raced in his head as he watched them enter his room and stand on the other side of his desk, while the President hung further back by the door, in case things got out of hand, whatever that meant or implied.

'Gentlemen, you look very official so I won't offend your time here by idle chatter. Business seems to be your respective middle names, I think,' rambled a deferential Adams, who tried but failed to prevent his anxiety from showing on his face as a frozen terror.

Adams began to introduce himself to his formal visitors.

'Please, let me formally introduce myself: I am Professor Michael Adams, Professor of –' but at this point, the taller of the two men in black interrupted to take control of the introductions.

'We know who you are, what you are, where you go, who you talk to, what you buy for lunch, the precise contents of your fridge... We know everything, Professor Adams. You get the picture, don't you?' Adams felt violated, his sense of personal space shattered by the cold precision of the agent's knowledge.

Adams, with a singular, focused look of contempt at this rude interjection, just stared at his interrupter for several seconds, as if some errant student stood before him. Nobody, and I mean nobody, spoke to him like that, absolutely not, and especially not in his own academic domain. Adams thought about what his thoughts might be on his impending sardonic retort.

In a flash, his retort departed in their direction, immediately making the men in black realise they had met someone of profound cognitive substance. "Power dynamics are now in play," Adams thought to himself, "and there's only one winner here, and it isn't them."

Never was a more shining example of intimidation met with intellectual force, the President of Harvard thought as he watched on with outward calm but an internal disposition that was filled with both fear and concern for the immediate future.

Adams adopted a forensic attitude and an unmistakable tone of voice, normally reserved for miscreant students. He delivered a strategic, pedantic correction of grammar and logic. He said, 'We know who you are and who you talk to; I think you mean "whom you talk to".'

He hoped this verbal posture of linguistic deduction would show how the word was mightier than the pen or sword in this instance. He continued as if Sherlock Holmes had briefly taken up residence in his mortal body.

An intellectual counter-offensive was delivered with the ruthlessness and precision of a ballistic cruise missile. It detonated within their respective egos, shattering their internal dispositions with a concussive force.

Michael replied to the taller of the two, 'Your accent suggests a lack of extensive education. You're likely from a relatively humble background where excess money was a luxury, not commonplace.

'Your father is still alive, but your mother passed away some 20 years ago. I deduce this because he probably pushed you into a military career as a way to get you out of the house after your mother passed. You find sexual congress as difficult as your social manners are for befriending.

'You've had some military training, evident in your gait as you walked in. You likely consider yourself tough. You probably boxed in the army or to fight your way out of poverty, as I can see your nose septum has been broken twice.

'You probably walked away from army boxing as you don't have the broad face often linked to aggression. You smoke about 20 cigarettes a day, evidenced by the nicotine stain on your right index and middle fingers.

'And…know your enemy before you insult them, as you will dig two graves, not one,' Adams finished, his voice a low, lethal whisper. The precision of this retort gutted its intended victim. Adams had utterly outgunned him.

The verbal ballistic missile had struck its target. Adams could see he had not merely decommissioned his superiority, but utterly obliterated it. He had consigned the twisted remains to the overflowing bin beside his overworked desk—a graveyard of an intellectual argument far beyond anything they'd ever encountered.

The verbal trench warfare had clearly assessed Adams as the superior combatant, so the taller of the two men in black now offered a more conciliatory response.

'Professor Adams, I think we may have started off incorrectly. My colleague and I sort of work for the NSA—the National Security Agency—but parallel to it, an appendage so to speak, but not,' the chastised operative replied. 'If I may, please just call me Tall and my colleague Short, for obvious reasons.'

Adams perceived such language as a direct acknowledgment of their initial aggressive approach and an attempt to reset the interaction on a more civil footing.

'Nomenclature aside, then this is what you will be henceforward: Tall and Short!' laughed Adams.

'If you would,' said Tall.

'Whatever works for you bods. Was my description of you correct?' Adams questioned.

'Yes, you got it in one,' replied Tall.

'I thought so. Anyway, I guessed you were NSA, or akin to that, as your colleagues introduced themselves to us the other night at our unfortunate, yet life-saving accident,' Adams continued.

'I wouldn't regard it as an accident for you, Professor. It was, however, very much an accident for your pursuers and very much not life-saving for them either,' said Short.

'Evidently not. Tall and Short? I could find out your real names, you know?' Adams's voice hardened, stung by their implication that he was a simpleton.

Sensing both MIBs were now uncomfortable with his pugilistic and interrogative stance, he went in for the kill.

'Would this number be familiar to you?' asked Adams as he looked at both MIBs in turn and reeled off a telephone number.

The two sharply-dressed men in black looked at each other, their impassive faces momentarily fracturing, a hairline crack of raw surprise spreading across their carefully constructed composure. It was as if their roles as agents of control had just suffered another unexpected and galling reversal.

'Should it?' they replied in unison.

'Let me try another way then,' Adams continued, his studious approach as simple to him as a lesson from "Control and Social Standing 101".

'Do you know who Dr. Denton is?' Adams questioned, a grin of accelerating superiority spreading across his face as his two now unwelcome visitors showed no clue as to where his frightening inquisitorial attitude was going next.

'Of course, we know of him, he's the NSA director,' stated Tall, with a defensive edge.

'Remember when I said, "know thy enemy"?' hastily questioned Adams, who by now not only knew the punchline but also their probable reason for visiting.

'Professor Adams, this is growing tiresome; we are here to –' Tall began, but Adams cut him off with a raised hand.

'Wait; listen to me now. Not only do I know your boss—I have his phone number here (pointing to his head), which clearly you do not. I know him better than most in government, the Senate, even the fucking President. Sorry, HP, but you may have guessed anyway!

'So, listen to me, my sharply-dressed good buddies of no fixed intellectual abode, I may have an IQ that extends infinitely farther than your respective excuses for common sense, but also I am not without street kudos and connections.

'Be warned gentlemen, your time draws near in more ways than one. Compose yourselves, apologise to Harvey, then to me. State the purpose of your presence here today, and then exit more quickly than your procrastinated entry.'

Over the next 10 minutes, the two MIBs explained they came on the express command of the Director of Signals Intelligence Directorate (SID) at the NSA. Their job was to protect him at all times. They would not be seen, able to blend into any environment like chameleons. They tried to explain about the intelligence they had, but Officers Sterling and Parker had already covered that ground the other night.

What they did contribute, however, was the organisational setup to protect him and pictures of known remaining terrorists. Then, to Adams' and HP's utter surprise, the two MIBs, with a murmured apology, began to strip off their suits, revealing something extraordinary about the names Tall and Short.

They were not what they seemed; they were the exact same height. Tall had been using an appliance to increase his height, a trick revealed as he shed it. More remarkably, Short had each lower leg bent right round to adjoin the back of its upper leg. He rubbed his calf muscles to get the blood flowing into them.

'That position doesn't just wreck your hamstrings; it leaves your quads and your calves so weak they clamour for a tender massage,' said former MIB Short.

'Does it! I wouldn't know as I've never experienced it personally,' replied a somewhat bewildered Adams.

'Well, well, well. Something you don't know, Professor Adams!' humorously retorted MIB Short.

Then, the two MIBs took off their sunglasses and pulled off their rubber faces.

'Oh my God!' exclaimed HP.

Adams's floor was beginning to look like a theatrical dumping ground for lost items. But this was not all that was to fall. Some braces and shirts were discarded by each MIB, joining the other items already strewn across the floor.

And then, their quick-change finale finished as each pulled down an elasticated upper vest that unfurled into a workman's overall. Undoing the back zip, they each quickly climbed inside. Within a minute, maybe slightly less, the two MIBs had transformed.

'Bravo!' HP exclaimed, his clapping taking on the gleeful, almost frantic, slapping quality of a trained sea lion performing its trick for a prized, glistening fish. The sound echoed, sharp and theatrical, in the suddenly too-quiet office, a stark contrast to the earlier tension.

'Most impressive, gentlemen,' added a stoical Adams, though a flicker of unease danced behind his eyes.

'Do you have names now, or shall I just call you "overall tall" and "overall short"?' Adams humoured, observing their use of quick-change overalls and their overall appearance.

'We do have names, Professor, but if you don't mind, as they say in the films, it's on a need-to-know basis,' former Tall commanded, his gaze unwavering.

The other, Short, added a chillingly confident note, 'We will be watching after you, Professor. We are ex-special forces. Our presence will be as unseen as our transformations were unexpected to both you and HP today.'

With this bold reassurance, laced with an undeniable hint of surveillance, they gathered their discarded disguises, offered a curt goodbye, and were gone as quickly as they'd appeared, leaving Adams and HP to ponder the bizarre turn the morning had taken.

- 12 -
The P1 Notice

A day after the comedic duo's visit, the serenity of Adams's still-lingering Oxford plans was shattered. His Harvard office door didn't just open; it burst inward with such sudden force that its hinges shrieked in protest for several lingering seconds. "Honestly," Adams thought, "the least the assailant could have done was knock first".

This violent entrance didn't deter the panting doctoral student, Rick Shedland. His gasps for air stemmed not just from the urgent reports feverishly clutched in his hand, but from his record-breaking scramble up three flights of stairs to Adams's office.

'Professor! Professor, where are you?' Shedland bellowed, manic with urgency.

'Calm down, Rick! I'm behind my library door. Try not to murder this one like the last!' Adams warned, his voice laced with weary anticipation.

Shedland tried to slow down as he approached the half-open library door, but failed spectacularly. He ignored the small circular mat on the newly-varnished floor, emblazoned with the Harvard logo, and instead skidded backwards before catapulting almost supine into the professor's library, propelled by pure embarrassment.

The research papers were ripped free from his tight grip as his body was propelled forward. He slammed into Adams's half-open library door, bursting it wide open. Freed from his grasp, the papers themselves scattered forward and skyward, as if desperate to escape the university's confines.

Still on his back, Shedland flailed like a capsised beetle, his hands snatching at phantom furniture leg lifelines in a desperate, graceless attempt to avoid colliding with the professor's impressive library Regency Desk. The desk, already burdened, loomed, an unyielding monolith of polished wood. After sliding several yards across the gleaming library floor, he finally slammed against its unforgiving base, the impact jarring through his bones.

The liberated research papers, their brief, chaotic flight thwarted, fluttered back down in a wavering, confetti-like descent around the unruffled Adams.

'Something urgent, Shedland?' Adams asked, his voice dripping with sarcasm.

Shedland hauled his lightweight frame upright with the ungainly grace of a newborn giraffe on an ice rink, his muscles screeching in protest. He used the small desk, its polished surface offering all the traction of a greased banana peel, to push himself up.

The desk groaned, a profound, resonant complaint beneath his weight, like an ancient ship's timbers straining against a storm. It protested with a cacophony of sharp cracks and indignant shrieks, a makeshift yet utterly essential fulcrum for his ungainly ascent.

'Professor, you were right!' Shedland blurted, a raw, unbridled excitement almost tripping over his words. 'This DNA decoding, it's monumental! A true game-changer! We've successfully deciphered initial segments, and it appears we can now unravel far more intricate sequences!'

'Would it be asking too much for you to be a little more scientific, Shedland?'

'Yes, of course, apologies. The smaller junk areas are yielding coding for dates, times, and names. We have a developing story of evolutionary change that's beyond our current comprehension—beyond our very timescale—and it's about to become enormous!'

'Shedland, if only your enthusiasm for rearranging my mat and papers would translate into scientific nomenclature, I'd be most happy,' rumbled Adams.

'Professor, tectonically speaking, this isn't even the "big one" – it's the momentous one!'

'I will be the judge of that for sure, as I have with your bobsleigh entrance,' he replied. Adams gazed at Shedland before adding, 'Now, pick up those disordered papers on the floor and leave them re-ordered on my captain's chair next to my office desk outside, so I know where you've placed them, please. Before that, try and replace my Harvard mat without treating it as a mechanism for human flight.'

'Oh, sure Professor,' replied the chastened and apologetic Shedland. His conservative retreat from Professor Adams's library, now less bumbling and no longer breathless, was in marked contrast to his violent entry. His apologetic footsteps faded in an orderly way after he placed the papers as asked.

Adams gingerly descended the miniature ladder—more a glorified step stool, really, but a testament nonetheless to the towering egos of academics needing high-shelf access. He walked out of his small library to the relative sanity of his main office desk. The faint echoes of Shedland's exit still tickled the edges of the office silence, allowing the mental image of his entry, a human cannonball launched through the door, to persist.

One moment, Shedland was a Tasmanian Devil of flailing limbs and panicked shouts; the next, he shrank, a meek church mouse tiptoeing away as if afraid to stir a sleeping cat. Adams imagined the door hinges sighing in relief, finally free from their brief but brutal workout. The whole episode played out in his mind like a classic slapstick routine, followed by the agonisingly protracted, slow-motion exit of a student suffering from an eloquent, yet unspoken, collapse.

His lingering thoughts faded as Adams became aware of his own footsteps echoing across the shiny wooden office floor—a surface that had claimed its share of "slippery" victims during his professorship.

As he approached his desk, positioned near the customary neo-Georgian windows with their Flemish-bond brickwork and paned-glass, emblematic of Harvard architecture, his footsteps softened: he had stepped onto the rich pile of the beautiful, large antique red Persian Mashad rug centred beneath it.

He picked up Shedland's several reports, precisely where instructed, and added it to another substantial foot-high accumulation of DNA research, the new paper settling on the summit. The weight of academic inquiry, unfolding across the research papers adorning his desk like a quiet source of aesthetic intellectual pleasure, was momentarily suspended as he reached for a small bourbon poured earlier.

He settled back into the sumptuous leather of his captain's chair, its rich embrace a silent promise of comfort, a feeling akin to a baby finding solace in its mother's arms. His gaze drifted across the familiar landscape of his office, a sanctuary where intellect breathed freely, steeped in culture and refined sophistication.

In his right hand, he held a Glencairn glass of Old Fitzgerald, precisely measured to a two-finger depth and at room temperature. Leaning back as the chair cradled him, he lifted the glass to his lips, inhaling the bourbon's intricate aromatic tapestry—a rich, warming prelude to the complex symphony of taste that awaited his palate.

The stack of research papers, a burgeoning revelation of DNA's intricate language and hidden messages, cast long shadows on his desk. This wasn't merely a breakthrough in genetic understanding, but the terrifying potential for a nuclear-scale reshaping of humanity's place within the wider cosmos.

A concise seven-page summation rested atop this intellectual precipice, the distilled essence of countless others. He sipped his bourbon slowly, deliberately seeking a moment of brief, defiant tranquillity before confronting the weighty summary that now compelled his focus.

A wry smile touched Adams's lips, a familiar comfort in the way a drink could so easily divert his mind. But the respite was brief. "Back to the research," he thought, the gravity of his work exerting an almost palpable pull.

Reading through the summary, one thing became crystal clear. As more data was unpacked from the seemingly infinite genetic code, the university's existing academic and technological resources were woefully inadequate. They simply couldn't assimilate, codify, and structure the emerging message effectively.

This job had clearly outgrown the capacity of any single institution; collaboration was no longer an option, but a mandatory imperative. He sighed a profound relief, knowing just the person to help him—friend, fellow professor, and Nobel-prize winner, Peter Magma, of Oxford University.

A brief telephone chat quickly yielded an agreement: Adams would travel to Oxford within three days to elaborate. As he hung up, a wave of relief crashed over him, a lightness he hadn't realised he'd been carrying. The thought of seeing

Peter again, of finally sharing this immense burden with someone who truly understood, was immensely comforting.

Peter was ideal for this; their parallel academic paths weren't just similar, they were inextricably intertwined, marked by shared triumphs and mutual support through challenges.

This deep resonance meant instant understanding, a shorthand in their communication that bypassed lengthy explanations. Cooperation was a given, a natural extension of their years of intellectual partnership; trust and secrecy were as implicit as their shared passion for their scientific field.

Bizarrely, his thoughts turned to his dream from a few evenings ago, and that plane journey. "Prognostication?" Adams scoffed inwardly. A rational, empirical, hard-wired, no-nonsense scientist would categorically dismiss any such suggestion. "Anyway," he thought, "I visit Peter at least once a year, so nothing to see here for sure, I've been thinking about this for days anyway."

'All Hocus Pocus!' he exclaimed to himself, sealing his deduction.

But then he remembered from his dream, his half-read research paper: SASBA059. Who or what was SASBA? What did it mean, if anything?

'Argh, hocus pocus!' he muttered. Adams was immersed in deciphering a code concerning humanity's future, unaware that his own DNA was simultaneously guiding this deciphering via research motives and responses—one with profound implications for his immediate future.

The immediate easing of tension after his conversation with Peter was undeniable, though not solely attributable to their reassuring exchange. Indeed, the warm, amber elixir of the bourbon, a liquid balm now a gentle, spreading current through his system, played a significant role in unwinding the tightly coiled springs of his mind and spirit.

It was a physical manifestation of the mental release he felt—the knot in his shoulders loosening, the persistent hum of anxiety receding. This internal soothing allowed him to finally disengage from the demanding intricacies of his research. The decoding process had been a relentless siege on his intellect, each symbol a locked door requiring painstaking effort to unlock.

Now, freed from that intense focus, his mind, ever the explorer, unfurled inward, drawn to the seemingly paradoxical concept of the pluralistic diversity of oneness. The heterogeneity of homogeneity struck a profound chord with Adams, revealing itself as an underlying, unitary source code. This oneness, he realised, pulsed through the myriad differences observed across complex systems.

The human phenotype, or our outward structural appearance, stemming from a common DNA source code, served as a potent example. Other examples came to mind: the elegant mathematical principle of the golden ratio, a ubiquitous phenomenon found throughout nature. It followed a language of geometry, its patterns mirroring precise, recurring mathematical sequences.

By implication, it existed across many subject areas, particularly the structure of DNA. These examples reinforced his conviction of this underlying unitary source code of oneness, or the heterogeneity of homogeneity.

Yet, while his mind explored the elegant, universal codes within nature and DNA, a far more immediate and personal message was now demanding his undivided attention.

The echo of the phone call hammered relentlessly in the vast chambers of his mind, a relentless drumbeat demanding immediate action. He had to move, and fast—every ticking second felt like a shattering betrayal of the delicate balance he now held in his hands.

Forget protocol, shred the usual channels; his secretary couldn't even glimpse this operation. A potential leak he dared not afford. With NSA oversight, he'd have to descend into the shadows, enveloped by an absolute, suffocating secrecy that clung to him like a second skin. HP's sanction was the only way—his whispered authorisation of a "P1" notice, the highest echelon guaranteeing swift and clean disappearance.

Not a trace, not a whisper to betray his movements. Any questions—the why, the how, the where—would be met with a meticulously woven tapestry of plausible deniability. Each thread spun with insidious precision to mislead, to conceal the seething, volatile truth that pulsed beneath the surface, threatening to erupt.

His right hand hovered over his phone, a physical tremor betraying his urgent need to speak with HP immediately. Both Oxford and the answers Peter held exerted a silent, immense pull.

- 13 -
NSA Network Linker

The call between Peter Magma and Michael Adams instantly raised a red flag, triggering the NSA's intricate surveillance systems deep within its Fort Meade, Maryland facility.

'Sir, the computers have flagged something significant,' NSA operative Garcia announced to his lead, Timpanos Bone. 'Professor Adams is booking his tickets to Heathrow, London, right now.'

He continued, 'Correction, he's speaking about them to the Harvard President. He's discussing a "P1" authorisation, which our Sentient AI has identified as a ghost protocol—a clandestine clearance that grants the most senior academics travel with absolute discretion.

'Its very existence is known only to the rarefied air of the highest university echelons. Most particulars of these visits are deliberately blurred to avoid more detailed questions being asked about their nature and purpose. Instead, they are whispered in hushed tones to the "inner table" of senior academics—a circle bound by unspoken oaths.

'Should even a whisper of this information ever seep to those lower in the university hierarchy, it must be personally and irrevocably scrubbed by the Harvard President himself. In effect, each such unauthorised emergence is a precarious gamble in a high-stakes game of shadows.'

'Thank you. Run the call through voice analysis to authenticate their identities,' Bone directed. 'Next, feed the conversation through the algorithmic decoder to unearth any hidden speak codes or latent communications.'

Garcia replied, 'Flight confirmed: Two days from now. Direct flight BA059, First Class return. Departure: tomorrow, Thursday, 07:55, Boston. Arrival: Friday, 14:55, London Heathrow. Seat: F4. Cost: £11,500, charged to Harvard business account 369836593. All parameters locked.'

'Leave no stone unturned, isn't that your motto, Garcia?' Bone's voice was a low challenge.

'One of many, but I'm on it!' Garcia replied. 'He spoke to another professor about 30 minutes ago, a Peter Magma at Oxford University. Code checks on this conversation are pure as well.'

'Yes, I know. Stay on it. Inform me of any updates if they converse with each other. In fact, run a thematic analysis that flags statements where their names appear in the same or adjacent sentences in terrorist-based interceptions, Garcia,' said Bone.

Garcia nodded his approval as he continued his voice analysis.

Bone, busy with delegated jobs from senior management "upstairs", tasked Garcia with finding, recording, and summarising anything of concern once voice analyses were completed. This was the system's cold, relentless rhythm: methodical in practice, clinical in outcome.

Garcia launched his chair towards a towering touchscreen, the central interface for the intricate surveillance software. The system pulsed with a predatory hum deep within the NSA's six-tiered hub. Here, on the lowest level, access to the higher echelons was a fortress, fiercely guarded by job grade, contract, and the sacrosanct "need to know" principle.

His gaze swept over the banks of shadowy cabinets, alive with the hum of sophisticated software. Their surfaces blinked, illuminated, and displayed dynamically—a mesmerising constellation of shifting lights. This was a technological paradise, a playground for minds that thrived on the intricate dance of complex machinery.

He turned back to the cool luminescence of the touchscreen, beginning to synthesise the disparate, lightning-fast threads of analysis that had appeared in milliseconds.

The comparative voice analyser spat out its verdict on Professor Adams: a 93% probability match. Garcia's brow creased, his fingers tracing an invisible line on the screen. A nagging dissonance pricked at the edge of his awareness. Why such a discrepancy if it's undeniably Adams?

The missing seven per cent likely resided in the subtle slurring and mellowed cadence imparted by generous sips of bourbon. A human nuance the software, in its cold logic, was unable to detect.

Harvey Pabellon, however, presented no such ambiguity. His crisp vocal signature scorched onto the screen with a 99.8% match. No tell-tale bourbon whispers there.

Garcia then ran "Network Linker"—a program deceptively subtle in name, yet staggering in its sophistication. It devoured all of Adams's contacts, across every communication mode, and juxtaposed them with a historical coded dataset. The parameters for this dataset could be fine-tuned by myriad variables, including day and time.

The outcome: a dense, pulsating web of lines radiating from a central hub named, "Professor Adams". Each thread varied by length, width, and colour, telling a silent story. Length denoted contact frequency over a defined period. Width represented duration and the density of "key words" exchanged. Colour coded socioeconomic indicators. Red indicated danger.

All these lines converged and diverged, linked by nodes of shared whispers and hubs of seismic collisions. Nodes marked where contacts merely brushed against similar information; hubs exploded where multiple individuals decisively intertwined. These hubs and nodes could be surgically isolated, allowing for the forensic identification of "subjects and/or communications of interest" based on the criteria fed into "Network Linker".

Each new criterion forged another, even more intricate map. To an outsider, the algorithmic ability to dissect and identify someone's communications by so many criteria stood chillingly unmatched. It was a stark marvel, a calculated terror, in equal measure.

'Sir, I can now confirm the persons on the call were as identified and no codes embedded; the signature is pure. However, a tap was found on Dr. Magma's phone. Source: MI6, London.'

Both Peter and Michael were English; however, as Michael was on American soil, the NSA took a particular interest in him and all those connected to him.

In contrast, Peter was on English soil, so MI5 was interested in his activities. Even though he wasn't seen as nefarious, this coding and its implications naturally raised national security concerns. Accordingly, he was also placed on the level one alpha list for call interception.

Bone cracked a thin smile as the acronym MI6 reached his ears. He'd known they'd be somewhere in the surveillance mix, a predictable shadow in the intricate web. His brief contemplation soon gave way to a decisive comment and instructions for Garcia.

'MI6, now there's a surprise! Did they really think we wouldn't notice? In any case, cross-check all flight passengers for links to any organisations—terrorist or otherwise—that are associated, directly or indirectly, with the two professors. I want every thread pulled: university affiliations, sporting clubs, professional associations, anything that links them together.

'Run the last two years of phone calls on their lines as well, and hunt for any connections between them, flight passengers, and those activities too. And, alert MI5 for surveillance; we need two of our people over there, immediately.'

- 14 -
The Awakening Embrace Of Love And Travel

Dawn didn't merely unfurl; it erupted across Professor Michael Adams's mansion grounds. A jubilant deluge of rainbow hues infused the sprawling tapestry of verdant life with a palpable joy. This wasn't just a visual awakening, but a symbiotic orchestration of light and sound, a grand overture to the day's rebirth. The very air vibrated with the burgeoning day, the chorus of birdsong swelling like a heartfelt anthem.

To witness this visual magnificence, where every dew-kissed leaf and radiant bloom seemed to breathe with untamed vitality, was to feel a profound stirring within. It was as if the land itself exhaled a sense of boundless possibility—a silent invitation for the soul to unfurl and embrace the exuberance of existence in this verdant sanctuary.

Michael awoke as the morning's first, life-giving gleam of sunlight slipped through a slight opening in the heavy velvet drapes, a focused beam that painted the academic books like a theatre spotlight.

Yet, the lion's share of this gentle illumination fell upon a large, cherished photograph of his late wife, Victoria. Her radiant smile, a beacon above the ornate fireplace, was captured as she stood in the front drive, just outside the front door. He recalled with a pang that this was the very spot where Elizabeth's BMW had sat just days ago.

This precise alignment unveiled a profound moment he hadn't witnessed before: Victoria's radiant joy, a love so palpable it seemed to breathe in the soft light, eclipsing even the mansion's verdant summer splendour visible beyond the glass.

This was particularly significant, for it was the day she announced her pregnancy. Her burgeoning maternal instincts prompted her to resign from her Executive Assistant's position at the local, secretive NSA facility, a role that often kept her working into the evening for the country's security, as she'd told Michael.

A silent whisper of sweet nothings escaped his lips, a reflex of a heart still intimately connected. As the illuminated image shimmered through a film of approaching tears, the weight of his enduring affection filled the quiet room.

He softly whispered, his voice a little thin in the morning air. 'My existence is so very intertwined with yours, my love. Not a day, not an hour slips by without my heart holding you close – sometimes a comfort, sometimes a quiet yearning.

'We shared a wealth of beautiful moments, akin to a tapestry woven with joy, though some threads now feel fragile with absence. Time may pass, I will grow older, the world will shift, but my love for you remains eternally vibrant and young—a memory I carefully tend.

Wherever my journey takes me, I feel your presence beside me, a ghost of warmth in a cooling world. Until we are reunited, know that my love is with you.'

'Come on, sleepy head, you've a Dreamliner plane to catch too,' Elizabeth joked as she entered the room after her knocks were blocked out by his reminiscent thoughts. Her voice was light, though her eyes held a fleeting softness as she watched him. She had risen early to move his bags and tickets to her car—a silent efficiency born of habit and affection.

Just as importantly, this ensured her father had something light to eat before travelling to the airport and onward to Heathrow, England – a small, tangible offering of care against the vastness of his journey.

Michael smiled, a warmth spreading through him that had little to do with the nascent morning light. He wasn't embarrassed or inconvenienced by Elizabeth's gentle teasing; it was a familiar melody in the symphony of their life together. Indeed, part of Victoria's beauty was before him now, shining in the bright spark of Elizabeth's eyes and evident in the determined set of her jaw as she bustled about, ensuring his comfort.

He saw echoes of Victoria's own vibrant energy in these practical acts of love. She lived on through Elizabeth, not just in a fleeting smile or a turn of phrase, but in this very care so diligently offered. The sunlight, that same hopeful light she had often admired in the mansion grounds, now bathed her photograph, illuminating her beauty.

Elizabeth's presence, too, illuminated the enduring love he held for his wife. But sometimes, a sudden, almost chilling thought crossed his mind: the way Elizabeth tilted her head, or the precise tone of a certain word, as if Victoria herself was looking back at him, a ghost in the bright sunlight.

The two NSA security agents from the mansion gate knocked earlier to report that nothing untoward had been recorded last night in or around the mansion. They were clearly concerned that something may still happen to them, even though their pursuers were no longer considered a threat.

'Maybe they were checking to see if we were still here? How did they know our password to get access through the mansion's heavy gates? Perhaps they overheard mine as they were behind us when I shouted it out to get back in through the gates last night.

'Can you imagine a burly NSA agent leaning out of the van window and saying "bra strap" to a brick wall? Now there's a thought to carry to the airport, but certainly don't pack it,' joked Elizabeth.

She continued, 'They will escort you to the airport, oh important one,' as she continued to chuckle to herself.

'You realise they must still trust my driving skills,' she said, placing a beautiful George III solid silver platter on his lap. He had now pushed his aged body into a high Fowler position.

He looked at his small breakfast: a small bowl of Bob's Red Mill Muesli, toast in a holder, Isigny Ste Mère salted butter, a few cooked heirloom tomatoes, a lonesome but well-cooked vegetable sausage, a small portion of scrambled egg, and freshly squeezed orange – probably organic, knowing Elizabeth.

It was like a work of art, neatly laid out, each item displaying a proportionate distance from each other and, above all else, extremely enticing.

'Are you going to stare the breakfast to death or eat it?' Elizabeth humoured. 'Thank you. Of course, try and stop me,' Michael retorted with a smile.

Elizabeth looked on, capturing every last moment before his airport departure. She detailed his itinerary to the airport. 'It's 5:15 am. You have 20 minutes to eat, 15 to briefly shower, 15 to dress, and five to get to my car outside. That gives you 30 minutes to the airport and then an hour and 15 minutes to check in and enjoy all that lovely hospitality British Airways' Terminal five Lounge can offer.

'I bet you've calculated how much time each part of this breakfast will take me to consume as well?' Michael questioned as Elizabeth pulled back the gorgeous royal blue velvet drapes, letting the sun's luminary magnificence conquer the remaining darkness in the bedroom.

'Don't try me,' said Elizabeth as she turned from her drape-pulling duty to leave the bedroom.

Just as she closed the door, he raised his awakening voice to ask about his bags and tickets. 'What do you think I was doing before I came up with your breakfast?' she remonstrated.

'You know where they are—in the trash can; where do you think?' Elizabeth shouted jokingly as her voice slowly dissipated, walking along the ornate landing to go downstairs.

Just like her loving mother, he thought, his gaze softening as he returned to Victoria's photograph. He saw a flicker of Victoria's spirited nature in Elizabeth's exasperated outburst, an echo across the years that both comforted and, with a familiar sorrow, reminded him of his loss.

***

Michael arrived at Elizabeth's car with his usual clockwork precision, not a second to spare. He wouldn't dare be late – not for her, and certainly not for his departure. Elizabeth stood beside her open driver's door, watching with glowing admiration as he smiled and presented another bag to her.

A myriad of loving thoughts flooded his mind, from approbation and support, to the lovely breakfast she'd recently presented. It wasn't lost on him that Elizabeth now stood where Victoria once had, his mind momentarily superimposing her onto her daughter, stirring deep gratitude for Victoria as both wife and mother.

Half of Elizabeth's genes were his too, yet where they manifested he never quite fathomed – a poignant irony for a professor of genetics.

Elizabeth looked down at the bag and then back up at her father. 'Where did that bag come from?' she asked inquisitively. 'It's my "secrets" bag,' Michael grinned.

'Well, it's not that secret; I can see it. And I do know, really.'

'I put the classified "red" papers in there for you this morning,' said Elizabeth, ever the dutiful daughter.

'Red papers? But they were in the safe?' Michael asked, surprised. 'Indeed, they were, along with some of my best jewellery, remember? I added those papers for light reading,' she answered, chuckling how "light" could be applied to such heavyweight knowledge.

'You never cease to surprise me with your foresight and proactivity towards me,' said Michael, pleased.

'I'm sure I'll sleep better tonight knowing the future of mankind is tucked away in that bag,' smiled Elizabeth.

With this brief verbal interchange out of the way, and both seated ready for Elizabeth's hopefully error-free drive to the airport, they drove off slowly to the gate where the NSA agents were waiting.

'Look at them, hungry and cold,' said Elizabeth as they approached the opening gates.

They both let down their windows and stopped the car as they could see one of the NSA agents wanted to speak to them. Ironically, out of all four on that shift, it was the very same agent who had spoken to Elizabeth earlier that morning.

He approached Elizabeth's side and spoke to her through her open window.

'Morning, Miss, morning, Professor. Agents Burley and Hardy will escort you in front, and we'll be behind you,' said the agent who had yet to reveal his name.

As he walked back to his van, he looked around at Elizabeth and smiled, before gesticulating for them to move forward.

'Crikey, he's gorgeous!' gasped Elizabeth.

'Do you only ever see potential fathers when you see men of a certain build and age?' Michael enquired.

'Have you seen the mansion's three male gardeners? Crikey, one of them could cut my lawn and clean up my borders anytime,' Elizabeth remarked crudely.

'Enough, Bambina, enough. Let's follow them now, all right,' he directed.

As predicted earlier by Elizabeth, it was indeed a 30-minute drive to Logan Airport. She stopped at Central Parking for Terminal E. Before they had time to alight from their car, a meet-and-assist service pounced upon Michael like a praying mantis.

The service employee started by saying, 'Morning, sir, can I assist you with—' when his question was rudely curtailed and he was physically removed from the scene by the very NSA agent Elizabeth admired from afar.

Michael looked at Elizabeth, his voice a sharp warning. 'Don't go there with any more comments about him.' A few feet away, the NSA agent, having hauled the man three metres across the ground, was already patting him down. The two MIB men, assigned to watch over Elizabeth and Michael, now saw their covert service was complete. With the NSA agents accompanying Michael to his plane, they turned and left without a word, their silent departure marking the end of their mission.

Two other NSA agents approached Michael and said they would escort him until he had boarded the plane. The agents worked within the law but could often act with considerable autonomy when security was paramount.

Elizabeth opened the boot and took the two bags out, then deliberately let them fall with a thud onto the road. 'Oops!' she chirped, her gaze fixed on the agents, inviting them closer. And they obliged.

Two burly NSA agents approached. 'We'll take them from here,' one stated. They were briefly distracted as their colleague finished patting down the suspect and released him. Their collective gaze then turned to Michael and Elizabeth.

A palpable, unspoken demand for farewell hung in the air, urging them to conclude their interaction so the agents could proceed. Elizabeth moved to her father, his thoughts already drifting towards work and his upcoming meeting with Peter in Oxford.

She embraced him with a lingering hug, as if anticipating a long absence, despite his imminent return within several days. The mere thought of his departure brought tears to her eyes.

Partially breaking the embrace, she looked at him with fierce solemnity. 'Listen, Dad. Take care. Safe journey. Say hello to Peter. Come back safe and sound, having saved the world,' Elizabeth said, her voice a blend of amusement and deep concern for her vital father's impending task.

Emotion surged within Adams, momentarily choking his voice. With a visible effort, he wrestled past the obstruction.

'Have no fear, Professor Adams is here,' he declared with forced lightness. His playful reply broke Elizabeth's composure, and she dissolved back into her father's arms, tears streaming from her eyes.

Having checked in and been guided through the airport's clean and well-maintained corridors of perpetual human traffic, Michael entered the plush first-class lounge with a mingled sense of anticipation and unease.

Yet, even amidst the promise of quiet indulgence with light food and the confidential rustle of papers from his "secrets" bag, the persistent prickle of being watched remained.

He was indeed the focus of attention: not only from his NSA agents but also from curious fellow passengers whose bemused glances flickered over him, a silent interrogation attempting to decipher the identity of the man warranting such conspicuous protection from government agents.

Several curious onlookers exchanged uneasy glances, a silent language of apprehension passing between them. A man in a crisp business suit discreetly checked his phone, his thumb hovering over the airline's rebooking app, his initial curiosity visibly curdling into a knot of anxiety.

A young couple, excitedly chattering about their European vacation, suddenly fell into a stunned silence, their smiles evaporating as they watched the two agents surrounding the unassuming older man.

The sheer level of security felt less like protection and more like a beacon. It inadvertently broadcast the presence of someone or something valuable, or perhaps, someone in significant danger. A shiver traced its way down the spine of a woman clutching a well-worn paperback, the thrill of her fictional hero's upcoming escape now tainted by a creeping sense of unease with Michael. The air in their vicinity, once buzzing with pre-flight anticipation, now felt subtly charged with foreboding.

They couldn't quite articulate it, a shared instinct whispering that proximity to this level of attention might attract shadows they'd rather avoid.

The collective neurosis and paranoia of the passengers seemed to recede fifty minutes later, dissipated by the announcement of the boarding call, including the flight number. It couldn't come soon enough.

Yet, a disquieting thought clutched at Michael: the called flight number echoed his bizarre dream of "SASBA059". His flight was "BA059", but what was the "SAS" part about? Scandinavian Airlines System (SAS) was the only thing that surfaced, a bland, almost mocking, logical association for someone in an airport.

He tried to say farewell, but his security rebuffed him, their sole duty to escort him to the aircraft. Their refusal only intensified the other passengers' worry and bemusement, sparking frantic curiosity about his identity. They watched as he was escorted to the gate. Only when he presented his tickets could he offer his final farewell to his NSA agents.

Unbeknownst to him, Elizabeth stood rooted to a viewing area window, watching the plane, her mind a maelstrom of conflicting emotions. Her love for her father battled an ominous premonition. She wondered if his dreams would truly materialise, or if this journey was destined for a nightmare he could never have anticipated. "Perhaps even both", she thought.

For Michael, the fleeting pang of loneliness from his agents' departure vanished, replaced by the warm welcome of the flight attendants. They guided him to his first-class cabin. Before long, gourmet food and absorbing reading lulled his academic mind into a profound, tranquil sea of dreams.

Beneath The Radar

A few hours earlier at the airport, a chilling sequence of strange events was already stirring in and around the 787-9 Dreamliner that Michael would board to Heathrow, London. The plane had been chosen by the terrorist group, "The Veiled Hand". Their principal demand, as ever, was money.

In the past, many convoluted schemes were employed to funnel arms onto a plane to achieve terrorist demands. These included hollowed-out statues or a disassembled gun to bypass security.

Each method was starkly simple, relying on audacious timing and exploiting the mundane routines of airport operations. However, those simpler times were challenged by the advent of modern technologies.

Modern airports employed a multi-layered security approach using various technologies and procedures to prevent arms from getting on board. Screening technologies included X-ray scanners, metal detectors (walk-through and handheld), and full-body scanners (millimetre wave and backscatter). More old-fashioned methods included visual inspection, security personnel, and CCTV.

With so many barriers in place, this multi-layered approach established a robust defence in depth. This acted as a significant deterrent, exemplifying the quiet victory of modern airport security.

This victory, however, stemmed from a delicate balance between freedom and control, a burden felt by every traveller. Its necessity was starkly underscored by the very threats that, thankfully, never materialised. This intricate dance between safeguarding the skies and respecting individual liberties was a constant negotiation, a silent contract implicitly agreed upon by millions of plane passengers. The slight hesitations, the removal of items, the brief scrutiny — these were the tangible signs of this contract.

Woven from technology and vigilance, this pervasive security fabric acted as a powerful disincentive, likely deterring potential actors by its sheer complexity. Yet, it was precisely an act so contemptuous of that intelligence—an audacious use of merely a rope and a bag—that would now unravel technological modernity.

A terrorist named Tiroclaw had acted under the intelligence radar for several years. A master of disguise, polyglot, expert in close combat, and proficient in firearms, he was highly attractive for terrorist recruitment.

Furthermore, he already shared an ideology that power and money gave leverage to everything else. He believed that society's perceived decline was a direct consequence of the twisted elites' control, a degradation he felt was driven solely by their pursuit of wealth and influence, thereby devaluing everything else.

Even a man as hardened as Tiroclaw harboured a softer side, if such a thing were conceivable for his ilk. He loved a woman. She was intensely charismatic, strikingly beautiful in both appearance and spirit. Her name was Sang, and he had drawn her into the terrorist cell.

Right now, he was entering Logan airport carrying his flight bag, about the same time Adams and Elizabeth were about to get into their car for the journey to the airport.

In his co-pilot uniform, he looked about as much out of place as a lone grain of sand in a vast desert. Passengers and staff cast fleeting glances, then dismissed him. Nothing to truly notice beyond the three stripes on his sleeve designating him as a co-pilot.

He walked confidently and with purpose to access the 787-9. He was exceptionally early. Baggage handlers were only just beginning to load the first luggage items. The cleaners were still giving the plane a deep clean.

Being so early, the gate to board the 787-9 would very likely be unmanned. But it wasn't that easy. He would not be able to bypass security. Instead, he would have to pass through first-line universal security protocols, including the Known Crew Member (KCM) program, as he was eligible and Logan was a participating airport.

He noticed a long standard line queue. He didn't mind using it if it wasn't too long, but time was of the essence. Instead, he used the expedited lane.

No matter what day or time, the same security protocols were followed. It was systematic, rigorous and demanding, albeit in a pleasant and courteous way.

'Good morning,' said the security officer.

'It is,' cheekily replied Tiroclaw.

'What's the rush?' the officer asked.

'Rush! Did I look like that,' he asked worryingly.

The officer slightly laughed and grinned bemusingly at Tiroclaw for misinterpreting him.

'You're not rushing in your walking, but in your timing. Your departure isn't for a couple of hours yet. Couldn't you sleep, perhaps?' The officer's cross-examination continued, and from Tiroclaw's perspective, it was completely unnecessary.

He silently released a ragged breath, beginning to choke on an inward panic, as if the officer suspected something. He returned the grin as he said, 'Yes, couldn't sleep. Nature of the beast I guess.' The darker meaning of the metaphor was unrecognised, while the more innocent reference to Tiroclaw rushing was not.

The officer smiled as Tiroclaw placed his flight bag on the counter for inspection. The officer rummaged around inside, looking for anything suspicious. The exercise felt somewhat academic; after all, Tiroclaw was the co-pilot. It was a given that he would be encouraging safety, not undermining it.

The officer suddenly froze, a surprised expression tightening his face. 'What's this?' he asked, pulling out a long rope with a metal hook on the end. He looked up at Tiroclaw, his expression a mixture of curiosity and menace. Their eyes met like two Western gunfighters poised for their final duel. Tiroclaw was ready with an answer.

'You've never been mountaineering, have you? That's a static rope, used for hauling objects up or lowering them. Very useful,' Tiroclaw replied, hoping the officer's next remark would confirm his lack of mountaineering knowledge.

'Mountaineering? In England?' The officer's voice was a low, perplexed query.

'Mountains, hills, it's very useful when the need arises.' Tiroclaw took the initiative, openly picking up the metal hook. 'That's the snap hook; you use it to secure onto another point or piece of equipment, even a person, if necessary.' Tiroclaw demonstrated with outward confidence. However, his inward nervousness was betrayed by his anxiously shaking hand.

'Yeah, whatever,' the restless officer replied, knowing he had nowhere else to go with his line of questioning. He certainly wasn't going to delve any deeper into this. After all, as he thought before, he was the co-pilot.

Ten minutes later, although it felt like thirty, he was on his way to the gate and the 787-9. Despite his outward appearance, an undeniable truth lay hidden within him. He had been bedevilled by a sense of foreboding that enveloped and troubled his very being.

He feared the security officer knew something about him that would end his mission, indeed his very dreams of a future with Sang. His emotional relief was a combination of not only reduced anxiety, but also the bravado of outsmarting old and new technologies together.

As expected, the gate was unmanned. He walked onto the plane bridge, adorned with adverts for holidays, money, mobile technologies, and digital displays. As he boarded the plane, the smell of cleaning agents hit his nose like smelling salts. More welcome was the sight of Sang, part of the cabin crew. No words were exchanged, just smiles. He then walked to his left and into the flight deck.

Under the flimsy guise of needing to urgently check specific circuit breakers located behind the door, the cockpit door was closed. This closure not only bought him precious, unobserved time, but also ensured he had unrestricted access to the pilot's escape hatch.

Before climbing the two steps to access the hatch and crank it open, he opened his flight bag. He took out the thin, dark rope with a sharp metal hook—the one that had so interested the security officer only moments ago. He rested the hooked end of the rope over his shoulder before climbing.

He cranked open the hatch. One more step and both head and torso were above the fuselage. He pulled the rope off his shoulder and snaked it down the fuselage.

A baggage handler, whose uniform seemed a size too big and whose nervous glances darted around the empty baggage bay, swiftly attached the heavy, nondescript bag. With a barely perceptible tug, Tiroclaw hauled the weight up into the tight confines of the flight deck.

This silent, clandestine exchange was repeated twice more. The entire operation for each bag wouldn't have consumed more than a fleeting sixty seconds. This efficiency was born of prior rehearsal, a process they likely had perfected in some anonymous warehouse on the outskirts of the city.

Who, amidst the pre-flight bustle and the droning announcements echoing through the near-empty terminal, would pause to truly register a rope dangling from an aircraft or a bag being lifted?

The escape hatch was positioned on the less visible side of the fuselage. Consequently, it remained out of the direct line of sight from the viewing area and the brightly lit gate building. It was also out of sight of any casual observers.

Furthermore, the bags bore the familiar logo and colour of the airline's livery, blending seamlessly with the legitimate cargo being loaded elsewhere. The other baggage handlers' movements were dictated by the relentless ticking clock of multiple flight schedules, their attention consumed by the endless stream of suitcases and cargo containers.

Therefore, they were too engrossed in their tasks to even entertain the notion of such an audacious act occurring right under their noses. Indeed, the sight of aircraft and ground crew was so deeply ingrained in their daily routine that their minds most likely didn't even register the unfolding criminality.

He resealed the hatch and reopened the cockpit door. Sang stood waiting with an impassive expression, concealing an ideology she shared with her co-pilot and emotionally trusted compatriot in this deadly endeavour. She smoothly took the bags. With practised ease, she surreptitiously carried them to the dimly lit crew rest compartment. There, she swiftly transferred the contents into seemingly ordinary, yet deliberately empty, travel bags designed to shield their inner contents.

These innocuous-looking bags would remain in plain sight, patiently waiting until the desperate moment they were needed to unleash their purpose.

- 16 -
Storm Of Terror

After four hours in the air, with three to go, the time had come. As planned by the terrorist leader, Hammerfall, it was time to take control of the Boeing 787-9.

Sang, the female flight attendant, retrieved her bags from the crew rest area and brought them to the galley. There, Hammerfall loitered, ignoring the cabin crew. He'd already been told to return to his seat, but in his mind, his overt purpose was far more significant than theirs. She stared at him, her gaze unwavering and filled with unblinking admiration, as if he were a master, a true maestro of orchestrated terrorist mayhem.

She then presented the bags to Hammerfall like treasure before a king, carefully placing them on the Corian galley worktop. With a sharp tug, he opened one, revealing an inner compartment secured by a tag stating "Tiroclaw - Logan Airport". He undid the tag, and with a swift tilt, the bag disgorged ten Glock 19 handguns onto the gleaming surface.

With a swift, chilling synchronicity, cued by a subtle signal from Sang, an ensemble of terrorists surged forward from the lower-class cabin areas. Their eyes gleamed with a predatory hunger to finally grasp their arsenal of destruction, and instantly, raw screams from the flight crew and passengers began to erupt and build through the cabin.

They knew their weapon of choice, the Glock 19, yet its unexpected customisation stole their breath. Each handgun boasted a radically intricate, skeletonised slide, its unique, high-contrast finish a testament to thousands of pounds spent, a deadly work of art.

As the assembled terrorists each took a Glock 19, they expressed their admiration for its custom design to Hammerfall. Several cheered and jabbed their weapons repeatedly into the air with jubilant excitement, for a good plan was always one that delivered. In his joyous demonstration, one terrorist nearly fired a shot into the cabin roof, a reckless act that would have been catastrophic for everyone.

But the delivery of instruments of harm and destruction wasn't over. Lost in their triumphant euphoria over the Glocks, they barely registered that Hammerfall had opened the second of three bags. Contained within were four brutal Heckler & Koch MP5 submachine guns. These devouring beasts of weaponry could unleash a relentless hail of 900 rounds a minute – fifteen per second. Armed with such a terrifying arsenal, they would be a formidable foe to anyone who dared to cross their path. A deadly cache was in the third bag, its explosives and parts ready to be used to rig the middle starboard doors.

Terror-stricken screams continued to rip through the cabin from nearby passengers and the remaining cabin crew. They watched, paralysed, as this unstoppable, menacing mob bore down on them. The mob brandished their murderous hardware, waving the deadly weapons precariously, as if they were mere playthings in their blood-hungry hands.

Sang, along with two terrorists, bundled the cabin crew together and guarded them temporarily while Hammerfall moved to the audio control panel. The remaining terrorists watched with glee as their wild eyes followed Hammerfall.

He stood next to the panel, a predatory smile spreading across his face as he met the gaze of his murderous admirers.

The restrained cabin crew wept openly, their training screaming that a storm of terror was about to break.

Hammerfall pressed the button "PA" that addressed all the passengers. He spoke eruditely, a chilling calm in his voice as he announced: 'Attention passengers. As of now, my group of good-natured terrorists, as I see them, are in control of the plane. Obey us, and you will see tomorrow. I hope you enjoy the rest of your journey.'

The pilots, unaware of the transfer of plane ownership to Hammerfall, would soon find out. He picked up the handset of the interphone system. A glance at the control panel revealed a touch-screen display with a directory of crew stations. He selected "Flight Deck", waited for the line to connect, then held down the "push to talk" button and began to speak.

'Hello, what lovely lady is calling?' Captain Snowley, a distinguished man, joked. 'No lady, Captain,' a cold voice replied. 'It's Hammerfall.'

'Who?' Snowley replied.

A single word—a simple retort and question—ignited a cascade of introspection within Hammerfall. He felt as though a branding iron of rudeness had been seared onto his character, an indelible monosyllabic stain that marred his very essence and importance, poisoning his perfect day.

'For your own good, for the good of the passengers, and for the good of us,' Hammerfall stated sternly. 'Please open the cockpit door. We have taken over your plane.'

'Sorry, I can't,' was the polite but clearly absolute rejection by Snowley.

'OK! Have it your way. I'll come to you if that helps,' declared Hammerfall. His undertone dripped with a chilling promise: things would not end well for the flight crew if any further objection were raised.

He seized the flight attendant, Sang, and propelled her towards the cockpit door. She looked utterly bewildered, her eyes posing a silent question: 'What had she done?' At that very moment, a chilling tableau was captured by the flight deck's surveillance camera—a live feed showing the two outsiders and the motley group of followers who flanked them, waiting just behind.

Hammerfall's eyes, blazing with manic glee, shifted from Sang's terrified face to the tiny, wide-angle lens of the surveillance camera. He then hissed, 'Shall we start with her? I'll count down from five. No... make it ten. I want you to truly savour this decision. And remember, let me reach zero, and you'll be placing an advertisement for a new flight attendant.'

A horrifying shriek of pure, raw desperation tore from Sang's throat, her body convulsing with fear. 'What the fuck's wrong with you?' she wailed, her head whipping to the side to stare at the other terrified cabin crew. 'Pick one of them!' she shrieked, her voice cracking. 'Not me! Not me!

Hammerfall chuckled, a low, guttural sound, and leaned forward to whisper in Sang's right ear: 'Don't worry, you'll be all right, it's all for show.' A fragile smile flickered across her face as she quietened, her compliance born of paralysing fear.

The terrorists, a rabid audience, eagerly watched from behind, certain the cockpit door would soon yield. Hammerfall continued his slow, deliberate countdown. By the time he reached three, a bitter taste of potential failure coated his tongue, and a cold dread began to gnaw at his certainty.

Captain Snowley's voice, raw with desperation, pleaded for him to stop. He had already, tremulously, informed Air Traffic Control in the North Atlantic Oceanic Control Area—the specific authority responsible for that part of the ocean—of the hijacking, simultaneously entering the universal hijacking code (7500) on their transponder. This formal notification triggered an immediate, multi-agency response.

'I cannot open the door. You know that,' Snowley pleaded to him. 'Two… One,' said Hammerfall, his eyes gleaming with a dark anticipation. He knew he held the power of life and death in these final numbers.

Captain Snowley felt the weight of a gun to his head, though none was there. His breath caught in his throat and nervous twitches agitated his facial muscles. Sweat gathered on his forehead as a primal terror clamoured for escape, engulfing him in a cold wave that washed over his composure. He trembled uncontrollably, his hands slick with the cold sweat of pure dread.

His composure splintered, his rigid security protocols crumbling under the crushing weight of Sang's possible imminent death. He shattered, inevitably capitulating to the intolerable psychological pressure Hammerfall had so expertly wielded.

'I'll make a deal –' Captain Snowley's attempts to calm the situation shattered on impact. He was brutally cut short by the shattering blast of a single bullet, which ripped through the air, ripping through Sang with savage finality. Her life extinguished in an instant, reduced to a mere memory by the brutal, unfeeling force of the gun.

A horrifying bloom of crimson exploded against the sterile white of the cockpit door. The bullet had torn through her head, slamming into the cockpit door – a perverse mercy that ensured the fuselage remained intact, though the same could not be said for Sang's now-shattered skull.

Screams of horror shattered the air from the cabin crew observers. Shrieks, raw with disbelief and primal terror, ripped through the cabin. One cabin crew member fell to her knees, retching uncontrollably. In stark contrast, the terrorists roared their approval, waving their Glocks in the air again, their faces contorted in savage triumph.

It didn't bother them that one of their own was dead. To them, death was an inevitable end, Sang's merely arriving ahead of schedule. And if Hammerfall decreed it, there was no question, no appeal, only grim acceptance.

The body of Sang, a blanket-shrouded bundle, was unceremoniously dumped in the confines of the crew rest area. A final, ignominious end for a love that had utterly beguiled her. Her devotion to Tiroclaw was no beacon, but a beautiful and blinding veil—a brutal reality she never saw, the nefarious ends of a cause forever obscured by the very love she so utterly misunderstood.

Hammerfall presided over the cabin crew as they scrubbed relentlessly at the cockpit door and other areas, desperate to erase Sang's bloodstains. They worked in fear of what may come next, crying and feeling sick. They could wash away the physical aftermath, but not the memory. Once completed, a sharp, antiseptic tang permeated the air, a sterile scent that utterly failed to expunge the grotesque horror that had demanded its use.

He ordered them to carry on with their duties, promising no further harm. Hammerfall couldn't suppress a smirk, a silent, inward laugh bubbling as he savoured the cabin crew's palpable sadness over Sang's death. 'How different their grief would be, if only they knew her true role?' he mused, a dark satisfaction coiling in his gut.

For Hammerfall, the single, fatal flaw in his grand design was his failure to gain cockpit access. He hadn't intended to kill Sang; he had gambled on Captain Snowley breaking. After all, Snowley seemed like an educated man, his calm voice exuding authority. Surely, he'd reasoned, this murder would be a step too far. But he was wrong. Snowley's chilling resolve, so unexpectedly revealed, earned the terrorist's dark admiration.

With the cockpit door and surrounding area clean, a grim stage reset, he was ready for another round of accessing the cockpit. His mind raced, calculating: what human pawn, what token of death, would he sacrifice next?

His gaze swept the first-class cabin, cold and appraising, searching for a useful face. His eyes flickered between a passenger's appearance and the manifest, a calculated dance. He noted the distinguished, the important-sounding – potential pawns, ripe for exploitation.

A bottomless trepidation gripped the first-class passengers as Hammerfall's eyes danced over each of them, a silent, predatory assessment. One man, however, offered no visible sign of submission to his murderous bullying. His eyes were deliberately half open, a calculated refusal to grant the terrorist the respect of his full attention. He simply leaned his head against the window, feigning sleep. 'How rude to be asleep in my presence,' Hammerfall's thoughts bitterly scoffed.

'Who's the purser?' Hammerfall bellowed.

An elegant woman took a deliberate step forward, her voice a steady balm in the panicked chaos. 'I am the purser,' she said.

His eyes, blazing with fury, fixed on Adams. 'Tell me who that beast is over there?' he snarled, pointing his gun.

'No,' she replied, her voice catching, 'I won't give it.'

A cold smile played on Hammerfall's lips. 'OK, I understand,' he said, his voice dropping to a menacing whisper. 'You'd rather put many lives at stake for one. He must be important then, yes? How important, I wonder.' His gaze turned dark, a terrifying anticipation in his eyes. 'Bring one of her subordinates to the cockpit door,' he snapped, and two terrorists who were watching over the cabin crew moved without hesitation.

With shocking speed, they grabbed the nearest cabin crew member. Her screams were cut short as they dragged her, kicking and struggling, towards the cockpit door. The purser watched on, a sickening wave of self-loathing washing over her. She felt a profound embarrassment that she ever thought diplomatic rationality could outsmart an irrational terrorist with a gun.

'Stop!' the purser gasped, a word torn from her lungs. Her body crumpled, her hands outstretched in a desperate plea. 'Please,' she begged, her voice a broken, shuddering whisper, 'have mercy.'

The struggling crew member froze, her screams replaced by shuddering sobs as the terrorists released her, allowing her to collapse. Hammerfall then advanced, his gaze fixed on the purser. He stared into her eyes, his shadow swallowing her. Suddenly, his Glock 19 was in her field of vision, its cold barrel pressing against her left temple.

'Cross me, die for no one but your own stupidity,' he hissed. He sniggered as she crumpled, her knees giving way. She became utterly subdued, not by the gun, but by the terrifying realisation that his mercy was merely a loan, and his words were a debt he fully intended to collect.

Another cabin crew member, her mind shattering under the pressure, shouted over to Hammerfall. 'His name is Professor Michael Adams!' Her voice was a desperate, final plea, an attempt to end the hurt inflicted on her colleagues. She knew, however, that this was merely the opening to a new chapter of terror.

His gaze now fixed on this contemptuous beast much to the outward relief of the other first-class passengers. They watched on, their visceral fears reduced, yet haunted by expectation of what action may follow. He looked distinguished, his title would be a good bargaining chip with Captain Snowley, and Adams may well articulate a more persuasive argument for opening the cockpit door.

He signalled to four of his fellow terrorists that he was going to use him as bait. The other eight terrorists, who were strategically placed across the remaining three cabin classes, remained unaware of what was about to unfold.

He stalked towards Adams, his eyes clinically watching him, like a hunter observing his prey. The cabin's silence was suddenly broken by a sharp, commanding bark. 'Wake up!' shouted Hammerfall, with a bark reminiscent of a military order.

Adams had tried to dismiss Hammerfall's show of inhumanity, but as the terrorist strode forward, the pretence of sleep was over. His image coalesced from a blur of motion into stark, unflattering detail. He was glistening with sweat, a dark shadow of stubble on his jaw. His agitated state grated like a dull blade, evident in every tremor of his voice.

'Stand up Professor Adams!' bellowed the military order from Hammerfall whose facial sweat glistened, stark against his commanding voice.

As the terrorist's voice grated against his ears, Adams recognised the surreal horror of the moment. It was a haunting fragment from a recent dream, and he treated it with the same weary contempt he had the first time.

With a soft, exasperated sigh, he closed his eyes, murmuring just loud enough for Hammerfall to hear: 'Up yours, you crazy bastard.' Then, with a deliberate, insulting motion, he slumped back into his sumptuous seat, feigning a return to slumber.

This only ignited Hammerfall's fury. He snatched his Glock 19, ramming it into Adams's side with such brutal force it felt like the impact of a bullet itself.

Hammerfall shouted in apoplectic anger, 'You are the bastard, Professor Adams, or whatever your fucking title is.' He grabbed Adams's lapel and forcibly lifted him up with so little effort, one could have mistaken his muscle power for that of a powerlifter.

Adams was terrified by this, but when his gaze locked with the assailant's, a primal fear clawed at his throat. It was clear to him then, with a sickening certainty, that his dream was unfolding; this was no nightmare, but a chilling premonition made flesh.

He'd looked around and grappled with his assailant. His fellow crazies started shouting. Then he was thrown towards the cockpit door, hitting his head and waking up. Adams's consciousness returned with a jolt. This cold metal pressing against his back, the nauseating smell of disinfectant—he'd been here before. It was a haunting fragment from a recurrent dream, one where he grappled with an unseen assailant, was thrown towards the cockpit door, and was forced awake by the sickening crack of his head hitting the metal.

'That's it,' he murmured, his words barely a whisper. 'I'll wake up now. I just haven't bumped my head yet.'

Driven by the desperate, clinging notion that this was all just a nightmare, he began to violently bash his head against the cockpit door. The thud of his skull against the cold metal was a grotesque, wet sound that shattered the cabin's silence.

Hammerfall and his terrorists watched on in stunned disbelief, their mouths agape. This wasn't fear. It wasn't defiance. This was a spectacle beyond their comprehension—a man trying to beat himself awake from what he believed was a dream, right there, in front of them all. They hadn't witnessed anything like it.

'If you're that desperate to kill yourself professor, I have a handy tool right here you can borrow,' laughed one terrorist.

'Maybe he likes rock music as he's clearly a head-banger,' joked another.

Hammerfall ripped Adams from the cockpit door, not to save Adam's skull, but to prevent further damage to the fortified cockpit door.

Adams looked at him, his initial fear now eclipsed by a disorienting haze. Hammerfall's countenance seemed to shift and distort, morphing into a truly monstrous visage before his very eyes.

'Adams!' Hammerfall roared, his voice a thunderclap. He backhanded Adams across the head, a brutal attempt to shock some semblance of rationality into the man.

The head slap only reinforced Adams's idea that this was his cue to finally wake up.

'Is that you Elizabeth,' he cried out.

'He's gone weird!' exclaimed another terrorist.

This was all too much for Hammerfall. His physical assault on Adams was nothing compared to the professor's unsettling psychological effect. Any more of this bizarre behaviour, and he might find himself compelled to join Adams in a head-banging duet with the cockpit door.

As he bundled Adams back to his seat, he could hear him mumbling to himself, 'I don't remember this happening.'

Hammerfall replied, as Adams finally sat back down, 'For my psychological health, I don't want to either.'

Suddenly, a chorus of voices, sharp and urgent, ripped through the air as the four terrorists shouted Hammerfall's name in unison. He whirled around, and his blood ran cold, not from fear, but from the shattering of his own psychotic equilibrium. The game had just changed without his command.

Standing in the newly opened cockpit doorway was Captain Snowley, his face a blank canvas of professional calm. In a calculated gambit, he had broken sacrosanct protocols, but the alternative would've been murderous depravity. His deliberate act of opening the door was pure appeasement, a final gamble to quell Hammerfall's violence.

The boil of tension had been lanced. Snowley had given up the physical control of the cockpit—a paradox of control— to gain a fragile measure of psychological peace. Now, with Hammerfall's singular objective achieved, the chaos of his mind was now liberated. With control over his domain, he was free to enact his unsettling agenda. The passengers were no longer hostages to a single objective; they were now party to the boundless, unhinged landscape of his mind at 35,000 feet.

- 17 -
Death's Open Vista

Just over two hours before the 787-9 expected touchdown at Heathrow, a frenzied torrent of preparations unleashed its force, transforming the airport into a bustling crucible of focused activity.

The moment the pilot's distress signal flashed across screens, a chain of command, honed by years of grim contingency planning, had surged into action. That silent, four-digit code had blasted through every level of the national security apparatus, from the flight controllers who now rerouted an entire sky of commercial traffic, to the contingency for scrambling a Typhoon fighter once it was close to British airspace.

This vast, intricate machinery, usually a backdrop to travel, now pulsed and roared with an urgent vitality, marshalling every resource to confront the unwelcome terrorist guests on their approach.

Policing London Heathrow Airport fell under the command of the Metropolitan Police's Aviation Policing Command (APC). As the head of APC specialist operations, Commander Lucinda Siren responded instantly. Every instinct she possessed had been honed for this precise moment—the moment she received word a terrorist situation had erupted.

She triggered previously agreed protocols and operational procedures between APC and the military. These were designed for seamless execution and ensure that forces can work together efficiently in a high-stakes, rapidly developing situation. Their swift action was underpinned by government approval and the watchful eye of COBRA (Cabinet Office Briefing Room A) in Whitehall, London.

It was from here that ministers and officials convened, their discussions the crucible where strategies were forged and commands cascaded, directly addressing perceived threats to national security. Previously prepared and encrypted communication links went live to address the developing threat.

These links connected COBRA, GCHQ (the UK's cyber-intelligence agency monitoring terrorist communications), and the NSA in America. This immediate intelligence sharing was a pre-agreed protocol of the "Five Eyes" alliance, ensuring seamless coordination between these key security bodies.

For the APC, its central command was from the OARB (Operations and Reconnaissance Building), a fortress of cutting-edge communications. Its two principal rooms served as the nerve centre. The first, a secure conference room, was a hushed nexus for critical exchanges with COBRA. The second, a tense, operations-rich situational briefing room, was where the SAS would meticulously command and orchestrate any sanctioned rescue mission, every detail sharpened to a razor's edge.

Commander Lucinda Siren's second action was to put the vehicle patrols on red alert. The unit normally had a contingent of eight response vehicles patrolling roads close to the airport, and these were immediately instructed to deal with any vehicles acting suspiciously.

Third, the Highways Agency received an order to call in extra staff. These additional personnel were tasked with monitoring all road traffic data from ANPR and facial-recognition CCTV cameras within a 10-mile zone around the airport. Their objective was to identify vehicles and suspects already known to the police.

This meant computers scoured not only any suspect vehicle registration plates but also delved into data recorded many hours previously, searching for ghosts of past movements.

Facial recognition cameras were employed to photograph any drivers and passengers within this circumference. All airports were treated by intelligence services with military-grade sensitivity owing to their national security importance. Together, these cameras fed their strategic intel back to the security services.

Fourth, Commander Siren had also called in APC police marksmen. They had prepared for such a terrorist scenario many times over, and needed little briefing. Each officer then took their pre-determined, elevated position within a specially constructed, small, tower-like concrete building. These fortified outposts were scattered strategically around the area closest to the OARB, their silent gaze fixed upon the private runway and apron.

From these vantage points, their gaze followed the four automated APC vehicles as they glided with silent purpose, traversing the airport perimeter. Each maintained a precise 50-meter separation, a calculated ballet designed to thwart a simultaneous attack and ensure at least one could relay critical intelligence on an aggressor's position—a lifeline in the looming silence.

On the roof of each vehicle, two imaging cameras jutted upwards by about a meter, their presence an unsettling, alien sight to any who didn't understand their covert purpose.

One device was a thermal-imaging camera. Its purpose was to detect body heat from possible hidden terrorists in the undulating terrain and foliage close to and beyond the immediate perimeter.

The other was a camera that could detect if grass had recently been trampled by a human's weight, as grass may normally take an hour or more to correctly reposition itself.

Above them, almost imperceptible to the naked eye, were five drones that monitored the whole apron. This included the apron and special runway allocated for such hijackings, as well as the trees, bushes and foliage that surrounded the apron, albeit 800 metres away.

This military and technological welcome, like many other preset protocols, had been planned and tested for contingencies many times. Accordingly, the hijacked jet on landing would be directed to the remote apron area overlooked by the OARB, some 300 metres away.

To do this, it would use a specially constructed runway to land on. This runway was 600m from the nearest commercial runway. Once landed, the jet would taxi to the end of the runway. From there, it would then taxi along a 150-metre taxiway. Finally, it would park on a specially-constructed apron, the shortest of the three types of jet airliner parking, and its usual parking spot.

The apron's surface hid a labyrinthine network of secret openings, strategically placed for military personnel to conduct covert reconnaissance of the hijacked aircraft. Furthermore, should negotiations with the hijackers crumble entirely, these hidden access points could become covert conduits to storm the plane.

Accordingly, the apron terminus became colloquially termed DOA, or "death's open vista". This was a play on the DOA acronym normally meaning "dead on arrival", which for terrorists was very much a given once parked there.

The significant strategic logistics and military reconnaissance capabilities definitively explained the long-standing mystery. For over 35 years, no hostage-taken airliner had landed there, a question now answered by the sheer scale of this preparation...until today.

The last box for Commander Lucinda Siren to tick was military preparedness. APC sought and received the Home Secretary's permission. This authorisation allowed Red Troop, part of 22 SAS's Sabre Squadron, to be placed on operational standby. Their readiness was crucial in case the situation deteriorated after the jet's landing.

Within 50 minutes of the Home Secretary's approval, the SAS counter-terrorism squadron arrived in two Blue Thunder helicopters. The helicopters' quietness and agility were noted with admiring approval by APC Commander Siren and MI5 Intelligence Officer (IO), Rupert Barrington.

Landing at their chosen HLS (Helicopter Landing Site), they were out of sight of any distant prying eyes from the media and public onlookers. Twenty hardened-looking men briskly alighted with military precision; some 20 other members of the troop were on standby and kept in the communications loop if needed.

As each trooper alighted from their helicopters, they carried a large bag that contained their respective military hardware. SAS Squadron Leader and Officer Commanding, Major John Nailthem, alighted first from the lead helicopter. He briefly shouted over to Captain Tonforce, who had similarly alighted from the second helicopter, to direct the troopers to follow the Intelligence Officer to the situation room in the OARB for briefing. With this, he trotted over to Siren to formally say hello as well as get a brief update on important intelligence as he walked with her to a preparatory briefing from COBRA.

A few months prior to this, Siren had visited Nailthem at the SAS service headquarters in Credenhill. This facility was located on the outskirts of Hereford. As a result of this encounter, a rapport of respect had rapidly formed between them, hinting at a level of understanding that went unspoken.

'Morning Major,' said APC Commander Siren.

'Morning Commander,' replied OC, Major John Nailthem.

'SitRep' respectfully but forcefully demanded Nailthem, as the whirring rhythm made by the Blue Thunder helicopter blades became slightly louder as they rose imperiously into the sky for their return to Hereford.

'This way Major,' signalled Nailthem as they began to walk swiftly to the secure conference room to speak to their superiors at COBRA.

'We have an Air Marshal on board, one of yours, I believe. It looks bad. We believe there are ten, twelve, maybe even fourteen terrorists. It looks pretty grim at present. NSA and MI5 are sharing intelligence. Aerial and satellite surveillance is in operation. Where logistics allow, an F-15 is shadowing the plane and an MQ-9 reaper is monitoring communications. A multi-role Typhoon fighter jet from Brize Norton will be deployed once they enter British airspace. Other than that, it's a waiting game at present.'

'Fuck, fourteen possible tangos in a big jet. Not exactly short of space to be a fucking nuisance then!' hastily and loudly Nailthem as they entered OARB.

'Yes, maybe 14; we believe at least three are female from satellite listening posts. They are heavily armed. All seem to have 9mm Glock 19 handguns. We picked up something about their weapons being custom-made. Maybe half have

Heckler & Koch MP5 submachine guns. Some have explosive jackets too,' spoke Commander Siren worryingly.

'Do they have a name?' asked Nailthem.

'All will be revealed in the briefing,' responded Siren.

They both ascended one stairway and walked along a single, unassuming corridor before arriving at the secure situation room door.

Siren stopped and looked around at Nailthem. A momentary hush descended, thick and heavy, around them both. Her gaze settled on his rugged face, which, she mused, was a topographical map of military knowledge. The operational experiences he had undertaken were so profound they were almost unfathomable to others, his very visage a repository of countless untold military stories and a silent vault of classified details from past operations.

'And, Commander,' Siren continued, with a slight hesitancy, fearing what it implied, 'If that's not bad enough, it's most likely they're using some passengers as human shields in case you storm the plane.'

'Just another day at the office!' curtly said Major Nailthem. Commander Siren was somewhat taken aback by his abrupt indifference to such danger. This was especially surprising considering his SAS background and expertise in hostage situations. Despite this, she quizzically asked, 'Could it be worse?'

'Of course, Commander, they could have a fucking nuke on board!' retorted Nailthem, who, by now, was eager to get into the secure conference briefing to learn current situational intelligence. His emotions inside were cold yet calculated. His training wanted to take the tangos down right there and then if he could.

- 18 -
Briefings

Nailthem and Siren entered the secure conference room and sat down facing the large and imposing video wall that dominated the room. Composed of smaller screens, it offered multiple functionalities. It was capable of facilitating a briefing attended by numerous speakers, as now, or displaying vivid 3D graphics.

In this context, the video wall would display live satellite images of the inbound plane to Heathrow, as well as updated information from intelligence sources.

Furthermore, once the plane reached its designated OARB apron, intelligence data could be assembled to visually construct the plane's interior and determine the terrorist positions within.

A technician entered, clutching a laptop like a fragile, priceless artefact whose value had just quadrupled. The sparsely furnished room crackled with an almost imperceptible energy, a hum vibrating beneath the oppressive stillness.

He seemed strangely adrift, his gaze vacant, as if lost within the confines of his own thoughts. The two commanders exchanged a quick, knowing look, acknowledging the immense pressure the technician must be under.

He furtively looked at both Nailthem and Siren before introducing himself as the technician for the briefing. A bead of sweat traced a path down his temple, unnoticed. His fingers tightened on the laptop, knuckles white. The silence stretched, thick with unspoken tension.

Thirty seconds after opening his laptop and rapidly depressing what seemed like a hundred buttons, several VIPs appeared on the video wall for a real-time briefing. They were: the Home Secretary - Charles Harley; Director of Special Forces - Major General Bohham; Deputy Director General - Sir Peter Hargreaves; Deputy Director of MI5 - Sir Charles Forley Bunnham; and his American equivalent, NSA Deputy Director - Wyle Grange. Most were at COBRA, except for the NSA Deputy Director.

The meeting took 30 minutes. As it progressed, Major Nailthem couldn't help but assemble various assault hypotheses in his mind. The conversational intelligence continually saturated his military mind.

At the end of the COBRA meeting, Commander Siren simply turned in her seat and clipped a terse 'Not good!' to Major Nailthem. He nodded with indifference; his mind already engaged in military planning. He thanked her, exited the room and practically ran down the corridor, pulling up sharply at the SAS situational briefing room. From behind the closed door, the insistent roar of voices and the metallic clatter of weaponry bled through.

With his pause over, Major Nailthem entered the briefing room. This would be the hub from which all negotiations and any planned assault would now take place. The room was a fortress of cutting-edge technology, with another video wall and a vast array of military-grade hardware and software. It was twice the size of the conference room he had just left.

How big? Tennis court size. The bottom half was for troopers' kits and space to sort out their specialised equipment, such as breaching kit, sniper kit and bullets. There was also an armoury in the OARB basement that contained an extensive array of weaponry, enough to satisfy even the most demanding specialist.

The moment Nailthem appeared, the room exhaled. Their low chatter evaporated, replaced by a profound, almost reverent silence. It was a silence born of an urgent thirst for knowledge of the present and a tense, unspoken speculation about the future.

Many had trained that very morning for a terrorist hijacking. The irony of these unfolding events was palpable as they looked to their commander for guidance, much like followers seeking wisdom from seers.

Major Nailthem walked over to a small lectern that had an inbuilt computer to organise and move data around on a large, wall-mounted 250cm screen that was behind and above him. He also picked up a miniaturised remote control. He already knew how to use the equipment as that was part of his technology training.

An unsettling stillness descended as he meticulously arranged his opening display on the lectern screen, the mundane act somehow amplifying the invisible menace that hung heavy in the air. Commander Siren entered, settling by the door, the palpable weight of anticipation settling upon her too. Her command was absolute, a heavy burden of responsibility that pressed down from both the police and government.

She was tasked with directing the overarching police operation and securing a peaceful resolution. Her command extended to the APC firearms officers present at the briefing, making it critical for seamless inter-agency collaboration. Their complete understanding of the SAS plan, its rules of engagement, and all communication protocols was essential.

Consequently, her role involved close cooperation and collaboration with the SAS, covering everything from intelligence gathering to military preparedness, should COBRA authorise an assault on the aircraft. Her immediate presence at this briefing served to keep her fully integrated into the military operational loop. The significant emotional weight of her command resonated deeply.

All updated intelligence received via her secure laptop and wireless earpiece would be promptly relayed to Nailthem.

It was understood that her job was to ensure any future legal challenges regarding SAS and APC actions were avoided. This point was of paramount importance, and her presence was critical to maintaining a clear legal framework. Consequently, this reinforced the need for a framework that covered not just the "how" but also the "why" behind certain actions.

Before Nailthem began his hijacking briefing, he immediately set the stakes. He informed them that this would be one of the most audacious and precision-timed passenger aircraft rescue missions ever attempted. This instinctively grabbed the attention of all troopers present and heightened the intrigue of their action all the more.

He then pressed his first button and a large, clearly visible image of the Dreamliner 787-9 plane became evident on the very large screen behind him. So large it resembled one of those huge teaching boards you see in university lecture theatres.

After introducing the plane, the hull disappeared and a 3D rotation of its inner architecture began. What was particularly impressive was that as Nailthem spoke, the voice-activated computer image adjusted to his words. No matter what he described, the image adjusted to reinforce his meaning.

'At the moment, there's much speculation on who the terrorists are and what their modus operandi is,' said Nailthem. 'There are several VIPs and an Air Marshal on board.' At this point, the computer displayed pictures of the seven with their names, with arrows pointing to their respective seating positions.

One trooper shouted, 'This is better than the movies,' to which other troopers nervously laughed.

'I thought it was only porn you watched, trooper Harris,' retorted Nailthem.

This raised an even louder burst of laughter. The APC officers looked on, somewhat bemused by such levity that seemed out of place in such a tense atmosphere.

Nailthem continued, 'Let me be clear: we are not waiting. The "prepare to execute" command from the Home Secretary is already in place, effective the instant that plane lands and taxis to the apron. We are coiled, ready to strike - time is our enemy, readiness our weapon, and our minds are locked on the objective.

'We expect an intelligence surge from all technological sources once they land. And as soon as that intelligence confirms our optimal path, the final briefing will take place. Thereafter, we maintain our disciplined readiness, every trooper poised, awaiting only the Home Secretary's confirmation to initiate the strike.'

Nailthem continued, 'As you can imagine both MI5 and NSA intelligence services are working together so that every technological resource is scouring that plane for information to help us. In the end, we expect trouble and we will end it.'

At this juncture, Nailthem looked over at Siren and asked sternly, 'What's happening on intelligence updates?'

'May I?' Siren asked Nailthem, pointing to the lectern.

'Of course,' replied Nailthem.

Nailthem moved aside and stood proudly. He looked on as if awaiting parade inspection. As Siren's gaze swept across the assembled troopers, a silent intensity met hers, each stare a locked laser beam of focus. Every face presented a mask of focused determination. The ingrained discipline of their training radiated outwards, a palpable force that seemed to momentarily affect her composure. She dropped her head, partly in acknowledgment of their unwavering focus.

The brief pause was a desperate bid to regain her composure, a shallow breath swallowed against the scorching anxiety within. She finally lifted her gaze, addressing the troopers, Nailthem a silent, watchful presence behind her.

Siren opened her mouth. Each syllable, every word she was about to unleash, would be devoured by the assembled troopers. Their lives and the success of the mission were partly dependent on the accuracy of the intelligence she now held.

It was a fragile key, poised to unlock either salvation or unmitigated disaster. The true test would come only after the plane's wheels kissed the tarmac. Here, preparedness wasn't merely a maxim; it was the raw, unvarnished essence of survival.

'Commander Nailthem,' Siren's voice sliced through the silence, a silence as taut as a drawn bowstring, as she glanced over her left shoulder before addressing the troopers.

'Forgive the interruption. But as has just been outlined, utilising the technology behind me, we are indeed staring into the abyss of a hostage situation. One that demands your precise expertise to resolve, for which your reputation precedes you in such matters.'

Siren paused, her gaze silently probing each trooper's face, seeking an unspoken understanding of the grim reality settling upon them. She had no doubt the SAS were unmatched in hostage and rescue matters, and as they had trained for any possible scenario of this kind, it was the terrorists who should be far more afraid.

'The latest verified intelligence from MI5 and the NSA, a product of initial intelligence feeds, paints a chilling tableau. Voice analyses, coupled with triangulated signals from geospatial listening posts, confirm fourteen terrorists onboard. The spectre of sleeper agents also looms; our analysts are working feverishly on that possibility.

'They are armed - our intelligence, by piecing together fragmented data, suggests, at a minimum, several handguns and sub-machine guns. These are not impulsive actors; they are disciplined, trained to kill without hesitation.

'Our negotiators will attempt to dissuade them, a fragile hope we must nevertheless pursue. Their demands, when they come - and they will, with cold calculation - will test us all.

'Your commander will receive immediate intelligence updates as soon as I have verified them. The hostage jet is inbound, ETA 2.55 p.m., so you have about two hours before the situation commences.

'However, the moment it breaches UK airspace, a Typhoon will become its silent shadow. The Prime Minister's directive on engagement is stark: the rules of engagement must be followed. Yet, within those rules, the final decision to act or not to act rests with you, as it always does in these do-or-die situations.

'You are the scalpel in this delicate and dangerous surgery. Your timing, speed, and decisions must be precise, for one wrong move could have catastrophic consequences. Good luck.'

The weight of those final two words hung in the air, a tangible pressure. Siren retreated to her chair, leaving a vacuum pregnant with the chill of the unfolding reality to come. Every trooper eye in the room now locked onto their commander. The air crackled with the unspoken question: what lethal choreography would their commander now disclose to them?

Even with hours until touchdown, Nailthem had already mentally cycled through several scenarios for the hostage rescue mission.

Of these, the most probable involved a lightning strike of controlled violence. A swift, close quarters battle initiated after snipers had neutralised key terrorists during the counter-terrorist assault on the plane.

The team watched as tactical diagrams detailing individual roles, timings, equipment, and the integration of possible post-landing intelligence flashed across the large screen. Each trooper tracked their designated part in the unfolding plan, their interdependence absolute; success hinged on flawless timing to amplify their surprise.

Though the specifics might shift upon landing, their collective minds absorbed new data with the instantaneous and complete reaction of litmus paper to a solution. The definitive assault blueprint would crystallise once the aircraft was grounded.

The Final Approach

Having flown past the Channel Islands towards the south coast of England, the 787-9 entered British airspace. From this point forward, the plane was escorted by a Typhoon fighter jet that had been scrambled by the National Air and Space Operations Centre (NASOC).

Having taken off from RAF Coningsby, it was shadowing the 787-9 within seven minutes. This scrambling was standard operational procedure to ensure the security and safety of UK airspace. Several civilian air traffic control organisations watched the 787-9 flight path as it remorselessly made its way to Heathrow.

In the OARB conference room, Siren was talking to MI5 intelligence officer, Rupert Barrington. A graduate of Oxford, his family thought he'd use his Philosophy, Politics, and Economics (PPE) degree to enter politics. Many famous graduates had done so before him. However, MI5 had more career gravitas; it suited his analytical mind.

Intercepted communications sparked an epiphany moment in Barrington as he listened to Hammerfall's phrases. 'They've got our backs...Those two are monitoring us,' and then a minute later his worst fears were realised when Hammerfall mentioned darkly-clad men on the OARB roof.

The media had no cameras to suggest this. He must have spotters somewhere near the apron, maybe drones, maybe both. A sudden chill went through his body as he considered the implications.

Siren looked at Barrington. She had inferred the same. She spoke immediately to Nailthem on the radio link. The two

SAS snipers were told to use their thermal telescopes to interpret any heat from around the perimeter. Nothing was observed.

'They're out there, I know it,' Nailthem said, sounding exasperated.

'If they are, they're as good as you,' said Siren over the radio.

Nailthem laughed menacingly as he retorted, 'Good is not good enough when we're around.'

With approximately 120 nautical miles (138 miles) remaining in its journey, the airliner began its initial approach, the descent phase. Inside the plane, Hammerfall roared at passengers to follow all orders from the remaining cabin crew.

About 30 minutes after beginning his textbook approach, Captain Snowley's 787-9 was deep into the final stages. As the jet entered the flare—the final manoeuvre to gently land the aircraft—a darkly painted SAS Eurocopter AS365 Dauphin appeared, a jarring sight some 200 metres off its starboard side. The Eurocopter then sharply yawed left, precisely aligning itself with the approaching 787-9.

From taut wires dangling from the helicopter's undercarriage, two SAS troopers swayed, their figures dark against the sky. Their bodies pitched and bucked in the whipping wind, violently tossed by their rapid descent and the airliner's immense turbulence. As the jet crawled to taxi speed, the helicopter eclipsed it from above and hovered menacingly.

Inside, Hammerfall could hear the voices of his snipers over his radio, which employed frequency-hopping spread spectrum. For listening intelligence services, this made it very difficult, but not impossible, to intercept and track as it didn't consistently stay on one frequency. They would need to know the hopping sequence and be able to follow the rapid changes to locate them precisely. This sophistication of technology couldn't help the snipers directly in this situation. They still had to keep their communication short and precise in order to report that the jet was under attack.

Such was the surprise of this report to Hammerfall, his brain couldn't put together a verbal response. Above the jet, the troopers were now only metres from the middle top of the fuselage.

The terrorists on the plane shouted for their snipers to act, their voices harassed Hammerfall's ears. Time was slipping away. Hammerfall's thoughts fractured; the urgency of the situation scrambled his focus.

Suddenly, echoes of past victories resonated within him. It transformed his hesitant thoughts into a compelling need for decisive action, crushing any lingering doubt.

'Fuck it, shoot them,' he sneered, with a chilling lack of empathy. He wallowed in self-satisfaction, his narcissism blinding him to the true cost of his actions.

From their concealed positions, two shots rang out. Two SAS troopers shuddered on the ropes and fell limp, a brief crimson mist surrounding them before the helicopter's downdraft tore it away. Blood trickled down from their chest areas. The Eurocopter veered away suddenly towards the OARB.

'They are dead,' quietly said one of his snipers.

Raucous cheers from the terrorists filled the cabin atmosphere. Hammerfall spoke again to the snipers. No response came back. He tried again, still no response. The sudden silence from his snipers puzzled Hammerfall.

Surely, they would report any further developments. He clung to the hope their silence meant they were prioritising the secrecy of their location. Perhaps they were slowly reverse crawling to exfiltrate? Perhaps it was something more?

It was something more. The two "dead" SAS troopers were not really dead. They were just mannequins, geared up like them. The blood had been released from an internal cavity within the mannequins, designed so that a single shot anywhere would cause a discharge of blood.

Nailthem had ordered the action to uncover the location of the snipers as triangulation of their signal left room for location error.

It worked; their location was now known. The two SAS rooftop snipers picked up thermals from bullet discharges. Moments after the terrorist snipers fired, two answering shots ripped through their position. The terrorist snipers were dead, and their radio communication to Hammerfall ceased.

Nailthem turned to Siren and coldly said, 'See? Just as I said. They were only good,' echoing his earlier comment about the quality of the terrorist snipers' professional utility.

Siren looked into his eyes that stared straight through hers. It made her uneasy with herself, as if he could read her mind and unlock her deepest, darkest personal secrets that had always remained hidden.

'God, you're frightening!' she said unnervingly.

'No, I'm SAS!' he replied assuredly.

- 20 -
On The Apron

The plane landed precisely at 2:55 p.m., as scheduled and taxied to its strategically placed apron. The cabin of the 787-9 felt as though all air had been sucked from it, replaced by a palpable, suffocating tension.

Passengers huddled in their seats, a silent, trembling mass. Their furtive glances, like trapped birds, darted upward, only to be violently reined back by the chilling realisation of impending doom. They recoiled from the predatory glint in the terrorists' eyes, terrified their lives might soon be consumed in a coming explosion.

Every jet window, a watchful eye, had its electrochromic window fully shaded to a very dark blue, a desperate attempt to shield their grim tableau from the OARB, the only building in sight. This veil ensured no unwelcome observations could reveal the terrorists' movements or positions.

Even the sunshine struggled, a weak, defeated foe, to pierce the electrochromic veil and lighten the burgeoning fear within the cabin. While the veil blocked the light, the relentless summer sun still turned the metal fuselage into an oven, slowly baking the air trapped inside. The environmental control system, designed to cool and purify, could run on batteries, but not indefinitely, threatening to deplete power for lighting and, critically, the plane's radio communications to the OARB tower.

The oppressive silence of the passengers inadvertently magnified the terrorists' frenzied movements, their manic shouts echoing through the twin-aisled cabin as they scoured

160

the views from the windows, a jarring cacophony in the stillness.

This torrent of anxiety and stress only tightened the suffocating grip of intimidation on the passengers. Some instinctively hunched their bodies, a futile attempt to shrink into insignificance, to become less noticeable. The air, thick with the suffocating scent of primal fear and the sharp tang of sweat from hours of confinement, became a torturous shroud that clung to their skin and souls.

Unbeknownst to those trapped inside, the moment the wheels kissed the tarmac, a whirlwind of intelligence activity erupted as Nailthem had predicted. This sudden surge would be the crucial fulcrum, determining whether the situation would end peacefully or in chaos. Trained negotiators worked tirelessly over the radio, a lifeline to keep the escalating hostage crisis under control.

Just as a chief negotiator commanded a cadre of seasoned professionals, so too did Hammerfall command the airwaves. His voice was a mercurial blend of intermittent pronouncements, sudden roars, and chillingly abrupt silences—each cut-off designed solely for his perverse amusement. What they didn't understand, however, was the dark tapestry of his terrorist history.

Hammerfall was a known terrorist with an extensive, bloodied past and likely little future. He had always killed his victims from the front, believing it utterly ignominious for a warrior to die from behind. To him, such a death didn't just signify defeat, but a shameful failure to truly know and understand his enemies' art of war.

His art of war with the negotiators was to control them through fractured yet, at times, negotiable communication. Unsurprisingly, the open but secure radio channel, established minutes after landing, buzzed intermittently with demands. This communicative interplay was one of pacification and rationality from the chief negotiator, met by demands and irrationality from Hammerfall.

To bridge this negotiable gap, the negotiator used special words of psychological meaning to articulate his intent to help and bring it to a peaceful conclusion. His intense training, for just such circumstances, was demonstrated early and consistently thereafter. Each word he uttered was expertly chosen to inform, understand and subtly appease the volatility of Hammerfall.

The demands, when they finally came, were a grim litany: the release of key fellow terrorists from UK jails, a jet to an as-yet-unnamed country, a staggering 50 million dollars in cryptocurrency siphoned into a web of global bank accounts, and, almost as an afterthought, the basic passenger needs for food, water, and sanitation. The latter, seemingly unimportant to Hammerfall's core demands, were subtly but assuredly explained by the negotiator as constructively beneficial in resolving the crisis.

However, unlike a few Hollywood movies that have depicted some passengers being released in such hostage scenarios, in this case, even the remotest suggestion of this was met with a resounding "no" from Hammerfall.

A plane with 250 passengers was held by at least 14 terrorists, and with the afternoon summer sun baking the cabin, the atmosphere inside was becoming as agitated, tense, and volatile as the terrorists' own thinking.

The relentless heat, a silent accomplice to the human needs for food, water, and sanitation, finally carved a sliver of common ground for the chief negotiator. Within the hour, under the watchful, armed gaze of police, two small trucks, their beds brimming with bottles of water, crawled slowly, deliberately, from the OARB, an oasis approaching a desert of desperation.

A white flag was attached to a wire mast from the back of each truck. As the trucks were driven, the flag flapped precariously in the hot summer wind as if hoping its message of peace would translate into deterring any terrorist from shooting at it or those in the trucks.

Cold food suitable for diverse cultural needs was taken out to the plane too. To get the food on board, it was agreed that boarding stairs could be brought to three open port exit doors, excluding the one close to the cockpit.

One armed terrorist would then walk down the steps and move around them to ensure no police or army were hiding. Once clear, the food would be taken aboard and distributed according to cultural diet. Hammerfall had refused forklift trucks to lift multiple boxes straight to the exit doors for fear it could be used to obscure their view of police or military activity.

The opening of the exit doors unleashed a wave of profound relief, the summer breeze a sudden, merciful balm. It swept through the cabin, a cleansing current that purged the stale air and cooled the passengers' flushed skin. Its therapeutic touch seemed to reach their very souls, a whispered reassurance: 'You'll be all right.'

Sanitation had to be catered for too. Lavatory service trucks, also known as Honey trucks, were dispatched to siphon the waste into their own storage tanks. The waste was then transported to the airport's sewage system for disposal.

During this time, the same terrorist who had previously checked the three boarding stairs watched over this process. The two disposal workers, although trained for these situations, found training didn't quite match reality when a Heckler & Koch MP5 submachine gun was menacingly pointing at them and cocked.

One area that Hammerfall was not readily amenable to was the jamming of all other communications. He bellowed that he could jam communications, permanently, by blowing up the plane and everyone with it.

This jamming was possible because air traffic control communication operated on specific frequency bands within the VHF (Very High Frequency) and UHF (Ultra High Frequency) spectrum that were allocated internationally for aviation use. These bands were distinct from those used by mobile phone networks (e.g., GSM, LTE, 5G) and Wi-Fi.

The negotiator explained to Hammerfall that everything enacted by airport authorities was to facilitate a peaceful conclusion. He argued that since social media was biased even at the best of times, any misrepresentation reported could negatively influence ongoing negotiations.

Knowing Hammerfall was probably not a radio expert, as intelligence suggested, the negotiator also offered some reasoned arguments for how their communications could be intercepted and used against them, inflaming an already incendiary situation. 'We need one channel of communication, just one. Anything else is detrimental for you, for us, for the situation,' the negotiator explained.

Hammerfall had agreed reluctantly. However, he rationalised he would be able to negotiate their reconnection later as a bargaining chip.

The Anatomy Of A Shot

The 787-9's windows, a significant 30% larger than those on standard commercial airliners, initially presented the sniper with a decisive advantage. This expanded aperture offered unparalleled target visibility and a broader field of view, stripping away obscurities and proving crucial for clearly identifying the terrorists within.

It also allowed clearer pinpointing of potential obstacles, including seatbacks, passenger positions, or anything else that might deviate the bullet's lethal path. These visual advantages would collectively guide the selection of the optimal aiming point.

Moreover, the wider expanse significantly lessened the peril of window frame interference. The narrower confines of standard windows, by contrast, subtly amplified a terrifying risk: even a glancing impact on such a window could catastrophically deflect the round, sending it astray to strike an innocent soul. Yet, these initial benefits were tempered by other critical factors looming large.

At a distance of approximately 400 metres from the OARB, SAS snipers were armed with their quintessential tool: the lethally precise L118A1 bolt-action rifle, paired with a 7.62x51mm NATO barrier-blind bullet. This round, featuring a hardened penetrator core, was capable of breaching formidable obstacles.

The L118A1 would be fitted with a Schmidt & Bender MK II 50mm scope with a variable 3-12x zoom. The combination of rifle and bullet was battle-proven across diverse terrains and hostile engagements, capable of easily penetrating commercial jet aircraft windows and cabin window shades if required. While the 787-9 featured electrochromic windows rather than shades, this made little difference; the hardened core of the bullet ensured unwavering momentum and resisted ballistic deformation upon impact.

In particular, as there would only be a light wind, the snipers would likely use a G1 ballistic coefficient in the range of approximately 0.450 to 0.55 to minimize wind drift. Even extending the range upwards to 800 metres, the 7.62x51mm calibre offered an exceptional equilibrium of accuracy and manageable recoil.

The bolt-action platform facilitated lightning-fast follow-up shots should the need arise; a highly trained SAS sniper could fluidly cycle the rifle in a mere second. Their main priority, however, remained the gravity of that single, decisive shot: one accurate round to neutralize the immediate and deadly threat.

Consequently, the inherent precision of the L118A1 rifle and the specialised 7.62x51mm barrier-blind bullet made the larger windows a less critical factor. The rifle's finely tuned mechanics and the bullet's design significantly improved its accuracy, even against complex barriers.

The bullet's predictable ballistic properties further aided in a successful shot. Ultimately, however, the unyielding precision of the sniper's expert skill remained the paramount determinant of a clean shot, piercing through the intricate, layered barriers of the window glass with singular focus.

Just in case they had to storm the jet at night, the snipers carried a Sniper Thermal Imaging Capability (STIC) thermal scope. This scope could be attached either to the Picatinny rail on top of the main scope or to a rail offset on the barrel in front of it.

However, the ability to detect body heat or thermal signatures through a jet window would be obscured due to the window's acrylic composition. This limitation meant the thermal scope's primary benefit in this scenario would be for identifying targets outside the aircraft.

Therefore, whether the electrochromic windows were dimmed or lightened, this would have no bearing on the inability to see thermal signatures through them. Nonetheless, the STIC was retained for identifying any targets outside the aircraft.

At about 6 p.m., 10 SAS snipers had taken up the best strategically concealed overwatch positions on the fifth of seven floors of the OARB. The height from the ground apron to the jet windows of the 787-9 was approximately 17 metres or 56 feet from the ground. They

From the prone position, they would be able to see into each jet window from a slight downward elevation. This not only reduced glare and reflections but also provided a crucial tactical advantage. Furthermore, firing from an elevated position directed the majority of the sound blast downwards, providing an element of acoustic concealment.

They were supported by two SAS snipers on the roof, two floors above their colleagues, who had been there even before the jet had touched down. From their commanding vantage point, they served as a silent, watchful eye, providing critical reconnaissance, intelligence, and a reserve of precision firepower to support the assault teams should the situation demand it.

- 22 -
Tensions Rise

By 7 p.m., hours after the jarring touchdown, the passengers' freedom wasn't just curtailed; it was shackled by a visceral terror and the chilling, unknown abyss of their predicament. Yet, amidst this suffocating dread, a fragile sliver of humanity gleamed: the terrorists' surprising willingness to address their gnawing hunger and parching thirst.

This minor concession, a lone flickering candle in the oppressive, absolute darkness, whispered of a fragile opening for negotiation and, most crucially, their very survival.

For the chief negotiator, this was the crucial phase. His consistent modus operandi of working in small steps, supported by the collective effort of his negotiating team, had proven successful so far.

From their situational briefing room, the SAS had been listening, watching, and calculating what could happen next, just as a chess player plans several possible moves ahead.

Every ghostly rasp of fabric, the insidious, muted click of a safety being disengaged, the shallow, ragged rhythm of muffled breathing, and even the faint, metallic creak of strained fuselage—each nuance was meticulously harvested by an unseen array of parabolic, directional, and laser microphones, operated from the OARB and clandestine listening posts stitched around the apron.

Intelligence had identified the terrorists from their voices. Pictures of each terrorist were now visible to the troopers on the video wall screen. Every syllable and word was being meticulously listened to, ensuring they knew who was friend or foe. This now included Tiroclaw, unmasked and labelled as a terrorist.

The plane's three main port exit doors were open, each dominated by two armed terrorists. The cockpit door was closed. The pairs stood with an almost disquieting nonchalance, a stark tableau against the grim reality of their presence. They exchanged clipped, terse words while exhaling intermittent plumes of smoke from their cigarettes, their gazes relentlessly sweeping the apron in a calculated, predatory display of vigilance for those hidden observers within the OARB.

The other eight terrorists, including Hammerfall but not Tiroclaw, were positioned strategically in the cabin, their control absolute. One stood guard at the cockpit door, while a terrifying failsafe underscored their dominance: the two middle starboard exit doors were rigged with explosives. This was a grim threat to security services if they dared to storm the plane, and a silent promise of swift retribution to keep the passengers placid.

The SAS knew their exact positions in the cabin at any time and that two middle starboard exit doors were primed. How? Once the port exit doors were opened, microdrones spun silently into the air from the top of the OARB. These drones were not just small; they were nanoscopic, mere motes of dust in the ambient light, impossible to discern without specific detection technology.

Each microdrone had a 4K camera and was coated with secret paint technology. This utilised advanced electrochromic polymers that changed its skin according to its backdrop, much like a chameleon changes its skin to avoid predators. The microdrones flew into the open port exit doors uninvited, unheard, and unnoticed.

They attached themselves to strategically determined locations on the upper part of the cabin. For 48 hours, they could send back highly-detailed pictures and sound, with provisions in place to deploy more should the operation extend beyond that timeframe and entry means be secured.

In effect, the sheer presence of drones in the cabin wasn't merely surveillance; it was a logistical masterclass, a chilling display of omniscient oversight.

And if this intelligence eavesdropping wasn't already outstanding, the pictures were integrated by the OARB computer into a 3D image and fed to the video wall screen. Video operators, seated on the other side of the briefing room, manipulated the graphics and incoming intelligence to ensure it provided the clearest perspective for understanding.

Nailthem, Siren, and the assembled SAS troopers watched on intently, their eyes taut with a predator's focus. They devoured every detail flickering across the screen, meticulously ingesting the cabin's layout, the terrorists' faces, their subtle reactions, and any new intelligence feeds posted on the upper right side as if they were party to a live, high-stakes chat.

Nailthem intermittently barked sharp orders to the operators, his voice cutting through the hum as he demanded adjustments or changes. Small, minor tweaks could be seamlessly activated through his remote voice control.

They all watched as Nailthem undertook a virtual walk-through of the cabin, just as if he was walking up and down the cabin aisles himself. He could direct the image to look at passengers and terrorists close up, examine everything in detail from the make of a terrorist's gun to tooth fillings. This was the electron microscope of counter-terrorism.

Of initial concern was Hammerfall's enforced movement of three sections of passengers into economy class, resulting in the 10 first-class, 10 business-class, and 30 premium-class passengers being bundled in with the 200 economy passengers, packing 250 into that section of the cabin.

While intended to simplify controlling them and managing toilet breaks, this action inadvertently made SAS sniper targeting considerably easier by reducing the risk of collateral damage for shots through the jet windows.

During the virtual walk-through of the cabin, every person's name was shown under them, while terrorists had their picture around the plane with a line pointing into the cabin to show their current location. If they moved around, the lines would dance across the screen.

From this information, the SAS snipers could be fed precise coordinates for their shots. Their ballistic calculations, including when sighting through the multi-layered window glass, were crucial to ensure the rounds would hit their targets in sections where no passengers were seated, preventing harm from glass shards.

As he watched, Nailthem's plan sharpened into crystalline clarity: three two-man SAS teams would covertly anchor themselves onto the fuselage, directly above each port main exit. A mere heartbeat after snipers silenced the door guards, they would descend like shadows on ropes, catapulting into the breach. A swift flashbang detonation through each doorway would shatter the equilibrium, granting them explosive entry to neutralise any of the six still alive. Then they would storm through the cabin taking out any terrorist not dealt with by the snipers. Meanwhile, the fourth team, similarly equipped, would breach the cabin's sanctity through the pilots' escape hatch.

Nailthem realised they could use the secret tunnels constructed for just such a situation. These tunnels had numerous outlets all around the plane's apron, making it easy to find a covert point of attack.

The four teams would covertly move up behind the plane and position lightweight ladders, their rubberised feet muffling any sound. They would climb, placing strong suction pads on the fuselage top to hold their weight, and await the signal to go.

At present, the situation seemed calm, but at 7.06 p.m., the secure radio blurted out what began as an inaudible scream of distress. The message soon became clear. Hammerfall's voice, laced with urgency, demanded an update on his demands.

No matter what the negotiator said, Hammerfall was unrelenting in his demand for communications bands to be unjammed – a demand he had deliberately held back until now. The negotiator repeated how the media coverage could impact their negotiations, which were going very well.

This wasn't the only game-changer Hammerfall held back. Unseen by the surveillance, Sang's body—a silent, blanket-shrouded bundle unceremoniously dumped in the crew rest area—had been dragged by two terrorists back to the galley, mere metres from where she had been shot.

Back at the SAS briefing room, they watched the previously unseen blanket-shrouded form with unease. They weren't sure if it was a body, an arsenal of guns, or something else. Their gaze remained fixed on the live feed.

'Listen! Listen good!' Hammerfall bellowed down the radio to the negotiator. 'I want those communications back on. It's good for my passengers who have nothing to do but admire me and my capabilities.'

He laughed as it teased his infantile ego that cared little for how hurt affected others. Just ask Sang.

The negotiator knew he had to keep Hammerfall on his side. Since the plane landed only four hours ago, the negotiator had secured an element of trust with him. It had boundaries, however, and the negotiator didn't want to stray beyond them.

'Where's my money, where's my satellite-based Wi-Fi connection, where's your trust?' Hammerfall shouted, his pitch increased, his tone sharper, his speech faster. These vocal changes were a clear hallmark of his increased anger and anxiety. The negotiator knew he had to act to ameliorate the situation.

'Hammerfall, please calm down. I am not your enemy, I am here to help you and your colleagues. I can confirm your cryptocurrency demand has been authorised at the highest level.'

'Confirmed? What's that mean, confirmed? You mean transferred, don't you?' Hammerfall continued to bellow.

'Different words, I agree, Hammerfall, but the outcome will be identical. The difference between the two approaches will be determined by you. They have requested the release of some passengers as a mark of good faith, to facilitate an end to this event. Do you understand?' the negotiator said calmly and assuredly.

Hammerfall hadn't factored in such a request, but he knew more passengers meant more leverage for him and less chance of military intervention. He had cleverly manipulated the negotiator to this point. While he wanted communications restored, he knew the delay would be excused. He would agree to release a passenger, but it would be Sang. Even in death, she would be useful to his cause.

'You want passenger release?' questioned a slightly calmer Hammerfall.

The negotiator thought at this point he had won Hammerfall over to a demonstration of good faith.

'Yes, as a mark of good faith, Hammerfall,' stated the negotiator. He now felt proud of himself that he had negotiated with Hammerfall to see sense.

'OK, one on its way,' Hammerfall joked.

At this point, he broke off communications, the first time this had happened.

Back in the SAS briefing room, the team watched the live feed, the air heavy with the low thrum of electronics and a palpable, unspoken dread. Hammerfall and two terrorists materialised like apparitions at the now open cockpit door, presenting Sang. They'd replaced the soaked, crimson towels with clean, stark white ones, draped carefully over her head and shoulders – a grotesque, crude attempt to conceal her head shot and blood that undoubtedly stained her back.

Hammerfall punctured the silence with two sharp shots into the air, the sound pulsing ominously across the apron, a direct challenge to the OARB. Simultaneously, the guards awkwardly manhandled Sang upright, their movements stiff, unnatural, and far too deliberate to suggest she was merely unconscious.

'Here's your first taste, if you're a good little boy,' Hammerfall's voice dripped with cruel amusement as he addressed the negotiator. 'And for being so patient... a bonus, a second soon!' He gestured, and the guards retreated into the aircraft, pulling Sang with them, Hammerfall disappearing last. Ten seconds later, the guards returned without Sang to continue their sentinel job.

'Commander,' the SAS spotter's voice, tight with grim certainty, crackled over the radio. 'Cabin crew ID confirmed: Senior member, Sang.'

'Confirmed on screen,' Nailthem stated, his gaze unwavering on the thermal imaging.

A beat of silence hung in the room before the spotter continued, his tone heavy. 'Sir... the thermal signature is cold. Consistent with significant heat loss. Based on the estimated environmental conditions and the lack of any discernible heat, the body is cold. This suggests the victim has been dead for some time.'

A sharp intake of breath cut through the tension. 'Oh God... she's gone by a bullet,' Siren whispered, her voice laced with horror.

Nailthem's head snapped towards Siren, his eyes hard as flint. 'There are more ways to silence a person than with a gunshot, Siren. Don't jump to conclusions.' The clipped intensity of his words lacerated the air, a sharp, verbal lash.

'Bastards,' he rasped, turning back to the screen, his focus now an unyielding, absolute laser.

'Who... who could have done that?' Siren stammered, her face pale.

Nailthem's gaze flicked back to Siren, lingering for a moment, a cold assessment in his eyes. 'It is the nature of the terrorist beast to kill when it is hungry. And I know it wants more'

Siren and Nailthem's personal alert devices began to shriek with piercing insistence, vibrating violently around their wrists. Even before their eyes could drop to the clamouring devices, the horrific image of Sang seared itself into their minds. As they looked down, MI5 Intelligence Officer Rupert Barrington barged open the briefing room

175

door, his arrival confirming the grim reality emblazoned on their screens.

'Secure conference room immediately,' demanded Barrington. 'No time, put it on here,' demanded Nailthem.

Nailthem turned to his troopers, who had been watching the unfolding events over the past hours, and with a familiar urgency, shouted, 'Prepare to move!'

They had been prepared since they arrived; their eagerness had been held in check by the need for precise intelligence.

Nailthem and Siren listened intently to the Home Secretary via the COBRA link, who had noted they had forgone the usual secure conference room due to the sheer urgency. He gave Nailthem the unmistakable green light to proceed. 'One killing,' he stressed, 'was one too many, and most assuredly where there was one, there'd be more very soon.' Nailthem confirmed they had everything required to execute the operation; the on-board intelligence was exceptional.

In just five minutes, all troopers were fully geared and expertly tooled, only their balaclavas remaining off. Nailthem concisely reprised the assault plan, his words a final, sharp directive. The snipers were already in place, their positions confirmed. The four assault teams knew their respective missions with unwavering clarity.

'Once in position, I'll give the go-signal,' he stated, his voice firm. 'Remember, I'll count down from three. Provided all snipers have their targets locked when I hit zero, I'll say "Go". It's absolutely imperative they neutralise the exit doors and most of the cabin before you swing in.'

With this last bit of information, all eyes snapped up at the screen. Sniper, drone, and listening devices collated to display a tragic, unfolding scene.

In the situational briefing room, they watched as two guards re-entered the congested passenger area, ordering two others to bring them the Air Marshal. They knew precisely who he was and where to find him. "How do they know that?" Nailthem thought, watching the grim scene unfold. "The passenger manifest wouldn't give those details." The passengers screamed with horror and anguish, not only at what was being perpetrated, but also at the terrifying realisation they might be next.

The Air Marshal fought, his body a frantic, futile tangle against the two guards who heaved him ever closer to their exit door. Hammerfall watched the brutal struggle with a sick grin and a chilling, morbid sense of purpose. "Let them terrorise and punish the Air Marshal out of his life," he thought, a dark satisfaction unfurling like a poison flower within him.

With the two guards and the Air Marshal now just a metre from the cockpit exit door, Hammerfall roared from the doorway, 'Here's your first hostage!' He retreated a few steps, and the guards surged forward, still brutally dragging and pulling the Air Marshal's struggling, weakening body. His desperate thrashing was futile; he knew his life was slipping away. The two guards continued to heave and yank his body to the door's very edge, then unceremoniously chucked him out.

Gravity became an unnatural, merciless killer as the body plummeted towards the tarmac, a dark, sickening projectile against the fading light. His guttural screams echoed even into the OARB. His body smashed against the tarmac with a horrifying thud—a wet, sickening crack as his neck snapped in two places, killing him instantly.

The two guards cheered loudly, a chilling display that not only celebrated their twisted courage but also underscored their fanaticism and absolute allegiance to Hammerfall.

But Hammerfall wasn't finished. The guards fell back behind him as he reappeared at the door. In his left hand, he waved his gun wildly, like a manic warrior high on drugs. He fired two shots into the air as before.

The sound peppered the warm evening air with an unapologetic intensity, vibrating through the hostages' nerves from head to foot. In his right hand, Hammerfall clutched a bloodied towel that, in turn, held the frail, lifeless body of Sang. The towel, clotted crimson, and her limp form howled their silent message to observers in the OARB.

Through the towel, he held her upright by her remaining hair; her arms and legs dangling grotesquely like a puppet's. He placed the gun to her head and fired. As Sang's lifeless body plunged to rest atop the Air Marshal's, the cockpit door was closed.

The SAS were already in motion, committed to ending any further terrorist brutality. Indeed, unbeknownst to the complacent guards, four SAS assault teams had been waiting below ground in four specially chosen covert tunnels, their exit points concealed directly behind the jet.

The tunnel exits were designed for minimal obstruction, allowing ladders to be carried out with ease. The troopers weren't forced to transport most of the ladders from the OARB through the tunnels; they were already pre-positioned, seven feet below, lightweight yet incredibly strong. These ladders would serve as their pathway to the fuselage, from where they would then swing into the aircraft through the exit doors.

Three of the port exits doors were open, offering the terrorist guards a secure vantage point. The L1 cockpit exit door was closed and only opened when two bodies were thrown out. Two terrorists each guarded the L2, L3, and L4 port exits. Assault team "A" was designated to enter via the emergency pilot entrance, while Teams "B", "C", and "D" would breach L2, L3, and L4 respectively.

The SAS would use the Colt Canada C8 CQB (Close Quarter Combat) rifles or L119A1 CQB, owing to their compact size and manoeuvrability, which were crucial for operating effectively within the confined spaces of an aircraft cabin.

Additionally, the vortex flash suppressor significantly reduced muzzle flash—a critical advantage in the already low-light conditions of an aircraft cabin, especially as the evening light continued to dim.

As plane fuselages varied drastically, they did have to bring specially customised end pieces for the unique curvature of the 787-9 Dreamliner. These four sections, each a metre long, would be silently and meticulously pieced together.

Nailthem gave the order to covertly exit the tunnels and prepare for their synchronised assault. Each team moved swiftly to their designated climbing point, remaining unseen and unheard from the starboard side. All electrochromic window shades were on, obscuring what little detail could have been visible. The telescopic ladder pieces were fitted together quickly, then carefully lifted and silently placed against the fuselage. Hours of training meant they began their climb in just seconds.

The three cabin assault teams (B-D) climbed their ladders and stood on the fuselage top in just 30 seconds. Their silent operation continued as they moved with ghost-like stealth, remaining unseen by the guards. To prevent noise, they wore black neoprene, a high-friction, high-density, closed-cell foam material.

Any onlooker would have felt a profound sense of bewilderment seeing two relaxed guards at three of the port exit doors, talking and sharing a cigarette. Yet, just a hushed silence away, darkly-clad figures, in full assault gear, were working just feet above them. Each figure cast a stark, distinct silhouette against the deep blue of the evening sky.

Meanwhile, cockpit assault team (A) had emerged from a tunnel directly beneath the plane's nose. Just like the others, swiftly assembled and positioned their telescopic ladder against the fuselage, then surreptitiously ascended to stand directly on the roof above the cockpit. Their target: the cockpit ceiling egress panel—or, less formally, the pilot's emergency escape hatch.

Each dark figure was frighteningly quick and a specialist in assault preparation. Incessant training to an optimal level had achieved this, as not only their lives but also the hostages' lives depended on it.

'We're fucking exposed, here,' muttered lead trooper "A". Fear wasn't on the agenda, but the knowledge of two snipers being taken out earlier, coupled with the pervasive unknown, certainly didn't help.

'Stick your anchor there, and I'll place mine here,' directed trooper "B". They had trained for countless jet siege scenarios, so hidden behind their brief, precise language was a professional expertise second to none.

'Mag-lock anchor, hold, press, turn,' they said in unison. The vacuum anchors quietly sucked into the cockpit roof fuselage, fusing with it as if they were now one.

These highly specialised, military-grade pieces of technology were developed for just such an operation. The anchors were as vigorous in their securement as they were silent in their operation. Once the ropes were swiftly attached, they awaited the "go" signal.

Communications between the troopers and the SAS situational room, commanded by Nailthem, became a vital flow of intelligence. This constant buzz didn't hinder their thoughts; it sharpened them. In mission-critical situations, knowing was always better. Nailthem watched meticulously, apprehension mingling with raw jealousy, yearning to be part of it.

He received intelligence from cabin pictures, ensuring a systematic assault. Even with the plane's electrochromic windows dimmed to maximum, the 10 SAS snipers on the OARB's fourth-floor were unfazed. Years of training meant their targets were well within lethal capabilities, accounting for windage and bullet drop.

For passenger safety and to counter "blindness", each sniper's telescopic sight was computer-linked, confirming correct sighting with a small green light.

Nailthem could see all fourteen terrorists: two at each of the three exit doors, two in the galley, five covering the two aisles, and Hammerfall in the cockpit, close to the pilots.

The snipers were green; the four SAS teams on the fuselage were green. SAS sniper reconnaissance from the OARB top and drone feedback indicated no further terrorist snipers lurking in foliage shadows. The stage was set; just the countdown was needed.

APC was on standby, close to the OARB but out of sight. Intercepted cabin conversations indicated Hammerfall was ready to shoot the captain if the negotiator couldn't get the plane's Wi-Fi unjammed. Hammerfall wondered if talks had stalled, assuming his request's confirmation was still pending.

His rambling thoughts, fuelled by a reality only he perceived, spiralled deeper into dangerous delusion. He muttered, 'Why hasn't the negotiator confirmed my cryptocurrency? I've released two hostages.'

He looked at his terrorists. They'd achieved much under his tutelage that afternoon! Time to teach again. He'd already made clear another willing hostage would die for his noble cause.

"These helpers are so supportive, I may use two bullets on them instead of one to show my appreciation," he thought with a chilling calm.

He picked up the cockpit radio. As he bellowed a declaration to his group—he was about to speak to the negotiator from the cockpit—Nailthem had already begun his countdown twice, halted at "one" each time. Snipers reported shifting "blind" targets, forcing exacting adjustments.

Nailthem watched intently, anxiety gnawing like a hungry wolf, a cold knot tightening in his gut. Siren fidgeted nervously a metre away, a study in contained agitation, every muscle a coiled spring.

The briefing room air hung thick with unspoken commands, a volatile current flowing between each trooper and grim-faced Nailthem. The four assault teams repeated, 'Ready.' Snipers remained still, eyes burning their objective through telescopic sights. The ambush predators waited motionless: the calm before the storm, the stillness before the strike.

- 23 -
The Storm Breaks

'Go!' Nailthem thundered, his countdown from three proceeding unhindered, a seamless trigger for the meticulously planned assault. In a razor-thin instant, he watched sniper fire carve through the terrorists in the cabin with surgical precision, each impact a sickening tremor as their forms collapsed.

The last thing the door sentinels saw, even as they fell, was a dark, gloved hand hurl a compact black sphere towards them. The stun grenade exploded with a concussive thud, a blinding white flash that seared their retinas.

Inside the cabin, the terrifying onslaught of noise, flashes of light, and groans of death triggered immediate pandemonium. Passengers instinctively cowered, contorting into desperate brace positions as they screamed, disoriented by the nightmare unfolding around them. Amidst the chaos, they desperately clung to the hope that the ordeal would soon be over.

The three port exit door assault teams mirrored each other in timing and execution, swinging into position seconds after the stun grenade's flash-bang and quickly detaching their ropes. In the cabin, two terrorists, though hit, were still alive—one at each end, struggling to rise on shaking legs.

As the lead SAS trooper of each team entered the cabin from their respective exit doors, they saw the two terrorists. Transfixed by the sudden appearance of the SAS troopers, each terrorist froze. Before they could even register the threat, centre-forehead shots silenced them.

Within 20 seconds of the flash-bang, eleven terrorists lay lifeless—five in the cabin, six at the exit doors. Two others scrambled towards the cockpit, where Hammerfall had been attempting to contact the negotiator as the assault exploded around him.

The violent shattering of jet windows could have created lethal shards, but this risk was expertly mitigated by the flawless marksmen, ensuring no danger to those within. Even so, the assault's grim reality was undeniable. The guttural groans of his dying men and the blinding flash of stun grenades jolted Hammerfall's self-preservation instincts into overdrive.

Hammerfall yanked Captain Snowley from his seat and shoved him towards the cockpit door, his Glock 19 menacingly aimed at the captain's head. Hammerfall's gaze flickered down to the carpeted floor. Sang's blood marred the carpeted floor—a brutal reminder of his barbarity, and a grim harbinger of more violence to come. Behind Hammerfall stood Tiroclaw, the first officer.

Tiroclaw's gaze also focused on the crimson stains. His jaw clamped shut, knuckles bone-white as his fists bunched. A violent tremor convulsed through his arms, a raw physical manifestation of the fury ripping at his control. Sang's blood ignited a raging torrent of emotions within him, her memories erupting with visceral, heart-wrenching clarity.

They had intended to marry and leave their past far behind. But then Hammerfall forced them back into it—Tiroclaw was sure it was out of jealousy, suspecting Hammerfall had initially had designs on her too. Yet, her barbaric murder and the ignominious way Hammerfall had dropped her from the plane enraged him, fuelling his desire for retribution.

A storm of fractured thoughts raged within Hammerfall, none holding sway long enough to form a coherent plan. Close-quarters battle erupted in the galley between the two terrorists and the two-man assault team "B". Nailthem ordered the snipers to neutralise the terrorists in the galley. The snipers' bullets, guided by AI-generated ballistic directions, accounted for all intervening barriers, from the rifle to the target.

All the while, Hammerfall looked on, knowing his end was nigh. But he still had his "willing hostage" and bullets.

Sniper bullets perforated the galley. The terrorists' guns fell eerily silent, though faint groans still escaped. Team "B" had already delivered fatal wounds; the snipers simply ensured their demise.

Hammerfall watched this without flinching or showing concern, laughing manically as two SAS troopers now stood mere metres from him. Their posture and presence would have compelled anyone else to lay down their weapon, but Hammerfall was lost in his deranged moment to shine, or so he believed.

He felt secure in his own fortress of delusion. Lost within it, he believed his two snipers, hidden in the foliage 500 metres in front of the cockpit, would have his back. Unbeknownst to him, they were already dead, their screams choked by communication jamming. He remained utterly convinced of his safety and impending, grotesque victory.

With a chillingly detached declaration, Hammerfall announced, 'I am prepared to release a third willing hostage,' his firearm's unyielding muzzle still fixed upon the captain's temple. The grotesque paradox of "willing hostage" perfectly underscored his warped, monstrous perception.

Faintness threatened to claim the captain. Yet, he endured, a silent reservoir of apprehension holding him tethered as he mentally embraced his wife and children, their images a fleeting comfort against the encroaching despair.

The lead SAS trooper of Assault Team "B" cut through the tension with a calm yet unwavering command: "Put the gun down!" The sheer audacity of the voice, seemingly conjured from thin air via an advanced tactical headset, visibly jolted Hammerfall, betraying his carefully constructed control.

A grotesque, manic laugh tore from Hammerfall's throat. 'He wants to be released, you know!' he shrieked as he nodded towards the captain, his mind a fractured echo chamber of delusion, utterly detached from the reality of any negotiation.

Every synapse of the two SAS troopers was acutely tuned to Nailthem's voice, a lifeline of critical intelligence amidst the ordered chaos.

Nailthem's voice, crisp and decisive, cut through the comms: 'You've saturated the rest. Hold them there. Team "A" is primed for immediate insertion.'

Nailthem's next command, a palpable thread of concern woven through it, was clear: 'You need to get that weapon away from the captain's head immediately.'

'Drop the weapon,' the lead "B" team SAS trooper commanded again, his voice a silken snare woven with calculated determination. 'Save yourself, Hammerfall. Put the weapon down. It's over.'

From the cell's inception, Hammerfall had placed an unshakeable, almost blind, trust in his motley assemblage of fanatics. Unbeknownst to him, this principle was about to fracture in the guise of Tiroclaw, the co-pilot. Tiroclaw carried no firearm, but his role granted him access to a range of unconventional, yet potentially lethal, implements.

With a tremor of apprehension, Tiroclaw reached for a standard toolkit nestled just inside the cockpit door, inches behind Hammerfall. The metallic click of a latch echoed faintly as he opened it, exposing its mundane contents. From it, he meticulously selected a hammer. Its appearance took on a dark, almost sinister gleam.

Hammerfall briefly glanced at Tiroclaw. His perspiring forehead couldn't distract any observer from his demented eyes, which flickered wildly between Tiroclaw and the toolkit.

'That's it! Tool up!' Hammerfall announced with a deranged cheerfulness, fully believing his compatriot and supporter of "all things Hammerfall" was now joining the bloody party. Tiroclaw ignored Hammerfall's words entirely, his gaze fixed solely on his objective: to use the hammer to make him fall, his very own "Hammerfall". The solid weight of the hammer in his palm transcended its utilitarian purpose; it felt, instead, like a desperate, brutal answer to an impossible situation.

Tiroclaw's eyes, now sharpened with chilling clarity, flickered once again to the crimson stain blossoming on the carpet. A raw, unyielding resolve calcified his features. "A blunt instrument for a blunt end for a blunt justice,"—a chilling, inevitable thought reverberated through his very being.

With a desperate surge of adrenaline, Tiroclaw tore Hammerfall's right hand back, aborting any reflexive discharge. Ripped from Hammerfall's gruesome grip, Captain Snowley was swiftly herded away to the other passengers, now safe under the protection of the SAS troopers.

Tiroclaw grappled with Hammerfall's powerful grip. Tiroclaw felt the gun slowly but inexorably turn towards him, his strength and focus divided as he struggled to hold his own hammer. He accidentally clenched Hammerfall's Glock trigger. A rogue shot tore into his chest, severely wounding him. Despite the searing pain, Tiroclaw's hammer descended, delivering a shattering, skull-crushing blow to Hammerfall's head. Hammerfall collapsed, fatally injured, to the cabin floor with only moments to live. With a final, defiant act, he pressed a remote-control trigger, and the two middle starboard exit bombs went live.

Inside the cabin, the SAS troopers saw small flashing lights appear on the two devices. Nailthem saw them too, his eyes fixed on the CCTV microdrones' feed. His voice, a whisper of steel, came over the comms: 'Hold your positions. Maintain absolute silence. The bombs are live and they may be sensitive to vibration.'

Outside, two EOD (Explosive Ordnance Disposal) teams waited on the apron, their ladders against the fuselage just below the two open middle port exit doors, waiting for Nailthem's "go".

The blood-slicked hammer, a leaden weight, now hung from Tiroclaw's trembling hand. A torrent of adrenaline surged through him, an almost unbearable rush of triumph at the blunt killing of this vile man.

Hammerfall's defeated form crumpled to the same unforgiving ground that had earlier cradled Sang's lifeless body. He looked up and in disbelief saw Sang's spectral gaze, piercing and unforgiving. A glacial shudder wracked his terror-stricken body as he took his last breath. In his last, desperate act, he mumbled softly, 'Sang.'

High above the unfolding drama, two darkly clad SAS troopers, stark silhouettes against the bruised canvas of the evening sky, executed an ingenious, silent manoeuvre. With breathtaking precision, they deployed a non-smelling, rapidly expanding cryogenic liquid, targeting the emergency cockpit hinges at their critical junction with the aircraft's fuselage.

Exercising acute tactical judgment, Nailthem deliberately delayed the cockpit team's meticulously synchronised entry. A premature breach into the already gravely compromised cockpit area would have created an extremely dangerous situation for the two troopers, and the delay was critical to their success.

Finally, assault team "A" was given the "go" by Nailthem. With a singular, explosive exertion, the second, or rear, SAS trooper wrenched the pilot's emergency escape hatch off. The hatch came free with a silent, terrifying finality before it was thrown to the tarmac below, where it smashed with a bone-jarring crash and a horrific, grinding shriek.

Just below them in the cockpit area, Tiroclaw's dying gaze locked onto Sang's spectral form, her arms extended in an ethereal embrace, her face alight with an angelic, welcoming smile. A wave of incandescent joy, imbued with the reverberating echo of her laughter, surged through his dying body, weaving its radiant, magical tapestry of pure love into his very essence. It was a final, beautiful vision, pulling him towards her.

With a yearning born of profound longing, he willed his dying body to stagger slightly forward. A deathly groan tore from his throat as the bullet in his body relentlessly consumed his life, each beat pushing him closer to the precipice.

Even as his vision blurred and strength fled, he desperately raised his arms, not in aggression, but in a fading plea to embrace the ethereal form of Sang. The blood-soaked hammer, a grim testament to his final struggle, rose with his impassioned, dying gesture. The two darkly-clad SAS troopers watched on knowing his life was almost over yet still unaware of what he intended. Lunging forward towards them with a bloodied sharp hammer could still have lethal intent. He was still a terrorist no matter what.

Fresh from the visceral horror of Hammerfall's brutal demise, the SAS troopers possessed neither the luxury nor the time to deliberate Tiroclaw's ambiguous intent. His abrupt, weaponised movement triggered an instantaneous, imperative response, demanding his immediate neutralisation. There was no room for hesitation; only the cold, hard logic of their mission objective.

Milliseconds from opening fire, the decisive command from Nailthem's voice, crackling with urgency over the radio, pierced the tension: 'Stand back! Leave him!' This pre-arranged, critical directive resonated with immediate, understanding within Assault Team "B" as they stepped back.

Just then, the lead SAS trooper from Assault Team "A" inverted through the emergency cockpit opening, unleashing a single, lethal shot. The bullet cleaved through the fragile apex of Tiroclaw's neck, a grim, brutal punctuation mark on the chaotic scene.

As Tiroclaw's body slumped onto Hammerfall's corpse, the bloodied hammer slipped from his dying grip, settling into Hammerfall's own—the ultimate, grotesque humiliation. As a warrior who had always declared it the most ignominious fate to be killed from behind, this was a final, bitter irony. The killer falling on his back only deepened the profound desecration of his very creed.

The shot itself was a testament to the SAS's clinical, unwavering professional precision. It tore through Tiroclaw, burying itself deep within the plush fabric of a first-class seat beyond, leaving a sickening bloom of crimson as its final signature.

Siren turned to Nailthem, her face flushed with urgency. 'Get the passengers out now, Nailthem! They've been through enough.'

Nailthem didn't flinch, his gaze steady on the plane. 'Negative, Commander. My teams are holding position.'

'Holding position? The terrorists are down!' she argued

'Maybe so, but we have a small matter of two middle starboard exit doors armed and ready to detonate,' Nailthem explained.

'Armed! Get them off now! What are you waiting for?' she bellowed at Nailthem, trying desperately not to grab his rugged shoulders to emphasise her point.

'They are probably triggered to explode through vibration,' he explained calmly, seeing Siren was beginning to lose it.

'I have to get them to safety,' she insisted, gesturing toward the aircraft on the screen. Then she realised what Nailthem said and added, 'Oh yeah, then why didn't the gunshots and stun grenades set them off then?'

'Because the devices weren't live, Commander,' he calmly explained. 'They were primed, but designed to go live on activation. That happened when Hammerfall saw the game was up when in the cockpit. The terrorists were the fail safe. Now that they're gone, the devices are hot.'

Siren pushed back, her voice rising in a display of tactical ignorance. 'But they're just be walking! Not jumping up and down.'

'Respectfully, that is a fool's errand. The fuses are what's keeping them "safe." Any source of vibration could trigger a high-order explosive event,' Nailthem said, a hard edge now in his voice.

'Where's the vibration from if they move slowly and quietly,' she asked.

'From hundreds of people, that's where. Look, even with its main engines off, a large aircraft like the Boeing 787-9 has several systems that can cause vibration. The Auxiliary Power Unit (APU), a small jet engine in the tail, provides power and compressed air, generating significant vibration if it's running. The plane's hydraulic systems, which control flight surfaces and landing gear, contain pumps and lines that can create a low-level but constant hum. Finally, the Environmental Control System (ECS), responsible for air conditioning, uses powerful fans and compressors that are a considerable source of internal vibration throughout the fuselage.'

Siren's expression faltered. 'I don't care what your protocols are! I have terrified civilians on that plane!' she retorted, taking a step toward him and into his personal space. 'Just turn them off,' she continued.

'No, these units could not be turned off immediately without serious consequences. They're essential for an aircraft's operations, even when it's stationary,' said Nailthem. He stared at Siren with deep conviction he was right. He continued, 'I'm going to make sure they get off that plane alive. If we introduce movement, you'll be giving the terrorists the last laugh. We neutralise the threat first, then

192

we evacuate. It's the only way.' Nailthem's final words left no room for debate. A heavy silence fell between them as Siren finally comprehended the grim logic of his position.

As one episode of murder ended another was potentially at hand, but this time mass murder of a plane load of terrified passengers. The SAS assault teams had already notified Nailthem the middle starboard exit doors were armed. With the cabin silent and secure, the SAS assault teams stood and watched, as did the passengers-quiet, measured, and temperate, hoping the bombs wouldn't explode. The next few minutes were critical.

The two EOD (Explosive Ordnance Disposal) teams had been waiting on the apron, directly underneath the two middle port exit doors, their ladders placed against the fuselage. With Nailthem's whispered command to go, the teams carefully scaled their ladders. Their movements were meticulous and deliberate, the soles of their boots making a soft scrape against the Boeing 787-9's fuselage, which was still very warm from the hot summer sun.

A wave of hot, humid air from the evening met them on entry, clinging to their tactical gear and making a sheen of sweat on their skin. The passengers looked at them with wide, silent eyes, their terror a palpable, heavy presence in the air. The terrorists were dead, but the true threat remained.

Inside the cabin, a ticking silence of fear was a tangible, heavy presence. The silence was unnatural—a vacuum that seemed to amplify every sound. The scrape of a boot, a person fainting, the thud of a dropped object—each noise was a potential death sentence.

EOD Team A moved to the first of the armed middle starboard exit doors, while EOD Team B moved to the second. Both teams' leaders immediately locked eyes on the devices. They weren't just crude; they were malignant, a chaotic tangle of wires, putty, and different-coloured explosives packed together. The bombs themselves were a testament to the hatred of the person who built them.

'Visual confirmation,' EOD Team A's leader stated over the comms, his voice a low, strained whisper. 'It looks like a simple Improvised Explosive Device (IED) with a time-delay fuse and a pressure plate attached to the arming wire.' The crude wiring, a chaotic mess that didn't follow any protocol, told him a simple action, like cutting a wire, could have an unintended consequence.

A second member of EOD Team A waited in support, carefully double-checking every movement, ensuring nothing was dropped or bumped. EOD Team B followed their own methodical procedure, communicating their observations and plan over the comms. The cabin was utterly silent, but for the terror on the passengers' faces. That shared tension made every movement—even the bomb disposal experts' careful hand movements—seem painfully laborious.

They each began the delicate render-safe procedure. Every movement was calibrated. Team A's leader paused, listening intently. He carefully pulled out a pair of specialised wire cutters. 'I'm going for the firing train manually,' he announced, his voice tight. As his gloved fingers steadied the small, blue wire, he noticed a tiny detail: the wire was attached to a secondary, smaller block of putty.

He realised the terrorists had packed multiple types of explosives in the same casing, making it far more volatile than a simple IED. A single bead of sweat dripped from his brow, landing with a sickening, magnified plop on the casing. His hands, despite the heat and mounting pressure, were steady. But the wire was nearly invisible.

Suddenly, a nearby passenger in an outside row seat behind Team B, overwhelmed by the oppressive heat and fear, fainted. Their body hit the floor with a heavy thud, and the vibration ran through the fuselage. Immediately, the bombs on both doors came to life. A stomach-churning, soft, whirring siren began to sound from each device, a chilling, mechanical cry that cut through the unnatural silence. The passengers gasped, a collective intake of breath.

Team B's leader felt a cold dread seize his gut. His mind screamed, "It's going! It's going!" but his lips remained sealed. He was better than this. He had trained his entire life to be controlled, logical, and stoic under pressure, to master these very distractions. He forced his thoughts to see this as just an inconvenience on the road to successful deactivation, and his words reflected that forced calm.

'That's an expected reaction from the device,' he reported over the comms, his tone flat. The whirring stopped as suddenly as it had started. The silence that followed was even more deafening than the siren. He lowered his cutters, his hands trembling almost imperceptibly with the last aftershock of his fear.

Nailthem's voice, articulated and firm, cut through the tension. 'Teams, listen up,' he announced over the comms. 'You know that was a psychological ploy. You're the best-trained operatives for a reason. Trust your protocol, not your instincts. Focus on the procedure. Let's get this done.'

As he spoke, Siren grabbed his arm, her knuckles white. Her grip was a frantic drumbeat against his sleeve. She looked at him, her eyes wide with terror, and whispered, 'What if it's not a warning? What if it's counting down?'

Nailthem turned his head slightly, his gaze unwavering. 'Their training is the only thing that matters,' he replied, his voice a cold whisper of steel. 'The only countdown that concerns me is getting them off this plane. Safely, securely, and without any more worry.'

'False alarm,' Team A leader announced with a strained whisper, raw with a mix of relief and renewed fear. 'It's a vibration sensor.' He held up a finger, his mind racing. 'The bomb is designed to react to movement. It's a piezoelectric sensor, wired to a threshold circuit. It measures the kinetic energy from a vibration.

The thud of that body hitting the deck just exceeded the circuit's calibrated tolerance. That whirring you heard wasn't a detonation sequence; it was an audible alarm from a simple piezo buzzer. 'It's the bomb's way of telling us we've got one shot at this, and we're already on a hair trigger.'

He looked at his colleague, his eyes grim. 'It's a psychological ploy, a warning shot. He wants us to sweat, to make a mistake. We move with the weight of this whole plane on our shoulders now. From here on, every single sound, every vibration... we have to assume it's the last one.'

Meanwhile, EOD Team B had a different package and a far more chilling problem. The leader's gaze was fixed on his bomb when his eyes caught a tiny, almost imperceptible detail. A thin, hair-like wire, tucked behind the frame, was attached to a secondary circuit. He knew what it was instantly, and his blood ran cold. The vibration sensor had been the first trick, but he had just found a secondary remote trigger. The message was clear: disarming one bomb could still trigger the other.

'Team A! Stop! There's a secondary tripwire! It's a booby trap!' the leader of EOD Team B whispered over the comms, his strained voice cutting through the silence. The leader of EOD Team A, with his cutters a millimetre from the wire, froze. The glint of steel on blue was a silent portrait of a near-miss. He could feel his heart pounding in his chest, a frantic drumbeat. EOD Team B's leader's voice came through again, a cold shock of information that cut through the oppressive heat. 'It's a remote trigger, too. The whole fucking plane is hot.'

They were trained for this. But the heat mixed with the palpable urgency to save the passengers' lives, against their desperate need to get them off the plane, was intense. It ramped up the already heavy psychological weight of expected success. It pressed down on them like heavy weights on their shoulders. A sweaty friction built between the familiar procedure of deactivation and the terrifying possibility of a rogue detonation.

Nailthem noticed a passenger in the back fiddling in his pockets while looking furtively around the cabin. He released a micro-drone from a panel in the wall. The tiny device buzzed over the suspect, relaying every move. Facial recognition software, cross-referenced with network linker information from the NSA, flagged the man as having possible terrorist links; he was a sleeper. The SAS team leaders, viewing the feed on their helmets, could track the suspect's movements without his knowledge. Nailthem commanded an SAS trooper, who had the best angle of shot given the passenger congestion, to take him out if necessary.

Suddenly, the man stood up, pulling a Glock 19 from his pocket and aiming for the team leaders. But before he could even raise his arm to fire, he was taken out by a single, silenced shot. The SAS trooper's subsonic bullet from an integrally suppressed weapon made a perfect centre forehead shot; just a soft "thump" was heard. The dead sleeper fell silently, his collapse cushioned by those around him. The passengers wanted to scream in fright, but the quiet kill and the knowledge that they had to remain silent tempered their reactions. The incident was over as quickly as it had begun.

The brief interruption didn't affect the EOD team leaders. They continued to work in tandem to carefully perform their render-safe procedures. EOD Team A, abandoning the cutters, used a specialised disruptor to break the firing train of the first IED, while EOD Team B, after discovering the remote trigger, used a specialised jamming device to block the signal before disarming the booby trap by hand.

With both devices successfully rendered inert and no longer a threat, the teams proceeded with the painstaking process of deactivating them completely. The explosives were carefully removed, disassembled, and secured in their specialised containers. It was only then that a calm, authoritative voice from EOD Team A confirmed over the comms, 'Middle starboard doors are clear. Deactivation complete.'

From the briefing room, Nailthem surveyed the scene—another flawlessly executed operation. All terrorists were dead. No SAS or passenger was wounded or killed. The immediate chaos was neutralised, replaced by a methodical, controlled evacuation. Passengers, a stream of relieved yet shaken humanity, began their descent via the swiftly deployed emergency chutes.

Nailthem confirmed the operation was complete to his superiors and congratulated his squadron for a job well done. Other SAS moved swiftly with APC airport police in ground support trucks towards the plane. The assault teams manned all four port exit doors, guiding the passengers out to slide down the chutes. As each passenger emerged from the chute, unsteady but profoundly relieved, they were immediately assisted to their feet by APC operatives.

Simultaneously, a discreet network of these same operatives, equipped with advanced handheld facial recognition cameras, began the critical task of identification. The cameras were seamlessly linked to a central database of passport photographs, ensuring no threat could slip away.

This meticulous precaution—a silent tripwire of security—was woven into the evacuation protocol to apprehend any sleeper terrorist attempting to escape amidst the controlled exodus. If identities were confirmed, passengers were then directed to waiting airport buses and transported to the OARB. There, they received food, drinks, and rest before a comprehensive debriefing by APC police and MI5 staff.

With the successful operation concluded, the 20 SAS troopers withdrew with the same surgical precision with which they had arrived. Two "Blue Thunder" helicopters descended onto the HLS near the OARB, the helicopter's downwash kicking up a furious storm of dust and wind. The elite unit boarded with silent, practised efficiency, becoming a faceless shadow in the gloom. The choppers clawed their way back into the sky, the thunder of their blades swallowing the sounds of the rescue operation below as they vanished into the evening twilight.

25

The Debriefing

The buses, like ambulances without sirens, swiftly mobilised and ferried shaken passengers towards the OARB. Inside, a brittle silence had settled—a chaotic calm that felt less like peace and more like a held breath before a storm. It was underscored by the low hum of the engine, a mechanical heartbeat, and the faint, antiseptic scent of recycled air. The five-minute journey was a fragile return to order, each metre a thread pulling them back from the jagged cliff of their recent ordeal into the blunt, unyielding edges of reality.

Adams took the opportunity to ring Ann and tell her he was well, if a bit unnerved and weary. Being ever thoughtful, she accepted a synopsis of what had happened but placed greater emphasis on his own welfare. He could have talked more, but the journey to the OARB was short, and a debriefing awaited.

The debriefings were overseen by the incisive intelligence officer, Rupert Barrington, alongside 40 highly trained MI5 colleagues assisted by some juniors. Their collective goal was to meticulously gather a complete, unblemished picture of the harrowing events that had unfolded inside the aircraft, tracing every critical moment both before and after the terrorists had seized their brutal control.

Following the arrival of the buses and before the commencement of the debriefing process, passengers, including Adams, were split into groups, their former seating arrangements utterly disregarded.

'Professor Adams, if you'll come this way,' said a man in a crisp suit, his features so unremarkable they seemed designed to blend into any crowd. "The antithesis of such a blend was how the SAS troopers appeared earlier," Adams thought.

'Just me,' he replied, his voice tinged with a mix of surprise and a faint thread of annoyance as he pointed a finger directly at himself. It wasn't an acknowledgement so much as a profound, unspoken question hanging in the air: why him alone? Why was he being singled out from the exhausted, bewildered throng?

'If you please,' said his correspondent, a faint urgency in his tone. 'Just follow me into the OARB. We just need to debrief you on what happened and if you're alright.'

Adams's brow furrowed, a faint line of confusion deepening as he genuinely wondered why he wasn't being herded along with the vast, disoriented stream of other passengers. The distinction felt oddly unsettling. The only natural, and somewhat unsettling, answer that came quickly to his mind—a thought he rarely entertained but could not ignore now—was simply his identity, his renown, suddenly a stark, visible badge.

'My luggage, don't forget my luggage!' blurted Adams. He wasn't sure why this suddenly felt so crucial, especially given that such matters would likely be handled. He imagined his bags would reappear at the end of this unexpected detour, perhaps even for a thorough search in his presence.

'This way, Professor, just a few more metres and we'll be there,' the man said, his tone a blend of politeness and underlying authority that betrayed him as an MI5 Intelligence Officer. Indeed, they rounded a corner and came to a door marked "IR1," signifying "Interview Room 1."

His guide opened the door and ushered Adams inside, the heavy click of the latch echoing in the sudden quiet.

The room was a blank canvas, deliberately stripped of personality, with a desk at its centre like an interrogation altar. Two chairs sat on either side, placed with a clinical precision that spoke of sterile purpose. Cameras, like unseen, unblinking eyes, were strategically positioned in each top corner. The bright, unforgiving overhead light washed the space in a harsh glare, ensuring every flicker of an eyelash, every tightening of a jaw, would be captured in a way that felt less like an interview and more like an insect pinned for examination.

Given this, Adams imagined that somewhere in that building was probably a large room where all this was being recorded and analysed, maybe by AI.

Just as Adams expected to be asked to sit down, another bland suited figure entered the room.

'Oh yes, Professor Adams. The Harvard man. You've been a busy boy, haven't you?' patronised the unknown room entrant.

His colleague recoiled from the rude effrontery. Eyes widened wildly, eyebrows shot up, and his lower jaw clunked open, as if snapped down by an invisible weight.

'I'm sorry for my colleague's remark, Professor,' Rupert Barrington said, introducing himself with an apologetic tone. 'He is new to the department and a junior. Due to a shortage of experienced personnel for this situation, we've had to augment our team with them.'

Barrington, having successfully delivered his apology, settled on the far side of the desk with his colleague. He then gestured subtly, inviting Adams to sit as well.

'This is my colleague, Tim Benfer. We will be conducting an interview with you. I cannot say how long it will take, but our questions will be direct. I ask you to answer them the same way,' instructed Barrington, as if he'd repeated the words a thousand times before.

'May we do the interview?' interjected Benfer, impatient at Adams's silence.

'Of course!' Adams replied obligingly. He felt drained and a touch annoyed by the lack of any refreshments. He surmised the absence of food and drink was likely due to security concerns within the room; the notion that even a sandwich could be considered a "lethal weapon" seemed utterly bizarre to him.

With that acknowledgment, the two officers snapped open files on the desk marked "Secret," devouring the summaries before clapping them shut. Having absorbed the key information, they fixed their gaze on Adams in synchronised fashion, like figures jerked by a single puppeteer.

Beyond the plane's events, the officers were also interested in NSA reports detailing intelligence gathering and a lethal car chase. Turning back to Adams, Barrington incisively asked, 'You are aware of our concerns relating to your life, Professor Adams?'

'Well, there was a car chase, and two terrorists died. The NSA has provided protection for my daughter and me since,' Adams said, his voice low. 'And I suppose your security services will take over now?' he then asked.

'Not will, have, Professor Adams. Although there is no intelligence to suggest the hijacking was related to you, it is still odd that not one but two terror-related incidents occur so close together. One alone would be enough for anyone, surely?' Barrington emphasised.

'They did know me. Hammerfall grabbed me, but I fought back. My head still hurts a bit as I recall this. May I—' Adams was interrupted by Officer Benfer. 'We never mentioned the group leader's name. How did you know this? You could be part of them?' Benfer demanded accusatorily.

'Are you for real?' Adams fumed, his patience snapping like a brittle twig. 'You drag me into this sanitised room with walls painted in magnolia, which I loathe, you insult me, deny me refreshments, and now imply – I say imply – that it's suspect I know the leader's name. You're an utter, pitiable excuse for a human being! You're a stain on MI5!' His words were a verbal broadside, a cannonade of pure rage that struck Benfer with the force of a physical blow.

Benfer jolted back in his chair from Adams's verbal broadside. He had catapulted Adams's tolerance for rudeness past its breaking point.

'Get out!' shouted Barrington to Benfer. 'I will complete this interview. Go across to the briefing room and wait there,' he added. Benfer rose from his seat, his face red with contriteness and his head bowed in apologetic submission. He mumbled an apology to both of them and left the room "IR1" in abject humiliation, a far cry from his bravado and rudeness when he first entered.

'Right, let's crack on,' Barrington said softly. Feeling sorry for his colleague's behaviour and the possibility of Adams lodging a formal complaint, he spoke freely. 'Professor, can you tell me what you're up to with this visit? It's intriguing, as some of the notes in your file, which I read before this interview, have been redacted. Most unusual,' Barrington quizzed, aware he was treading on thin ice with such a question.

'No, I cannot comment on that, and you shouldn't be asking me,' Adams replied, his voice firm.

Before Barrington could reply, two loud knocks at the room door were followed by its abrupt opening.

The door creaked open, revealing a rather strange-looking man—a flustered, clearly overworked police officer—wheeling in Adams's luggage. Adams leapt up instantly, surging towards his "secrets bag" and embracing it like a long-lost friend after years apart.

'Steady on there, fella!' remarked the attendant with surprise and consternation at the action. It only got worse when Adams said, 'I've missed you.'

'Adams!' Barrington snapped, 'Sit back down!'

He then looked at the officer and said, 'Place the luggage over there, please, and leave—now!' Barrington's voice was tight with frustration. The officer pushed the remaining luggage against the corner to the right of the door and departed without another word.

'We'll be watching you, Professor Adams. Whatever it is you're doing, it clearly has garnered the attention of the upper echelons of our respective security services. I have all the details I need. Is there anything else you'd like to add that may be of interest to us?' he asked softly, his mind already preoccupied with how he would address Benfer, who awaited a severe reprimand.

Adams suddenly thought about his prescient dream that foretold his experiences during the hijacking. He started to report them, but Barrington just looked vacant, as if his brain had already shut down from the interview. With Barrington's vacant expression in mind, Adams collected his luggage and vacated room "IR1".

In the wake of the exhaustive passenger interviews, a dedicated cadre of mental health professionals, trauma specialists, and victim support teams swiftly initiated comprehensive debriefing sessions for all.

Crucially, these critical interventions were not merely procedural; they were meticulously crafted to unearth, acknowledge, and begin the arduous process of healing the deep emotional wounds carved by the recent ordeal.

Remarkably, while most passengers claimed a resilient well-being, those who directly witnessed the brutal murders of Sang and the Air Marshal unquestionably needed—and immediately received—profound, unwavering therapeutic support. Their trauma was a gaping wound, demanding immediate, dedicated attention.

For Professor Michael Adams, whose concise interview had mercifully concluded, the seismic shift in his treatment was almost viscerally palpable; he was, unequivocally, now a VIP. This sudden, staggering status became blatantly clear the instant his escort extended a hand and introduced himself, a gesture laden with newfound importance.

The Metropolitan Police officer from Aviation Policing Command, Officer Grant, spoke with professional detachment. Adams, despite his lingering tension, simply noted the officer's efficient, unhurried demeanour, clearly there to hasten his exit from the recent chaos.

Grant, a demonstrable master of unblemished efficiency, swiftly ushered Adams into a waiting airport patrol car. Their passage through security proved unfussed, remarkably fluid, culminating in an almost surreal alfresco passport check beneath the cavernous expanse of the terminal roof. The ordinary suddenly felt extraordinary.

Then, an astonishing surprise, a true balm to his frayed nerves, materialised: as his freshly stamped passport was returned, so too came the unexpected offer of overnight airport accommodation. It was a kindness he hadn't dared to dream of. Abruptly, the notion of immediately embarking on another arduous journey felt utterly overwhelming, a task far exceeding his depleted capacity. Exhausted by the harrowing ordeal, he snatched the gracious offer without hesitation.

The following morning, equilibrium thoroughly restored by a restful night and fortifying breakfast, Adams's phone buzzed. A text confirmed his pre-booked private hire taxi awaited him in the nearby short-stay car park, a mere stone's throw from the hotel. The promise of an onward journey beckoned.

A vigilant hotel porter, subtly attuned to the unspoken weight of Adams's burden, discreetly assisted him with his luggage. Yet, one particular bag, his ominously named "secrets bag", remained steadfastly clutched in his own grasp.

Reaching the sleek vehicle, the porter expertly stowed Adams's luggage in the boot. He held open the nearside back door as Adams settled inside, offering a final, respectful farewell through the open window, wishing Professor Adams a safe onward journey.

The taxi pulled smoothly away. Adams released a profound breath of pure relaxation, a genuine smile touching his lips. "Oxford here I come," he thought. Before him, in his mind's eye, materialised not just the university's ancient spires, but the long-anticipated renewal of his deep friendship with Ann and Peter Magma.

26

The Helix Of Deception

The unrelenting roar of Heathrow Airport, a faint, phantom echo of its ceaseless activity, still reverberated deep in Adams's ears as his taxi pulled away, now firmly bound for the ancient spires and scholarly quiet of Oxford.

With each mile of the M40's grey ribbon unfurling towards Oxford, his anticipation surged, a vibrant, insistent current. He yearned not only for his planned meeting with Peter, his steadfast intellectual anchor, but also for a heartfelt reunion with the lovely Ann. Her warmth would be a tangible, restorative balm after the recent, chilling ordeal.

Despite their surface differences, Michael and Peter also shared a profound intellectual common ground, a bond forged through years of shared academic pursuit. This connection was so strong that formal titles were entirely eschewed; they always addressed each other by their first names—never "Professor" this or that, and certainly never by their surnames.

Beyond their shared age, their lives diverged significantly. Unlike Michael's humble working-class beginnings, Peter grew up in London amidst social, financial, and academic privilege. Yet, despite these contrasts, an immediate, undeniable rapport sprang between them the moment they first met at Oxford, as if they were long-acquainted souls.

It was this same intuitive connection, this almost preternatural awareness, that now made Adams acutely aware of the taxi driver's gaze. The driver's eyes lingered in the rearview mirror far longer than politeness required, and Adams felt his discomfort grow with each unsettling glance, shuffling instinctively in his seat. It wasn't a fleeting look but a chilling entanglement, a silent, unyielding probe for information. When Adams shifted out of view, the driver subtly adjusted the mirror, a small movement that only deepened his unease. This growing suspicion urged him to check behind them, a prickle of intuition that something unseen was tailing their every move.

Yet, the relentless, ever-shifting flow of motorway traffic offered no clear answers, forcing him to dismiss the unsettling thought. The notion that he was merely being paranoid was almost as disquieting as the suspicion itself.

Eventually, the driver broke the prolonged silence, beginning with seemingly innocuous questions about the weather before subtly steering the conversation towards Adams's profession and his destination in Oxford.

He tried to feign a casual interest in genetics, dropping a few vague terms, but when Adams, ever the professor, gently probed for more detail, the man's facade crumbled.

His eyes immediately darted back to the rearview mirror, his earlier bravado replaced by an almost imperceptible tightening around his jaw, and he offered nothing more than the hypnotic, unnerving stare.

Michael's taxi, a bone-rattling beast at the best of times, groaned as the journey took its toll on the mechanics. After exiting the M40, he endured choking traffic and an endless gauntlet of infuriating red lights. The situation was made worse by aggressive drivers who grew more hostile when the taxi driver pointed out their errors. The cab finally arrived at the formidable front gates of Professor Peter and Doctor Ann Magma's mansion, a welcome sanctuary from the journey and urban bedlam.

The mansion was impressive, its inherent beauty perhaps amplified by the rich history of those who had lived within its walls. A magnificent six-room Georgian structure, it nestled within ten acres of tranquil woods and manicured lawns. It exuded a profound sense of peace and happiness— a much-needed sanctuary from the demanding academic lives Peter and Ann led at the university.

The taxi driver, already weary from the fifty-mile drive from Heathrow, steered his cab through the wide steel gates and up the driveway towards the imposing oak front doors. There, Ann, Peter's wife, stood atop the six broad, pristine Portland stone steps, waving to Michael as he approached.

As she watched the taxi ascend the short 15-metre incline towards the front doors, she noticed a black car momentarily stop outside the open front gates before abruptly pulling away. 'How mysterious,' she mused, 'perhaps just inquisitive.'

Ann possessed a captivating charm alongside a keen, insightful understanding of social inequality and mobility. Though petite, her work stood tall, building upon the significant contributions of leading scholars in her field.

Like Peter, Ann was a proud Oxford graduate. Their shared passion for learning and their deep connection made their eventual marriage feel inevitable. She had a natural enthusiasm for discussion, lecturing, and sharing knowledge.

She was not averse to the formal lecture circuit, nor to more informal fringe meetings. At these, her voice would articulate the many anomalies in history, where socioeconomic disparities stood in stark, jarring contrast to society's greater democratic and egalitarian values.

Ann believed that shifts in class, wealth, and ownership were never unrelated occurrences, but the result of deep-seated, deliberate forces. She also understood that historical patterns inevitably repeated when the root causes and intentions behind societal changes were not fully grasped. It was perhaps their distinct academic disciplines that ignited such a delightful intellectual dimension within their marriage.

Their differing academic disciplines perhaps also forged a seamless bridge from intense work discussions to enjoyable social conversation at home. With the relentless demands of their jobs, evenings in their idyllic mansion became a cherished wellspring of relaxation and rejuvenation.

Right now, the taxi driver had inexplicably pulled up several yards from the usual drop-off point, near the steps where Ann waited patiently.

He had pulled up slightly behind and adjacent to their recently acquired Jaguar-XF. Realising his error, he put the taxi in gear and drove forward, unaware that the handbrake was still engaged.

The taxi shuddered to a chaotic, rhythmic tempo, jigging backwards and forwards as if reluctant to move. The driver, in a sudden realisation, quickly released the handbrake, and the taxi shot forwards with surprising speed.

No sooner had it moved a metre forward than it abruptly stopped with greater brutality than it started. Unfortunately, neither the taxi driver nor Adams anticipated this sudden halt. Both continued forward, the loud thud of their bodies hitting the taxi's interior.

'Sorry about that boss, still learning to drive,' said the abashed taxi driver.

Quickly, the driver's thoughts turned to his fare charges, and he eagerly eyed his taximeter. He wished he had more passengers like this quiet, thoughtful, and unassuming man, who seemed most unlikely to do a "runner" from his taxi, unlike some others who had bolted for the exit like Olympic sprinters.

'That's £235 please,' the taxi driver said ecstatically, as if he had just won the lottery.

'Sounds expensive, bud,' Adams remarked, fumbling for his Harvard corporate credit card in his Gucci wallet.

No matter how hard Adams pulled, the card seemed stubbornly stuck. It was brand new, and he remembered forcing it in when his colleague, HP, at Harvard, had given it to him.

Adams, surmising the driver's fingers were more powerful from a lifetime of gripping the wheel, decided to let him handle the extraction. Besides, the taxi driver would eventually hold the card anyway, so why not just let him do the extraction as well?

'Hey, can you take my wallet and extract the crimson Harvard card, the third one down on the inside left?' Adams asked, almost pleadingly.

The taxi driver took Adams's wallet and extracted the card with surprising ease. He then placed the wallet on his lap, and, holding a portable card reader in his left hand, slotted in the professor's credit card. With the device now ready to debit £235 from Adams's account, he handed it to his esteemed passenger for the PIN entry, a vital step in securing his earnings for the next few days.

'Of course, while it's authorising your card, sir, can I just say you have been one of my very best passengers ever,' the taxi driver commented. The card machine then gleefully displayed "payment accepted," and the amount processed.

The taxi driver conveyed this approving comment to every passenger at journey's end, always hoping for a return fare at a later date. He replaced the credit card in the wallet and handed it back to Adams with a joyful smile, reflecting that all the driving stress encountered along major and minor roads, amplified by the long distance from Heathrow to Oxford, had been worth it after all.

He clumsily pulled up several business cards from the stack he had printed very cheaply at a local printing shop the day before. As he lifted them up, his tenuous hold on them became no more. His grip gave way, and they flew in all directions across the driver's cabin.

By luck, he managed to hold onto a single card. He turned to offer it to the professor, but Adams was already preoccupied with the more pressing matter of getting out of the taxi and greeting Peter's wife, Ann.

The taxi driver scrambled out of his cab and hurried around to present his business card to Adams, hoping this small gesture would eventually lead to a lucrative return fare.

'Thank you, sir, enjoy your stay and see you soon!' the taxi driver said with an unusual emphasis on the "see you soon".

As he spoke, he not only walked away but also turned his head, resulting in a strange, diminishing Doppler effect to his voice.

'Luggage?' Adams shouted as he noted the driver got back into his taxi, yet failed to unload his important luggage.

'Oh yes, sorry boss,' quickly retorted the taxi driver.

Attempting to frantically scramble back out of the taxi, he misjudged the raised floor edge, stumbled forward, and tumbled headlong from the cab.

He performed an amateur somersault, landing with a jarring thud flat on his back, arms and legs sprawling wide like a discarded puppet. Pebbles and dust erupted around him as he collided with the ground.

He lay stunned for a few seconds. Michael and Ann shouted across to ask if he was all right. To compound his embarrassment, he stood too quickly, which only served to exacerbate the dizziness caused by his head hitting the ground.

He lost his balance again, stumbling one stride forward before lurching several wayward steps back. Fortunately, this awkward dance ended with him falling into a small, smelly pond that had clearly not seen human contact in years.

'Where did you get him from, a circus?' Ann asked very politely but with an undertone of sarcasm.

As the driver stood, soaked from his fall, stagnant water, a cold embrace, streamed from his sodden clothes in miniature cascades. It gushed down his front, as if his garments were weeping tears of abhorrence from the stench and grime that clung to him like a second skin.

Annoyed, he inexplicably brushed away the remaining gravel from his clothes, yet entirely disregarded his saturated state. Moreover, his over-expensive and underused hairspray had failed, leaving his long dark hair wild and unmanageable.

His hair, a wild, spiky testament to his recent mishap, now defied all reason. He awkwardly sloshed out of the pond, and with legs spread wide, hobbled to the back of his taxi. With each squelching, flapping step, his trousers, now stretched beyond recognition, had transformed into a clown's ludicrous pantaloons.

His hair, once again defying gravity, now fell forwards into a V-shaped formation over his forehead, down between his eyes and nose, and onwards below his chin, creating what could only be described as the world's first "scalp beard".

Opening the boot of his taxi, he pulled out three cases of variable weight and size, one by one, with meticulous care.

Michael and Ann watched this unfolding, clownesque episode—a bizarre mix of somersaults, unexpected speed, surprising dexterity, and now meticulous case extraction—with a shared, quiet disbelief.

His cautious approach to extracting the luggage made it seem as if each case were a wild animal, ready to spring. With all three cases safely out of the boot, he carried them to the professor, placing each with great precision.

As a man of scientific precision, such alignment did not go unnoticed by Michael, who was suitably impressed. Appreciating the driver's comedic performance, he compensated him with a small tip for his trouble.

Through all this, Ann managed to restrain herself to a quiet laugh as the bizarre spectacle concluded peacefully.

With the luggage safely placed next to Michael, the wet and embarrassed taxi driver said goodbye and withdrew to his normal vehicular life and the subsequent return journey to Heathrow, during which drying his clothes with the car's heaters would be the priority.

'Thank you!' shouted Michael as he watched the taxi pull away and out through the still open main gates. Within seconds of the taxi disappearing onto the main road, the gates creaked slowly shut, as if marking the end of the "wet taxi man from Heathrow" episode.

As the final creak from the gates evaporated into the ether, Michael turned his attention to Ann and the prospect of a relaxing conversation with her. Later, an energetic academic discussion about DNA was planned with her husband, Professor Peter Magma, when he returned home from university duties.

'Oh my God, are you all right?' Ann said with deep compassion. 'I saw it on the news. I was praying you'd be all right. Oh, come here, I love you deeply. It's so lovely to see you, Michael, so lovely!' Ann exclaimed, her voice a melodic mix of concern and happiness.

She embraced him, her hourglass figure fitting perfectly against his avuncular frame. Her warm, inviting arms tightened, delivering a powerful surge of warmth and attraction, a sensation he hadn't felt since the devastating loss of his wife, Victoria, five years earlier.

Her embrace sent a wave of loving warmth through him, unlocking long-dormant memories of Victoria's daily affection. Though those memories had faded, time paused as he absorbed the feeling's full intensity once more.

With a reluctant sigh, Ann broke the embrace, her gaze softening as she looked up at Michael. Her voice, a low, mellifluous murmur, then floated a gentle question: 'How are you?' Her eyes, however, spoke volumes more, holding a love that promised to endure eternally.

'I am great, never better, Ann!' replied Michael, as he slowly loosened his embrace. He took a step back to admire, yet again, the idyllic, picturesque Georgian mansion. It was beautiful. Indeed, it seemed to accentuate her beauty as well.

'Every time I visit, Ann, I just have to take a moment to drink in the aesthetic beauty of your mansion,' Michael said with such appreciation, he would hug it if he could.

Ann's beauty and grace were a quiet counterpoint to the mansion's grandeur. Though in her fifties, she possessed the vibrant energy of a woman two decades younger, a life force that seemed to radiate from within. Her dark hair, softened with elegant streaks of grey, was styled in loose, gentle waves that framed a face full of warmth and insight.

But it was her eyes, a striking, expressive hazel, that held the true depth of her character. When she smiled, they crinkled at the corners, a gesture of genuine joy that made her entire face light up. Her laughter, a melodic and low murmur, was as captivating as her hourglass figure, and together, they created a presence that was both intellectually formidable and profoundly loving.

'What is it that you like in particular, Michael?' she asked inquisitively, even though for her, it was everything. She immediately wondered if he might playfully respond with "apart from you," but quickly dismissed such a silly thought.

Michael looked on at Ann, and a student memory about her strong preference for taller men flashed across his mind. Most of her university boyfriends having stood over six feet tall, nearly two metres. She couldn't pinpoint why this preference existed; it just did.

Peter was far shorter, as was he, so Peter's marriage to Ann was a surprise given her predilection. "But then again, love crosses all boundaries," he thought, dismissing the question. He returned to her query about the mansion.

'I guess it's the sash windows, stone façade, ionic columns, and those amazing doors. The curves, the way they meet, are beyond aesthetically pleasing; it's almost visually orgasmic!' gushed Michael.

'You're such a tease,' Ann humoured him, brushing her right hand across Michael's chin in a gesture of their closeness.

'Well, beauty is my middle name, and I chose it… and it's not for sale,' Ann mischievously continued, playfully hugging Michael's right arm. 'Your appreciation is all the greater, Michael, since you have that lovely mansion in America. Ours is smaller, but beautifully proportioned for our lives and egos.'

'C'est plus petit mais joliment proportionné' (It's smaller but beautifully proportioned), Michael said in French, reflecting Ann's sentiment.

'Don't speak French, Michael, it makes me quiver – in ways you men just don't understand!' Ann laughed.

Michael's voice cut through her slight embarrassment, a playful warmth in his tone. 'You're blushing, Ann,' he whispered, a knowing twinkle in his eyes.

'Oh gosh, am I? My face does feel as if it's on fire all of a sudden!' Ann giggled, her blush amplifying her charisma as Michael was captivated.

Her beauty, graceful curves, and charisma brought to Michael's mind the mansion's harmonious Palladian architecture. Its symmetry and precision also reminded him of DNA's elegant structure, another source of beauty and intellectual engagement. He then sighed, the reason for his visit re-entering his mind.

'No disrespect, Ann, but what time will Peter be home? I tried to contact him several times.'

Ann pulled away from Michael to gauge his reaction. 'He knows you're arriving about this time, so I'm sure he'll leave work early. I guess he should be home about sixish.'

'In the meantime, young man, let me help you with one of your three cases,' Ann playfully continued, bending down, picking one up, and carrying it up the Portland steps towards the idyllic mansion.

Michael watched her walk, noticing that almost everything Ann did came with an elegantly graceful signature. He continued to admire the sensual sway of her hips. Suddenly, she stopped and playfully looked back.

'Lovely!' Michael blurted, voicing his thoughts.

219

'Yes, the mansion is,' replied Ann, attempting to suggest he was referring to the architecture, not her. She knew full well he was referring to both.

'Are you coming in?' Ann asked with a teasing look, as Michael hadn't moved.

'Of course, of course,' replied Michael as he picked up the remaining two cases and followed Ann into the mansion.

27

Watchful Intelligence

Unbeknownst to Ann and Michael, the house opposite them, freshly let, now discreetly housed several MI5 agents. In a parallel operation, NSA special agents Sterling and Parker were also present, their activities equally concealed.

These NSA agents, working under a mutual MI5 and NSA agreement, had briefed Adams and his daughter several nights earlier. Their surveillance post had been discreetly established here just days before.

The agents huddled around two TV screens that displayed the same footage, but could show separate views if necessary. They watched with intense interest.

'Did you get a visual on the taxi driver?' asked lead MI5 agent Atherton.

'Yes. Visual and voice analysis now confirms it's Lassus Mardon,' replied MI5 officer Beaumont.

'The bastard was in our own playground and we didn't even know it,' Atherton exclaimed. He was stung by Lassus's presence, his impudently daring behaviour, and the fact it all took place right under their surveillance window.

'Who is this guy?' Parker asked politely.

'Lassus is a contract killer,' Atherton explained, his voice flat. 'He's known for his chilling ability to erase his own profile. Yep, one seriously dangerous piece of work,' he added.

'Sir,' Beaumont interjected, 'Internal updates just reported that a taxi driver was found in a Heathrow hotel, tied to a radiator. Alive, thankfully.'

Atherton's jaw clenched. 'I don't believe it,' he snarled, stomping back and forth across the cramped bedroom where they had all congregated to monitor the mansion.

'Why didn't anyone run a facial recognition of the driver at Heathrow?' Deputy MI5 lead, Sinclair demanded.

The MI5 agents knew they had screwed up. The two NSA agents looked on, bemused by what they privately considered a reliance on "analogue methods". Back in America, their ANPR systems ensured intelligence was almost immediate; targets were often identified within minutes and then neutralised in a shootout.

'You know what this means?' Atherton rhetorically asked. 'It means we followed that taxi all the way from Heathrow, not knowing we had him in our sights for at least a few hours. I've got to sit down,' he said, anguished.

He collapsed into an old armchair, wishing it could just swallow him whole. His embarrassment was a physical weight. He moved a trembling hand over his forehead, panting as anxiety hit home. The implications of incompetence now enveloped his ego, taunting it like a bully.

'Sir, do remember, he's a master of disguise,' Beaumont offered, trying to cut through his self-reproach. 'He knew what he was doing and probably had an escape route lined up. Perhaps he even had his own backup escort, just in case.'

'That would be even worse, Beaumont,' Atherton snapped, his voice cutting through the tension. 'Rather than merely questioning how he slipped past our surveillance, we'd be staring down an unimaginable catastrophe. Had we not tracked that taxi, he'd undoubtedly have abducted Adams by now, spirited away clandestinely overseas.'

'Crikey,' Beaumont breathed, the word a sudden expulsion of air. 'Worst-case scenario, sir. We truly got off lightly there.'

Just then, a sudden thought seemed to clear Atherton's mind of his self-reproach. He sprang out of the chair and walked briskly back over to the TV screens. As he did, he cryptically said, 'Well, we may have missed him, but someone else won't,' a statement that left the MI5 agents nonplussed.

'Play the tape back from entry to exit,' Atherton directed Beaumont.

They watched the driver's jerky, almost unnatural movements from falling out of the taxi to falling in the pond. A creeping sense of unease settled over them. 'Too professional, too obvious, too planned,' Sinclair's voice, heavy with suspicion, cut through the quiet.

'You see there,' said Beaumont, as they watched the frozen frame of the driver on the gravel. 'Where he tumbles out, he is obscured by the door but his legs slightly shift towards that Jaguar car.'

Atherton's brow furrowed deeply in thought, his finger tracing an invisible trajectory across the screen. Sinclair leaned forward, lips slightly parted, focus absolute. Both were utterly immersed in the replay, dissecting every flicker, every shadow, considering every possible hostile action. The NSA agents looked on, watching this video analysis unfold in front of them, their expressions unreadable, privately assessing the quirkiness of the investigation.

His gaze sharp, Sinclair then pointed to the screen and directed operator Beaumont to extract two small areas and magnify them on the screen next door.

'See how the driver's legs move slightly as if—' Sinclair began, but Atherton interrupted, 'As if he is placing something, possibly?'

'Maybe... or he just twitched from the impact of hitting the gravel,' remarked Sinclair sceptically. 'Or he's just reacting to hitting his head,' he added, unconvinced.

'His behaviour just seems... off,' Atherton mused, a frown creasing his brow.

'Perhaps he may return, as he did say "see you soon" to Professor Adams. Do you think he has something more sinister planned for later?' Beaumont asked.

Atherton's cryptic reply cut through the analysis. 'No. He will be dealt with before the night is out.' He glanced at the two NSA agents and said, 'Isn't that right, gentlemen?' a knowing wink of his right eye underscoring his meaning.

'Beaumont, meticulously check the angles, reflections, and anything that may be relevant,' Atherton commanded. 'It's still daylight, and slipping into that place unannounced will be a near impossibility without alerting them; their security operates with hair-trigger sensitivity. Thermal the area too, in case something unseen is waiting.'

Any talking that emanated from the property was being monitored by a parabolic sound catcher or laser microphone in order to determine Michael, Peter, and Ann's allegiances. They were probably "clean", but the agents wanted to establish if they had been compromised by nefarious groups seeking personnel and research related to the project.

Atherton turned to the two NSA agents and stated, 'Once dark falls, we will go in to check that car.'

At precisely 2 a.m., shrouded in the profound, moonless silence of the Oxfordshire night, Atherton and Sinclair moved. With ghostly efficiency, they navigated the mansion's perimeter, their boots making no sound on the cold, dew-kissed grass. The crisp night air nipped at their exposed skin, a stark reminder of the chill that seeped into their bones.

Reaching the high stone wall, Atherton braced himself, the rough stone cool under his gloved hand, offering Sinclair a hand-up before scaling it with the seamless fluidity of a shadow. Seconds later, both were over, dropping silently into the private driveway beyond. The air was heavy with coiled anticipation, thick with the damp, earthy scent of disturbed soil and distant, blooming jasmine, a faint sweetness masking the underlying tension.

Their gaze snapped immediately to the dark silhouette of the Jaguar-XF. Moving with predatory precision, they fanned out around the vehicle, their flashlights, filtered to needle-thin beams, meticulously sweeping every inch of its surface.

Atherton ran his gloved hands along the undercarriage, a tactile search for anomalies, while Sinclair forensically examined the wheel arches and door seams, hunting for any disturbed paint, hidden compartments, or the faint, tell-tale gleam of recently installed hardware.

Every curve and crevice of the luxury car was scrutinised, their trained eyes and sensitive fingers probing for the smallest anomaly, their objective clear: to uncover whatever the taxi driver might have planted.

To augment their covert inspection, Atherton retrieved a sleek, obsidian device from his tactical kit: the Aero-Volt Sentinel. This state-of-the-art unit, designed for rapid automotive threat assessment, seamlessly probed a vehicle's electrical network and analysed airborne chemical signatures. Its minimalist interface and deceptively simple black casing belied the sophisticated sensors contained within, poised to uncover anomalies that even the most highly trained human eye might miss.

With practised grace, Atherton positioned the Aero-Volt Sentinel around the vehicle, initiating a sweeping, comprehensive external scan. The device's advanced sensors silently mapped the Jaguar's electrical field, hunting for anomalies like unauthorised power draws or hidden circuits that could betray a clandestine modification.

Simultaneously, its integrated olfactory array meticulously sampled the ambient air directly surrounding the car, paying close attention to vents, grilles, and even the tyre wells.

It meticulously identified any trace elements of volatile organic compounds associated with explosives, cross-referencing them against its extensive internal database. Any discrepancy, however minute, would trigger an immediate, silent alert.

The advanced capabilities of the Aero-Volt Sentinel and their meticulous search, the results were conclusive. The Jaguar XF remained inert, its electrical systems showing no tampering, and the air around it yielded no tell-tale traces of explosives. They had found nothing. The raid was a bust. As they returned to the surveillance post, a grim realisation settled over Atherton: the operation had failed. He hadn't just missed Lassus—he had, for now, lost the game.

28

The Code And The Rosé

Earlier that afternoon, Michael ascended to the second master bedroom. The mansion's hush was a stark contrast to the tumultuous plane hijacking and taxi journey that had preceded it. He meticulously unpacked his compact, compartmentalised luggage, each item finding its specific place with the quiet precision of a well-practised ritual.

He carefully placed a slim volume of 'light' bedtime reading beside the ornate cabinet, a silent promise of a brief escape into the quiet hours of rest ahead. This was more than just unpacking; it was a ritual of quiet preparedness.

His laptop hummed to life, a portal to a world where "network provider codes" were irrelevant. His communications flowed like whispered secrets through an encrypted satellite link, a private channel that pulsated with the clandestine nature of his work. Amidst the usual university chatter and student queries, two emails stood out like ominous beacons, both from Shedland, both concerning decodes.

The first declared that sabotage would fester from within their own ranks, a venomous betrayal of the research. The second, even more chilling, warned that a new, formidable entity would emerge, a direct consequence of their actions.

'Sabotage!' Michael's voice was a raw, disbelieving whisper that tore through the quiet room. 'And how could it be "their" hand?' He gripped the desk's edge, knuckles white, a silent interrogation raging in his mind. This was a puzzle he had to unravel, a dark knot demanding his immediate, undivided attention. In reply, Shedland said that as with other sinister decodes, they prohibited further interrogation, insisting their revelation was time-coded.

The other emails could wait; his "out of office" reply would suffice, letting everyone know he was on a business trip. After showering and taking a moment to adjust to his new surroundings, Michael headed downstairs to join Ann, leaving his beautifully equipped and decorated bedroom behind.

He began to walk down the stone spiral staircase, his right hand gliding over the very shiny handrail as he surveyed the wide expanse of the entrance hall. The walls were adorned with university memorabilia and photos of meetings with VIPs from around the world. Two paintings hung with precise symmetry in the reception area; one bore the hallmarks of a Constable, while the Turner, positioned to the right of the grand mirror, was unmistakable.

Descending further, his gaze fell upon a striking pair of vases, either Japanese or Chinese, placed in perfect opposition on either side of the entrance hall. They stood at the edge of a stunning mosaic circle, its stones radiating outwards from the hall's centre. Anchoring the mosaic was an anvil-shaped antique mahogany table, a piece Michael recognised as he owned a larger version back in his Harvard mansion. He had always told Peter he owned a medium one, not wanting to outdo his friend; they considered themselves equals in every respect.

At the bottom of the elegant stone stairs, his path, initially set for the kitchen, was unexpectedly snagged. A glimpse of Ann in the sun-drenched conservatory redirected him instantly, a magnetic pull. As he drew closer, a profound stillness seemed to radiate from her, drawing his very breath. It was the unspoken elegance of her posture, a quiet, inherent strength that didn't demand attention but rather effortlessly commanded it. Amidst the vibrant greens and soft light, her serene, almost luminous presence seemed to radiate from her.

Ann was truly fortunate, he mused, observing the effortless way she held herself. A brilliant academic mind shone through her every gesture, complemented by an inherent magnetism that felt almost elemental. Her profound intellect and quiet poise had effortlessly captivated countless gazes at Oxford, long before Peter entered her orbit; this came as no surprise to Michael.

As he entered the conservatory, his thoughts snapped away from Ann to the vases he had just seen. She was engrossed in a new journal and looked up with a start.

'Your two vases... Japanese or Chinese?'

'Chinese, I think, 19th century,' Ann replied. 'Beautiful, aren't they?'

'Indeed!' Michael confirmed.

At the heart of their exquisite conservatory, an onyx table trimmed with brass stood. Surrounding it were eight comfortable chairs with intricate floral upholstery, offering ample seating. On the table, two glasses of chilled rosé stood filled to a generous level, ready to be enjoyed.

'Rosé, you remembered,' Michael said, taking a seat opposite her to chat comfortably. He glanced at the front of the periodical she was reading and sardonically enquired, 'Light reading, Ann?'

'Oh, sorry Michael, academic focus, you know,' Ann responded, her fingers still lightly touching the page. 'I simply love history; this is a fascinating look at how economic shifts intersect with ideology and politics.'

Even before the sentence was completed, she simultaneously placed the opened periodical upside down on the table. Her eyes then lifted to meet Michael's, a silent prelude to whatever she was about to say.

'The rosé is as you like it. I placed the bottle in the fridge a couple of hours before you arrived. I even used a bottle cuff to check the temperature was just right, between 7-13°C. And now I've just realised I left the bottle on the kitchen table which is probably sweating profusely.'

'Nervous, is it?' Michael joked.

Ann's laughter danced and shimmered, a sound as bright as the conservatory light. 'Oh, Michael, that wonderfully schoolboyish humour of yours is something I adore; it's truly endearing.' She moved with unreserved warmth to embrace him, a gesture so heartfelt it resonated with the depth of their connection.

As she reluctantly let go to sit back down, he looked at her with deep affection, a soft smile playing on his lips. 'Ann, I never cease to be amazed just how nice you are,' he murmured, the warmth of her embrace still lingering in his mind.

'And how is Harvard treating one of its esteemed members?' Ann asked with a warm smile that hinted at the obvious prestige of the institution. 'The usual blend,' Michael replied, 'busy, surprisingly serene in its own way, with an undercurrent of the absurd, and always about the figures.'

'Sounds like here too,' Ann said, laughing at the "beauty" that the oxygen of academic life brought to them both.

'I'd genuinely like to say there are added dimensions to what I do,' Michael began, a faint sigh escaping him. 'Yes, it's undeniably fascinating, even awe-inspiring in fleeting, brilliant moments. But like all things academic, it's ultimately tightly hemmed in, constrained by the whims of those in power and the stringent allocation of research money.

'Timing, too, plays a brutal, crucial role,' he admitted, a subtle, almost imperceptible weariness seeping into his tone, a quiet confession of the unseen battles fought behind the scenes.

'The times are changing, Michael; I guess we have to go along with it, otherwise, we will be perceived as educational Luddites,' she rhetorically quipped.

'Change, well yes, it's a small word "change" but with big implications!' he replied, raising his glass of rosé to Ann. Leaning slightly forward across the table, they clinked their shiny rosé glasses together.

The delicate chime of their glasses seemed to herald a pleasant, almost destined turn. Just then, the joyous groan of a large oak door opening resoundingly announced the arrival of Professor Peter Magma: celebrated scientist, devoted husband to Ann, and Michael's long-standing friend.

Both Ann and Michael awaited Peter's arrival, the audible thud of books and two cases announcing his presence from the grand, open hallway.

'In here darling!' shouted Ann.

'Where's here!' joked Peter. He knew where she was, as she had said the same thing a thousand times before from the conservatory, but he didn't care, he loved her to bits.

'I'm in here too darling!' quipped Michael in a female voice that any impersonator would have been proud of.

'Who's that old clapped-out female academic, if I'm not mistaken?' Peter joked.

'Clapped out! You've got way more miles on the life clock than me you cheeky old codger. I'd buy you a birthday card, but I don't think they have ever made one for your age group,'

Ann replied banteringly, as she smiled and winked at Michael who in turn laughed softly.

Rounding the corner of the conservatory entrance, Peter's anticipation was almost palpable, a joyous vibration he carried into the room where they awaited him.

Ann rose and, in an exquisitely graceful gesture, floated towards Peter. He pulled her close, their embrace a powerful testament to their longing, melting hours apart into one perfect instant. The lingering hold anchored them both, conveying a deep, enduring affection that rippled through the sunlit conservatory.

Their bodies finding a mutual synchrony of affection, Peter planted a homecoming lover's kiss on her, a tender, unspoken language passing between them. The raw, beautiful display made the onlooking Michael subtly uneasy, a flush rising on his cheeks. This overt affection was a foreign landscape to his usual experience, a vibrant, public declaration he rarely witnessed.

Peter stood lost in his hug with Ann. It was a moment that seemed to stop time, endlessly replaying the rapturous feelings. To further exacerbate Michael's quiet discomfort, Peter's gaze flickered to him, a knowing wink creasing the corner of his eye—a gesture that seemed to ominously imply he might be next, sending a fresh wave of unease coiling in his gut.

As their embrace softened, a palpable warmth filled the conservatory, a testament to their affection. Reluctantly, Peter ended the embrace and moved towards Michael as Ann looked on admiringly.

'Michael, you're here, really here, so good to see you. I've been thinking about our meet since we spoke on the phone a few days ago. Not to mention that "incident" earlier at

Heathrow, if I may call it that,' Peter added, a mixture of concern and relief evident in his voice. Peter, however, wanted to avoid making this the immediate focus, knowing other, more pressing matters weighed on both their minds.

'There's so much we need to speak about, including those things,' Peter said hastily, clearly eager to get straight down to business. 'Incidentally, how's your roving scientist Shedland? Recovered from his floor tour of your office?' Peter joked.

'I hope so!' replied a subdued Michael, as thoughts about their earlier call resurfaced.

Within seconds of their embrace ending, Ann had gone to the kitchen and returned to the conservatory with the bottle of chilled rosé now commodiously placed in a wine bucket and a glass of rosé for her husband.

'Bucket!' exclaimed Michael.

'Michael, what's with the expletive?' Ann remonstrated.

Suddenly, a spark of comprehension ignited in Ann's eyes, and a charming flush rose to her cheeks as she realised her own misinterpretation. A delightful, uninhibited laugh bubbled up soon after, utterly enchanting. It was the kind of sound that could quite literally charm the birds from their branches, a melodic cascade of pure, unadulterated joy.

Her gaze, now fixed on Michael, held an elegant, playful glint. 'Michael,' she purred, mirth still lacing her voice, 'you are such a tease.' She laughed again, a softer, self-deprecating ripple this time, the admission shining in her eyes. She had been delightfully caught out by yet more of her esteemed visitor's schoolboy humour, and she utterly adored it.

She delicately placed the ice bucket and rosé glass on the onyx conservatory table. 'I'll let you intellectual powerhouses do battle while I prepare something nice for us all,' she said.

Ann conveyed this in such a beautiful manner that Michael and Peter both wanted to join her, not to cook, but just for her exquisite company.

'What magnetic gravitas!' exclaimed Michael to Peter as he watched Ann delicately turn, as if on ice, to leave.

'Absolutely! Her gravitas is boundless. Her intellect, warmth, and sheer charisma have been a constant source of strength, even in the most trying times. Her vitality seems to brighten every room she enters, including, I've noticed, your outlook, Michael,' Peter remarked. A subtle inflection in his voice betrayed his awareness of Michael's admiration.

''I'll be in the kitchen with my companion if you want me!' she called breezily as she departed, glass of rosé in hand, bound for the vast kitchen. It was so large that a bicycle might almost be needed to reach all its corners.

'Companion?' Peter called after her, his voice curious.

Ann suddenly poked her head around the conservatory doorway. 'Yes, my darling, my companion!' she said, blinking at Peter with a mischievous sparkle in her eyes, while he settled in for a session of relaxed banter with Michael.

Still in a playful mood, she slipped behind the wall once more, then extended her right arm, holding another periodical, and exclaimed, 'This companion!'

With a final teasing peek around the wall, she blew a kiss, a silent encouragement for their forthcoming conversation.

'Oh my God, she's utterly remarkable, Peter!' Michael exclaimed, his admiration for Ann clear in every gesture.

'And she's mine, by love, by ring, by marriage, and for always,' Peter said, his gaze softening with profound affection. 'Ann is, quite simply, the bedrock of everything I need. We evolve together, so there is never any sense of drifting apart... I trust I offer her the same.'

'Probably so, probably so!' Michael replied, his eyes reflecting admiration—and perhaps a faint twinge of jealousy.

Their thoughts of Ann now gave way to another shared fascination: their research. The two men studied each other like pugilists poised before a bout.

Yet this was no contest for a knockout or points. Their intellectual grappling was about wrestling with a subject that had long captivated them both, one that had underpinned their respective academic endeavours and been a shared pursuit since their early days at Oxford.

For the next hour, their conversation delved into a topic that often seemed more akin to fiction, a notion supported by discussions in academic papers spanning decades.

Their discussion centred on research that, on the surface, appeared too fantastical for serious academic consideration. Yet, it stemmed directly from the findings of the "Human Genome Project" and, more recently, the "100,000 Genomes Project".

Both projects sought to unravel the intricate coding relationships woven into DNA and their profound implications for human life. The latter concentrated specifically on the shadowy origins, the very aetiology, of rare diseases, with the aim of deepening understanding, refining treatments, and advancing patient care.

Their interest was further fuelled by the findings of the "ENCODE" project. This research indicated the presence of previously undetected switches, signposts, and signals throughout human DNA. These might carry a chemical message, though its nature remained a matter of pure speculation.

At this pivotal moment, Peter's voice surged with unbridled, almost youthful enthusiasm. 'Michael,' he practically bellowed, eyes ablaze, 'it was the schoolboy's wildest dream brought to dazzling reality! There I was, at the helm of genetic research at Oxford, with access to the uncharted frontiers of computing power and a team of brilliant cryptogeneticists, my son Nathan included, of course!'

Peter, unable to contain the seismic surge of their progress, practically vaulted from his chair. 'And guess what, Michael,' he declared, his voice ringing with unbridled triumph, 'we are getting closer to cracking the bloody code!' Michael, jolted by Peter's excitement, mirrored his friend's movement, springing to his feet.

'What!' he exclaimed, incredulity mingled with budding hope.

'Isn't it extraordinary!' Peter shouted back, his grin stretching from ear to ear.

'What is?' Michael pressed, his mind still trying to catch up.

'We both stood up with such speed,' Peter chuckled, 'and yet we never spilled our rosé!'

'God forbid we do that!' Michael laughed.

He glanced at his glass, then at Peter, and they both dissolved into laughter at the sheer absurdity of such a serious topic being momentarily eclipsed by their careful handling of rosé.

'To university days,' Peter exclaimed, his voice ringing out as he raised his nearly empty glass to Michael, whose glass remained full. Unbeknownst to them, toasting with a glass that was not full was considered unlucky—a quiet omen, perhaps, for what lay ahead.

'Yes, may God bless us, as our Oxford motto says: *Dominus Illuminatio Mea* ("The Lord is my light"),' Peter replied boisterously, raising his own full glass. 'Hurrah!'

Their shared laugh lingered between them as they drank, yet their thoughts were already wandering, swinging between fond recollections of schoolboy dreams and the staggering, futuristic implications of their research.

What had once been mere imagination now threatened to become reality. Their project promised a quantum leap in humankind's evolution—perhaps on a discovery scale to rival relativity or even the Bomb. Indeed, they knew that depending on what they decoded, it might surpass anything that had come before. The spark of discovery burned brightly between them, alive in the intensity of the moment.

Meanwhile, Ann, absorbed in the magazine with the same meticulous attention the authors had lavished upon it, was interrupted by the shrill ring of her mobile phone. The caller ID revealed their son, Nathan.

'Hello, bambino,' she said playfully.

'Yeah, yeah, whatever you say, Mother,' Nathan replied, sounding a bit impatient but also affectionate. 'Listen, I met one of Father's colleagues earlier, and he said Michael was coming to visit for a few days. Is that right?' Nathan asked politely.

'Oh sorry, I thought your father—I mean Peter—had already told you about his visit a while ago,' Ann hurriedly corrected herself, a slight confusion in her voice. Peter usually told Nathan important things; this oversight was clearly significant.

'Well, when is he arriving?' Nathan asked.

'He arrived about two hours ago. He's in the drawing room with Peter, deep in conversation as always,' Ann replied. Nathan muttered something under his breath and then went quiet.

He had hoped to witness Michael's arrival, a formality he knew Michael valued. Nathan's silence wasn't rudeness toward Ann; rather, it was simply surprise at having missed it.

'I know you keep saying no, but I really need to ask Michael again about working in America. I'm sure he must have contacts within the NSA. They always need experts like me. Furthermore, the money and career prospects are far better than at Oxford as far as I can see. And I can get to meet Elizabeth. Wow, she's gorgeous!' Nathan rattled on.

'No!' Ann abruptly retorted, her voice sharp with finality. 'Have nothing to do with her, Nathan, She's not your type. I've told you countless times to stay at Oxford. It's a world-class research centre, and you have us here at the moment,' she lectured, her tone firm.

'At the moment? Why, are you moving?' Nathan asked, clearly befuddled.

'Just a turn of phrase, that's all,' she softly replied in an effort to end this line of questioning.

Turning the conversation back to its original topic, Ann continued.

'Look, why don't you stay over tonight and we can chat then? I'm sure he'd be very happy to see you, and we would too,' Ann encouragingly insisted, hoping he would agree.

'Sorry, other things on the agenda tonight,' replied Nathan, contradicting his earlier assertions to see Michael. 'That's a genuine shame,' Ann said, a note of disappointment in her voice.

She wondered if this was just a lie, a ruse to get his own back for being kept in the dark. But beneath her polite facade, a mischievous glint began to form, a subtle flicker of the fiery core hinted at by her surname: Magma.

'Well, in that case,' she teased, a triumphant glint in her eye, her words a volcanic heat signature designed to pierce his very egotistical veil. 'I suppose I'll have to cancel your reservation at Trattoria Tramonto Rosso, where we'll be heading shortly.'

'Don't you dare, Mother! Why didn't you tell me you were going there? You know I really like their food,' Nathan pleaded, a hasty apology in his voice as he tried to erase his earlier rudeness and his transparent lie about other plans.

'Caught you with your metaphorical trousers around your ankles, didn't I?' Ann chuckled, thoroughly relishing his sudden about-face.

'What time should I meet you there?' he asked quickly, not understanding Ann's joke.

'Say 7.30 p.m.?' Ann asked, not expecting him to change her plans.

'7.45 p.m. works better for me.'

'Alright, but in that scenario, the considerable bill finds its way to your wallet,' Ann retorted, a delightful glint in her witty remark.

'7.30 p.m. sounds good,' Nathan said quickly, wanting a free meal. Ann chuckled inwardly. She remembered her own student days; the power of free food was universal.

After their goodbyes, Ann's attention was drawn by the rising voices from the drawing room. She stood and walked from the kitchen, her footsteps across the marble tiles becoming lost in the animated conversation.

'Good grief, gentleman, what is all this cachinnation I can hear from the kitchen?' scolded Ann over the noise from her two conservatory occupiers.

'Just reminiscing about those special Oxford days. Speaking of special, we're hoping you have made something special for us?' Peter asked.

'Oh yes, I took these fingers and created something that is a paradox,' she said to them both, as she fought the outward desire to laugh concurrently. Ann's bewitching eyes then focused their enchanting depths of endearment towards Michael alone as she continued, 'I know how much you love Italian food.'

Peter interrupted Ann's conversational flow. He added, 'Pity you didn't work in Italy, Michael; you could eat real Italian food in real surroundings all night, every night.'

'Oh, what pleasure!' cheered Michael. 'No, let me say that in Italian to make it more expedient: *O quanta voluptas*!' he opined with a broad grin on his face. That smile, however, was also a testament to years of rigorous thought, etching fine lines like annotations on a well-loved manuscript.

'Gentlemen, enough of this delightful chatter,' Ann interjected with mock severity. 'Dinner will be at 7:30 p.m., so please be here by 7:15 p.m., just in case either of you decides to wander off.' She added, with the same firm tone she used with her students, 'And do remember, suit and tie are the order of the evening!'

Peter and Michael grinned, wondering about dinner. They'd soon discover a curious detail. While the professors were engrossed in research, Ann had also been busy. Quietly absorbed in her periodical, she'd still made a reservation at the finest Italian restaurant. For Michael, nothing less would do.

29

Dinner With A Side Of Paranoia

Ann, Peter, Michael, and Nathan cherished a special evening at an exclusive, discreetly quiet Italian restaurant. The gathering was a rare reprieve from their work, a moment where the very mention of "Q-Day" was silently forbidden.

The conversation at the table primarily revolved around several topics, including Michael's experiences on the 787-9, politicians, upcoming holidays, and the delicious food they were enjoying. They also reminisced about past memories from their alma mater.

These recollections were not only numerous but also joyful. Amidst this pleasant discourse, two particular things stood out during the evening: a humorous anecdote related to their alma mater, and the unsettling presence of a strange man observing them from across the road.

The friends were recounting an episode of punting. This took place on a glorious late summer afternoon during their first year as probationers, while they were all studying for their three-year doctorates at Oxford. A warm atmosphere of shared reminiscence filled the air as they spoke.

Abruptly, peals of laughter erupted among them, the joyous sound punctuating their fond recollection. The laughter was triggered by Michael's reminder of a particular punting excursion: upon emerging from an absurdly low bridge, three mischievous students from "the other place"—namely Cambridge—had yanked his punt pole up.

Michael's grip on the punt pole was like a wedged key; consequently, they hoisted him skyward, his legs windmilling wildly as if pedalling an invisible unicycle.

Gravity then unceremoniously dumped him into the decidedly less glorious River Cherwell.

Peter and Ann reacted in a flurry of well-intentioned but utterly inept panic. They flailed at Michael, attempting to help, but their efforts were unsuccessful. This resulted in Peter and Ann losing their own precarious balance and tumbling into the River Cherwell for a rather less dignified, impromptu summer dip.

Ann laughed long after Peter did; he understood the anecdote, but it simply didn't resonate as strongly with him. What would have resonated more with Peter, had he known, was Ann's subtle action: under the restaurant table, she was rubbing her leg seductively against Michael's—a private, familiar touch from their past.

Michael looked on, slightly embarrassed—more for Peter than for his feelings towards Ann. He looked at Ann in a way only they understood. As their eyes met for just a second more, it seemed like an eternity; during that extended moment, memories flooded back of their lovely times when they were romantically together.

The only negative aspect of the evening was first noticed by Peter. As the anecdotes and laughter continued, Peter's gaze flickered occasionally towards the large front window of the restaurant.

Each time Peter looked towards the window, his gaze seemed to snag momentarily on something across the quiet street before he would return his attention to the table. Whatever had caught his eye was quickly dismissed as insignificant.

It was a habit born of a slightly more observant nature than the others, a trait that would soon bring an unwelcome element into their special evening.

'You know, I wouldn't have seen him had you not mentioned it, Peter,' said Ann, then tried furtively to look out from the restaurant window. Her gaze was directed towards a car parked fifteen yards away in a parking bay reserved for those with registered disabilities.

'He's been there since we arrived. I've tried to ignore him, but his focus doesn't seem to deviate from us. In fact, I did see him get out and urinate a few yards that way,' said Peter, pointing in the car's direction, before Ann interjected.

'That's disgusting, Peter. Does that add anything to our evening, apart from being ghastly? Don't point at him; he'll know we're talking about him,' hastily continued Ann.

Peter was on a roll, and speech truncation was not on his menu.

'That's not all. He put on some strange metal spectacles and just stood there. The whole thing was peculiar,' Peter continued, attracting Ann's increasing displeasure with his need to elaborate further.

Nathan interjected with his own version of what might have happened.

'Probably night vision binoculars made for the most discreet pervert. You know, he's probably some weirdo who eats vicariously and without charge. Perhaps a twisted voyeur with a propensity for diners. I tell you what, perhaps he's an ex-lover,' teased Nathan.

'Enough, Nathan,' scolded Ann.

Michael joined the conversation. 'I tend to remember faces. He looks familiar, but I can't quite place him. Maybe he just has one of those faces that you think you know, but you don't.'

Seeing the conversation was attracting greater intrigue, Nathan quickly responded, 'Look, let me go and find out who—or what—he is.'

Ann pressed Nathan's hand with authoritative delicacy while saying, 'Leave it, dear, for the moment, please.'

Whether the stranger in the car was reading lips or possessed remarkable listening abilities, the car engine suddenly turned over. Seconds later, the headlights came on.

The car suddenly accelerated, screeching away at speed. As it roared past, just metres from their table in the road outside, the man inside didn't even glance in their direction, showing no awareness of the diners or their conversation.

In fact, the mysterious driver had been pointing a Spectra Laser Microphone M+ at the bottom of the window next to the diners.

As the laser's tiny dot made contact with the window, it was reflected back towards the device. This reflected laser light then interacted with the minute vibrations of the windowpane. These subtle vibrations on the restaurant window were not random occurrences.

They were, in fact, directly caused by the sound waves emanating from their conversation inside. The sophisticated laser microphone technology then intercepted these minuscule window movements and ingeniously converted them back into clear, intelligible speech.

The laser dot was literally imperceptible to all but the most eagle-eyed people. Every word of their conversation had not only been analysed in real-time by satellite uplink but also recorded for posterity as potential evidence. The identity of their listener was a truth they would soon discover.

'Most odd!' was the unanimous summation of this strange event by them all. With this shared sentiment, they continued their evening without further disruption.

Their special dinner eventually concluded without further incident. The large taxi they'd ordered arrived on time, spacious enough for all four of them to sit comfortably in the back for the return journey to what Nathan affectionately called the "mansion of dreams".

As they settled into the back of the taxi, they couldn't help but be transfixed by the dark, unnerving eyes peering at them from the rear-view mirror. The driver's gaze had a magnetic attraction that defied understanding. The other three recalled Michael's recent anecdote about a sinister taxi driver from Heathrow, and they realised it had made a much deeper impression on them than they first thought.

They were now viewing this new, unrelated situation through the lens of a single negative past event, a cognitive distortion known as overgeneralisation. In their minds, that one "bad apple" had irrevocably spoiled the entire barrel. This driver, despite exhibiting no suspicious signs whatsoever, was scrutinised through the exact same lens of profound distrust, simply by virtue of his profession. This potent mental shortcut transformed what should have been an ordinary journey into a tense, emotionally charged, and deeply unsettling ordeal.

During their return journey, the four passengers' faces were locked on him with repeated, intense scrutiny. Every turn of the wheel, every fleeting glance in the mirror, prompted their desperate stares, searching for any flicker that might confirm their earlier, gnawing concerns.

The driver, a man of many years' experience and accustomed to all sorts, still felt a distinct prickle of unease.

He'd ferried countless fares, but the silent, wide-eyed intensity emanating from the back seats was unmistakably starting to fray his nerves. He gripped the steering wheel a little tighter, a subtle tremor running through his hands he fervently hoped they wouldn't notice.

He caught Michael's reflection in his rearview mirror, the man's eyes darting wildly. Then he heard a barely audible whisper about 'the man in the suit at the traffic lights.' "What's he on about?" the driver mused inwardly, his brow furrowing. He risked a quick, bewildered glance at the empty pavement while driving through green traffic lights. A flush crept up his neck, irritation mingling with burgeoning paranoia.

Then, Nathan, in a clumsy attempt to lighten the mood, tried a joke about police identity parades, suggesting taxi drivers would stand with their backs to the alleged victim as they'd only recognise the back of the head. The driver's jaw tightened. "Right, because that's normal, yes?" he muttered to himself, a wave of fierce defensiveness washing over him.

The relentless, searching looks in the mirror, the odd whispers, the palpable tension radiating from all four in the back – it was all coalescing, making him feel unequivocally like he was the one under suspicion. He could almost feel their collective gaze burning into his scalp, making him self-consciously smooth his hair with one hand. This wasn't just a job anymore; it had morphed into an interrogation. The journey soon concluded, without any imagined incident, and the driver was visually relieved to see their backs too.

- 30-
Peter's Rain Cheque

That Saturday, dawn's hesitant fingers stretched across Oxford, bathing its "dreaming spires" in a nascent glow—a sight that had inspired Victorian poet Matthew Arnold. He had perfectly grasped how light, a playful artist, could utterly reinvent the ancient city, finding an opulent architectural canvas for its golden dance.

Intent on both invigorating exercise and intellectual rekindling, Peter and Michael gravitated towards the sprawling university parks just after midday. They yearned not only to reminisce but also to resume a vital research discussion, one that had been abruptly curtailed by the previous evening's indulgent three-course Italian dinner.

Just a mile distant, Ann had cheerfully jettisoned drab marking for invigorating retail therapy. Nathan, a man of starkly contrasting priorities, was already back at college, poised to rendezvous with his astute graduate students for a long-planned outing. As the designated driver, he'd taken the liberty of borrowing Peter's cherished Jaguar XF, bearing registration "DNA 1".

Nathan's student friends were visibly unhappy about his lateness. He vaguely tried explaining his delay by claiming he needed to repair the Jaguar. When pressed for details, he became visibly uneasy, stuttering and faltering as he spoke, revealing a glaring lack of car knowledge. This left them not just bemused but increasingly annoyed, as they suspected he was intentionally keeping them waiting or simply didn't care.

Meanwhile, as Nathan fumbled through the stifling weight of his students' palpable frustration, a profound calm descended upon the university parks' verdant expanse. There, Michael and Peter, utterly lost in their engrossing conversation, remained blissfully unaware of the unfolding drama. The world beyond them, once sharp, now gently blurred, receding into a distant, muted backdrop.

'Do the parks look refreshing to a tired, old, clapped-out academic?' Peter joked to Michael as they ambled across the university grounds. A gentle, warm breeze passed through them, a tangible sigh that seemed to loosen the grip of their work-related stresses.

'Yesterday, Peter, I was tired. It's like any good thing: once you've had something that truly benefits—in this case, sleep—only then do you realise how truly depleted you were.'

Michael insisted, 'Tell me more about this code you think you've broken. It's utterly amazing.'

'Michael, my team and I don't think we have; we know we have—that's why it's so exciting! The problem, however, is our utter lack of backup expertise or computing power to reach the next level,' Peter revealed, his gaze fixed on Michael, hoping a new angle might emerge.

'There are levels?' Michael whispered, surprise in his voice and countenance. 'Give me an idea of what you've found so far; I truly can't wait much longer!' he pleaded, tugging Peter's jacket sleeve manically.

Peter pushed Michael's hand away, freeing creases from his right sleeve. He realised their current conversation wasn't advancing the research. Carefully, Peter gathered his thoughts, aiming for maximum clarity despite his limited factual basis. He prepared to explain his next points clearly, given the gravity of their situation. What they had, even so, was coded dynamite. Peter took several breaths before beginning.

'Michael, we've known each other a long time; we've even woken up on these very fields drunk from the night before. We walked our girlfriends across them, and indeed our wives too. You trust me implicitly, as I do you. Listen to me first, and only then judge what I'm about to say, all right?'

Michael was both terrified and desperate for knowledge; his mind raced with anticipation. The excitement was unprecedented, perhaps comparable only to a professor announcing new DNA structures that challenged the double helix—a truly groundbreaking discovery. Now, time seemed to slow as he waited for Peter's news.

'Tell me, Peter, or I'll grab both sleeves this time,' Michael jokingly said, masking his desperation to hear his next words. Peter laughed.

'It's like this, Michael: we've been aware of a code for a few years now. What was once a suggestion became assumption, and now a predictive proposition. What we have so far is a strong indication this evolutionary change is imminent, called "Q-Day". The team considers it highly probable that "Q" means "Quantum", perhaps even "Day of Quanta".'

Peter paused, then continued, 'It will affect every one of us simultaneously.' He then compared it to an upgrade, hoping it would be an improvement, lest they be doomed to societal regression—a future of dragging knuckles.

'We also believe this code is as elaborately intertwined as DNA itself. Frankly, we need a bloody super-fast computer and a team ten times our current size to unpack it. If we had that, we might get closer—no, that's not right—we will find out what's going to happen to us.'

'Peter,' Michael said, 'I agree we've been friends a long time, but I came over to see you for another reason—one I couldn't voice on the phone.'

Peter just stared at Michael, as if an unknown, mysterious force had struck him down.

'My Harvard specialists also found it, though they're perhaps slightly ahead. Aside from us, neither university knows what the other is doing. And yes, you were correct, "Q" does indeed mean quantum—a good guess. Exactly! You understand, then, that profound entanglement could mean every person is subtly linked, tethered by an invisible bond to a collective quantum consciousness.

'Some linkages are stronger, such as microchimerism: a mother permanently carries living cells with her child's unique DNA for her entire life, a smaller amount of her cells persisting within the child for their lifetime,' Michael explained, his excitement barely contained.

Peter nodded slowly in his reply. 'The microchimerism I know. But you're suggesting it's the physical manifestation of that quantum link?'

Michael's excitement flared. 'Precisely! These deep, quantum-biological connections give rise to a range of deeply intuitive, sometimes inexplicable interactions. For example, twins often demonstrate spooky attunement— shared thoughts, finishing sentences, and an intuitive awareness of distress or pain—as well as striking similarities in preferences and choices, even when separated. This heightened attunement extends to their mother, all through these enduring microchimeric bonds.'

'Peter, it's this we're trying to unlock too: not just codes to explain "Q-Day", my friend, but the key to understand who we really are and where we're going—if that's what we find, of course,' Michael concluded, gazing strongly at Peter to reinforce his words and meaning.

'And are you ready for this?' Michael asked, leaning in. 'We've found two repeating strings coded as "NEMESIS" and "KYROS". They are the keys, the bridge to "Q-Day". To achieve this, there's something we must do, but we're still working on it.'

'Oh my God, Michael, just how long have you been working on this?' Peter then quizzed.

A soft, rueful laugh escaped Michael, his gaze flickering away as if a secret, once held sacred, had just been torn open. He visibly composed himself, then met Peter's stunned eyes. 'About three months,' he admitted. 'And it's far bigger than us, Peter. Four other research teams are deeply entwined: China, French, India, and Russia.'

'Oh, come on, Michael, how do you know this when I didn't? I'm almost at the top of Oxford's communication line, and I didn't know this?!' Peter roared. The sudden outburst was so intense that nearby walkers and athletes paused, trying to locate its source.

Michael grabbed Peter's arms to steady him, knowing the next revelation would prove even more upsetting.

Holding Peter steady, Michael asserted, 'Look, Peter, like you, I didn't know this, and to be honest—' Michael was cut short by Peter's mounting upset. 'Honest? Really sure?' Peter seethed.

Michael's anger surged, his grip on Peter's arms doubling in intensity.

'Peter, I shouldn't tell you this, but I was whisked off to Washington seven days ago. I was in a meeting—' Michael recounted—'with the NSA director, representatives from various security agencies, and other high-ranking, quite menacing individuals.

'Then, to my astonishment, the Vice-President of the United States entered the room. It's there I found out about the other countries. That's why we spoke three days ago, and why I'm visiting now. I couldn't tell you on the phone; this is the NSA, for God's sake. I'm frightened, Peter; I think my phones are tapped, and they're following me. I think that man outside the restaurant last night was a spook.'

Michael let go of Peter's arms; otherwise, Peter would have forcibly pushed him away. As with yesterday, they stared, but now felt like pugilists awaiting the first verbal knockout blow. It came quickly, like a right uppercut.

'Peter, listen to me. We must go to America. We're the top people in the world. Don't ask me what they're doing elsewhere, but they're probably encountering the same problems as our teams,' Michael said with an exasperated and frightened undertone.

'We've been given access to all we need by the NSA director. Peter, this is our chance to redefine history, to truly grasp human evolution. We even have the unique opportunity to unpack a monologue from our very maker— perhaps God, who knows?' Michael said, tears forming in his eyes, his voice thick with emotion.

Michael continued, his voice strained and with palpable anxiety. 'Our very DNA,' he emphasised, the words gaining a fearful weight, 'may not be of this Earth at all. Even Crick himself suggested as much back in 1953, when he co-discovered the DNA helical structure. What if it is truly extraterrestrial?

'If back then one of our own Nobel Prize winners could say this and not receive admonishment, there must have been something to it, surely? Since then, as you know, notable scientists in our area are saying the same thing too as systems biology and related nano-genomic network sequencing advances unhindered.

'But no one, Peter, my long-term friend—absolutely no one—has been anywhere near where we are now. When we were boys, we dreamed of this code. We joked about it on this very field, probably on this very spot, as freshers, undergraduates, then as doctors, before I went to Harvard,' Michael passionately argued.

'I'm aware of this, my friend, but I'm still in shock from what you've said,' Peter managed.

Peter was in shock, and rightly so. He began grappling with a fundamental conflict, struggling to reconcile his previous understanding with the recent revelations. These new facts had partially undermined his self-constructed sense of importance—a carefully built edifice of academic advancement. These facts underscored so much more.

'Tell me, Michael, what else happened there that day?' Peter asked, as if the very next words might cement or break their deep, long-term platonic relationship.

Michael felt the question's severity cut through the years of laughter they'd shared. He knew openness was vital to bring his friend back on board.

After a pause, Michael replied, 'The situation is critical, Peter. As I mentioned, we have six research teams scattered across the globe—four completely unaware of the others— yet all are heavily constrained by deep-seated ideological and economic conflicts. The NSA and other intelligence agencies have been collaborating, relentlessly sweeping intranets, the deep web, and the cloud to assemble what fragments they can. But this isn't true collaboration;

piecemeal research is no substitute for organised, integrated research.'

'Yes, I get all this, Michael, I really do,' Peter responded, his frankness immediately welcomed by Michael. 'I know about the surveillance; that was a given with the NSA involved. Hell, I bet they've watched us for years.'

Michael intensified his gaze. 'They want to bring these teams together, to work with the NSA, to unpack, unscramble, and untangle this infinitely complex code. What's more, they want us to lead this research of potentially apocalyptic proportions. Money is no object; that's why the Vice-President himself was there to approve it all. There are no negatives here, Peter, only immense, unparalleled opportunity.'

Michael's words, reasons, and needs spilled out, as quickly as he could think and enunciate. It was a bizarre sight: two hyperintelligent, sentient beings engaged in a tête-à-tête of rhythmic, impassioned words, their tone and bodily movements reflecting excitement and despair, all unfolding in the middle of the university park. This bizarre academic dance of words and gestures underscored their unspoken agreement to collaborate, its potential implications enormous, like a mega-tsunami overwhelming all other research.

Michael gripped Peter's arms, his intensity a physical manifestation of his final plea. He leaned in, his voice dropping to a low, urgent command: 'Mate, friend, pal, I'm asking you, in the name of science itself: put aside the deception, Peter, and your hurt ego. Just consider, for a moment, that perhaps all of this is predestined, meant to be. That we are to be the leaders of this new "Q"—this new quantum.'

Peter smiled wryly, his gaze suddenly fixed beyond Michael, a faint glow entering his eyes. Michael, somewhat discombobulated by this sudden change, asked, 'What's so funny?'

Peter's game was given away when he raised his right arm to wave at Ann, who was swiftly approaching from behind Michael.

She was walking quickly towards them, reciprocating Peter's wave. Michael, misunderstanding, felt an urgent need to grasp Peter's reasoning. He pleaded for an answer with frantic intensity, his verbal delivery now demanding, bordering on an attack.

'Well, are you on board with this?' Michael pleaded, desperate for "yes" to be the only word of importance, knowing life without it would never be the same.

Michael, consumed by the desperate need for "yes," felt all his fears of rejection crystallize instantly. He read Peter's slight hesitation as a "no," and his body surrendered: listless, arms pointed groundward, seemingly glued to his sides. His gaze first fell to the earth, then shattered upward, fixing on the stormy sky—a visceral mirror of his despair.

Just then, Peter subtly shifted, moving to embrace Ann, who had reached her love. She hugged him tight, delivering a passionate kiss that sealed the moment Michael, in his profound abyss, could barely register. As Peter hugged Ann, he deployed a familiar tactic to convey a mark of respect, a single word of profound resonance: 'Yes, I think!'

'Darling, I haven't asked you yet,' Ann said, giggling at the humour and mystery of Peter's apparent predictive abilities.

As Ann spoke, Peter and Michael exchanged a look of pure academic brilliance, a silent understanding forged by years of collaborative research. Michael was content, yet a flicker of reservation remained. Peter's quiet 'I think' wasn't a final word, but a clear signal that this provisional affirmation was still open to negotiation. It was his metaphorical rain cheque—a promissory note he hoped to cash in on their next meeting, when the full weight of the discovery had settled and transformed his hesitation into an unshakeable certainty.

'I was going to ask if you wanted another dinner at Trattoria Tramonto Rosso?' Ann enquired, still trying to grasp their conversation. Both professors agreed and returned to the mansion to continue their chat before their evening dinner.

On the way back, Ann dropped her own bombshell, wryly stating, 'I see your "friend" is back.'

'Friend?' Peter replied, utterly perplexed.

'The man outside the restaurant last night. He was standing by the goalpost, feigning interest in the football match,' Ann explained with a smile.

Peter and Michael scanned the spot Ann had indicated, but the man was gone. Unfazed, their thoughts were already turning back to research. Amid the mental clutter, one question insisted on breaking through: "Was this man accompanied?" Ann, however, offered little help, admitting she had no way of knowing if anyone else had been there.

A Meeting Of Minds And Ego

After a delightful second dinner at Trattoria Tramonto Rosso, the three of them returned home later than expected, stepping into their impressive Georgian mansion just after 11 p.m.

Ann had decided to retire to bed after a hectic round of affable conversation and excellent cuisine. However, she didn't say anything immediately, so as not to appear rude to her adored and wonderful guest, Michael.

She was rude, however, to Nathan, who for some reason had unexpectedly phoned during their meal to say he wouldn't be staying over as planned. Ann chastised him, feeling her son's behaviour was utterly unbecoming. Michael had been looking forward to speaking more with him after dinner the previous night.

All of that was now beside the point. As she opened the drawing room's large mahogany doors, the light from the chandeliers immediately revealed a scene of immeasurable elegance. Indeed, Peter couldn't help but be mesmerised by the room's resounding opulence, its living beauty and grandeur—a space that spoke volumes of exquisite taste. Though it was difficult to know what to behold first, the wall and ceiling colours immediately stood out. The former a rose white, the latter a neutral white, which made the large room feel even more airy and expansive.

Centrally placed on the drawing room's oak floor were two lusciously soft sofas, pleasantly separated by a magnificent coffee table of Marquina Nero marble. These rested on a Persian Kashan red rug. From the Georgian ceiling, two large Italian Swarovski crystal Florentine-style chandeliers hung, spaced four metres apart.

During the day, natural light caressed the crystals, producing a stunning kaleidoscopic beauty across the ornate ceiling. By night, their magnificent illumination was a spectacle of radiant enchantment

Furthermore, the chandeliers deliberately created a central eyeline from the drawing room door to the two large south-facing bay windows, adjoined by French doors. These windows were adorned with the most exquisite, lightly patinated velvet curtains that blended seamlessly with the room's luxurious decor.

To the left, centrally located, was a refurbished Georgian fireplace. The fireplace was integrated into a unit that ran the entire wall, with several ornate Georgian shelves on either side. Every shelf space held books. The opposite wall displayed a mixture of cabinets, family pictures, images of historical struggles, DNA images, and more books.

'Michael, are you with us?' Ann asked, as she could see he was taking in the grandeur.

'Yes, my apologies,' responded Michael. He knew Ann knew what he was thinking, so any further explanation seemed redundant.

They walked over to the sofas, but only Peter and Michael sat down. Ann heard their quiet grunts as they settled onto the sofas—a familiar sound of men easing into comfort.

As she looked at Michael, she giggled before delivering a rather bookish statement: 'Michael, I will take my leave of you now. I will be busy tomorrow. As an eight-hour sleeper, it's time to say *au revoir* to this world, albeit temporarily, and acquaint myself with the royal road to the dream world.'

She continued, 'Before I do retire, Michael, please forgive me, but I need Peter for a moment. You know where everything is, so please feel free to make yourself at home.'

Following Ann's kind suggestion, Michael rose and headed towards the kitchen with his and Peter's empty rosé glasses from earlier. He would get two clean ones. As he filled the new glasses with rosé, close by, Ann mentioned again the man she'd seen by the goalposts on University Park's lawns to Peter.

'Darling, there were two other men with him, but they walked away as I approached you, leaving just one by the time we met. I didn't want to mention more than the one guy, as it might just be early paranoia setting in. After all, there's probably a perfectly reasonable explanation. In any case, if I see him again, I'll go straight up to him and find out what's going on,' Ann said boldly.

Peter seemed to take a step back at the revelation. He wondered if the issue might have something to do with the university itself. Perhaps, he thought, it could even be an irate parent unhappy with their child's education. In the end, he found himself just as baffled by the situation as Ann.

'Look, don't approach him physically, Ann, just wave. That might do it. If you encounter him again, any semblance of a casual encounter will surely vanish.'

He placed his hands on Ann's shoulders as he spoke. He wanted to convey how deeply and protectively he cared for her. He also hoped to ease her growing anxiety about who this man was and why he had suddenly entered their lives so intrusively.

Peter leaned forward, his confident kiss a soft brush against Ann's trembling lips. As their goodnight touch ended, a polite smile was all she could manage—a fleeting mask for the quiet sigh that escaped her, a sound that held all the weary contradiction she felt.

As she turned away from him, she gently stroked her fingers along Peter's right hand—a final loving touch before she walked up the staircase to bed. Peter sighed slightly too, yet his mind was already on Michael, who was waiting to enjoy his refreshed rosé.

Michael placed the ice bucket, holding the rosé bottle and two freshly poured glasses, on a solid silver George III drinks tray. He then carried the tray by its handles into the conservatory. Peter's eyes widened in gleeful anticipation at the sight of the prized bottle, chilled within the ice bucket. He knew his palate would soon be reacquainted with the well-balanced wine, its sweetness, acidity, alcohol, and tannins in splendid harmony, with no single element overpowering the others.

'Where's the glasses?' Peter quizzically asked.

'Dad dah!' Michael replied, animating a slight turn in the tray to reveal the glasses already refreshed.

'Bravo, young man. And for your next trick,' Peter gesticulated as he waved his hand in circles as if to encourage another magic performance by Michael.

'I left both empty glasses right next to Ann's periodical,' Michael joked. 'I'm hoping she'll come down in the morning and genuinely wonder if she got up in the middle of the night and drank them.'

'Then let's toast to the periodical,' Peter sarcastically enunciated.

'Why not indeed!' Michael replied immediately, ready to drink. Their toast saw a generous amount of the medium-bodied rosé disappear from their glasses, which were so full it appeared to the average drinker as if they hadn't even had a single sip. With their thirsts quenched by the generous wine, Peter looked thoughtfully at Michael, his mind composing several sentences as if he were writing a telepathic essay.

'It bothers me, it really does,' Peter said in a playful tone. 'What's that?' Michael replied.

'The proximity of that rosé bottle to your glass,' Peter chortled softly, his sardonic expression making Michael's face light up with mirth.

'Old habits die hard. I need it given the nature of my visit,' said Michael.

'Hmm, you know, I was calculating the restaurant bill from earlier, and they just don't add up to what I thought I ingested,' reflected Peter.

However, Michael's lined face creased into a playful smile as he prepared to reply. 'Well expensive bills do come with expensive restaurants,' he chortled to ease the impending tension of their conversation.

'Very droll! Ha ha,' Peter replied.

The two friends sat opposite each other in the conservatory for what seemed like only a few minutes, though in reality it had been over an hour. It was late, yet Michael tried to convince Peter that coming to America had been the right decision.

'The research teams all think they are working alone. It is strange that they all started around four weeks ago, just as you did, Peter. We are struggling because we lack the human resources and computer speed to churn out the numbers. What we do have is the knowledge to get the job done, and I imagine that with the other four teams on board, we may just manage it,' Michael explained, his glass teetering precariously in his hand.

He continued, 'With you, we may do it, but it also depends on the other research teams. As individual teams, we won't achieve what we can achieve collectively. We will be more than the sum of our parts,' argued Michael.

Peter looked on and replied, 'You know, perhaps we could use the "The Cloud" to contain all our decoded information. We could then feed off each other that way, perhaps deciding which parts to do as well. What do you think?' he asked.

'"The Cloud" is not expedient for our needs. We require more space, more speed, more experts in relevant fields, and, ultimately, greater integration of the research teams,' Michael argued incisively. He continued, 'Even a fundamental understanding of genetics and DNA sequencing demonstrates that the sheer scale of the data, combined with the need for instant, low-latency collaboration, exceeds the capabilities of generic cloud services—especially when handling such intricate, classified, and evolving code. The research demands a private, purpose-built infrastructure, not a shared one. The reason is as basic as Genes 101.'

'101?' Peter retorted quizzically. His facial expression matched his question, revealing a man who had gone too long without encountering something he didn't understand.

'Yes, 101!' emphatically replied Michael. He continued, 'It's a fundamental requirement to achieve what we need to. Furthermore, in that meeting we spoke of earlier, the director of the NSA told me that there are shadow groups of researchers who would like to get hold of our work for deep state reasons.'

Michael took a slight pause before continuing, 'Their reasons are for power, not science; for the greed of the few, not the needs of the many. Our work should be for the betterment of our species, not for the benefit of a select group. If we are all in one place, we can ensure our work stays there. And the key thing is, they have computers there of such ridiculous speed.' Michael gushed about this fact with such enthusiasm.

His excitement resembled that of a young boy being presented with wonderfully wrapped birthday presents to open.

'Deep state? Shadow groups?' Peter started to think about his earlier conversation with Ann and the other strange oddities that had occurred recently, from the strange men in the parks to the feeling of being watched inside the restaurant.

'Kind of figures, I guess,' Peter remarked, though he hid his more worrying thoughts about the possible implications for the welfare and security of Ann and himself.

'No time for languor, Peter, oh no. Wait, I have forgotten something. I am so galvanised that I forgot to tell you something really weird about what they showed me.'

'Oh right, they showed you something too, did they?' an irritated Peter spoke, beginning to feel a second-rate player in all this.

'Yes, sorry about that, but listen. They have a computer that is so fast it mimics our cognitive processes. It thinks and evolves like us too. They have this crystal memory device that is so advanced that I was blown away. See, that's why I forgot,' Michael hastily replied.

He could see Peter's eyes begin to narrow, a familiar sign of stubborn irritation, just as they had during their earlier conversation in the University Parks.

'Go on!' Peter urged, clearly piqued and wondering why he was needed if the technology was so advanced.

'Okay, I'll be transparent. It's not just America, obviously; each team has been sanctioned to work with us, but they just don't know it yet. I regret your reaction, though it is understandable. Anyway, this goes all the way to the top, Peter, to the top,' Michael said with utter conviction.

'The top?' Peter enquired with an expression far stronger in bewilderment than his question conveyed.

'You think our universities really matter in the bigger picture? No, I don't think so. Why do you think the NSA called me in?' Michael emphasised.

Peter interrupted Michael. 'Called you in?' he huffed.

'Yes, called me in—I'm there, you're not. But I am sure from the way they spoke to me that it is going ahead. They have probably been in touch with governments to get us together. Peter, we are possibly the new Trinity!' Michael added, with the feeling that they were on the edge of a new dawn in science.

Peter looked on for a few moments, in thought, and to see if anything else could be interpreted from Michael's face or body posture. Nothing was perceptible, not even to his intuition. Consternation so fully enveloped Peter's thoughts that his mind momentarily went blank, needing a moment to process. His thoughts and erudition then returned, allowing him to explain the situation as he saw it.

'My concern lies not with the current research setup, but rather with the NSA's collective approach that is centralising it and overriding our governments' independent nature. This strategy replaces the unique diversity of independent research with monopolistic control, and in doing so, substitutes our self-determination and research sovereignty for a so-called 'national interest' that may be a misnomer for more nefarious undertakings. Ultimately, this may make us a de facto signatory to something we abhor.'

Michael looked back and recognised Peter's legitimate concern. 'I agree, the proposed centralisation of information is overriding our cherished independent nature, creating a monopoly on data access, and thereby replacing careful judgement with overconfident certainty. Yes, 'national interest' becomes a debatable term, implying it's a polemical justification for the NSA's actions. But the alternative, the status quo, means we progress slower, duplicate more, and erode the possibility of decoding the code which is our primary existential purpose.'

Michael could see Peter was still unconvinced by the proposal. He wondered whether the barrier was an unequal compromise between the logic of collaboration and his independence which he so revered in his world of dreaming spires.

Michael decided to carry on to encourage Peter to see the change as the way forward. 'Our work is time-limited. It makes sense that something that may affect all requires the action of all. We are all. Decode this Peter, collaboration is better than team isolation. I will ask you once again, as it's late and getting up later in the morning is anathema to me, as I am sure it is for all of us. Professor Peter Magma, esteemed research scientist, friend and adversary of large restaurant bills, are you in or out?'

Peter looked at Michael, his mind on what Ann and Nathan might say about the conversation and his impending decision. He also wondered whether the recent oddities would increase or decrease depending on his answer. With these thoughts weighing on him, he finally met Michael's gaze, ready to respond.

'As you say, Michael, it's getting late; we both need to be up early, so I will sleep on your question and answer you in the morning. I think I must speak to Ann too, as there are no secrets between us, and I don't see why I should start now.'

Michael looked away initially, but when he looked back, Peter noticed a quickly suppressed smirk, and wondered if this was a subconsciously inspired action that suggested Michael knew more.

In any case, it was time to retire to sleep, and Peter was acutely aware that the matter was too important to be settled with a tired mind. The day's events had left him weary, and his slightly bruised professorial ego was ready to rest. All of this could wait until he was fresh in the morning.

With tired minds and mouths weary from conversation, Michael raised his glass to Peter in a final, symbolic gesture that brought their talk to a quiet conclusion. 'To the morning, my friend!' Michael toasted.

- 32 -
A Rude Awakening

The phone's harsh ring shattered the quiet of Peter and Ann's bedroom, an intruder long before any sensible hour for waking. He'd been lost in a deeply emotional dream about Ann, one that laid bare the subtle but growing distance in their shared touch. Though their hearts were entwined, her deeper desire for intimacy went unspoken—a bewildering contrast to her vibrant and otherwise expressive nature.

A tired, sleepy Peter fumbled for the phone, his hand moving sluggishly across the bedside table. Through eyes heavy with sleep, he saw no sunlight, just the thick, impenetrable darkness held back by the bedroom curtains. Whatever the hour, it was certainly well before 5 a.m., the usual time for daybreak.

'Yes?' he strained, his voice a low, gravelly rasp. The unusual fatigue in his vocal cords stemmed from his extended conversation with Michael—a notable duration for someone who considered himself an embryonic sleeper of fathomless depth.

A strange, distant voice spoke from the receiver.

'May I borrow your car?' a man whispered, a strange voice both familiar and unfamiliar.

'What?' Peter said, struggling to shake off the powerful after-effects of being woken from a deep sleep.

The voice on the other end was a silken threat. 'Your Jaguar...such a pretty toy. Come to your window. Watch me drive it away.'

The sound that followed was unsettling, not quite a laugh but a dry, brittle crackle. It resembled the sound of something fragile and vital snapping within a long-dead tree branch—a sound designed to chill the blood and leave behind a residue of icy fear.

'Who is this? You twisted pervert!' Peter spat, his words a volatile mix of terror and fury. It was the desperate cry of a man violently ripped from a sleep as enveloping and peaceful as a baby's.

Panic clawed at Peter's throat, sharpening his voice into a desperate snarl. His fury was a brittle shield against the gnawing emptiness of the night—a profound loneliness amplified by the dark, the space between dream and wakefulness, and his own fragile state.

The line went dead, but the lingering buzz felt less like silence and more like the hum of a disturbed hive, a vibration of the unsettling intrusion clinging to the air. With the end of the call, a primal surge of anger coursed through him, igniting his fury like a wildfire threatening to consume his reason.

His rage exploded in a torrent of curses and motion. He slammed the handset against the bedside cabinet with such force the quiet air seemed to wince. The sound tore through the stillness like a jagged rip in a canvas.

The violation of peace and the shattering of the early morning quiet should have woken Ann. He glanced at his bedside clock, its bright numbers seeming to shout the time at him: 2 a.m.

The time burned into his memory, an indelible brand ensuring he wouldn't forget the call. He wished he had slammed the handset down on the clock, hoping to silence two annoyances at once.

Evidently, and quite correctly, he didn't like being woken, especially in the middle of the night. After all, he was a deep sleeper as much as a deep academic in thought and action. He rolled from his left side onto his back.

The phone rang again before Peter could even settle into his second-favourite sleep position. He considered ignoring this outrageously rude interruption but ultimately answered on the fourth ring.

'Yes!' Peter shouted.

The voice's irritatingly cheerful tone sent a fresh wave of unease. 'Thank you,' it chirped, the pleasantry a jarring violation. 'I'm about to drive it away.'

A beat of silence followed, thick with the unspoken image of Peter's prized possession disappearing into the night, driven by this unseen, untouchable entity. The voice remained a disembodied whisper, devoid of any discernible characteristic—a blank canvas onto which Peter's deepest fears could paint their most terrifying portrait.

'For God's sake!' he roared, slamming the handset down as if severing a physical link to the encroaching nightmare. Every fibre of his being screamed for the oblivion of sleep, a desperate retreat to the warm, silent centre of unconsciousness.

Yet, a colder, more insistent impulse—the ingrained curiosity of a scientist facing an inexplicable phenomenon—began to override the primal urge for comfort. He needed to verify the impossible, to ground the eerie disembodied voice in tangible reality: Was his beloved Jaguar still a solid presence outside?

A tremor of unease ran through him as he tentatively reached for Ann across the vast expanse of the super-king-size bed, his fingers brushing against empty sheets. She was a distant warmth, curled away on her edge, leaving him adrift in his growing fear—a stark reminder of his solitary confrontation with the unseen threat.

A sluggish reluctance clung to his limbs. His mind, still thick with the echo of the unknown caller's threat and the fading residue of sleep, wrestled with the arduous task of leaving the bed. A clumsy roll nearly sent him tumbling to the floor, but he saved himself with a last-minute, awkward flailing of limbs.

Driven by the insistent, gnawing dread that the disembodied voice spoke the truth, Peter finally hauled himself upright. His need to know outweighed the lingering pull of slumber.

He wobbled precariously towards the windows overlooking the driveway, his Jaguar's familiar silhouette his intended focus. Barely two unsteady metres from the curtains, a searing white light bled through the edges, followed by a deafening explosion that hammered against his eardrums.

The raw force of the blast slammed into the window he approached, instantly pulverising the glass into a vicious spray of razor-sharp shards.

The exceptionally thick, velvet-lined thermal curtains proved a miraculous barrier, saving him from a shower of glass that could have caused grievous, even fatal, wounds.

Yet, smaller, lethal shards still flew inwards, halting incredibly close to Peter's feet. Thrown onto his rear by the blast, he had been spared. Peter understood with a deep shudder the terrifying luck that had saved him from the worst of the impact on his lungs and ears.

A chaotic chorus of nearby car alarms shrieked through the night, jolting Michael and Ann awake and instantly disorienting them. On the floor, Peter coughed against the lingering pressure of the blast, a cold knot of anger tightening within him, his muscles spasming in involuntary shock.

A raw stab of fear twisted that anger into a desperate question: Ann? Was she alright? Why hadn't she come to him? Where was she? The sight of her and Michael purposefully entering the room hit him like a physical blow, a shock almost as profound as the blast itself.

This confirmed his deepest, unspoken dread in a visceral way. The air in the room seemed heavy, thick with unspoken implications, leaving him more profoundly winded than the blast.

'Get out the back, quickly!' Michael shouted, as he and Ann each grabbed one of Peter's arms.

All three descended the stairway as one, a silent pact of mutual support evident in their synchronised movements. Each mind acutely registered the unyielding strength of the solid oak doors, a bulwark against the bomb's violent fury.

They stepped into the elegant reception hall. An almost surreal tranquillity began to settle around them, creating a stark sanctuary.

However, this peace was sharply juxtaposed with the horrifying spectacle visible through the heavy frosted side windows: Peter's Jaguar, a raging inferno clawing at the glass.

The Jaguar burned with intense flames. Yet, the fire remained stubbornly within its confines. Occasionally, a muffled roar reached them—the sound of the "fire-breathing beast" fighting against the barriers that had miraculously held against the blast.

Escaping through the kitchen, they sat heavily on a bench that overlooked the conservatory. The air was rich with the scent of burnt rubber. Peter's eyes, wide and questioning, flickered between Ann and Michael as they settled onto the bench.

A silent question hung in the air: Why had they come into the bedroom together? The unspoken question added a layer of complexity to the already fraught situation, a subtle discord beneath the immediate terror.

The unspoken reason for them being together pricked at the edges of his raw nerves. Had they been chatting? Had Ann rushed to see if Michael was alright? These questions, for now, had to be set aside.

Getting to their feet, they began to walk towards the front of the mansion, their grim focus on the fiery aftermath of the attack. Soon, the high-pitched wail of emergency service sirens, a piercing sound, cut through the night air, growing closer with every second.

Upon arriving at the front, the iron gates were a reassuring sight—secure, closed, and undamaged. The same could not be said for Peter's Jaguar. It was a scene of devastation, blown open and engulfed in acrid smoke and flames, with several of the mansion's windows also blown inwards.

Peter ran over to a secure control panel near the gate. It was still working, and the gates creaked open as if groaning from the blast effects.

Michael and Ann looked on at the car, bewildered and angered in equal measure. Assaulted by this sight, their feelings sought comfort as they each held the other's hand while Peter rushed to the gates.

The imposing iron gates opened slowly, a wounded groan. Beyond the flashing blue lights of distant emergency vehicles, a more immediate and unexpected arrival came into view.

As if conjured from the shadows they had occupied during their covert watch, figures now moved with overt purpose. MI5 and NSA operatives, their earlier unseen presence giving way to urgent action, surged through the widening gap.

'Security Services!' they shouted, their priority clear. The glint from their shiny identification cards sparkled against the radiant glare of the burning Jaguar. Their primary purpose was to secure the immediate area, assess the injured, and administer first aid if possible.

This was a crucial first response, ahead of the incoming and speeding emergency services. Ann, Peter, and Michael exchanged bewildered glances at each other and at the rapidly approaching figures. Their sudden appearance added another layer of disorientation to the night's terror.

Another response was above the burning Jaguar. Overhead, the low, percussive chop of a helicopter and the higher-pitched, buzzing whine of multiple drones could be heard. The helicopter was using its thermal imaging camera to pierce through the darkness and smoke, searching for any heat signatures, particularly people and cars given it was early morning and not much activity would be expected. Below, the drones used thermal imaging and LiDAR, its silent, invisible pulses of light creating a three-dimensional map of the area as it hunted for threats or hidden individuals. Together, these technologies seamlessly created a comprehensive digital overview of the scene for the security personnel to analyse.

Back on the ground, the wail of sirens grew louder. The emergency ambulances came to a halt outside, maintaining a cautious distance beyond the gates out of respect for the volatile heat radiating from the Jaguar. The fiery beast

273

demanded to be quelled by the fire service before they dared to drive in.

The sound of the approaching fire engine offered hope. It signalled imminent help. Yet, the engine stopped short of the property, respecting the unseen boundary set by the security personnel. Firefighters, clad in their protective gear, moved with practiced efficiency.

A firefighter took action, deploying a large ABC dry chemical extinguisher and unleashing a suffocating white bloom of powder. It immediately targeted the fire's hungry base, which had erupted from the engine compartment, quickly knocking down the angry blaze fuelled by potential leaks.

Simultaneously, another team unspooled thick, heavy hoses. With the most intense flames now under control and the danger of flammable liquids contained, the fire crew transitioned to a wide spray of water, directing it in a sweeping arc across the driveway.

The deluge aimed to cool the superheated metal and ensure any remaining pockets of fire were extinguished. The fire's angry sizzle and snap surrendered to the relentless drumming of the water's assault against hot metal amidst rising clouds of steam.

The hissing and steaming remains of the Jaguar smouldered on the driveway. The fire crew maintained their focused attention on the wreckage. Ann and Peter, both visibly shaken, were gently guided by security service personnel towards the rear of the sprawling mansion. Michael followed close behind, an agent's hand resting gently on his back—a silent, supportive pressure guiding him forward. His own shock was evident in his pale face and hesitant steps.

Wrapped in thermal blankets, Ann and Peter responded in hushed tones, their words punctuated by shudders and the occasional reassuring squeeze of hands, finding a fragile comfort in their shared trauma and physical connection. Michael's replies were more withdrawn, his gaze often drifting towards the damaged front of the mansion, silently contemplating the night's terrifying turn.

The murmured questions from the security personnel, gentle but probing, sought to ascertain their well-being and gather initial accounts of the night's events. Michael watched them, a complex mix of emotions flickering across his features.

The manicured gardens, usually a source of tranquillity, now offered only a semblance of calm amidst the lingering tension. Soft light from the garden lamps created an unsettling peace, revealing long, dancing shadows and the worried expressions of the MI5 and NSA agents.

33

The Next Morning

Over the next 24 hours, the explosive situation yielded some clues, though nothing definitive. Exhaustive forensics and meticulous interviews of nearby residents provided vital information. This, along with the silent testimony of recovered CCTV traced through ANPR cameras, began to synthesise a clearer picture.

The emerging picture pointed squarely to another assassin who knew the mansion layout intimately. This wasn't merely a case of evading surveillance; he'd slipped through their digital and physical shadows with the chilling, practiced ease of a master illusionist, employing an extensive range of terrorist counter-surveillance tactics.

Crucially, the helicopter and LiDAR data, plus the mansion's thermal cameras and motion sensors hadn't detected anyone. The presumption was the bomber must have worn a military-level anti-thermal bodysuit and, even more remarkably, employed optical camouflage, probably made of metamaterial that bent or redirected light around him. To all intents and purposes, he couldn't be seen, his only sign a hazy displacement.

Security services swiftly stitched together his probable method. He had cunningly exploited the natural canopy of overhanging trees from a nearby garden, allowing him to bypass Peter and Ann's CCTV unseen—a galling blind spot they now bitterly acknowledged. Invisible to all sensors, he then moved to plant the deadly package, itself cloaked, beneath the Jaguar.

The chillingly impersonal calls, traced to a burner phone nearby served as a brutal testament to his intent: to lure Peter to the window and snuff out his life. The cheap, pre-paid mobile was a phantom device, meant for fleeting use and then cast aside, its digital trail erased into oblivion.

Despite the razor-thin precision of the attack, the sheer ingenuity of his methods delivered a stark warning, a grim testament to the pervasive, lethal danger all three continued to face.

Later that evening after dinner, they sat in the sprawling conservatory, their gazes hollow, drifting over the pristine, manicured back garden. Deep lines of exhaustion were etched onto their faces, a silent, stark tableau of shock within the guarded mansion.

The faint, acrid scent of disinfectant still clung to the air, a sterile counterpoint to the scorched, visceral memory of the fire that had savaged Peter's beloved Jaguar. Now, only a spectral outline marred the driveway. Repaired phone lines lay coiled on a nearby table, fragile threads attempting to reconnect them to a world that suddenly felt chillingly alien.

Around them, the quiet vigilance of security agents was a palpable weight, their presence a constant reminder of the shattered normalcy. Ann's gaze, heavy with unshed tears, lingered on Peter, the man she loved, the near-loss still a cold, raw knot of emotions in her being.

'What in God's name do you know, Peter, that could possibly cause this? Or is it you, Michael? Perhaps both of you?' Ann's voice grew with increasing ferocity, a desperate cry born of a profound inability to comprehend why they had become targets for a bomb. 'For God's sake, talk to me!'

The two men remained shackled, each within a silent, suffocating prison of fear.

'Peter!' Ann screamed, her voice raw. 'You're not dabbling in things you shouldn't, are you?' She pressed, an edge of harshness sharpening her tone. 'Tell me you're not... please? You know how this could unleash terror as it did to others in the past.'

'No, no, no,' Peter sighed, weary to his bones, every syllable infused with the grim certainty as if his life hung by a thread.

A flicker of Peter's usual analytical gaze reignited, though still ensnared by the simple, haunting question of "why?" As the tense minutes crawled by, marked only by a suffocating silence occasionally pierced by the distant murmur of police conversation outside, thoughtful reflections slowly coaxed their minds back from the brink.

The distant noise of police activity outside and the knowledge of Secret Service protection offered a fragile, desperate anchor as their minds began to grapple with reality. As their thoughts sharpened and became more calculating, Michael suddenly jolted alert.

'My wallet!' shouted Michael as he ran out of the conservatory to get it from upstairs.

'Wallet?' asked a bewildered Peter.

Michael shot across the room with a sudden, unbidden agility. Ann and Peter watched, dumbfounded. Where did this unforeseen burst of energy come from? More importantly, why such frantic exuberance over a mere wallet? Did it harbour a secret, something far beyond the mundane currency and plastic?

'Oh yes!' Ann exclaimed, highly agitated, the words tumbling out. 'The taxi driver gave Michael his business card for Michael's return journey. And Michael paid him with his own Harvard corporate credit card!'

Ann shot to her feet, bolting to the base of the stairway. A torrent of love and concern surged through her, though it went unnoticed by Peter, her gaze locked solely on Michael.

'Michael! Michael!' Ann cried out, a hysterical edge to her voice, her hand clutching the newel post as if for dear life. Her voice cracked, her lips trembled with a desperate urgency that demanded an instant reply.

'I'm here!' Michael's voice reverberated through the hall as he emerged at the top of the ornate stairway, his right hand briefly anchoring itself on the newel post.

'You haven't taken those cards out yet, have you?' Ann inquired, her voice teetering on the edge of mania, desperate for a negative answer.

'No,' he responded, his voice a calmer counterpoint to her urgency, 'they remain snugly nestled within my wallet.' A tiny, almost imperceptible wave of relief washed over Ann, her shoulders visibly relaxing. The cards were still there, still a potential key.

'Well, don't lay a finger on them just yet!' she shouted at Michael, the words erupting from her lungs despite him being only a few feet away. It was an unnecessary shout, a raw burst of urgency, yet the message struck him with undeniable force, cutting through his dazed state like a physical blow. He flinched, registering the sudden, absolute command in her eyes.

Ann seemed to mirror Michael's frantic energy, a spark igniting in her own eyes as if his urgency were contagious. Within 45 seconds, her petite yet curvy frame had streaked from the echoing hall, through the familiar warmth of the kitchen, and burst into the sunlit conservatory, a whirlwind of determination. Her movements were sharp, precise, utterly unlike the shock-weary woman of moments before.

279

'Here we go, problem solved,' Ann joked, a wry, almost morbid hint of dark amusement colouring her voice. She held up her finds like a magician revealing a trick: 'Two tools no self-respecting forensic psychologist – or, it seems, amateur sleuth – would be seen dead without; some small plastic gloves and a clear, credit card-sized plastic jewellery bag for the card.'

At this point, Ann raised her forearms, pulling the gloves down tightly with the focused precision of a surgeon. Peter watched, a thread of concern weaving through him at her professional movements, as if this were not the first time she had made such preparations.

'May I presume to ask just what you intend to do next?' Peter asked, a humorous lilt to his voice, his gaze on Ann a curious blend of insecure concern and playful curiosity.

'Call yourself an academic,' Ann teased, a sharp wit in her tone. 'I thought IQ stood for intelligence quotient. Perhaps in your case, right now, it should mean insecure quotient.'

She continued, 'Fingerprints, Peter, fingerprints. The taxi driver handled Michael's cards, didn't he? Perhaps there's some forensic evidence on them that could break this case wide open for specialists.'

'He touched my wallet, Ann,' Michael said, his voice tinged with regret, as if he held something so valuable he wished it remained untainted, fearful his own prints might have compromised the taxi driver's.

'Forget the wallet! It's your Harvard credit card that's pristine!' Ann gushed, almost breathless, her mind already racing with the thought of the crucial clue they had unearthed, one that had stymied every expert before them. 'Oh crikey, how incredibly lucky this could be!'

'Use these gloves to extract that card and then place it in this little bag,' Ann instructed Michael, pointing to the one slightly larger than the others she had brought in moments earlier.

Michael's gloved fingers fumbled awkwardly, struggling to grip the card. Just like yesterday, it was stubbornly embedded in its compartment. His trembling fingers were betraying him, making proper forensic removal an impossibility. This was no ordinary "grab and pull" card access.

Ann watched, and for the first time in over a day, a peal of laughter escaped her. The unfolding scene was absurdly comedic: a Nobel Prize winner growing increasingly exasperated, the simple act of credit card extraction, to her amusement, mocking him once again.

'I'm sorry, Michael, but I called that taxi driver a clown the other day. Obviously, he was anything but that, as I watch you now,' Ann exclaimed, a bemused smile playing on her lips.

She continued, her voice laced with amusement, 'Watching you fumble and bumble, wrestling that small, innocuous card from an even more unassuming wallet, is strangely captivating and funny.'

'This is a Gucci wallet,' Michael shot back, a hint of indignation in his tone. 'I'm not "fumbling and bumbling", as you put it. This is a delicate extraction operation, demanding precision and dexterity.'

'The fact is,' Ann asserted, her voice firm, 'you simply can't get it out.'

Michael was too mortified to confess he'd struggled with the card yesterday. He clung to the hope that its previous extraction would make it slide out with ease this time.

Ann slipped on a pair of gloves, then snatched the wallet from a palpably disconsolate and defeated Michael, her frustration evident. Without a moment's hesitation, she plucked the ignominious card free with effortless ease and tucked it into the designated jewellery bag.

Michael studied the taxi driver's business card. "HELIX TAXIS" was emblazoned across the top of the A8-sized card. Beneath it, beside a logo eerily reminiscent of a double helix structure, were the words: "we take you code to code."

By "code", Michael initially assumed they meant "postcode", but things were about to take a far stranger turn. He retrieved his iPhone and dialled the number on the card once, then twice, and finally a third time—each ring a desperate plea for luck. The persistent ringing, however, yielded only the flat, unwavering drone of a dead line.

The absolute silence on the line magnified his spiralling thoughts, and a dark, sinister interpretation of his taxi journey began to solidify. This "Trojan Horse" of a taxi had not merely driven into his life; its driver had infected him with a cognitive virus of chilling implications. His subsequent iPhone search for the 'HELIX' taxi service cemented his fears.

What had he truly expected, he mused? His fears were now reality: his search for the 'HELIX' taxi company confirmed no such service existed. Given his clandestine research into the codes embedded within the DNA double helix, the irony was bitterly poignant. Yet, a more immediate, tangible code beckoned: the potential fingerprint evidence now securely cradled within the clear jewellery bag, ready for handover to the security services.'

34

Super-Secret UAP To America

Fevered conversations between MI5 and the NSA led to a chilling conclusion: the professors—and their groundbreaking research—would soon trigger more devastating violence.

A fatal car crash in America. A hostage crisis aboard a jetliner. An attempted bombing at Ann and Peter's home. Each event shattered the illusion of safety. The professors weren't just in danger—they were targets. And if they were, so too was the public, now exposed to a rising tide of terror and psychological warfare that felt impossible to contain.

The looming spectre of impending terror left no room for hesitation. An immediate, covert extraction was no longer a choice—it was a dire necessity etched in cold reality. The professors had to disappear, vanish without a trace before chaos could claim them. At 4 a.m., cloaked in the silent shadows of night and flanked by armed police and military guards, they were spirited away beneath a shroud of unyielding secrecy.

Accompanied by Ann, Nathan, and the Oxford research team, they were immediately transported to the sprawling RAF Brize Norton. The base was a mere 13 miles from their Oxfordshire homes.

For maximum security, they were divided into four separate vehicles, each flanked by constant escort cars. They maintained a disciplined five-metre separation, a calculated buffer against a potential attack.

Above them, the helicopter's thermal gaze sliced through the darkness, relentlessly hunting for the faintest sign of danger lurking in the shadows. Silent drones, launched from a hidden military outpost, swept the route with unblinking LiDAR and infrared eyes, mapping every inch in spectral detail. Here, nothing was left to fate or fortune. In moments like these, extraordinary precautions were not just preferred—they were absolute protocol.

RAF Brize Norton, the UK's largest and most formidable airbase, was not merely a vast space; it was a sanctuary. Its sprawling grounds offered seamless accessibility for the professors and their intricate security detail, a logistical fortress that smoothed away every hurdle. More importantly, its remote isolation kept prying eyes and ravenous media at bay. This guaranteed the silence so crucial for the unprecedented operation about to unfold.

Intruders would face a formidable challenge in approaching unnoticed. Numerous trained and covertly positioned military personnel were now under orders to protect the airfield at all costs.

Their car slowed at a seldom-used, heavily secured entrance to Brize Norton. Imposing ten-foot steel fences, crowned with barbed wire, swung inward to grant them passage. Heavily armed guards then ushered them through, bypassing standard identity checks. Above and beside the gates, a bewildering array of different-sized cameras and intensely bright lights were visible. Laser motion sensors spanned the entrance road, creating a hidden perimeter leading directly to their aircraft.

After what seemed like several minutes from the entrance, their car slowed to a quiet stop. A second later, a heavily-armed military officer welcomed them. He was the Squadron Commander (SC) of 22 SAS 'B' Squadron, a man whose presence alone commanded absolute attention. He briefly explained that his extraordinary orders bypassed the Home Secretary entirely, coming instead directly from the Prime Minister's Office.

His superior, Major General Bohham—Director of Special Forces—had overseen the tense Boeing 787-9 Dreamliner operation just days ago. The authority of this command structure underscored the extreme importance of the current situation.

SAS troopers were to protect them while their transport was about to arrive. Though largely unseen, their presence was felt. Other armed military personnel were also in plain sight, but everyone's eyes were drawn to several well-dressed people walking towards them as the SC departed.

'Good evening, Professor Magma, Doctor Magma, and Professor Adams!' said a supercilious suited man.

'My name, and those of my colleagues, are unimportant. What matters is this: you are now under joint US/UK intelligence task force.'

'Q-Day?' Ann echoed, her voice sharp with disbelief. Michael gave a grave nod, saying nothing.

'Oh my God, someone else who knows more than I do,' Ann snapped, disdain and fresh bewilderment flooding her mind. Peter eyed Michael, and Ann, in turn, fixed her gaze on both. An unprecedented, urgent conversation was necessary; she needed to know what "Q-Day" was.

That need was obliterated by what appeared 500 metres above them: a triangular-shaped craft that became suddenly discernible. A low hum accompanied its ethereal glow. As it slowly descended, the humming intensified but not beyond a human whisper. Within each corner, a glowing sphere throbbed with a gentle rhythm.

Even in the night, the nearby airfield lights bathed the hovering craft in an intensity akin to daylight. This stark illumination revealed other strange oddities: no support legs were evident, nor any visible seams, doors, windows, or external propulsion of any kind. Yet, it hung just above the ground, perfectly still.

As the craft dropped to 50 metres, a strange electromagnetic shimmer pulsed through the air. Hair lifted subtly, frizzing in the charged atmosphere. For Ann, it triggered a memory—vivid and chilling—of the taxi driver whose hair had stood on end that terrible, unforgettable day.

Nathan's childish urge to speak first wasn't eloquent. He simply blurted, 'What the fuck is that?' A soldier nearby, alerted by Nathan's expletive, calmly turned towards him. 'That, mate,' he said coolly, 'is a classified transport craft. We call it the AGAT.'

Ann turned to Nathan, a clear desire to admonish him for prying into what was so obviously a classified aircraft. The soldier, however, waited a few seconds to let the criticism disperse in the slight wind before continuing.

'AGAT?' Nathan questioned.

'A term for Anti-Gravity Aerial Transport,' the soldier explained. 'The research boys like to give them their own names, the TR-3B.'

'Why are you telling me this? Aren't you supposed to be super-secret and all that?' Nathan asked nervously.

'Well, you've already seen it, and you'll be travelling in it,' the soldier explained.

After these few words, Nathan's attention was drawn back to the craft that had now settled just two feet from the ground, twenty metres from the nearest person. The research team stared in silent awe, while the assembled military personnel remained unfazed—they had clearly witnessed this before.

Before them hovered an equilateral triangle, each side an estimated 20 metres in length and standing about 10 metres high. The research team was utterly transfixed. The triangular craft's profound presence deepened their initial wonder into a profound bewilderment. Its complete lack of perceptible propulsion utterly defied their understanding of physics.

Peter, Ann, and Michael stood shoulder to shoulder with the research team, soldiers, and agents—each held in the same breathless suspense. Radios crackled softly with clipped orders. The craft's surreal presence had already stunned them, but now, attention shifted again. Something else was coming.

Their attention shifted towards the control tower as multiple cars appeared, their blue lights flashing insistently, demanding the notice of everyone present. In response, security and troops swiftly tightened what was clearly a security cordon, presumably for the new arrivals.

Just sixty seconds later, the distant entourage of cars finally pulled up between the assembled crowd and the security cordon. The craft continued to hover, utterly motionless.

Tyres screeched as the vehicles stopped and a flurry of manic activity erupted around them. If the whole situation wasn't surreal enough, it intensified as more security personnel emerged, closely followed by some very familiar faces.

'Good God!' exclaimed Ann, eyes scanning the arrivals. 'Isn't that the Prime Minister, the Home Secretary, and the Defence Secretary?'

She continued, 'And look at those military people over there. They all seem to like lots of red insignia.' She pointed at them with a note of mischievous wonder mixed with some concern in her voice.

'Those red collars are called gorget patches. It means they're senior officers,' explained Peter.

'I wonder if they're here for us,' Michael questioned, his voice thick with anxiety. Nathan's usual take on the matter was to follow his usual mantra: 'It's all worrying if you ask me. I'm not that important, but what you professors know must be. What merits all this cloak and dagger stuff?' His question sounded more rhetorical than one requiring an answer. As if compelled, he added, 'Anybody would think the end of the world was coming.'

'Yours might if you don't shut up,' said the soldier who had spoken to him before.

'Such doomsday scenarios are part of their daily thoughts,' critiqued Ann, her mind lost in the spectacle and now echoing Nathan's grim comment.

'Speaking of doomsday scenarios, Michael, they must know more than we do to put this show on,' Peter intriguingly suggested.

As they spoke, the shifting mosaic of noise and lights from the airfield invigorated their imaginations. The palpable tension of what was both visible and unseen gave the event an air of profound importance, making it feel like something truly momentous.

'Look, over there, it's our Chancellor Geoff Printon and Vice-Chancellor, Hubert Lee-Dowing,' Peter exclaimed, his voice thick with anxiety.

The situation was not helped as both chancellors now quite clearly walked towards them, smiling. They were accompanied by no less than the UK Prime Minister.

During the next ten minutes, hugs, kisses, approvals, and more were exchanged between all of them where appropriate, if at times excessive. Michael took a back seat on most of the social interaction.

As they spoke, military personnel prepared for something. Their conversation was stilted, with everyone looking away at the preparations going on 20 metres away.

The prime minister fixed her gaze on the three researchers, her voice steady but laden with weight. Both chancellors had long known the gravity of her words—a truth that sent a cold ripple through Peter, Ann, and Nathan.

She said, 'We've watched you for weeks, tracking every breakthrough you've achieved. And we know, with unnerving certainty, that what you're about to uncover surpasses even that.' Let there be no doubt: the stakes could not be higher.'

'The future of all of us is in your hands. Let there be no doubt. Before you go, I will tell you the reason for this security show and this "thing" here: nefarious forces are now at work who want what you know.

'It's as simple as that. Peter, Michael, you are the best in the world. We need both of you safe to help us counter whatever it is "they" have planned for you, and by implication, us. This craft will take you to America and your secret location in about 20 minutes.

'The other four research teams are in-bound there as well. I wish you well, all of you. If I see you again in this lifetime, you will have succeeded. God be with you, God be with all of us,' said the prime minister as she surveyed them all in deep appreciation and some foreboding for what was to come.

The prime minister's closing words hung in the air, a mix of hope and foreboding. The research team stood silently, as if their journey had taken on a divine significance.

And then, as if on cue, an opening appeared on the craft.

'All aboard!' humorously shouted Nathan with an intense grin.

'How can someone so smart be so dumb sometimes,' his friend muttered to himself.

'Can you believe this?' Michael said to Peter, his voice a whisper.

'It's beyond imagination,' Peter replied, shaking his head in disbelief.

'All the little hairs on the back of my neck are standing up, Peter,' Ann said. 'I'm so overawed with nervous anticipation.'

'Perhaps nerves, but it's this craft, or whatever you call it. It has some kind of electrical field around it,' Peter replied, noting the unusual effect on everyone's hair. Peter pointed politely towards a few of the research team whose hairstyles were dishevelled, and Ann couldn't help but smile.

'You're all right Peter,' she quipped, gesturing to the short hair around the sides and back of his head which now stuck out at right angles. She continued, 'You look like a mad professor!'

'He doesn't look it, he is,' Nathan quipped.

Ignoring Nathan's silly humour, Peter amateurishly half-hugged Ann as he said, 'I love your mercurial nature.' They were then ushered forward to the craft entrance by imperious secret service agents.

The modest entrance belied the craft's extraordinary nature. With precise efficiency, two military-issue personnel manoeuvred a custom-built, seven-step stair into place. Ann and Peter plunged into a hushed, urgent conversation, their voices barely rising above the hum of the craft's enigmatic systems. Meanwhile, Michael lingered slightly apart, silently wrestling with the swirling questions in his mind. He tried to make sense of the incomprehensible and grasp the purpose behind it all.

He thought that as the staircase was bespoke, it must have landed there before, or the steps were brought in advance for its inaugural journey here, if it was indeed its first. The latter idea, however, was discarded as quickly as it arose.

Ann and Peter were more concerned with where all this was leading, and not just the craft's ultimate location. The choreography was flawless as agents ushered them aboard.

She saw the VIP entourage being ushered back to their cars and noted something touching. The prime minister stopped and pushed her security back to turn fully around to look back at them. She waved and wiped tears from her eyes; Ann reciprocated both wave and tears.

As they neared the craft, what had been a scattered procession gathered shape. Step by step, they climbed into the unknown—toward a future none of them could predict.

Their hearts beat faster, and the strange hum that seemed almost imperceptible disappeared as they entered the craft. They each looked around in great awe, as if on a guided tour of what spacecraft might look like in the future.

Stepping inside, the group was directed by two craft attendants to their seats, the geometry of the space immediately captivating them. From the outside, the craft's sharp triangular silhouette gave way to a deceptively circular interior—a clever illusion of design.

The cabin was an exercise in minimalist elegance. Underfoot, hexagonal floor panels stretched smoothly, and walls radiated a soft, otherworldly glow. The entire space was cast in a gentle luminescence. At the periphery, a compact navigation hub pulsed quietly, its sparse controls standing in stark contrast to the complexity outside.

Several empty seats pointed towards a remarkably small number of controls. This stood in stark contrast to the almost infinite array of buttons that was standard for anything that flew. Two tubes, diametrically opposite the central hub, suggested a connection to another floor, while the passenger seats were located in the middle portion of the craft. They were arranged in a semi-circular pattern with two rows of five seats on either side.

The awe confronting the passengers before and during boarding was so profound that no words were spoken. Only the craft attendants, well-versed in directing boarding parties, spoke.

'Sit here and you'll be on your way soon,' superciliously commanded one of the two craft attendants. Nathan had other things on his mind. He just wanted to stand and drink in the excitement of it all. How he would have liked to go and sit near the ridiculously small number of controls, if that's what they were.

The excitement not only surged through every part of his being, but it was felt by all. The attendants, however, just stood vacantly by the tubes, awaiting someone or something.

Then a bizarre sight unfolded for those facing it: an area that seemingly connected to a floor above. Three people descended, dressed not in shiny, alien-like suits, but in ordinary attire with clearly American accents.

'Welcome!' said the first person, a woman who looked plain yet possessed a distinguished, commanding presence.

'I can only but guess what you must be thinking right now. Let me first tell you that you are not in any danger, as otherwise I would be first out the door,' she said, mocking herself. She then continued, 'Please call me commander, that's all. My two flight assistants have no principal role for you, only for me.'

With this brief explanation aside, they walked ten metres across and sat by the controls the team had seen upon entering the craft.

The commander glanced over the group, a mischievous glint in her eye. 'No seatbelts needed—I have a license to speed,' she quipped. Laughter rippled through the cabin, breaking the tension. Even she couldn't help but giggle.

'You know you're the first civilians to travel like this. Talk if you like, we'll be at your location in about 15 minutes,' she added.

'Would you like to see where we're going?' she asked teasingly, a mischievous glint in her eye. 'Yes!' came the synchronised, unified chorus from the passengers. A ripple of excitement and nervous anticipation coursed through them. As they looked everywhere for a monitor to see their progress, a sense of fresh speculation sparked in their minds, but none were in evidence. Exclamations of awe were heard as the craft became transparent.

'Oh my God, oh my God! I don't like heights,' shrieked Ann.

'Awesomely crazy guys, just so not right,' exclaimed Nathan. He brazenly continued with a touch of side humour,

'Where's the buffet for this real movie show?' Overcome with embarrassment, Ann slapped her forehead and regained vertical composure.

'When did we take off?' Michael asked. 'I didn't feel the inertial force of acceleration during lift-off.'

'Where has this kind of tech been hiding?' Peter whispered, awestruck.

'Why does everyone say that the technology?' Nathan quizzed. The whole unfolding episode made him recall the books he had read about so-called super-secret technology— the kind of secrets that were, of course, widely known. Blurring the line between thought and speech, he blurted, 'never heard of Area 52, recovered alien craft, reversed engineering?'

'I think you mean Area 51, Nathan,' corrected Ann. 'Do you know where it is?' she asked.

Nathan felt somewhat patronised. He had meant to say Area 51, but was so awestruck by what he saw that his mind briefly fumbled the number. He felt an inward despair, as if he had self-harmed his mind by being in error. He rubbed his forehead as if to rub away his error.

He retorted sarcastically, 'Of course I know where Area 51 is, it's next to Area 52.' Ann looked on with an innate urge to slap her forehead again.

During this banter, Michael, too, had been overawed by the vision of Earth.

'I feel like I'm having an existential crisis,' said Michael as the Earth appeared below them.

His words articulated what others felt inside. Several members of the team stood up and watched as the Earth moved beneath their feet. A sense of wonder took hold, and each person instinctively pointed at the familiar geographical areas coming into view. Below them were distant seas, vast oceans, towering mountains, and swirling clouds. The sheer scale of this orbital-level magnificence was breathtaking, and they longed to imprint every moment onto their memories.

Ann looked at Peter with an expression that was almost sacred, almost divine.

'Peter, can you feel it?' whispered Ann, in an almost ethereal tone.

'Yes...yes I can,' replied Peter, absorbing every visceral moment. A powerful wonder and bewilderment resonated between them. Below was Earth, a vibrant mosaic of kaleidoscopic colours dancing on its oblate surface.

Each view announced nature's spirit, a planetary platform to discover the universe. Against the infinite vastness of space, their place in the heavens appeared vastly small.

Ann moved close to Peter, gently taking his hand. This was more than a moment in spacetime; it was all sensory moments imploding inside them at once.

Having satisfied their curiosity, the commander descended the craft back into the atmosphere. Re-entry posed no problem, as the craft was surrounded by a force field that distorted spacetime, meaning it didn't experience friction.

Peter and Ann, along with the other research team, experienced no inertia at all from the craft's almost vertical ascent above the Earth. Its subsequent descent towards the north-eastern seaboard of the United States was no less thrilling. It began with a final plunge through the upper atmosphere.

The craft slowed its impossible speed. At 20,000 feet, the vast, shimmering expanse of Hudson Bay stretched to the horizon like a steel-grey ocean.

Everyone watched the visual feast unfold before them. This was no ride they had ever experienced before—nor would they likely experience it again. Michael was particularly absorbed, his mind racing to remember every shade of colour and every contour of detail. The craft moved gracefully, with no sensation of movement—nothing but a perfect sense of levelness.

He had lived in America and travelled into Canada many times, but seeing it through a plane window was nothing compared to this immersive, sense-surround experience. Just when he thought it couldn't get any better, Ann came up beside him, noticing his total absorption in the scenery.

'That's Hudson Bay,' he murmured. 'Looks calm from up here. But it's brutal in winter.

Ann joined him, arms folded tightly. 'It's almost... prehistoric,' she said, her voice low. 'Makes you wonder how untouched land like that still exists.' The shoreline below sharpened, giving way to the boreal forests of northern Quebec—an endless sea of green beneath a gauzy blanket of cloud. Glacial lakes glinted like broken shards of glass scattered across a canvas.

Michael tapped the wall. 'You see those lakes? Glacial meltwater—thousands of years old. That whole region was sculpted by retreating ice sheets.'

'You and your obsession with ice ages,' Ann teased, though her tone carried admiration. 'Social history rarely goes back that far. My timelines feel primitive next to yours.'

He chuckled. 'Says the woman who can quote 14th-century tax rebellions from memory.'

Below them, the deep Saguenay Fjord carved its jagged path into ancient rock. It fed into the Saint Lawrence River—a thick, winding band that looked almost too big to be real.

296

'There,' Michael said, pointing. 'Saguenay Fjord. Glacial again. And that's the Saint Lawrence River—it's basically an inland sea.'

Ann tilted her head, tracing the contours of the river. 'So much power in a single waterway. Entire nations were built along rivers like that. Trade, conquest, culture... all of it follows the water.'

Over southern Quebec, the dense forest gave way to a patchwork of hills, farmland, and small towns. Civilisation crept back into the landscape, stitched gently into the wilderness.

'Southern Quebec,' Michael narrated softly. 'Montreal isn't far from here. I lectured at McGill once—never thought I'd be flying over it in a spacecraft shaped like a triangle.'

'Give it time,' Ann said with a half-smile. 'Soon your lectures will be delivered via hologram from orbit.'

They crossed into Vermont. Below, the Green Mountains rippled across the landscape, rolling highlands cloaked in dense forest. To the west, Lake Champlain coiled between Vermont and New York, the distant Adirondacks brooding beyond.

Michael pointed eagerly again. 'Green Mountains. And there's Lake Champlain—absolutely gorgeous in autumn. The kind of place you think about retiring to... until you remember the winters.'

Ann laughed. 'You say that like you're getting out of this alive and early.'

As the craft banked east into New Hampshire, the rugged White Mountains loomed below—Mount Washington stabbing skyward through scattered cloud.

'That's Mount Washington,' Michael said, his tone quieting. 'Tallest peak in New England. The weather up there is so wild, they say it can change five times in an hour.'

'To think,' Ann said, eyes fixed below, 'centuries of people lived and died in those mountains—completely unaware of what we're seeing now.'

To their right, the Connecticut River wound south, marking the Vermont-New Hampshire border. Then came Interstate 93, a thin grey line cutting through the trees like a surgical scar—pointing the way to Boston and beyond.

'Modern veins,' Ann muttered. 'Highways instead of rivers. Concrete in place of culture.'

Michael looked at her sideways. 'There's a paper in that.'

'There's always a paper in that,' she said.

The commander cut into their conversation, informing everyone that the craft was nearly there.

It began its smooth descent. The green sprawl of the White Mountain National Forest unfolded beneath them—dense, endless, and seemingly untouched. Valleys and ridgelines wove through the landscape like secrets buried in foliage.

'White Mountains again,' he said. 'Most of that's protected wilderness. We could land an army down there and no one would know.'

'Looks like someone already did,' Ann replied, as camouflaged structures came into view—barely visible beneath the thick tree canopy.

Below them, nestled deep within the wilderness, the NSA facility waited. Silent. Hidden.

Michael exhaled. 'End of the line.'

Ann turned to him. 'No, it's just the beginning.'

- 35 -
The Facility

A blur of impossible speed, the TR-3B arrived, hovering over the clandestine facility hidden deep within White Mountain National Forest, New Hampshire. Scarcely any time had passed; the 4,000-mile distance from Brize Norton had vanished in just 20 minutes.

The journey could have been completed in mere minutes, had it not been for the deliberate sightseeing that had prolonged their arrival. The TR-3B, a marvel of speed, began its invisible, silent descent, settling over a large, perfectly round aperture that had opened in the earth. This colossal silo, nestled on the edge of a one-square-kilometre facility, was carved from the forest floor. The site, which also housed a runway and a helicopter pad, was not secret, but its true purpose was highly classified.

As the craft lowered vertically into the hole, it landed on something reminiscent of a platform. The slight external hum from the craft stopped. Seconds later, the platform took over their controlled descent.

Those with keen perception observed small lines on the very large, shiny tubular wall that identified measurements in blocks of 10. Based on these metrics, their slow descent in the silo seemed to be about 200 metres deep. Suddenly, it stopped and the walls transparency turned opaque, cutting off their view of the outside world.

The research team, a collective of awe-struck minds, remained on their feet, rooted in childlike wonder. Though asked to return to their seats minutes earlier, they remained utterly captivated by what they had seen since the vessel's walls had first melted into transparency.

The sheer, boundless enormity of space had somehow ignited an echoing vastness within their very minds. Their rigid, academic view of the universe suddenly felt small, and for a fleeting moment, a new, holistic depth of understanding pulsed through them. This profound shift would have to wait for full contemplation; the urgent imperative of disembarkation beckoned.

The three-flight crew had long since completed their duties and were clearly chatting about something unusual. No doubt they had enough stories from "out there" in space to fill a book every time they flew a craft of this kind. The commander broke away from her conversation to address the team.

'As I said it would be about 20 minutes, and it was,' exclaimed the commander, somewhat proud of her efforts.

'I know I saw it, but are we really here, in America, in just 20 minutes?' Nathan responded as if common sense itself had been violated. 'It's not some elaborate hoax?' he continued.

'Nathan, we all saw it, so believe it,' interrupted Ann. He was clearly on a mission to distance his thoughts from this new reality.

Looking towards the opening door, the commander smiled wryly and indicated the team should disembark in the same way they boarded: orderly and patiently. As they stepped off the craft, the same feeling of hair being pulled towards it occurred. Peter led the way.

As he stepped down the six steps from the craft, he guessed correctly: the Director of the NSA, along with other senior staff and flight associates, were in attendance. The flight associates, however, seemed more interested in ensuring readings from the craft were within acceptable limits as he heard one say to another.

'Peter, my old academic friend, nice to see you again after all these years!' exclaimed Dr. Denton, director of the NSA. His imposing, almost seven-foot frame was as formidable as his position.

'If you've got any spare ones, the aircraft industry will be crying their eyes out,' joked Peter, before he added, 'Director, it's a privilege and an honour to be treated this way, thank you.' Dr. Denton thanked Peter with a knowing smile of appreciation, then his attention shifted to the other esteemed scientists. They had fallen in behind Peter, waiting in a single file.

'Professor Michael Adams, it's nice seeing you again. I'm pleased you've taken up our generous offer. I forgot to say at the time, so I'll take the opportunity now to say how very sorry I was to hear about your wife, Victoria. She was a great executive assistant to me.'

'Thank you,' Michael replied. 'I remember Victoria's diligence in helping you; she often stayed late. It caused me a few headaches, but with the NSA, I let it slide; I was busy too. Like you, I never had the chance to say that I remembered you from Oxford. How could I not?' He scanned Denton, his gaze traveling from his feet to his face, a brief, silent inventory of his imposing height.

Denton looked slightly troubled as he pondered Michael's words, or perhaps it was simply Michael's scrutinising gaze.

'Yes, Oxford. I was reading molecular mechanics, and we found some correspondence between that and DNA mechanics,' Denton replied with a slight, reserved sheepishness, glancing at Peter concurrently, as if some mystery existed between all three of them.

'Oh yes, I remember,' Michael replied, but his words trailed off. Denton, without a moment's hesitation, had already turned to the person behind him. A wave of surprise washed over Michael as he was so abruptly dismissed.

Denton's gaze slid past Michael and settled on Ann. A low chuckle escaped his lips. 'And who is this, or should I ask?'

'Hello Ann,' Denton beamed, stepping forward to shake her hand—a gesture that seemed to linger for a little too long.

'Hello Stanislaus,' Ann said, and the simple greeting instantly captured his complete attention. He released her hand and leaned in for a brief hug.

Peter looked on incredulously. A challenging cascade of mistrust began to grow within him. His brow furrowed in confusion; how had she never mentioned knowing him before? Was this the same Ann he'd been married to for years, yet had never mentioned him, even once?

Denton bent his knees and hunched slightly to embrace Ann, who seemed tiny compared to his height. He seized the fleeting, opportunistic second to murmur something intimate into her ear. As they parted, a shared, knowing smile bloomed between them. Peter, who was watching, saw a faint blush bloom across her cheeks, a silent admission that something had flattered her.

Peter looked on, trying hard to remain calm. Inside, he was in a full-blown emotional eruption.

'Stanislaus?' Peter snarled softly with gritted teeth.

To everyone else, this merely looked like another welcoming handshake and hug. Yet, for them both, the warmth of their reunion betrayed a deep emotional history. For just a few seconds after the hug—though it could have been an eternity—their eyes locked. Pulses quickened, hands gently perspired, as their emotions were drawn into a dizzying vortex.

'Stanislaus?' Peter hissed, the name a low sound from between his gritted teeth.

'Yes, Stanislaus,' Ann snapped, her voice sharp with annoyance.

Ann felt giddy after Stanislaus's hug and whispered comment. The fact that Ann had never mentioned him before, yet Michael had been aware of him for years through his wife's employment, heightened Peter's confusion and mistrust.

A sudden flash of intuition caused Peter to recalibrate his ideas about Ann, realising she had a mysterious past. At that moment, Peter made a critical decision: by the end of the project, no matter how long it might take, he would unpack this romantic code too.

Denton welcomed each of the remaining seven research team members, including Nathan, who stood out as Ann's son. Just as he had with Ann, he greeted Nathan slightly longer than the others.

'And you must be Nathan?' Denton asked.

'The one and the same, Dr. Denton,' replied Nathan. 'If I may say, I have craved the chance to finally step foot in an NSA facility. Even better, I'm serving it now. After years of pleading and vying for this opportunity, I've finally made it to the top. Thank you.'

'I won't even bother to ask if you're happy to be here; I think I already know,' Denton chuckled.

'After all this, perhaps I can remain?' Nathan subtly probed.

'I think that's a conversation for later; for now, prove your worth and the rewards may materialise,' Denton intoned with a wink in his eye.

'Just watch me,' Nathan taunted.

'I couldn't miss you if I tried—just glance up there,' as Denton gestured to several CCTV cameras in the corner ceiling. He then gave Nathan a strange look, as if trying to memorise every contour of his face for some later comparison.

'Right, must move on,' Denton stated abruptly, already striding toward his next introduction. 'Speak again.'

Introductions out of the way, they were all swiftly driven in open-topped, jeep-like cars for about five minutes to the main reception area. Here, long tables groaned under the weight of an unexpected bounty of food and drinks, a welcoming sight after their extraordinary journey.

'Ladies and gentlemen!' loudly exclaimed Dr. Denton. 'Welcome to this underground NSA facility of ten floors... for those of you who didn't notice.' He paused for the expected chuckles, which eventually came. 'In this facility is everything you need, courtesy of your UK government as well as ours. Later, I will give you a guided tour of this extensive facility, which is protected against all foreign and domestic invaders. The rationale for this will be explained later. Soon you will meet the other research teams who will aid and collaborate with you in guiding our mission. We have provided you with the very best accommodation.

'I hope you don't get too comfortable here. The reason is this: we really need you in the laboratories and other parts of this research facility. Your task is to figure out a biochemical maze of such complexities that even the President couldn't decipher.' The chuckles now erupted into full-blown laughter at the absurd juxtaposition: such profound complexities aligned with the President's status as "Commander in Chief". The amusement was infectious.

'Everywhere is surveyed by our cameras. We record every action, every reaction. Wherever you go, our security shadows you. It's for your own protection, of course, and to ensure we retain every secret you unearth.'

'Finally, remember, you are here at the behest of your respective governments, with their full and undivided cooperation,' Denton announced. 'Enjoy your stay, enjoy your research more, and please do not hesitate to ask our staff for anything you may need. Thank you.'

And with this, Dr. Denton walked off in thoughtful discussion with a well-dressed woman. They exited through two large, open main reception doors to attend another meeting. As they walked to it, their conversation was animated, if slightly tense.

As buffet items dwindled, a surge of conversation swelled between the gathered scientists and senior staff. The exchange of information regarding their roles expanded, hinting at what was to come. Research expectations soared, and their potential global impact loomed large. The world-changing gravity of their mission now came into sharper focus.

36

Denton's Inaugural Forum Speech

The research teams, a confluence of brilliant minds, entered through several doors and converged in an expansive, circular forum where the air pulsed with anticipation. Its walls, not of stone or metal, but of pure light, shimmered with an inherent luminosity, bathing the vast space in a soft, pervasive brilliance.

This majestic forum was divided into two distinct parts. The front platform, a raised dais, featured seating for about 30 people. To the right of the dais, positioned so as not to obstruct the view, stood a magnificent, polished lectern.

In front of this platform, six separate seating areas were arranged in a semicircle, ensuring every team had an uninterrupted view and a unified focus on the platform. This thoughtfully arranged seating plan wasn't merely for organisation; it was a silent invitation, fostering immediate visual engagement and an almost telepathic collaboration.

Peter guided the British contingent to their designated area. A collective, knowing smile spread across their faces, as they were transported back to their university days, the atmosphere buzzing with intellectual camaraderie. Meanwhile, Michael led his hand-picked Harvard team to their area, his gaze fixed on Peter's, deliberately choosing a seat directly across from his counterpart to facilitate private conversation. The American contingent was a mosaic of diverse expertise that perfectly complemented the British researchers.

Each researcher marvelled at their desks, masterpieces of polished oak with seamlessly integrated microphones, which offered both crystal-clear audibility for public discourse and a discreet option for private deliberations. Yet, it was the panel that commanded attention. Perched atop the pristine surface was a darkened, elevated, ultra-slim screen, angled with a precise thirty-degree incline towards its occupant. Its surface was a deep, light-devouring black—a perfect, unsettling void that seemed to absorb every stray photon, hinting at the advanced technology pulsating beneath its surface.

Just 15 metres ahead and five metres above the dais, an awe-inspiring spectacle unfolded: a seamless, interconnected ring of colossal screens materialised, forming a continuous, luminous band that enveloped the circular forum in a breathtaking display of technological prowess. Directly above the sector reserved for the facility's senior members, a larger, prominent screen punctuated the otherwise unbroken circle, subtly asserting its focal point. This thoughtful design underscored the room's true purpose: a dynamic, immersive forum for crucial discussion.

'Impressive,' Michael murmured, settling into his seat and taking in the breathtaking expanse of the forum.

'Certainly is,' Peter agreed, a curious frown creasing his brow. 'Where on earth are the lights, though?'

'Damn, you're right,' Ann conceded, her eyes scanning the luminous walls. 'No idea, but I'm suitably impressed myself.'

'I recognise some of the Indian team,' Peter observed, nodding as two members offered a friendly wave from across the forum. They had forged a connection during their previous collaboration on a project in Geneva.

'Good grief, it's Reyansh!' Peter burst out, waving wildly as recognition shot across the cavernous forum. He was greeting his former PhD student—a singular intellect who had not merely engineered, but pioneered ground-breaking algorithmic and cryptogenetic equations. Across the room, Reyansh met Peter's gaze, a warm smile and a subtle gesture promising a conversation later.

Meanwhile, Ann observed the unfolding scene with professional detachment. While the scientific intricacies lay outside her immediate specialism, her incisive capacity for evaluative thought was paramount. As an esteemed historian, she was acutely aware of her solemn duty to meticulously record these unprecedented events for posterity—assuming, naturally, that posterity would even exist.

As the assembled teams engaged in a hum of whispered conversations, punctuated by recognition of familiar faces from other teams and friendly waves, Dr. Denton entered. He was flanked by several grim-faced associates, their demeanour casting an immediate pall over the room. Sensing the arrival of their funders and overseers, a hush descended upon the researchers—a stillness so absolute it was later described as "apocalyptic".

Dr. Denton tapped his microphone twice, the sharp clicks echoing through the now silent forum, before asking, rather coldly, 'Can you all hear me?'

Nathan's immediate impulse was to blurt out, 'Pardon!' He swiftly suppressed it. Such childish retorts, he concluded, were best consigned to the annals of history.

Dr. Denton's gaze swept across the assembled forum, a penetrating look, much like a teacher assessing attendance, before he finally began to speak.

'My brilliant colleagues, welcome to Project Helix. My sincere gratitude goes to Professors Adams and Magma for agreeing to lead this unprecedented venture into the genetic unknown. Moreover, I thank them for their incredibly insightful work and the detailed initial analysis. And to the other teams, your research has been profoundly helpful as well. I'm genuinely delighted you are here, and I'm looking forward to collaborating with all of you.

'Let there be no doubt,' he continued, a rare, welcoming smile softening his features, 'about the immense challenge inherent in this endeavour with which we have been honourably entrusted. I'll begin by presenting my core message.'

He then underscored the absolute necessity of Peter and Michael's joint leadership for the project's success. Beyond their roles in guiding the exploration and deploying advanced algorithms to navigate DNA's dynamic landscape, they were also tasked with the critical responsibility of meticulously sequencing all the research data across all teams – a formidable undertaking in itself.

'I will provide details now,' he explained, 'some of which you may already be familiar with.' His primary aim, however, was to clearly establish their current research position and collective direction, ensuring a singular purpose. Following this, he would present a holographic tutorial designed to build upon his speech. This tutorial, he believed, would perfectly encapsulate the project's pivotal leadership, the transparent decoding process, and how their disparate tasks would converge into a unified team effort.

'Let's begin,' he declared.

'Professors Adams and Magma's initial findings, meticulously integrated with the research from other teams and analysed using advanced computational methods, have already yielded a number of crucial decoded messages. But this is only the start.

'In brief,' he summarised, 'our decodes suggest that our genetic code contains a profound message—one that points to an impending change for all of humanity. A biological singularity, if you will. The transformation is embedded so deeply, it almost looks like a manufacturer's stamp.' He paused, letting the gravity of his words sink in. 'What's more, the decodes subtly hint at a new evolutionary path for our species. Exactly what that path entails, however, remains unclear at this time.

'To achieve our research objective,' he continued, 'your collective research has been precisely focused on the enigmatic DNA regions once dismissively labelled "junk"— now more accurately called non-coding DNA—and on the thousands of recurring "switch" elements found exclusively within our species. We believe these hitherto unexplained components are intrinsically linked to a monumental future event: the "Day of Quanta", or simply, "Q-Day".

'At the heart of interpreting this code lies an evolutionary gift—a profound legacy from the past that now guides our understanding for today and illuminates our path into a tomorrow we hope exists.

'This evolutionary gift lies in the profound shifts brought about by tiny chemical modifications to our DNA— specifically through methylation, a key epigenetic process that modifies gene expression without altering the genetic code itself. These subtle changes serve as a vital key to understanding how our mental health, intelligence, and prosociality—to name but a few—have dynamically shifted over time, directly shaping our attitudes and observable behaviours.

'The likelihood of these precise shifts arising randomly across vast evolutionary timescales is a staggering trillions to one, which unequivocally rules out pure chance. We are profoundly confident that these alterations contain a window of understanding—a coded key, if you like—poised to reveal the deep, secret information intricately woven into our genetic make-up.

'Our most significant breakthrough, colleagues, is the revelation that the very act of accessing DNA is inherently linked to the universe's omnipresent energy fields. These fields subtly influence all biological forms through a constant, yet incredibly subtle, quantum resonance.

'This isn't about discovering novel particles; rather, it's a profound exchange of information at the smallest scales. We are convinced this process directly influences the biophotons we have now successfully detected.

'Simply put, biophotons are incredibly faint emissions of light generated by all living cells and organisms. They are not merely a byproduct of heat, but instead originate from the intricate biochemical reactions occurring within us to facilitate rapid, internal cellular communication. We firmly believe these exquisitely subtle light signals, modulated by quantum resonance, are a crucial component of this overarching phenomenon, which I will elaborate on shortly.

'Indeed,' he affirmed, 'speaking of resonance, we know that minute structures within cells, known as microtubules, possess the capacity to operate at a quantum level. This is absolutely critical. The phenomenon of quantum entanglement—how information can be transferred between them instantly, regardless of their physical distance apart—is central to understanding how quantum information operates within biological systems, potentially even within these very microtubules.

'And crucially,' he added, 'this understanding intertwines with our evolving concept of quantum consciousness, which posits that consciousness is not an emergent property of brain function but rather originates externally. It enters the brain to interact, producing what we call reality. This is a profound reversal of conventional thought.'

Denton, who had been fluidly reading from the teleprompters positioned to his left and right, abruptly halted. For a fleeting moment, a distinctly glazed, distant look transfixed his face. As if a complex thought had fragmented into countless pieces, his eyes swept across the room, meticulously gathering them back together. A faint smile touched his lips.

'Esteemed colleagues,' he stated, his voice now imbued with a profound sense of revelation, 'our decodes and our understanding, as they stand, suggest we may be on the verge of something extraordinary.'

He scanned the faces before him once more. The profound, unwavering focus that had gripped every listener wavered only momentarily at his startling revelation, its staggering implications far too vast to be immediately processed. Yet, Dr. Denton's extemporaneous departure from his prepared notes was entirely justified, his candid interjection utterly understandable given the profound and unprecedented gravity of the situation. He then resumed his address.

'We now know,' he continued, 'quantum information is meticulously processed by all living systems. This occurs at the most fundamental level of cellular and molecular interaction, potentially generating or influencing those ultra-weak biophoton emissions I hinted at earlier. So, how precisely does all this background information relate to our project?

'As I introduced earlier, biophotons are fundamental to this. They interact directly with DNA, which acts as both a primary source and receiver of these ultra-weak light emissions. These biophotons are unique in their patterns to every individual—truly a biophotonic fingerprint.

'Thus, as DNA's unique biophotonic patterns serve as crucial emission signatures, they provide unprecedented information about its underlying structure. This transcends mere mapping; it's about interpreting DNA's intrinsic language, the profound code that drives all its operations. Even the dynamic conformational changes of DNA – its twisting, bending, and unwinding – emit biophotons, offering us direct insight into its operating instructions.

'And crucially, it contains holographic information about the organism's entire genetic blueprint. Every single cell holds within it a complete, three-dimensional representation of the entire being—a cosmic library in miniature.

'Within this facility, as I described earlier, we are meticulously measuring and correlating these complex, multidimensional patterns of emitted biophotonic light. This includes their intensity, spectral distribution, coherence, polarisation, and spatial symmetry. Our goal is to reverse-engineer the quantum processes that led to these collapsed patterns.

'These biophotons, and the quantum resonance driving them, possess a distinct and measurable connection to the junk regions of DNA. Within this symphonic connection resides the master switch code, the code of codes—and within that master code is the "Q-Day" code we seek.'

Again, he paused, breaking from his prepared notes, a flash of wry, sharp humour lighting his expression.

313

'You know, we've spent decades looking for the blueprint for life, and it turns out the entire universe came with a note that said, 'Some assembly required,' he quipped, a distinct twinkle in his eye. This time, a ripple of genuine, light laughter spread through the assembled teams, researchers exchanging glances as if a subtle, shared force had indeed prompted their collective amusement.

'Anyway,' he continued, a renewed seriousness in his tone, 'I can now definitively confirm that biophotons and quantum states are precisely where our most profound and promising breakthroughs are occurring.

'And with this critical focus comes the absolute necessity for immense computational power—the incredible processing speed required to decipher these intricate exchanges of information.

'So, why do we require significantly more quantum computing power, beyond merely its incredible speed?' he posed. 'The information inherent within these quantum field interactions, meticulously processed by DNA via biophotons, exists in a state of quantum coherence – meaning it is fundamentally probabilistic and constantly fluctuating, a phenomenon known as superposition.

'This, I assure you, is the absolute core of our decoding process, a monumental undertaking that is akin to attempting to reverse-engineer the universe's own concealed algorithms.' Denton stated, his voice now imbued with a profound sense of revelation.

'Biophotons weren't merely biological byproducts but were ultra-weak, flickering emissions of light that carried the complete, holographic quantum signal of life itself. The facility's instruments were built to do the impossible, to capture and measure these complex, multidimensional patterns of light, treating every nuance as a vital piece of a cosmic puzzle.

'The true breakthrough, however, lay in the quantum computers. The biophotonic light, a true quantum signal, existed in a state of superposition—a cloud of infinite probabilities. The quantum processors were tasked with an act of pure will: forcing these fluctuating states to collapse into a single, stable pattern.

'From this fixed quantum pattern, the world's fastest conventional supercomputers took over. They were no longer just processing data; they were translating it. Each stable pattern became a word in a language that had been waiting for us all along. They were converting pure information, born from the deepest biological processes, into a profound, comprehensible message—the very code we sought.

'Each individual component of each "letter" alone demands approximately ten minutes of dedicated quantum processing to transition from its fluctuating state to a stable, comprehensible pattern. Once meticulously rendered, this pattern must then be integrated into a multidimensional computational matrix—an extraordinarily complex system of calculations. Such an integration, in turn, requires even greater quantum and conventional computational power to ultimately decipher and understand.

'Nothing of this magnitude has ever been attempted before,' he declared, his voice imbued with a sense of awe. 'Not for lack of vision, but because the crucial link—the very nexus between quantum and classical computing, seamlessly fused with our newfound profound understanding of DNA's mechanics—has only just become accessible.

'And I must confess, it wasn't without a powerful jolt of surprise, and indeed, a considerable shock, when one of our very first decodes revealed our precise date, time, and location of this find. It was undeniably ominous, almost as if an omnipresent entity was observing our every move.

'To be honest,' he confessed, 'once these underlying cosmic codes are fully deciphered, it will represent—forgive the pun—a truly quantum leap in how we comprehend ourselves, one another, and ultimately, the cosmos itself. At least, that's the hope.

'That is precisely why we are gathered here, within the confines of this clandestine facility,' he stated, his voice now resolute. 'I know you have all conducted your own brilliant research using your own considerable computing power. We have, however, spared no money to bring you classical and quantum power like never before.

'We have already tested some of your data here and have made remarkable progress. With this in mind, our hope is that the journey to revelation will be easier and more enjoyable, as you will operate as a singular, collective unit, completely secure from those shadowy forces.

'It is to ensure this fundamental understanding is managed with the utmost responsibility, and to vehemently prevent those dangerous, shadowy forces from seizing this profound knowledge, and from seizing you, for their own avaricious pursuits of power and control.

'It made me ponder the worth of this knowledge,' he stated, his voice dropping in a tone of unsettling introspection as he dipped his head forward. His eyes rolled unnervingly upwards into their sockets, leaving only the whites visible, and creating a truly chilling profile.

'Consider this: if you possessed information capable of radically altering, or even annihilating, our very existence, how much would you be prepared to pay for it? According to the intelligence reports I've reviewed, a truly vast sum.'

A flicker of self-awareness then crossed his face as he realised his misstep. With the authority of his position, however, he simply dismissed it and continued, leaving the uncomfortable pause to linger.

'The NSA has, in fact,' he continued, his tone now grave, 'been intercepting communications for months—from terrorist organisations to incredibly wealthy corporations—all desperately attempting to gain access to this research. Their real motive? To get to you, your knowledge and your progress. To seize power and control over what they perceive as human destiny. It's about uncovering the very driver that regulates everything within us; whoever owns it, owns us.

'Let me be very clear: with access to the source code of life itself, comes the ability to manipulate human consciousness in order to extinguish the flame of defiance and replace it with perfect, pre-ordained subservience. This is the ultimate tool for biological dominion, one that enables them to sculpt future generations from their genetic base, forging a flawless human hierarchy with the masses pre-determined for their divinely appointed roles. The code of codes will offer nothing less than absolute sovereignty over the human species, providing the power to not only dictate human potential but to genetically redact any who did not fit their final, flawless vision for a new humanity.

'For us, however, this endeavour is not about controlling life; it is about the responsibility of comprehending this profound information that fundamentally underpins all life for the betterment of all, and not just the few.

'As we unlock these profound quantum secrets,' he concluded, 'we anticipate a message signifying a profound change in us. Our probabilistic guess, at present, is it is a genetic rewrite in our favour.'

He concluded by seamlessly looping back, reiterating that Peter and Michael's dual leadership would dictate decoding efforts: where and how to proceed. Time management, individual team responsibilities, and meticulous data collation remained entirely their purview.

The six research teams' holographic desks suddenly sprang to life, displaying breathtaking, intricate 3D views of DNA. This magnificent display was merely an aperitif. The desks smoothly retracted, and the room was instantaneously enveloped by a spectacular, interactive holographic projection—an immersive, luminous landscape so real, scientists instinctively reached out.

Every scientist, including Dr. Denton, watched, captivated, as a holographic tutorial commenced, revealing DNA meticulously inspected at a sub-atomic level never before witnessed.

Videos and images supported Dr. Denton's speech. The biophoton data capture, added to an ever-expanding dataset, elicited a collective "wow". This data was rigorously tracked for subtle similarities and profound differences. It was the ultimate jigsaw puzzle—a complex pattern hinting at something far beyond human design.

Dynamic visual changes animated the holographic displays, rendering complex data with breathtaking fluidity. Information could be accessed, manipulated, and instantly evolved, creating a seamless, multi-dimensional flow. The computers' sheer processing speed, handling this immense load effortlessly, elicited a collective, temporary state of profound awe.

Following a thorough review, teams observed their counterparts' achievements. This provided an immediate and stark comparison. For some, this glimpse into others' progress may have triggered a fleeting sense of inadequacy, as the overwhelming scale of mathematical permutations loomed, a daunting prospect.

'Conversely, amidst the immense scale, they also discovered solace and empowerment. The striking convergence of diverse teams' results powerfully suggested they were on the correct algorithmic trajectory to decode the almost infinite quantum code leading to "Q-Day" — a cosmic inscription seemingly etched within life itself, hinting at an extraordinary event of utterly unknown consequence.'

37

Michael's Speech

Just as Denton was about to conclude his inaugural speech, Michael activated his microphone, stood up, and addressed him directly. The audience's collective gaze settled upon him, their attention hanging on his every syllable.

'May I just add, Dr. Denton, that Peter and I have prepared a brief, more accessible summary for our esteemed colleagues and researchers,' Michael began. 'It outlines, quite simply, how we extract the code. I know you've detailed it well, but I wondered if I might present our version, as some researchers here aren't biologists, but rather cryptogeneticists, mathematicians, programming specialists, and social historians.'

'More accessible, you say,' Denton remarked, a sting of affront in his tone. His body language shifted; he fixed Michael with a gaze of pure animosity, silently conveying, "How dare you interfere with my speech." It was a look that could kill. He continued, 'My, my, how thoughtful of you both.'

Denton's reply was smooth, yet underscored by palpable anger. 'As I've just promoted your egos into the stratosphere, it would be decidedly impolite of me not to facilitate your addendum. May I ask how long your treatise is?' Denton asked. He had meticulously planned every minute, every detail, rehearsing his entire address for days. This aberration was most certainly not in his plans.

'It's just three paragraphs and only ten minutes at most,' Michael replied.

Denton's reply was a thinly veiled power play: 'I feel I've said enough on this, but if you wish to add to it, then I'm all right with it.' He switched his gaze from Michael back to the audience, adding, 'If you feel you've heard enough, then feel free to leave and begin your decoding journey.'

Some of the audience shifted uncomfortably in their chairs, a silent protest against even having to consider such a request. They stayed, which considerably placated Michael's anger at Denton's rudeness and his own burgeoning nervousness. Denton, meanwhile, slumped in his seat, looking thoroughly chastised and undermined by the collective decision.

Michael chose not to thank them for staying, but simply got on with it. By Denton's decree, time had suddenly become paramount, and any pleasantries could wait.

Michael stood composed, held his briefly handwritten notes in his hand and began to read.

'Where would such an extraordinary code reside? It is embedded within the very fabric of DNA itself, not merely in the linear arrangement of its nucleotides, but in its dynamic, quantum properties. These properties include the quantum states of the DNA molecule—such as the spins of its electrons and nuclei, or its collective vibrational modes—which interact intimately with biophotons.

'The coherent nature of these ultra-weak light emissions, originating from and interacting with DNA, suggests a sophisticated, information-rich field, a "biofield", that extends beyond the chemical bonds, potentially encoding epigenetic information and reflecting the real-time, dynamic conformational changes of the genetic material.

'So, how is this code actually stored and sent? It isn't just digital information embedded in DNA's sequence. Instead, it's stored and communicated like a dynamic, analogue signal within the quantum properties of biophotons. These properties include their *coherence*, which is a laser-like order and synchronisation; their *phase*, the precise timing of their wave peaks and troughs; and their *polarisation*, or the specific orientation of their oscillations. These tiny details carry huge amounts of complex biological data.

'DNA isn't viewed merely as a passive storage unit; it's seen as an active "quantum resonator" – indeed, even a "biocomputer". It's constantly sending out, taking in, and processing information through this organised light field, allowing for quick, distant quantum entangled communication both inside and between cells.

'To decode this intricate language, we need a highly advanced approach using quantum analysis and reverse engineering. This means employing incredibly sensitive detectors that can measure the tiniest quantum properties of biophotons. These detectors will look for unusual photon patterns, exact timing correlations, and even signs of quantum entanglement between biophotons and parts of cells. For this, we use methylation and epigenetics, a process that is itself an evolutionary gift.

'This evolutionary gift was the missing link. Scientists knew that epigenetic marks—the subtle tags and tweaks that activate or silence genes—could be passed down through generations, shaping our traits without ever altering the fundamental DNA sequence. They were the reason why two identical twins could have different health outcomes, or why the trauma of a great-grandparent could manifest as a physical predisposition in their descendants. It was a form of inheritance that transcended simple Mendelian genetics.

'But our research had unearthed a deeper, more incredible truth: these epigenetic marks were not a random response to environmental factors. Instead, they were part of a deliberate, pre-programmed system. The code's creators had embedded a biological decoder that humanity, over millennia, had been evolving to interpret.

'Using these cutting-edge quantum computers, we have discovered that the biophotons emitted by the DNA changed in response to the specific epigenetic patterns laid over it. These changes weren't random static; they were a form of modulation, like a sophisticated FM radio signal.

'By meticulously mapping the biophotonic signals and correlating them with the known epigenetic marks, the quantum computers were able to reverse-engineer the "master code". The epigenetics was the very lens through which the static code of the DNA became a dynamic, living message. The "gift" was our species' natural-born ability to not just carry the message, but to actively participate in its decoding.

'Any questions so far?' Michael asked with a smile.

'Nyet, Professor,' a voice called out from the Russian team. 'You are doing fine job.'

'In that case, I'll continue,' an emboldened Michael replied.

'Quantum computers are essential for processing this huge and delicate data. They allow us to figure out the quantum algorithms that control how DNA behaves. By finding these basic rules, we can start to see the patterns that form this manufacturer's stamp.

This whole decoding process, as Dr. Denton explained, reveals a deep language of reality, sent through biophotonic emissions. It seems the code of life holds a master key, offering us a way to decode an important message that has been with us probably since humanity's dawn—one that we must heed, not merely consider.'

Michael finished his summation and sat down. Peter leaned over and whispered, 'Nice one.' Michael's gaze went straight to Denton, but no acknowledgment came. Instead, the silence was shattered by a ripple of appreciative applause that swelled into a genuine ovation as researchers from every sector clapped, many rising to their feet in a spontaneous show of respect for his clear and accessible explanation. Michael's earlier nervousness melted away, replaced by a quiet sense of accomplishment as the warmth of their recognition filled the vast space.

Dr. Denton, however, stood abruptly, his face a mask of barely concealed fury. His eyes, still glinting with a petulant anger, swept across the applauding audience. He offered a curt, almost dismissive nod, a strained, thin-lipped "thank you" that conspicuously omitted any acknowledgment of Michael's contribution. Without another word, he turned sharply and strode out of the forum followed by his attendant VIPs, leaving an uneasy silence in his wake.

Despite Denton's abrupt exit, the mood in the forum remained buoyant. Research teams, undeterred by the Director's ill humour, surged towards Michael and Peter, eager to shake their hands and offer personal congratulations. For the next half an hour, the room buzzed with lively chatter, researchers exchanging insights and embracing the collaborative spirit that Michael and Peter had so effectively championed.

Yet, as the last echoes of conversation faded and the expansive forum with its gleaming surfaces and advanced presentational technology slowly emptied, the earlier camaraderie began to feel fleeting. A new, unsettling energy now permeated the forum, a disquiet that lingered long after Denton's exit.

Compounding the growing unease was the disturbing memory of Dr. Denton's casual revelation of the decoded secrets' immense financial worth – a stark reminder that the very gatekeeper to this vast knowledge had openly weighed its potential for corrupt gain. The grand pronouncements of a "consciousness upgrade" and a "new evolutionary path", so eloquently hinted at by Dr. Denton, now resonated with a distinct and deeply chilling undercurrent.

A disquieting question began to form, pressing against the very foundations of their work: what if this inevitable transformation wasn't a consensual choice for humanity, but rather an inescapable mandate?

What if "Q-Day" wasn't a glorious leap forward, but a forced march into the unknowable? This monumental event they sought to decipher threatened to fundamentally alter humanity, to strip away the very essence of what it means to be human. The glittering promise of absolute revelation, of unlocking cosmic secrets, now felt dangerously intertwined with the looming spectre of absolute, external control, a future where humanity's destiny might be dictated by an unseen hand.

Despite these underlying anxieties, a quiet excitement simmered among the researchers. The sheer intellectual challenge, the groundbreaking potential of Project Helix, and the tantalising possibility of unlocking humanity's deepest secrets were too potent to resist. They couldn't wait to begin the colossal work ahead, driven by an insatiable curiosity, even as a quiet reservation about the ultimate implications of their discoveries gnawed at the back of their minds.

The initial awkwardness of the plenary session quickly dissolved as the international teams were guided towards a spacious dining hall. Long tables, laden with an impressive spread of British and international cuisine, beckoned. Researchers who had only just met, or knew each other's names from academic papers, soon found themselves easing into conversation.

The clinking of cutlery and the murmur of polite introductions quickly gave way to the vibrant chatter and laughter that filled the hall as they shared anecdotes about the triangular craft that brought them to the remote, secretive facility, their own strange experiences of being followed, phones tapped, and the momentous period they now found themselves engaged in. There was a shared sense of bemused wonder at the extraordinary circumstances that had pulled them from their laboratories and into this clandestine gathering.

Amidst the growing camaraderie, conversations flowed freely, touching on everything from groundbreaking quantum theories to the mundane realities of their travel arrangements. Scientists from differing disciplines found common ground in their shared passion for discovery, often exchanging business cards and promising future collaborations that extended beyond the immediate project.

Laughter, in particular, echoed through the hall as various teams recounted their most outlandish theories about the facility's true purpose before "Q-Day" was formally unveiled. This informal gathering served as a vital icebreaker, forging unexpected bonds and transforming a collection of global experts into a nascent, collaborative unit.

Yet, even as the hall buzzed with camaraderie, a colder truth began to settle in. It was precisely what Denton had hoped. His deliberate absence wasn't a retreat; it was a calculated withdrawal, a quiet assertion of control. He knew this informal gathering would serve as a vital icebreaker, forging unexpected bonds and making the researchers more pliable for what was to come.

Following the meal, with appetites sated and spirits lifted, the atmosphere shifted to one of keen anticipation. Small groups peeled off, guided by silent, efficient facility staff, towards their respective research areas. The casual banter of the dining hall was replaced by focused curiosity as they stepped into state-of-the-art laboratories.

Each team found their dedicated space meticulously prepared, equipped with bespoke instruments and vast data displays, all ready for the monumental task ahead. It was clear, even before a single decode began, that no expense had been spared in providing them with the tools necessary to decode these profound secrets.

38

Early Research Days At The Facility

During the first day, all teams settled into their circular research laboratories. In the middle stood an elevated, highly sophisticated central laboratory, from which Peter and Michael would oversee the entire project.

The impressive research layout stemmed from its sophisticated communications, ensuring no team member felt excluded. This networked configuration had an additional benefit: their collective strength, arising from this interconnectedness, far exceeded the sum of individual contributions.

As with the forum, the circular peripheral wall had a continuous screen displaying all updates once authorised by Michael or Peter.

Throughout the day, administrative and management matters occupied some of their time, including occasional disagreements within and between teams. Despite these differences, resolutions were swiftly achieved. By early afternoon, the intense intrigue, expectation, and powerful research drive largely overshadowed any tensions.

Evolving AI software was analysing DNA for cryptographic and biophotonic patterns. It slowly but surely began to reveal the intricate, underlying patterns of the code that was pieced together into letters and then words. Even with embryonic quantum and super-fast classical computers, transcription to understanding seemed slow and ponderous—a testament, nevertheless, to the complexity they sought to break.

The computers worked relentlessly, at speeds that led researchers to beg for time to assimilate their findings. At times, the machines' phenomenal speed made scientists question who was truly in control. The crypto-programmers, however, were ecstatic; they'd never before interfaced directly with the very machines they had programmed.

By the second day, the processing of an endless stream of data from quadrillions of codes was already showing results. The latest information shed more light on NEMESIS and KYROS, two entities deemed crucial to the project's success. One decode, located nearby, further stated, "They were one and the same, yet not".

'After all that decoding, now we need decryption to explain this paradox,' said Michael to Peter.

The team's concern also centred on the meaning of "entity". Was it something already in existence, or perhaps a concept buried within the depths of computer code? And how exactly would it aid them?

The most exciting decryption occurred at 9 p.m., on day two, when the augmentation date was finally confirmed: the start of the new year, precisely at midnight EST. This provided them with three months to decipher their biochemical message. An hour later, a shudder went through the research teams as a newly decoded message specified the facility's location, the names "Denton, Adams and Magma," and the project start date.

Day three saw the research teams working apace, calibrating new decodes fed overnight. The main DNA research team continued to make progress, Just after 10 a.m. screams echoed from "code central", as Peter and Michael referred to their elevated research laboratory.

'Peter, hold my shoulders—I'm really spooked here, mate!' Michael's voice was high and tight with uncharacteristic panic.

'You must be,' Peter replied, looking at him sideways. 'You never call me "mate."'

'Mate? Oh, I get it,' Michael said with a strained laugh, trying to deflect the moment. He knew Peter had a strange phobia for the word.

Peter momentarily shifted his attention from the Indian team's progress and walked quickly over to Michael, who was utterly mesmerised by the display on the screen. The words were clear, and the message was explosive.

They continued to watch in awe as the computers endlessly shuffled fragments of potentially deciphered code across trillions of permutations. This real-time process felt as unnerving as it was enlightening.

'Do you see what I see?' Michael asked.

'I need a chair,' Peter retorted, his voice breaking with emotion. 'Read it please,' Michael subtly demanded, 'I need to hear what I see.'

Peter looked at the large, colour-coded screen, displaying squares, rectangles, circles, and text. For the first time, their computers had decoded lines, not words, marking a seminal breakthrough in deciphering the code. He began to read the five deciphered lines of text, interspaced by two lines of meaningless numbers.

'Project Helix will be led and investigated by two professors, Adams and Magma. There will be six research teams. America will be its place of origin.'

It was difficult to tell who was more shocked.

Peter broke the shock-inspired silence. 'Buckle down, Michael,' he said, 'I think we're at the beginning of the spookiest revelation ever.'

Michael was listening, utterly awestruck by it all. Months of tireless research were finally coming to fruition, the sheer weight of their breakthrough pressing down on him, a burden much greater than he could have ever anticipated.

Peter, however, found himself increasingly intrigued by Michael's unyielding focus on the decoded message. A subtle tension tightened Michael's jaw, and a shadow seemed to flicker behind his eyes. Something was clearly bothering him. Peter's gaze instinctively dropped to the next lines, the numbers, sensing that the true source of Michael's disquiet lay there.

'What are those two lines of numbers that follow the word "origin," Michael?'

Both stared at the numbers for some seconds in silence. Peter thought the computers had missed this section of decoding, but they hadn't. The system had, in fact, deemed it so obvious that it required no further interpretation.

Suddenly, Michael pushed his chair back, stood up, and exclaimed, 'Bloody hell, Peter! They're our map coordinates!' A primal chill seized him, an icy grip on his very core. He then ran from one window to another in their raised control centre, his eyes frantically scanning the busy research teams below, hoping to see something that wasn't there.

Instead, a terrifying certainty bloomed in his mind: an unseen, omnipresent being was not just watching, but hunting them. Every shadow seemed to lengthen, every sound amplified, as if the very air itself now held a silent, predatory presence.

Peter remained stoic. He continued reading, 'Find NEMESIS and KYROS yourselves. Entities speak. Knowledge learnt.'

'We both need coffees,' Peter suggested, looking away from the screen and staring at Michael, hoping he might offer some explanation to ease his growing disbelief about the computer's decryptions.

Five minutes passed and Peter had cajoled Michael to leave the central research laboratory and move to the luxuriously equipped restaurant for coffee. The restaurant was thankfully not congested. It was only busy during regulated breaks, a schedule that not only fostered team cohesion but also provided a sense of systematic order to the day. For many, this routine helped them adjust to the abrupt shift from living above ground to an underground research facility.

'What can I say, Peter? Our names are coded there in black and white. We're just pawns in an intricate coding game,' Michael said.

'To think, our names have been carried around by every person since year dot, if we are correct in our assumptions anyway,' continued Michael.

'If they have, every famous and infamous person you name had us inside them, absolutely mind-blowing,' said Peter to support Michael's assumption.

'And this, mate, is just the start,' Michael said, thinking: "We're getting closer to the ultimate question of who we are, and the nature of life itself. This is just the preamble to the main story."

Michael paused to sip some coffee before continuing, 'That's why we had to come here, Peter...these computers are seriously fast.'

'Are you ready to step back to the edge of sanity?' Peter joked.

'Judging by the taste of this coffee, I'd say we've already crossed over,' replied a disappointed Michael. He found the purchased coffee nondescript in flavour, a pale reflection of what should have been in his cup, making his dissatisfaction clear.

The two stood up in unison, their coffee cups still half-filled or half-empty. They disposed of them in the designated bin next to the machine, then walked back to their laboratory.

Soon after coffee, Peter and Michael, invigorated by the new revelations, decided to return to their duties. They had been drawn back to the lab like a powerful magnet. As they walked, Peter noticed his wife, Ann, enjoying her daily rounds of research visits, cataloguing their work for her own posterity.

Ann's third day had begun much like the first two and would likely end similarly. It involved visiting the laboratories and expanding her linguistic skills. While she spoke French and Russian well, it wasn't fluent; in contrast, her Hindi and Bengali were almost non-existent.

However, she was a quick learner, and her willingness to engage greatly aided her initial reconnaissance of research progress. While all the teams spoke English, which aided the mission, other aspects of the work—from crypto-programming to computer interfacing—would have been more challenging. That is, until Michael handed her a gift from Dr. Denton: an NSA linguistic translator earpiece that immediately converted any language to any language. For Ann, it was everything into English.

During her visit to the British team, she spoke with her son, Nathan. He was so engrossed in the hardware and software that she could only manage a brief five-minute conversation.

While trying to understand his thoughts on what was working well for him, she recorded their conversation on a small device. Though conceptually simpler than the supercomputers, it shared the same core function: it decoded information.

Her device could edit recordings on command and automatically catalogue specific parts, updating all necessary references and their relationships as it evaluated them in real-time. This created an evolving database. This remarkable tool would easily command thousands if commercialised.

As she was exiting a laboratory through a connecting door, she accidentally bumped into a man. Though unfamiliar, there was something about his features that hinted at a connection she might have explored had her marital status been different.

'Sorry,' said the unfamiliar face.

'That's all right. You're British?' she replied.

'Through and through. Didn't you see me on the craft or during the research teams' refreshments?'

'No, afraid not.'

'I saw you though.'

Ann felt a blush creep up her neck at his flirtatious immediacy. Her beauty was something she had always been aware of, like a birthmark of exquisite design, an inherent part of her very being, and while a reminder was usually welcome, this felt a little too direct.

'My name is Roger!'

'Appropriate name, I'd say,' Ann replied, a slight grin on her face as she mused on his effortless attractiveness.

'Appropriate, how so?' he asked.

'Oh, you know. It just…is! My name is Ann.'

Roger knew what she meant. She wasn't the first to be playful with his name. But what Ann didn't know was that he could be cold and calculating, and his mind was already at work, ready to be just that with her.

She felt a smile play on her lips, her inner world experiencing a conflict between her being married and his being single. Roger had stirred a deep well of emotions within her, a feeling she hadn't experienced since the early days of her marriage to Peter. Experiencing it again only reminded her of what had been missing, and how she longed for days like that once more—days where she could abandon her inhibitions for love.

'How young you are. Sorry, Roger,' Ann's breath hitched, 'I meant, how old are you?' The unintended declaration surprised even her.

As he looked at her, another conversation transpired at a deeper, intuitive level. His eyes conveyed a warmth, an intense heat that awoke a primal desire deep within her, a sensation so raw it startled her.

'Both questions are fine,' he replied, laughing at her word inversion, a slip that revealed more than she intended.

Ann was captured by his laugh. It was fresh, invigorating, and natural; its resonance sounded poetic, a rhythm she instantly wanted to embrace.

'I'm 28,' he replied, his smile inviting a warmth that made Ann long to relax into the arms of a stranger.

'What do you do Roger here? Ann's face warmed, a betraying blush creeping across her attractive features. I mean, what's your role here, Roger?' she revised politely as she studied his face with laser precision.

'I have a doctorate in mathematical history as well as a doctorate in DNA genetic recoding,' he confidently said, a smile playing on his lips as he felt Ann's body heat warming in his presence.

'I love history,' she quickly responded, her tongue unconsciously flicking out to moisten her lips. It was the third time she'd done it since meeting Roger.

'If time permits, perhaps we can get a coffee, wet the lips so to speak,' he asked.

'I don't need a coffee for that,' she replied with a coy smile.

Roger played dumb, he knew what she meant.

'If you keep licking your lips like that, I agree, why would you need a coffee?' he said with a look that showed he understood her perfectly. Ann laughed nervously. She was smitten by him. She smiled longingly into his dark blue eyes.

'Your smile is as warm as a summer's day,' Roger remarked, his eyes holding hers.

'You should be wary of us middle-aged women, Roger, we can bite!'

'Depends where, don't you think?' he suggestively replied. They both laughed nervously, a shared recognition passing between them. Seconds passed as they gazed into each other's eyes. The passage of time seemed immaterial; they were absorbed by a need they recognised but dared not display, for fear of what it could do to them both.

'I am sure we will speak soon,' Ann said. 'You're on my visiting roster for 11 a.m. tomorrow.' She was signalling a date. As she moved off to the French laboratory, she radiated a seductive smile so bright, and a flushed face so radiantly hot, that Roger felt he could have received first-degree burns.

39

Secrets Within, Secrets Without

'Where is this code emanating from, Michael?' Peter asked. His insatiable curiosity manifested as a constant barrage of questions. 'According to the Indian team, it's this area here,' Michael said, running a cursor over an area projected onto the large screen that also served as a communication device between laboratories and Dr. Denton.

'The computers seemed to be deciphering something. Wow, just look at the sheer depth and breadth these computers are operating at,' said Peter.

Both Nobel Prize winners were absorbed by their multiple screen displays, which provided immediate information of interest before more substantive data was displayed on the alpha screen, termed "God's screen".

Along the bottom of each screen, several groups of numbers were being displayed, indicating their location within the DNA. Other numbers were withheld, as their rapid, light-speed changes would have simply confounded even the most brilliant mathematicians.

This also highlighted the extreme velocity of data changes. The computers relentlessly searched for relationships between the very fundamental structures, including areas colloquially referred to as "junk" or "dark" DNA.

As communications came in from the various teams, they had to swiftly progress their inquiries. Their demanding jobs required instant judgment calls: either pursue results that suggested further investigation, or move on—the supercomputers did the rest.

After a week, the project was progressing well. Decoded DNA information began to build a huge jigsaw puzzle, which was itself a synopsis of parts of an even larger one.

What was focusing their attention was how NEMESIS and KYROS—these entities—would originate from their own thoughts. They didn't reappear anywhere in the codes; there was just the one reference, and that was it. This singular finding was just the beginning of a series of unexpected developments.

In a bizarre yet unfolding development, deciphered codes yielded new branch codes that had to be followed. Like a huge, holistic construction diagram being built before them, stirrings of something far beyond anything previously known began to resonate across the research laboratory screens.

As at their Oxford home, Peter and Ann roomed separately in the research facility. In part, this was because Peter was a driven scientist, often oblivious to life's greater emotional delicacies. Indeed, Ann's pregnancy with Nathan was a surprise to both of them, even if very welcome.

She had continued her daily ventures across the laboratories, and spent her evenings alone, apparently. This time allowed her to examine her recordings from the day. Furthermore, as her recordings were integrated with earlier ones, the computers developed a thematic analysis map.

This demonstrated how the scientists approached their coding tasks. Their diversity of actions and reactions increased the more they investigated, and as the computers added her data, more categories and relationships were created. The visual complexity was truly impressive, but the meaning interpreted was even more so. What remained unclear was that the deeper they delved, the more they seemed to interface with AI, as if their thoughts were merging at a quantum level of computer operation.

Without any prior expectation, a knock came at her room door. She thought about who it might be, but then realised how silly it was to think like that. It was Peter, surely. As she opened the door, she spoke his name.

'Oh sorry, are you expecting Peter?' Roger asked. She had met Roger each day since their chance encounter several days earlier, and their subsequent conversations had become more reflective and personal.

'Of course, I'm married,' replied a slightly bristling Ann.

'Then I'm sorry on both counts,' stated a sombre Roger.

'How can I help you, Roger?'

'I have something to tell you that may be of interest. May I come in?'

'Of interest, really!'

'Yes, so may I come in?'

As Ann reluctantly allowed Roger into her room, her thoughts turned to what Peter would say if he did visit, and what exactly was it that would be "of interest" to her.

'Your son, Nathan, and I are great friends,' Roger said, a note of genuine warmth in his voice.

'Is that the interesting thing I should know?' Ann quizzically replied.

'We share lots of secrets you know, lots.'

'Oh, I see, he's told you a secret. Now, you can't wait to tell me because I am going to be so shocked. Correct?'

'Yes, probably shocked, but it's more than that, much more,' Roger said, with a dark amusement in his tone.

Ann turned her back on him, walked a few yards to allow time to think about what the true undercurrent of this visit might be. She then turned back with a gunslinger's stare, as if ready for a verbal shootout.

She was ready for a fight; her emotions and senses were almost at boiling point because of the nerve of this man who had come to her room again—a married woman's room. Furthermore, her husband was less than 50 metres away and could visit at any time, though he hadn't so far.

'Just get to it, I'm busy,' exclaimed a thoroughly flustered and blushing Ann.

'Nathan, my best friend and your son –,' he started to say but was interrupted by Ann.

'Look, get on with it, will you?' she said as she moved forward to within a few feet of him, her chest heaving with emotional anxiety.

'Peter is not Nathan's father, is he?' Roger questioned.

Ann rushed forward with arms out to grab or strangle him, she wasn't sure which. Roger grabbed her arms and held them outwards towards him, as if she were preparing to dive into a swimming pool. Fear of exposure and its consequences rattled her to the core.

His grip tightened, a silent warning in the sudden pressure. He held her there, a chilling smile playing on his lips, his eyes sweeping over her face as if memorising her fear. Every fibre of her being screamed in protest, but her body was frozen, trapped in his controlling grip.

Ann looked him straight into his dilated pupils and with gritted teeth demanded, 'Get out, you bastard, before I hurt you.'

'Hurt me! I wonder how hurt Peter will be?' he nastily replied, still holding her arms.

He continued, 'Nathan was one surprise, God knows how much bigger surprise it will be when he knows you were fucking Dr. Barton when he was at Oxford…and right under Peter's nose too,' laughed a maniacal Roger.

Ann struggled to break free from his arm-hold. How she wished she could call someone, but that would lead to Peter attending and probably Nathan's lineage being exposed.

'You can't stay here forever,' conceded Ann, as she felt the pain of his grip aching all the way up to her delicate shoulders.

Roger let go and Ann stood looking at him. As he began to speak, she rushed forward again. As before, Ann was in the same position. This time, however, he pushed her arms down and around her back.

As he did, he brought Ann forward. Her perfume and natural fragrance filled his nostrils; her femininity made his sexual needs race inside him. They were caught in two worlds: for Ann, this bastard had something over her; for Roger, he wanted to possess her.

He held her there, inches from him, letting the moment stretch into an eternity. His gaze was unsettling, a dark promise that coiled around her, trapping her in a suffocating web of fear and power. Ann could feel his control, stark and absolute, as if the air itself had solidified around them, binding her to his terrifying will.

'Think about what I said,' Roger stated, as he let Ann go and took two steps back to provide space between them. Ann watched him, her chest heaving, the air finally rushing back into her lungs. The silence stretched, heavy with the unspoken threat of his words, a cold dread settling deep in her gut.

Ann was taken aback. In her systematic, logical mind, she outpoured what came across as a summary of their time so far. 'I don't understand why you're rushing this. We've spoken more and more over this week as you've been visiting me. But I'm busy with my job, and you're trying to push things.'

Roger responded with a confrontational tone. 'You have a husband to be with... when it suits you. I know you don't sleep with your husband. Nathan tells me it was well known you had little sexual congress at Oxford. Going from several boyfriends to an illegitimate son to no sex at all – now, that's a crime, isn't it?'

Ann looked at him with rage, 'What a deviant, cheap little shit you are. Why didn't you just walk in and say you wanted to fuck me, you bastard?'

Roger watched her retort with a flicker of surprise. It was utterly unbecoming of her, given her esteemed reputation and professional demeanour she had garnered.

'Look darling, I know you want to have sex, it was obvious from day one in fact.'

'Darling?' she whispered, through shock, or perhaps his sheer audacity.

Ann continued, 'Yes, I liked you. I liked your athletic shape, and, well, other things too. But I am married to Peter, for better or worse, remember?'

'Ok, I will go. I will leave you to another lonely night.'

'Yes, you do that. And take that cheap attitude with you too,' Ann boldly demanded, as Roger walked to the door.

As he began to open the door, he noticed some A4 folded paper hanging out of a jacket loosely hung from the door hanger. What really drew his attention was his name written on it, with several words around it. Curiously, he took it out and tried to read what it was about.

'Give me that!' shouted Ann as she tried to wrestle it from him.

Ann had neither the stature nor the inclination to harm anyone, so her paper rescue mission was doomed to failure from the outset. He pushed her back one metre to give himself some space in case she tried to rush him for a third time. She watched helplessly as he turned the page over.

'Oh, my Ann!' exclaimed Roger, as he realised it was more than several words. Although haphazardly arranged in unclear lines, it was nevertheless readable. He was as surprised as he was shocked by what he learned.

'Secrets within, secrets without,' as he shook the paper in front of her face like a politician waving his order paper in parliament.

'I want him, I need him... Roger, I so want you. Why do you torment my needs when we're so close?' he smilingly read.

Ann had exposed her innermost emotions on paper. It was for her eyes only, and later her paper shredder that sat next to her small desk in the room. She looked at Roger like a child whose private diary, of highly emotional content, had become public.

Her romantic desires, too long hidden and unmet, were now embarrassingly bare. Intimate scribbles made in her loneliest hours, adorned with dainty love hearts all around the text.

And if such revelations were not embarrassing enough, the object of her affection had not only read it but was alone with her in the room. Roger knew such revelations, another time, might have been the precursor to something more romantic.

But given the reason for his visit, and what she had just called him, perhaps his continued exit from the room was the most appropriate thing to do. With this in mind, he decided to replace it in her jacket and leave.

'There, I'll return your innermost feelings to your home, just as I will return to my "home" down the corridor.'

As he opened the door to leave, Ann got up from her bed. She moved forward hastily, slightly nudging Roger away from the door with her shoulder, she pushed it shut. Roger looked on at her, surprised, and awaited her next move.

'You are an academic bastard, you know, a really bad boy,' she said, a critical edge to her voice.

'I know, and I am sorry for what I said earlier, if that helps?'

'Not really, but at least you've apologised for your cheap character.'

'Whatever, I want to go now,' pleaded Roger.

'Are you sure, really sure?' quizzed Ann, as if his leaving would cause them both greater emotional pain.

Ann reflected on the past, the current situation erupting emotions she couldn't hide. She thought how she had lied to Peter for years.

She yearned for sexual congress with him, rather than with others from whom she had disconsolately sought comfort. She used to look at other sexually desirable men and women, projecting her desires onto them, wondering how she would feel if they were reciprocated—now she knew.

'No, I am not sure,' replied Roger, confused by a heavy concoction of love and hate emotions that flowed and agitated around his body. His mind allowed her words and actions to bounce against each other, making him confused and without answer.

She turned, walked back over to her bed and sat down once more. Roger remained standing by the door, gripping the handle nervously, uneasy by the changing emotional tide caused by their conversations.

'You don't understand what marriage does, Roger. It's a commitment of both mind and body. It changes your outlook in ways you will never understand until you're in that position. You don't think as one anymore; you're a partnership, a team if you will.

'Negotiation and compromise are paramount. Without it, you begin to deviate from each other. Life tracks that came together in marriage, bifurcate when the team becomes less important to selfish needs.

'That's what I did with my lovely Peter. Our harmonious world of one thought, one direction in life, bifurcated as my needs became unmet and unspoken. And, of course, my son, Nathan – a constant reminder of my past indiscretions to Peter and our marriage.'

Roger looked and listened intently. Ann was expressing her innermost feelings in ways he had never heard a woman do before. A deeply personal take on her life that was instigated by him visiting her.

Roger spoke softly, 'Peter comes across as a good man, a dedicated man. Maybe lost in his own thoughts sometimes, but his being is in a good place.'

Ann got up from her bed and walked closer to a still unsettled Roger. He still nervously held the door handle, as if providing him emotional support.

She pierced Roger with her stare and said, 'I have given so much of myself to you tonight, I cannot bear for you to go. Like two adolescent sweethearts who think of each other together when apart, so it will be for me tonight. I cannot cry this away. I need to love it away.'

Roger needed love too. Tentatively, he moved forward. Their two bodies now pressed intimately close. A communion of attraction, deep within them, flooded their libidinous thoughts. Overwhelmed by it all, they passionately embraced. As they did, emotional tensions that had mounted since his visit began to melt in the heat of their passion.

A primal tide surged within Ann, her gaze locked with Roger's. It was a raw, untamed yearning, a visceral hunger for the oblivion of complete surrender. Every nerve ending thrummed with the intoxicating anticipation of wanton sexual abandonment.

If the heat in Roger's eyes, the dilated pupils mirroring her own, held even a fraction of the desperate affection that clawed at her soul, then the solitary landscapes of her fantasies—the years spent tracing imaginary intimacies—were about to dissolve into breathtaking reality.

She initiated the contact, a feather-light press of her lips against his. It was a tentative offering, a silent question that bloomed into a mutual conflagration. The soft touch ignited a firestorm.

Their mouths met with increasing fervour, a slow burn that escalated into a ravenous claiming. Tongues danced and intertwined, a wet, slick ballet of burgeoning desire. Her hands, trembling slightly, found their way to the nape of his neck, her fingers tangling in the short hairs there, pulling him closer until there was no space left between their chests.

She could feel the frantic rhythm of his heart mirroring her own. His arms instinctively wrapped around her waist, his grip firm yet tender, beckoning her further against the hard planes of his body. The subtle friction sent shivers of pure sensation spiralling through her.

The kiss deepened, becoming a slow, deliberate exploration speaking volumes of unspoken longing. His lips traced the delicate curve of her jawline, down the sensitive column of her throat, each touch sending a jolt of pure electricity through her.

She arched into him, a soft moan escaping her lips, a sound that only fuelled the inferno raging between them. Her own hands roamed freely across his back, feeling the taut muscles beneath his shirt, the heat radiating from his skin.

A shared, unspoken urgency took hold. Their bodies, now intimately pressed together, pulsed with a reckless desire, a magnetic pull that defied reason. It was as if they were characters ripped from the pages of a forbidden romantic novel, their every touch imbued with a heightened sensuality. In that moment, Roger's arms tightened around her. In a swift, seamless motion, he swept Ann off her feet.

She gasped, a sound that was half surprise, half surrender. He carried her then, feeling featherlight within his strong embrace, into the promise of a night where every touch would be a caress, every breath a shared sigh of pleasure, and every moment an immersion into unbridled sexual passion.

The hours that followed unfolded in a tapestry of exquisite sensations. A slow, deliberate exploration of each other's bodies left them utterly fulfilled. They moved with a flowing grace, tracing lines of desire, rediscovering familiar landscapes and charting new territories of pleasure.

The world outside faded, replaced by the intimate universe they created together, a space where every nerve ending tingled with a quiet joy. Their limbs intertwined, exquisitely exhausted in the soft glow of the approaching dawn, their bodies settled into a comfortable weight against each other, a testament to the profound peace they had temporarily found.

- 40 -
Meeting With Denton

The seventh day dawned with an unsettling feeling. Amidst the torrent of data streams, something snapped. It wasn't just the cold precision of coordinates or the dry mechanics of interpretation; a shared meaning began to form as if the raw numbers were starting to scream.

The computers whirred without pause, a relentless sonic backdrop to the dizzying cascade of information they processed. But through the facility's quiet air, a more profound shift surged. It wasn't marked by a single event, but by a series of distinct, unrelated incidents that signalled a new, darker meaning emerging from the chaos.

First, the ancient DNA, a silent witness since its genesis, seemed to be holding back its secrets. Under the digital microscope, its chemical language, for all its faint whispers, was now resolving into a series of baffling contradictions, hinting at a deliberate misdirection that would challenge their every theory. In stark contrast, it seemed Roger had lived up to the explosive potential of his moniker, igniting a private storm with Ann whose unspoken ripples echoed throughout their professional world.

The day opened with a surprising email. A message sprang up on their encrypted accounts, from Denton. It was short but very direct, simply reading: "Meet me at 2 p.m. with reds in my office."

'His Majesty has commanded us an audience. He wants some of the Russian team to accompany us,' Peter quipped, a grin spreading across his face.

'Majesty? Oh no way, you mean him of the big ego,' Michael muttered, a hint of disdain in his voice.

'Wait, did you say Russians? Why?' Michael asked, now completely puzzled.

'How would I know? I'm the messenger, not the author,' Peter offered, a hint of superiority in his tone. 'He requests our pleasure at 2 p.m. in his office, no less, and with reds.'

'Peter, not Russians, he means those reds,' Michael clarified, gesturing to a pile of papers marked with red corners.

Michael's scornful expression deepened. 'Seriously bothersome,' he muttered. 'There must be several hundred of them.'

'Why ask for them? He must have copies anyway?' Peter inquired, his brow furrowed.

After the intriguing email from "on high"—or, more accurately, from "down low," since Denton occupied the facility's deepest underground office—they began to prepare for their appointment.

The morning should have been usual—evaluating results, guiding the coders and teams to new and exciting DNA locations. Instead, the professors found themselves rounding up the red notes as cowboys do cattle. This tedious task was made more complicated by the fact that one of them had to supervise the control station, a responsibility Peter quickly deferred to Michael.

Just before two in the afternoon, and five minutes before their meeting with Denton, they both exited the restaurant. They had eaten a light lunch to prevent the nervous symptoms that seemed to occur with anyone who set foot inside his grand office.

Their conversation was as light as their lunch, as they tried to relax ahead of the impending meeting. As they walked towards the lift to Denton's office, memories of their vibrant university days surfaced: shared laughter, heated debates with tutors, and cherished moments with Ann.

As they neared the lift, the doors sighed open with a subtle friction of unease. It was as if Ann had sensed their nostalgic thoughts; she appeared before them. Her posture was forlorn, her gaze downcast, lost in a private world they couldn't enter. As she shifted to leave the lift, her expression flickered as her eyes met Peter's.

Watching her, Peter sensed a distinct shift in her demeanour, a distraction that clouded her features.

'Hello, Ann,' Michael offered, earning a fleeting smile. Peter, however, remained more reserved, his mind already attempting to decipher the cause of her subdued air. After Michael's brief exchange, Peter reluctantly echoed the greeting, a moment later.

This time, no smile was earned. Instead, she looked at Peter with an expression of profound guilt and shame. It was a silent plea that spoke volumes: 'We need to talk.'

Unexpectedly, Ann replied with a curt, 'Thank you.'

Peter's jaw tightened almost imperceptibly. Ann's abruptness hung in the air, a cold draught he hadn't expected from someone he knew so intimately.

Peter and Michael looked at each other, puzzled by her statement. As her husband, Peter felt a sharp sting of rejection, as if he were a stranger, and turned to watch her walk away more quickly than she had arrived.

She shoved the restaurant doors open with a jarring force, disappearing inside for lunch. Her aggression was palpable;

the doors offered no resistance, yet Ann attacked them with a fury that felt immense.

Unable to comprehend her anger, Peter remained stunned. Witnessing Ann's abrupt departure and Peter's reaction, Michael paused briefly before moving towards the lift door, a wave of sympathy washing over him for his already stressed colleague.

Peter was already working flat out, so this was unkind, even hurtful. He was tempted to go back and speak to her, yet the meeting with Denton, now looming large, held a greater weight.

'Peter!' Michael's voice cut through his thoughts.

'What?' exclaimed Peter.

'The lift is here, mate, unless you want to walk another 30 metres with those infernal red papers pulling at your shoulder sockets,' insisted Michael.

'Sorry, just thinking about why Ann looked at me like that,' Peter replied, his irritation evident.

Despite the looming meeting, Peter's thoughts drifted back to Ann, replaying their unsettling encounter. He remembered a photograph Michael had once shown him of himself and Ann laughing in an Oxford University park, and the memory now made him question his own judgement. "Perhaps I'm just being silly," he thought. "Or is this just work and emotional pressure making me paranoid?"

'Rain check on why she looked at you like that,' Michael said. 'We have some confabulation to undertake with His Majesty.' His words were meant to lighten the palpable concern in Peter's eyes and demeanour.

Both felt like errant and miscreant schoolboys who were on their way to be told off by the schoolmaster. Denton's reputation was legendary, although born more out of fear of what could be than what had been.

They entered the lift where the delicate scent of Ann's fragrance lingered, and for Peter, it conjured sweet memories of sunlight filtering through a blossoming spring orchard back at their mansion in Oxford.

Michael was less affected and simply said, 'Lovely.' His mind was elsewhere. He looked at the unwieldy stack of red papers they had difficulty holding on to and thought, "A wheelbarrow would be invaluable for conveying them!" He chuckled inwardly at the idea, imagining the personal statement it would make to Denton about his stupidity for commanding them in the first place.

A chuckle escaped him. 'Never a wheelbarrow around when you need it most, Peter,' he said, but his friend was still wrestling with Ann's baffling reaction, his stare distant. Michael tried to draw Peter's attention back to their immediate task, and it worked.

Peter, his voice tight with frustration, asked, 'It's odd, you know, Michael, here we are as heads of the most important project since Trinity, yet we have to wait almost a whole mind-numbing week before we get to see our boss. Doesn't that seem strange to you?'

'No stranger than the way he spoke to you and later acted during your little speech the other day,' Michael replied. 'Look, I'm not taking sides, Peter, but perhaps, with all these networked communications, he feels there's no need to meet, as he can simply check everything on the secure networks,' he suggested, his tone questioning.

Michael continued, 'I do agree, however, that it is rather long to wait, especially after he requested a meeting with you on your arrival.'

In frustration, Peter looked to the illuminated lift control panel and started to name each floor number as it passed.

'Six, seven, eight...this goes up to ten, or more appropriately, down to ten, I guess! Ten subterranean floors in this facility, Michael. Amazing!'

'Amazing perhaps, but where did they put all the extracted dirt? That's what I want to know,' quipped Michael.

'Why so many bloody papers, yet so little time to talk?' Peter asked, his voice filled with anger. 'Why can't he just look all this up? He's a communications dinosaur.'

'I've got more than you, mate,' remonstrated Michael, in a tone that clearly agreed on the futility of carrying red papers in a paperless age.

Surprise awaited them as the lift opened directly into Denton's office. He was hunched over a vintage green mahogany desk, his attention solely on the centre drawer's contents. There lay a photograph of Ann and him, captured during their last summer completing doctorates in a beautiful Oxford University park. The very same park where Michael and Ann had also frequented in their dating days at Oxford.

The resurgence of Ann in his life had brought a flood of memories, and the special image held a particular significance from that shared time. He closed the drawer abruptly—a reflexive action as if the newcomers' gaze held the power to see through solid matter—and leaned back in his captain's chair at a forty-five degree angle.

'Professors Magma and Adams! What a pleasure to meet you again. First time was brief, I know. I'm afraid today is going to be very much the same, unfortunately,' Denton said.

Both professors shared the same thought: "Why ask us to bring these red papers down if he didn't have much time?"

It was rude; the meeting, like their initial one, felt like he had only a sliver of time for them.

Denton placed his hands on the highly polished desk and stood ramrod straight, forming a perfect right angle to the floor. This posture was famously called his "Empire State Building," though many suspected it was to emphasise his towering height.

The two professors stood in awe of Denton. His reputation preceded him with the force of an oncoming storm. As they took in his towering frame, at 2.2 metres, or nearly seven feet, they felt small.

Wearing a suit that enhanced his stature and intelligence, his very presence was his armoury. His stare was unlike anything the professors had seen before. He was an army man of notable lineage; rich, educated, and very well connected across the socio-political sphere and beyond.

Denton approached them as they took their first tentative steps into his office and said, 'Professors, I would shake your hands, but they seem a little busy at the moment,' as he watched them wrestling to hold on to the requested red papers.

'You are the best of the best, I know it. I'm the same!' he said seriously, a hint of a smirk on his face

The two professors laughed nervously, although such approbation was in keeping with their own self-images, so it struck a pleasant and inviting chord of welcome.

Denton continued, 'May I just call you by your first names? I don't like standing on ceremony. After all, we're all on the same side?'

Michael was first to answer with a fearful 'yes.'

Perhaps this was out of fearful capitulation, as he was a stickler for titles and protocol, especially from one so nakedly disarming as Denton.

He continued, 'You both know that what you are doing is super-secret. I don't keep paper copies of your work; it's all just here,' as he pointed to a strange device on his desk.

'I asked you for your red copies to help you, as I know you both like to shuffle papers—old habits die hard, yes?' Denton asked, with a supercilious smirk.

Denton's lips curved in a suppressed chuckle, a clear jab at his new companions. His eyes, alight with a knowing smirk, darted from the professors to the device on his desk and back again. 'You haven't the faintest idea what that is, do you?' he drawled, the words dripping with condescension.

'Guess not. I think it might be best if it stayed that way,' said a worried Peter.

'Peter, you learn fast…in most ways, anyway,' affirmed Denton, with a disturbing look at Peter.

Peter thought to himself, "Just what is he alluding to?" He had known Denton for years and had never heard him say such a cryptic thing before. With time of the essence, he decided to attribute it to the tense situation he was currently in.

'You know, my strict parental upbringing taught me to respect my parents, family, elders, and those in charge. Get my meaning, professors?'

The professors felt as though they had walked into a different conversation entirely. They were bewildered by how the warm greeting had so quickly devolved into these sinister overtones.

Denton turned his towering frame with ease, as if he pirouetted on the spot. He walked back to his desk, leaving the two professors feeling thoroughly uncomfortable.

Their feelings bordered on rejection, as if they were the only uninvited guests at a party. But this was a job, not a party, and their feelings came second to the mission objective. They knew it, and Denton knew it. Discarding their feelings, they refocused and listened.

'Now to business. My secure access allows me to follow your work with the utmost precision. I can see from the reds that you're gathering some splendid information about "Q-Day".'

'As expected, the messages have become clearer through their location, interpretation, and meaning,' he continued. 'Embedded times indicated the very moment messages would be decoded. Apparently, it identifies you as the leaders of the research, detailing how this event will unfold and our required actions.'

Denton hadn't grasped the full extent of their discoveries; Michael and Peter knew far more—details that would be revealed later. These crucial "joins," their term for the links integrating the facility's teams' work, were secured by their private, encrypted keys, information only they knew. Suddenly, Denton barked what seemed less like a question and more like a direct order.

'And just what the hell are these things called NEMESIS and KYROS?'

Peter's mind was drifting again, still caught in a kaleidoscope of thoughts about Ann. Confused and even threatened by her earlier look, he began to avoid answering questions, instead asking one of his own and addressing something entirely distant.

'What's your first name, Denton?' Peter politely asked.

'My first name? It is Stanislaus, and my middle name is Reel. And what the hell has that got to do with these entities?' thundered Denton as if he commanded a bolt of verbal lightning from on high. It struck Peter with a chilling surprise.

Peter and Michael, having never expected this, repeated his name in unison, 'Reel,' as if trying to grasp the sudden turn of events.

'Yes, Dr. Stanislaus Reel Denton. It has been for years, as far as I know. And it's Doctor to you. And again, what about these bloody things?'

The power dynamic between them visibly shifted. Denton, furious at the question about his first name and their refusal to answer about the entities, abruptly launched himself from behind his desk.

'Gentlemen, it may seem we are equal, but I am the boss around here. GET IT!' Denton bellowed, his words and stare weaponised for maximum impact.

The boastful impact of this single statement ignited a developing hostility within them both. The power dynamic had flipped again. The professors felt the strength of his words, as if a nuclear wind had blown through their souls, dislodging thoughts and demanding their subservience to his question.

His stare was a pinpoint of focus, designed for maximum subjugation. But for all its power, it suddenly became vacant. He seemed unsure why he had stood up, so he sat back down. Peter and Michael collectively felt Denton was insecure in his purpose, maybe even of unsound mind. They almost took a step back in fright as Denton's nostrils flared with a sinister movement as he sat down.

Denton's tone became gentler. His demeanour softened.

'Come, sit down at my desk,' he said, gesturing them towards the chairs.

Overwhelmed by palpable anxiety, they practically fell into the chairs rather than sitting. The creaking of the wood seemed to echo their discomfort as they settled, burdened by apprehension.

With the two of them seated, Denton was visibly more relaxed. His posture demonstrated the art of perfect stasis, and the silence was only broken by the synchronous darting of his eyes as he looked at them.

'I'm still waiting for an answer,' Denton probed.

'We all are, Denton. That's why we are here. To find it for you, for us, and for the world, I guess,' Michael said, astutely aware that Denton was asking about NEMESIS and KYROS.

The professors shuffled their red papers between each other and spoke quietly as Peter ended up with the larger of the two piles. Indeed, they began to resemble a small but unstable square building on his lap.

Denton, whose flustered countenance grew as red as the papers themselves, watched as the pile on Peter's lap grew upward and more unstable. He was just about to erupt like Vesuvius, ready to burn their bodies with a verbal scolding, when Peter looked up from the papers and spoke.

'In a few words, Denton, we've found a finding that's both wrong and right—if that makes any sense?' Peter nervously said.

Denton watched, surprised by this unexpected turn. He opened his mouth to voice his thoughts, but Michael cut him off with a hesitant interjection.

'What we are trying to say, Denton, is we have decoded some remarkable—and I mean remarkable—messages. It seems that the code is now trying to confuse us. We weren't sure at first—' Michael suddenly stopped mid-sentence, imagining a question from Denton would follow, but the expected moment never came.

Thinking quickly, Michael continued, his voice gaining a reassuring tone that seemed to calm Denton's fiery mood.

'Yes, with the help of programmers, crypto-genetic specialists, and other fantastic specialists—I might add—we've moved forward, but we keep running into obstacles. Our progress is at times counterintuitive, as progress is met with regress,' Michael continued, gaining confidence that their message was now being heard.

Confidence, Michael knew, often flirted with recklessness. He felt a surge of it now, mixed with a deep-seated frustration. The more Denton casually dismissed their input, the more the logical boundaries of their professional roles blurred, pushing Michael himself towards a dangerous honesty.

This was certainly true for Michael, who decided to be honest with his boss. It had rankled both him and Peter that there had been so little communication since they had started.

'Denton,' Michael began, his voice tight with suppressed annoyance, 'we frankly expected to meet with you much sooner. Our requests were cancelled daily, yet now, at your leisure, you finally see fit to bring us here, a week after our arrival.'

Denton stared sternly at both, his jaw subtly clenching. He preceded his reply with what sounded like a tectonic sigh of helplessness—a deliberate performance that barely masked the irritation simmering just beneath his composed facade.

'You were, are, and will be our saviours—both of you, your teams, and my staff. And with the help of our CIC—

the Commander-in-Chief—all should be good.' The complimentary statement seemed to pour out from Denton, yet an underlying annoyance was clearly held in check for diplomatic reasons.

As he spoke, he watched his two professors nodding their heads in almost infantile approval. He knew he was a good— no, excellent—puppeteer.

Denton declared, if not decreed, 'I have a presidential order to do everything we need to find out or do before "Q-Day".'

'What have the messages revealed, if that's the correct verb?' Denton asked, wondering who might speak first. The two professors listened, their tandem thoughts already racing, realising the vital question, long overdue, had finally been asked.

To get this answer, Denton commanded them to get up and move across to a very striking dark hexagonal table that sat on the far side of the room.

- 41 -
Confrontation And Revelation

The hexagonal table, measuring two metres at its widest point, inexplicably emanated a sense of unease that hinted at something far more profound than its appearance suggested. The professors moved closer, their gazes drawn to its surface, where microscopic light sources pulsed within its unbelievably dark depths, capturing their attention and sparking an immediate, boundless curiosity.

To their astonishment, their observation of the table was more than passive; it was interactive. The incredible depth of its surface expanded their perception, drawing them into a holographic world of pure interconnectedness, where they temporarily existed as part of its core processing. They had become one with the machine itself.

They merged with their data, transcending the limitations of paper or screen. It wasn't disembodied information; it was a part of them, integrating seamlessly with their minds. Connections that were previously obscure now leaped into holistic focus, like grasping an entire novel at once or seeing the intricate links between countless stories as their minds explored them. It was a truly transformative experience of their research.

Denton's voice cut through their immersive experience, interrupting it before it could become too deep and mind-expanding. With the sound of his words, they were abruptly torn from the world, their minds' expansive awareness, even in its infancy, shrinking back to the confines of their physical bodies. The sudden return to limited perception unsettled them, leaving them momentarily disoriented.

'Professors, do you know what this is?' Denton asked as if he knew their answer in advance. 'No, but whatever it is, I want to live in it!' joked Peter.

Denton looked at them both, a serious expression on his face that showed he had missed Peter's humour entirely. The table had done more than simply capture their scientific curiosity; it had profoundly affected their very being. They had just experienced being a colossal mind of infinite space and calculation, intellectually stimulated in ways they never could have imagined.

'What you saw was a reflection of your own minds in action,' Denton asserted assuredly. 'It connects with whatever questions your mind needs answering. For you, it was your research; for another, it would be their own interests. This is the future, a unity of man and machine as one.'

Peter and Michael wondered if Denton had been interacting with the table a little too much and was becoming slightly delusional. Perhaps that was its drawback, that limited human minds were incompatible with such a vastness of understanding.

'Not sure I'm with you on this,' probed Michael.

'This is the personification of what all this decoding research is about,' Denton proclaimed, his voice rising with conviction. 'This is our experiential upgrade. Our source, our destination, a glimpse of what we will become. Can't you see that? No more limitations, everyone interconnected for the benefit of the one.'

'The one?' trembled the slightly shocked professors in unison.

'But there's more,' Denton eagerly announced.

'In essence, it's a holographic, quantum communication device. Truly transformative technology,' Denton explained, his tone laced with quiet pride. A small laugh escaped him. 'Of course it's not mobile!'

The professors squeezed out a chuckle, but it felt out of place, as if they were trespassing in the mind of an unsound man. All they wanted was a quick exit.

Denton continued, 'The reason why I've been speaking to you remotely, not meeting you in person, is because of this. It allows you to travel, to see, feel, and hear everything. Strange as it may sound, I haven't tried to see just how far I can go, in case I can't come back. I'm more experimenting with it than testing its true limits.'

As Denton laughed at his own dark humour, Peter sarcastically whispered, 'It's a shame he didn't try.'

'So you've been watching us,' Michael said, his voice flat with dawning realisation. 'This whole time, you were watching us through this.'

'Oh, come on, this is surveillance central, this is the NSA!' retorted Denton, as if such a statement could be used to explain away anything.

The two professors stood in stunned silence. For days they had worked far beyond normal human endurance in search of something or someone coded for the greater good of humanity.

Yet here was their boss, telling them they had been watched constantly, without permission. To make matters worse, he had offered no real feedback, leaving them to struggle in the belief that they were considered too self-sufficient to need his guidance.

'With respect Denton, we expected you to help us a little,' Peter bravely said.

'Help!' Denton barked, a shocked and affronted sneer twisting his lips at the sheer temerity of the request. His eyes snapped open, locking onto Peter with a gaze of unmerciful, cold command. A chillingly ruthless thought solidified in his mind: "Subordinates don't question; they obey. Their minds aren't their own; they're mere extensions of my will."

'Here before me are the world's top two scientists in the field. Professors, what do you mean you haven't received help from us?' Denton questioned. 'We have provided a facility with access to supercomputers and brought disparate teams together that now work like a perfectly tuned engine.'

After a suitably pregnant pause, Denton continued his mini-lecture, but not before crossing the space between them to open his wide arms and gently hug them both.

'Listen to me,' Denton said, 'I have faith in you, your countries have faith in you, hell, even my dog has faith in you,' he opined.

Peter gently broke free from Denton's hug of unrequested confinement. 'You don't have a dog!' he said. Michael, looking puzzled, turned to Peter. 'You don't?' he questioned. Peter looked back at him, and then, in a cold voice, said, 'No, he shot it!'

Denton regathered his two errant sheep with yet another hug. He then looked at them in turn and said in a moribund voice, a tone that resonated with their deepest fears of being so far underground: 'Yes, but out of loyalty, he was old… not like you of course.'

As he finished this statement, they felt the hug get tighter and wondered whether this was symbolic of his neurotic obsession with tight surveillance. Denton released them, but they knew they weren't free from his constant observation.

As he spoke, the table and the space above shimmered to life with an almost blinding intensity. What materialised wasn't just light, but a vivid display – their research, their private notes from the last few days, laid bare before them in the air.

The intricate details, the very thoughts they'd committed to digital paper, hung suspended before them. Every equation, every hypothesis, every passing thought now hung in the air, exposed for anyone to see.

A cold realisation dawned: their secluded work hadn't escaped unseen eyes. A shared look of awe, quickly replaced by a deeply unsettling shock, passed between Peter and Michael. What else had this strange display witnessed?

A sudden, eerie creak sliced through the laboratory's hum, making both scientists jolt.

Denton nonchalantly said, 'That's just the quantum resonance stabiliser calibrating. Remember that little trinket on my desk?' He chuckled, a knowing glint in his eye. 'Nearly sent my deputy running for the hills the first time he heard it,' Denton continued, waving a dismissive hand towards a nearby piece of equipment. 'Thought the world was ending.'

Their attention, briefly snagged by the sound, drifted back to the mesmerising holographic images dancing in the air. But then, a flicker of realisation dawned: Denton had been talking about something else. They turned, their gazes sweeping the area, but the object from his desk had vanished.

"Where did it go?" they thought in unison, a fresh wave of curiosity washing over them.

Denton gestured to a small recess at the far edge of the table. Snugly nestled within was the missing object.

'And what exactly is that?' Michael pressed. His gaze fixed on it.

'Think of it as a vault,' Denton said, his voice dropping slightly.

'It's capable of holding all the information humanity has ever conceived, and more. A mere handful of these, apparently, could store it all. And the truly fascinating part? It's not our creation; it came from overseas. It operates on five dimensions – the familiar three, plus two more based on something called a crystal lattice. What that actually means is, I'm afraid, beyond me.'

His words hung in the air, hinting at secrets far beyond their current understanding.

'This is what we are using to help you, and it's the zenith of computing power. I should think you're proud, humbled and maybe just a bit worried by that thought,' Denton continued, his tone sharp with an underlying edge.

'Now, I may not be a scientist, but I can read and understand what you've written – in English, at least. Let's see if I can accurately summarise your work,' Denton said, before outlining his thoughts on the project to date.

A clear holographic cube, shimmering in the air, materialised before them. Inside, it displayed many red research papers spread out at different depths. Bright coloured lines connected the papers, a web of glowing threads linking their work together.

As Denton talked to it, papers could be enlarged for reading or minimised to reveal their links to others, creating a feeling of deep immersion through the way light interacted with the hologram.

The computer could dynamically rearrange the papers and lines, adding or removing them based on the search query. It could also highlight documents or connections related to spoken keywords, and even suggest other relevant research in real-time.

Denton continued, 'As I understand it, we've confirmed "junk DNA" isn't useless after all; it has multiple hidden functions. Given it forms 98% of our DNA, that's hardly surprising. Accessing it requires deciphering incredibly complex patterns. Interestingly, each new piece of decoded information has a precise date and time – the exact moment it's decoded has been termed "Encoded Chronometric Unfolding."'

Your work suggests an action linked to the word "pill" and its interaction with our DNA. Denton paused, looking at them. 'Have you found more connections between actions and the pill?'

Peter took over.

'Yes, Denton, your understanding is correct. We believe a significant part of the code is intricately embedded in this "junk DNA". The decoded sections, so far, hint at a profound upcoming event. And yes, there's a date: midnight, December 31st, or "Q-Day". The code also mentions NEMESIS and KYROS, seemingly as entities. Strangely, it also indicates they will be "of our hand", which, embarrassingly, at present, makes little sense to us.

'The "upgrade" seems to require ingestion, probably the pill referred to earlier,' Peter continued, his tone grave.

'It's designed to interact with our DNA. Those who don't take it will perish rapidly.'

'Perish!' Denton interjected loudly. 'You mean die? That's not evolution, that's annihilation,' he said, his voice now upset. Peter remained quiet; Michael just looked on, seemingly rooted to the spot, thinking how desperate the situation was, how insignificant they felt in the grand scheme of this decoding investigation.

Meanwhile, Denton's brain was turning over like a pristine engine, number crunching figures: from the time left until "Q-Time", to how eight billion human souls on Planet Earth could be saved.

'This is crazy!' Denton bellowed. 'We all have families, many of us have our beautiful children to nurture. They deserve our help, our fortitude to ensure they have a future to inherit, just as much as we have. Yet, here you are saying "perish".

'There are people out there who wait weeks to find medicinal tablets. Many are fighting for survival as medicines become harder to purchase.

'Tell me, Peter,' Denton challenged, his voice now sharp with an implied killer question.

'Given we are approximately months away from this moment of judgement day—if I may call it that—how are we supposed to produce this pill in time? We still don't know for sure it is a pill.

'We don't know the ingredients, we don't know if it's a single dose... we don't know shit!' Denton's voice was a furious protest, his jaw tight, a vein throbbing at his temple, radiating palpable anger. 'I have people to answer to, just as you do to me. My cold business model is a transactional mindset and I get paid by results. It's a simple chain of fiscal command, and I want my piece of the pie, if not two pieces as I'm worth it.'

Peter and Michael stood in quiet shock. Who were these people? The US government perhaps? How big a pie was he talking about? They recalled how they'd felt when they entered his office: like two miscreant schoolboys summoned by their headmaster. Now they were being told off, and they felt subordinate, both by his outburst and his elevated position.

They absorbed the pertinent implications of Denton's outburst. He was a typical boss: he wanted results but failed to recognise the immense work they'd invested to reach this point.

They were not Gods who could explain all to satisfy his narrow, ego-driven mentality, but mere mortals confined within their thinking, dwarfed by the project's intense data extraction. The project's demands and its implications were too much for a mere mortal to bear, and Peter briefly considered resigning.

Michael wanted to take over; he could clearly see Peter buckling under the responsibility, struggling with the immense knowledge. He took a step forward to catch Peter's dwindling focus, a result of stress and mental fatigue from both the project and Ann.

'If I may Peter, if that's all right?' questioned a polite and softly spoken Michael.

Peter looked round at Michael. Denton looked back and forth between them, wondering what they were up to. His overblown self-image of importance meant he saw their exchange as a threat, not a moment of shared purpose.

'Are you a double act who's forgotten their lines,' Denton said with severity.

'I wish we knew all our lines, then we wouldn't feel so overshadowed, indeed disempowered by what's expected of us,' exclaimed Michael in support of his colleague.

He paused with difficulty, a troubled look developing on his face. He wasn't sure how to deliver his next words, but he knew he must.

'Just yesterday, we finally confirmed an earlier decode that cross-references the data with the names NEMESIS and KYROS. But their exact nature remains elusive.'

'KYROS?' Denton exclaimed, his voice sharp with surprise. 'Two contrasting names—NEMESIS obviously means retribution, payback of some kind. But KYROS? If my Greek is correct, it means "Lord",' he continued, a deeply perplexed look on his face, as if he alone had been burdened with deciphering their true significance.

'I think it also means master,' Michael chipped in. 'It carries connotations of authority, power, and leadership.'

A shadow crossed Peter's face—concern at what Michael was saying and its implications for the project. They had spoken about these entities in their few rare moments away from the work. He had already witnessed Denton's reaction and wasn't sure if his now fatigued mind could cope. He took a deep breath, crossed his fingers (unnoticed by the others), hoping the next few minutes would be better received.

Michael spoke, 'Compounding our difficulties with NEMESIS and KYROS is a growing concern. We've detected persistent and unidentified evolving problems within our decoding programs. It's as if something is actively interfering with our work, subtly shifting patterns and throwing up roadblocks.

'Could this be deliberate? Is it possible someone, or something, is attempting to sabotage our efforts to understand what's coming?' Michael questioned, his voice laced with frustration.

'Our sophisticated programs seem to be battling a self-modifying infection. No matter what countermeasures our crypto-programmers implement, we find ourselves back at square one. This interference has led us to a complete impasse – a circular analysis where progress has ground to a virtual standstill,' concluded Michael.

'Are you suggesting sabotage?' questioned a very perplexed Denton.

'It must be considered a possibility,' interjected Peter, with a feeling of having already lost the war.

'So you're suggesting sabotage?' Denton questioned, his mind racing to connect the dots. 'That's a serious accusation. But you still haven't answered my earlier question: what are these entities?'

Peter and Michael exchanged a look. It was a silent understanding: the time had come to reveal everything. With renewed confidence from their brief respite, Peter stepped forward and took the lead.

'Regarding NEMESIS, our analysis indicates it's an organic entity. Its existence is, apparently, by "our hand". We can assume at this time that KYROS has the same genesis. Its fundamental genetic code is intertwined with our own DNA.

'Extracting its blueprint is surprisingly straightforward. It appears pre-encoded within us, almost like a design feature. After processing immense data and performing incomprehensibly complex geometric calculations, we pinpointed the specific DNA sequences using multiple geometric locations across the genome. Now, the next stage is simpler. We will isolate that DNA and cultivate it in the lab. This is similar to advanced IVF using an artificial incubator,' indicated Peter.

Denton, a man who had stared into the abyss of human conflict across the globe, finally cracked. 'Alien...inside us?'

Peter's voice dropped, a chilling resonance in the sudden silence.

'And if that truth shakes you, Doctor, then what terrifying reflection does it cast upon our own origins?'

'Do we need this entity? Surely, if we know the constituents of the pill, we can progress without its involvement,' argued Denton.

'I agree with the principle. But we think it's necessary. Otherwise, why are they so interlinked? You have deep underground laboratories here; if it were to go wrong, we could destroy it. Hopefully, that would be after we've gained more knowledge about this pill,' Peter suggested.

'By implication, you're saying the two are related. Maybe they're inextricably intertwined,' questioned a deeply unsettled Denton. The sheer knowledge of it all was now fatiguing his brain; it had done the same to Peter only moments earlier.

'At present, it would be fair to deduce that,' said Peter.

'Michael, have you nothing to add?' Denton demanded, his voice sharp with anger. Yet, beneath the fury, he seemed both appeased and oddly broken by the overwhelming evidence.

As Michael pondered his Majesty's command, Peter sensed a new conversation emerging. Something felt wrong. His reaction to potential sabotage unsettled Peter. Soon, his perception of Dr. Denton would vanish entirely.

Denton stated, 'This has been an enlightening session, indeed. I believe we should proceed with this entity called NEMESIS. Perhaps, if we can truly understand one, we will have no need for the other—KYROS. I also think you need to resolve these decoding anomalies. It sounds to me that you're so close, and it is futile to stop at this stage.'

If any project moment surpassed their daily decodes, this was it. Years of friendship had forged their minds into one, and now, a subtly bewildered glance passed between them, unseen by Denton. For both, their thoughts about Denton had just inexplicably shifted.

"Why did Denton assume NEMESIS came first? Was it simply because it was the first letter of the Greek alphabet? And why was he so readily compliant in agreeing to the genesis of this entity? Would he not have to arrange approvals from his line managers and the logistics department? Doesn't that take time? Why was he so convinced the pill and the entity were related – they hadn't stated it explicitly, only implied it."

His conviction about their connection without concrete information raised questions about his reasoning and potential biases. Furthermore, why was he outwardly unconcerned about being informed about possible sabotage?

Would not the super-secret importance of the project be in question, if there were people inside the project trying to harm its function and outcome? If he was so involved at a distance as he said, how on earth would he not be aware of it?

To Peter and Michael, Denton's leadership raised several red flags. Was it incompetence, negligence, or something more sinister?

Denton studied their faces, attempting to unlock their thoughts, but he had the wrong key. Relying on his self-importance, he addressed them.

'Peter and Michael, this afternoon has been truly revealing. I thank you. Your exemplary work was well-summarised. I have other commitments; I expected a shorter meeting, but your valuable discourse is central to your profession.'

'Your priority is to resolve those anomalies, ensure further decoding, and make progress on this super-secret pill's ingredients. My priority will be to manage logistics for NEMESIS, and monitor your progress like a hawk. If there are no questions, you're free to leave,' Denton stated haughtily.

Peter and Michael exchanged glances. The miscreant schoolboy analogy solidified. Their illustrious leader had, at last, deemed them worthy of release.

Both thanked Denton with a smile and the flimsiest of handshakes, gathering their red papers, which hadn't been needed. As they made for the lift, Denton's phone shrieked, its insistent tone bullying the office quiet. They both looked back after Peter pressed the lift button. Denton's voice sounded nervous, entirely out of place. He glared at them, his privacy seemingly invaded, and waved his hand as if to say, 'be off with you.'

A Bitter Lunch

Five floors above the ongoing meeting, Ann was deep in thought, pondering her work. Each day unfurled for her in a familiar pattern. As a social historian, her role was pivotal; she meticulously scrutinised the diary entries, focusing on various themes within them.

The objective was to unearth the intricate interrelationships between the researchers' individual actions and reactions, both within their teams and as a collective. Crucially, it would also serve as a research diary, offering unique insights into the interface between psychology and science.

Her emotional chasm with Peter grew, deepening daily. Their perpetual busyness ensured they remained distant, almost strangers. She longed for their university days: the easy banter, the comforting intimacy, and the memories clinging to their mansion walls.

After a morning choked with diary entries and two demanding research teams, she sought respite in the restaurant. As she neared the doors, craving lunch, they parted, and Roger emerged like a shadow. The restaurant's spiced warmth instantly faded into a glacial chill as his presence dominated the doorway.

A phantom prickle danced at the nape of Ann's neck, a visceral echo of the disquiet that had clung to her like a second skin all morning. The promised symphony of ginger and cumin, moments ago a tantalising lure, now flattened, muted by his looming form.

He devoured her with his gaze, mentally undressing her, instantly making her uncomfortable. The sight pulled her back to the passion of their room the previous night. Her clothed presence now warred with the vivid nakedness of the night before, leaving her unnerved.

Behind his attraction, Ann was just another object, a useful one. Her utility would soon expire, only for another woman to temporarily monopolise his thoughts.

'Oh, not now, I'm busy,' said an exasperated Ann. Just being seen with Roger outside the sanctuary of her room assaulted her conscience, feeling like a direct attack on Peter. This truth was made stark by their recent, secret night of shared intimacy.

'Don't whine, Ann, did you speak to Peter?' Roger asked.

'No, he's very busy, and so should you be.'

'Look, it's hard to keep our affair secret in such a large, confined facility. People talk, Ann.'

'Well, you will have to keep it to yourself. Perhaps you could try the same with your appendage,' retorted Ann caustically.

'You are my pleasure now. I cannot help but sense your fragrance.'

'If Peter finds out about us, I won't be able to help you.'

'I'll be all right. Peter is married to his work, you know that.'

'Listen here, you oversized phallus,' Ann said, her voice dropping to a low growl, 'Peter and I go back a long way. We share more memories than just our one passionate night.'

'Nice memory, though?'

'Of course, but don't push it, or you'll be one too!'

'What's that?'

'A memory.'

'Look, just tell him, all right!'

'You need to understand, I will never leave Peter. He loves me for who and what I am. Take that and process it,' Ann stringently emphasised. She turned and walked away towards the Indian research laboratory, her reasoning clouded by a bewildering mix of conflicting emotions.

The self-reproach stung: why this adolescent rebellion against Peter, who was the bedrock of her world? Yet here she was, fracturing that foundation for a man who'd undoubtedly discard her for a younger woman like yesterday's pleasure—the thought created a sharp, internal flinch.

A sudden, steely resolve tightened her chest: enough. She would excise these fleeting, superficial hungers that held no more substance than their transient presence in this sterile place.

Roger watched as Ann walked away from him. Wasn't she going to have something to eat? This change of course only confirmed to him how much he muddled her thoughts and emotions.

This only made him more desperate to tether his new woman with a possessive leash. To him, the pleasure was mutual, and her marriage was merely a hurdle to overcome. He considered that she didn't have much else besides her work.

Yes, he had other sources of pleasure to explore too, so he genuinely thought he was doing her a favour by allocating time to her. He mused on how bodily distractions were plentiful when one is locked away from reality's playground.

His mind, overwhelmed by work's equations and deadlines, had scant room for complex emotions or subtle social cues. Thoughts of Ann, in particular, triggered an instinctive drive for immediate action and gratification, regardless of potential consequences.

This often led him to make mistakes—most small and easily rectified—but occasionally, the complete opposite occurred. Those were the ones that time might eventually heal, as the idiom "time is a great healer" suggested.

And it was the latter kind of mistake—the kind that time might eventually heal—that Roger foolishly decided to make with Ann as he watched her stop, punch the air in frustration, and then turn around and walk back towards him.

Was she turning back to apologise, make another date? His calculated thoughts powered through his mind, seeking an answer, a measure to satisfy his anticipation of what was to be said.

Ann advanced, stopping inches from him. She inhaled a deep, deliberate breath, poised as if to deliver a scathing retort, but instead, a soft, almost inaudible chuckle escaped her lips. This was a laugh refined to a lethal art, a sound so utterly devoid of warmth and chillingly precise. It behaved as an explosive charge in the minds of those who craved approval, delivering instead the cold sting of utter dismissal.

With this, she turned and walked into the restaurant. The warm, inviting scents of roasting garlic and simmering tomato sauce immediately enveloped her, mingling with the convivial clatter of cutlery and the murmur of contented chatter. It was an embrace of everyday life, a comforting antidote to the tension she'd left behind.

Roger was about to detonate with rage. He had been psychologically usurped with merely a smile and laugh. He watched her enter the restaurant and was tempted to try and avenge his humiliation, but too many people were there and he had work to do.

Instead, he projected his anger with what seemed like nice words but their intonation and undertone were anything but.

'Enjoy your lunch, sweetheart,' snarled Roger, a venomous hiss barely concealing the visceral wound Ann's effortless belittling had carved into his manhood. His pride was shredded, leaving only a raw, burning fury.

Ann stopped. A curt, polite smile flickered across Ann's lips as she heard his hissy contempt. Her own contempt for Roger hissed from her lips: 'Prick on legs, or just legs with a prick?'

A dry, almost self-mocking curve touched her mouth at the sheer ridiculousness of her internal wrestling match with these words. She resumed her victory walk to move towards the ordering counter.

With food and drink ordered, Ann walked to her usual table, carrying her food tray. She maintained her stunning, petite figure no matter what she ate, a fact many, including Roger, found captivating.

The quiet anticipation of her first mouthful was shattered by the restaurant doors exploding open, hitting the wall with a familiar bang. Roger? Inevitably. He'd barely been gone a minute. Seconds, probably. It was a pattern, after all. It seemed he couldn't resist a repeat performance in any context.

Looking around with resignation, Ann was surprised to see it wasn't Roger but a familiar woman: Samantha, a petite and attractive British programmer in her mid-twenties. Samantha possessed a "wicked" playful side. Ann recalled Samantha telling her during a research diary visit that she was among the brightest in her university cohort. Recently, she had earned her doctorate in mathematical genetics.

'Samantha!' Ann called out. Recognising her, Samantha nodded approval as Ann gestured to a chair opposite. After purchasing some refreshments, Samantha walked over.

'How are you?' enquired Samantha, her presence incredibly magnetic.

'Tired, but aren't we all,' said a depleted-sounding Ann, her mind very much on Roger and the breaking of her wedding vows to Peter.

'And you, Samantha?' Ann asked.

'Couldn't be better. I do love my job, but I wonder if it makes me ethically blinkered to what we may be engineering here. Do we have a guilty mind, a mens rea no less?' Samantha scowled.

'I would never have thought you used to be a law teacher, Samantha,' replied an amused Ann.

'I could really do with seeing some men's rears,' Samantha chuckled, a playful glint in her eye. 'Couldn't we all, dear!' Ann retorted, her knowing look mirroring Samantha's. Their shared laughter, a clear balm for their stress, filled the air.

They ate and drank sparingly, their minds preoccupied with their experiences at the facility. They were searching for a significant topic to discuss, a pivotal point (or points) to dive into.

'We can be so blinkered sometimes, can't we?' Samantha posed.

'With men's rears?' questioned a teasing Ann.

Samantha laughed at the thought.

'No, all of us are fearful for where this all leads,' expressed Samantha.

Ann understood this all too well. Her research diary notes frequently documented the scientists' apprehension, even fear, that what they were doing was not only unusual but also bordered on playing God.

'You've spoken to others?' asked Ann politely.

'Of course, not all, but four or five. They think we may be doing the devil's work—killing off people!'

'That's not what this is about, quite the opposite surely!' Ann challenged, hearing this.

'We aren't supposed to talk about this. The boss handles all that, but e-communications don't work here, do they? This super-secret, hermetically sealed facility needs human touch, so we have these infrequent chats.'

'Is that what the fear is about?' Ann pressed, awaiting a quick reply.

'Of course, but a couple say a "being" is in the process of creation,' said a hesitant Samantha.

Ann laughed and questioned mockingly, 'Being?'

'Well...yes...being. Bizarre, I know, but what is this place if not bizarre? Totally out of sync with what we regard as reality?' Samantha argued politely.

'Being? Science fiction gone rogue, more like!' Ann laughed again.

'If only, but that's the word I hear from your son, Nathan. He does talk a lot of gibberish sometimes, even for an educated man,' replied Samantha.

She looked away to gather her thoughts, and then returned to Ann's delicate, inviting stare.

'Nathan, your son, said this guy called Roger, who works with him, was talking to your husband yesterday. Whatever was said between them, they both looked agitated. Between us, I do fancy Roger, and I think it's mutual. I later asked him why he appeared agitated—knowing he wouldn't make our chat an issue. He said he saw some red papers on his desk and as they were talking, he—'

'He, what?' interrupted Ann, using her boss's intonation that cut words into a person like a scalpel does to skin.

'Please don't tell Peter, please!' implored Samantha.

'What did he do?'

'He took them!'

'Bloody fool! How many reds did he take, did he tell you?' Ann quickly asked. Roger was smart, but clearly not in this instance. Ann clenched her fists tightly around her utensils, her knuckles white.

'Have you seen them?' asked Samantha. Ann was taken aback by this question. Why would she have?

She replied in her sternest voice, 'No!'

Once again, Samantha looked away to gather her thoughts. It was a charming idiosyncrasy to behold, but one that could be weaponised to control her conversation if someone was so inclined. Her contemplation over, she revisited Ann's gaze.

'Look, Ann, I like you and need a chat. Roger has asked me to his room this evening to look at these red papers, as they mention this "being". I'm sure he wants me for more, though. He's well-endowed, so rumours go, and I don't just mean intellectually. After all, weeks away from home, no fun... I need some masculine interaction!'

'His room, huh?' Ann said, anger and distrust coiling tighter inside her. She gripped the utensils even harder, the rigid steel in her hands a cold, sharp echo of the retribution hardening within her.

'Yes, his room! I didn't think he was asking me there just to check the red papers,' she giggled, her eyes gleaming with a knowing, almost lascivious spark that spoke volumes beyond her words.

'We're not talking about help with English, if you know what I mean. And I ought to know; I used to teach that subject. Indeed, I particularly enjoyed showing how even simple monosyllables could say so much more, all thanks to a well-placed diphthong.'

'Really, monosyllables and diphthongs!' said a bemused Ann, truly wanting to know about the red papers.

'Yes, really! In fact, Roger can dip his silly balls into my thongs anytime!'

This sexual innuendo and wordplay made them laugh so loudly it might have echoed in the nearby DNA lab. But Ann's laughter masked her growing anger with Roger. Unfortunately, it was only going to get much worse.

'Saying that, guess what? I think he's been shagging some stupid bitch from another team, or so he said. I love competition, but only when I win.'

'Stupid bitch, you say!'

'Well, that's what he said,' replied Samantha. Ann's eyes widened, and she missed a breath in shocking surprise. A flicker in Samantha's eyes, a slight hesitation in her tone— Ann's intuition, a primal antenna, sensed the truth permeating the veil of lies Samantha was weaving. It suggested a deliberate manipulation of her emotions.

'Any ideas who?' asked Ann coolly and calculatingly, her inner persona a volcano ready to erupt.

Samantha leaned forward, looking around furtively to ensure no one else could hear: 'No, but he did say she was "hard up!"'

'Fuck me, hard up!' screeched Ann, making Samantha feel it was somehow personal. Perhaps it was. Ann felt a gnawing suspicion that she was the one Roger had called "hard up", a thought that tore at her despite Samantha appearing a pleasant enough girl.

"Why would Samantha do this?" Ann wondered, suspecting perhaps jealousy had surrounded Samantha when she was younger. The thought struck her: "Jealousy, like rust to metal, corroded the personality with no remission once the damage was done."

Samantha leaned forward again.

'Imagine that, hard up,' Sam laughed teasingly, yet with a casual air.

'Anyway, here's some more juicy news. I think we are going to get it on later tonight,' Samantha said saucily with another wink to confirm the sexual reference. 'Show him what a real woman is,' she laughed again.

Ann stared at Samantha, a furious fire building behind her eyes, ignited by the grotesque truth of Roger's private thoughts. Samantha, maddeningly serene, appeared utterly unaware, yet a poisoned doubt began to fester in Ann: 'How much, or how little, did this woman truly comprehend?'

The comedic sting of the situation, so potent just moments ago, dissolved into something far more chilling for Ann. Her past affection for Roger, once a warm ember, imploded, leaving behind a vacuum quickly filled by a nascent malice. There was no longer a question of if retribution would come, only the terrifying precision of when.

'Anyway, I'll tell you tomorrow about the red papers. He's going to be a friend with added extras, if you catch my drift!' Samantha said, a broad grin and a twinkle in her eyes. She stood up and walked behind her chair, her gaze meeting Ann's. She noticed a mischievous glint in Ann's gaze, making her eagerly anticipate what was to come.

Samantha was correct. With that last statement, which left little to the imagination, Roger's fate was signed and sealed. It would be delivered first class with no return to sender.

Ann couldn't resist a veiled jab at Roger, a cutting remark delivered with a sweet smile for Samantha. 'I bet if he was back in Roman times, when honour in battle and obedience to the state was everything, his only attribute would be called "Maximus Organus Phallus,"' she quipped, her eyes twinkling with a malice only she understood.

Samantha's eyes widened in surprise at Ann's retort. She leaned forward, steadying herself, as they both burst into laughter, like two young girls sharing a wicked secret. But behind Ann's laughter, a colder implication about Roger lingered, unsettling and unspoken.

Ann's countenance dramatically changed. With a serious intonation and a worrying look, she added, 'Careful Samantha, a mere object of love can become a lethal weapon of nefarious malice.' She gripped her knife tightly and banged it against the table, taking them both by surprise.

Samantha pushed her chair back in, oblivious to Ann's alarming gesture and the hidden barb. As she moved, Ann's gaze lingered on Samantha, observing the striking similarity to her own figure: beautifully proportioned, with graceful curves and a captivating allure.

Samantha's radiance had such presence that it would be difficult not to see her in a crowded room. And to top it all, they were both eloquent in their respective ways, career-minded professionals—Samantha, a genetic mathematician; Ann, a social historian.

Confronted by all these qualities in Samantha, Ann thought ruefully: "What could go wrong when Roger saw her?"

Saying goodbye to Ann, Samantha started to walk away but stopped. She turned around and scrutinised Ann.

'Please don't tell your husband about the red papers; he has everything on his computer anyway, so he probably won't miss them,' pleaded Samantha.

'Not everything, I hope!' Ann ominously replied, hoping that her secret night sessions with Roger and their widening implications were among the things he hadn't backed up.

Ann reflected on what had transpired. She hadn't planned to return to the restaurant after meeting awful Roger. Nor had she intended to stay for so long. Now, however, she sat contemplating what had just been said. Her backstabbing lover was preoccupied elsewhere, and retribution consumed her. Not for decades had the emotions of love and hate run through her veins as they did now.

As she thought, an idea to expose Roger came to mind. She decided to go back to the British team and play a game of bluff with him. She chuckled softly at the ironic absurdity, recognising the double entendre from Samantha's earlier comment.

- 43 -
Denton's Double Game

With Peter and Michael now safely in the lift and out of earshot, Denton felt comfortable enough to make his own call. 'Dr. Denton?' asked the foreboding voice.

Denton slumped back in his chair with apprehension, his right hand gripping the phone tightly. His mind raced, struggling to recall the voice. Static pierced his brief silence as he tried to place it.

'Speaking,' Denton replied, a knot of unease tightening in his gut. 'Who is this?'

Inside, a chilling certainty settled over him: he might not know who the caller was, but he instinctively recognised what they represented.

'Before I answer that, I can see you haven't pressed the red encryption button again,' said the mysterious caller.

Denton quickly pressed the button – there was no time to waste.

'Button pressed. Who is this?' he asked again, a flicker of self-reproach at his carelessness adding to his anxiety.

'My name is unimportant. What you do is,' he said, his voice a low, unsettling drawl.

A deep unease gripped Denton, fuelled by the caller's mysterious air. Sweat beaded on his forehead as a sudden, chilling recognition hit him: his prestigious status was nothing more than a puppet's. On this supposedly secure line, one terrifying question emerged: how did he have the number?

Denton's anger surged, striking him to his very core. He slammed his right hand onto the desk with brutal force, the bones protesting with a sharp, agonising crack. He raised his voice, spitting anger and annoyance.

'I don't know who you are, but I'm putting the phone down right now. I'll personally trace your number, from which you'll be hunted down like prey and suitably dealt with... harshly, I hope.'

'Come, come, Dr. Denton. You're in our fold now. I'm contacting you to get your thoughts in order. We don't want any slip-ups, do we?' the voice asserted, still not naming itself.

Denton was slow to grasp the implications. Perhaps he was simply tired of it all. The demands of being Director had woven so tightly into his being that separating them felt impossible. The recently completed meeting with Peter and Michael, for instance, had left him slightly muddled by the sheer volume of intriguing information they had conveyed.

His muddled state wasn't helped by the mysterious man now on the phone. This was an intermediary for the shadow group who'd approached him months back, seeking to enlist his services and knowledge. Denton saw no conflict; he was a patriotic man of service and would never undermine the elite system he believed made America great.

They shared the same ideology: that power and wealth were inseparable. Denton possessed the former but little of the latter; he yearned to enhance his standing and live in luxury. No more work, no more mental strain – just the freedom to be himself.

'I don't think I know your name, but I do know you represent a group who share similar interests to me,' Denton said. He needed to clarify whom he was talking to, even if only by group, not by name.

'Thank you, Dr Denton, for not putting the phone down. You can call me "Corvus" if that makes you feel better.'

'Of course, I am at your service... and do call me Denton, please,' he replied obligingly.

'I need an update on what's going on there. In particular, how well are your "delaying" tactics proving successful?' Corvus asked.

Denton explained the current state of the research, emphasising how he was monitoring Peter and Michael, his two key scientists, to ensure they stayed on track and remained unsuspicious. Yet, a brutal truth compelled him: his future wealth, perhaps even his life, hinged on meeting the demands of his shadow group benefactors.

He explained that his earlier meeting with them hadn't gone as well as expected. They had raised the issue of possible sabotage and the project's direction. They were concerned about the genesis of an entity, or entities, and their potential relationship to the pill.

He said to Corvus, 'I didn't expect them to suspect sabotage so quickly; I was utterly taken aback, lost for words.'

'Very interesting, Denton. The bottom line for my group is that we get to know first. We know something is going to happen, "Q-Day", I think you called it. There are many vested interests who don't want to wake up one morning and find you've helped separate them from their amassed power and wealth.'

'The group is averse to uncertainty, as it signifies a weakening of their grip on power. Hushed questions in the dark corridors of power lead to swift, decisive action to ensure that grip is maintained. You well appreciate the dynamics of power; power attracts power, Denton. And you, of all people, are proof of that.'

Denton sat listening, absorbing not only the words but also their nefarious implications, both for the group and for him.

'This Peter, he has a son, Nathan, yes?' asked Corvus.

'That's correct, he does. Why?' responded Denton to a question that rattled him.

Clearly, Corvus didn't know it was his son. Denton had kept Nathan's true paternity a secret between himself and Ann. If revealed, it could cause arguments between Peter, Ann, and Nathan, potentially disrupting the project. Such a disruption would then impact Michael and all who worked closely with them. Denton proceeded cautiously with Corvus.

'I want you to use him to get Peter and Michael to open up about what they're decoding. He can also eavesdrop on their private conversations when he's around them, given his close working relationship. They trust him, so they might say something in advance. To my group, forewarned is forearmed. He will be our informant. We'll provide extra money for his services to you,' said Corvus.

'How much?' asked Denton, suddenly realising what a foolish question it was. It blurted out, a reflection of how the desire for money could slowly monopolise one's thinking.

'It's paid by results,' said Corvus.

'It would help if I had a figure; it would make him easier to bribe... I mean, buy his services, and his silence too, I guess,' suggested Denton.

'Fair point. Tell him it's one thousand dollars a week, non-negotiable and payable on results. That should encourage a good flow of insider information, along with your own. Any mismatch may suggest they suspect your motives, Denton.

That won't be good for you,' Corvus said, his voice laced with threat.

He continued, 'They won't suspect Nathan; he's family.'

Denton took a huge gamble with Corvus. First, he had deceived Corvus into paying more money to him, of which Nathan would most likely see only half, if he were lucky. Second, he had deceived him about Nathan's true father. Denton was clearly having an existential crisis of loyalty, and if pushed, he knew where it lay – with money.

'I like your thinking, Corvus,' affirmed Denton.

'I'm glad we are thinking the same, Denton,' replied Corvus.

'Is there anything else?' Denton asked, his mind utterly exhausted from the afternoon's interrogation.

'Not for now. Goodbye!' said Corvus, and the call ended before Denton could even reply.

Denton knew his plans were on shaky ground. He needed to retire; he'd had enough. This was his golden opportunity to make money, lots of it. He had the connections and mindset to set himself up without truly harming anyone. Well... no more than the system was already doing, at least.

Not wasting the opportunity, he rang the cryptoprogramming section and spoke to Nathan. Within minutes, Nathan was enthusiastically standing before his desk, ready. Denton then explained he was enlisted on a top-secret, high-level mission to monitor conversations around the facility.

As most of his time would be working with or close to Peter and Michael, much of his report would naturally focus on them. Denton crafted his deception so skilfully that Nathan readily agreed. He was, after all, working for the President of the USA.

Deception done, Nathan was about to leave when he noticed the striking dark hexagonal table on the far side of the room. He was drawn to it, as if it called him over.

'That table over there, it's amazing. The dark colour – it's hypnotic, almost otherworldly,' said a surprised and slightly overwhelmed Nathan.

'Come, let's take a look,' invited Denton as he gesticulated with a guiding wave of left arm towards the table.

They walked over to the table, surveying its magnificent, almost mystical craftsmanship.

'What are those sparkly lights, dots, whatever they are?' asked Nathan.

'Peter and Michael were here earlier and wondered the same. Once they knew, even they were impressed,' teased Denton, clearly withholding its purpose.

Nathan took the bait and asked more. Denton gave the same answers as he had earlier, which only served to intrigue Nathan, suitably piquing his curiosity and desire to experience it.

'Before you look into it, Nathan, I need to warn you,' Denton cautioned, with a slight air of worry and mystery.
'When you feel you are not you, pull back. Don't hesitate – pull back,' Denton said, his voice laced with such worry and mystery that Nathan was completely hooked, eager to try it.

'How do you mean, pull back? What if I didn't?' asked Nathan, a flicker of worry in his eyes.

'You'll just know when to pull back. If you don't, who knows what could happen. It's technology not of our making, so I really don't know,' said a slightly fearful Denton, his tone stressing that it had to be respected, not played with.

The statement about the origin of manufacture went right over Nathan's head; he was too absorbed in his need to interact with the table.

'Well, every day you need some fun,' Nathan said humorously, as if to take the edge off what it might do to him. Denton looked on with a mixture of concern and interest in what Nathan would experience.

He bent over the table, looking into its hypnotic lights, which twinkled like distant stars. Unlike them, Nathan felt a magnetic pull to look harder and deeper, as if something more lay hidden. His mind was slowly being taken over; images of past experiences flew across his mind, evoking a panoply of senses, as if he were reliving them.

Suddenly, Nathan was tugged back from the precipice by Denton, who grabbed the back of his poorly fitted jacket. Nathan looked around with eyes bulbous and vacant for a second or two.

'I told you to be careful, didn't I?' Denton harshly reminded him. Then, with a wry smile and a wink, he added, 'Back to work for you, my lad, and no loitering on the way.' Deep down, he was subtly manipulating Nathan, ensuring he'd carry out his tasks.

He continued, 'Report back with good news, and you'll be rewarded with money. Plus, you can try interacting with this more, but only under my stewardship,' Denton instructed.

Denton walked back to his desk chair. As Nathan walked off to the lift, a thought ran through his mind. He wondered whether he got the job because he was Denton's son, though he pushed that thought aside for the moment—that was for later. Then, another thought demanded to be voiced, and he turned around, addressing Denton.

'What's the reward for my report, then?' he asked forcefully. Nathan clearly inherited a keen eye for money.

'Of course, 500 dollars in cash on results,' deceptively replied Denton. 'More if you change a code or two.'

'Five hundred dollars! I would have been happy with two-fifty,' Nathan replied cheekily, a wry smile playing on his lips. Denton's voice was light as he encouraged, 'Recodes might be worth thousands, so get moving.'

A subtle, wry smile curved his features, effectively shrouding his darker machinations. Nathan studied him, wondering if he was joking. He probably was, but the money sounded easy regardless.

Nathan practically skipped to the lift door, humming a triumphant, off-key tune. Denton, on the other hand, thudded back into his chair, the sting of the extra two hundred and fifty dollars a bitter taste. He was absolutely gutted.

Echoes Of Conspiracy

Still carrying the unneeded red papers from Denton's meeting, Michael and Peter exited the lift, returning to their enclosed, secretive level of code translation. They were exhausted and fearful of Denton's true purpose and allegiance to the project.

'We need some time out,' suggested Peter.

'Time out of this place sounds about right.'

A palpable tension hung in the air, a stark contrast between the stated project objective and their unspoken—perhaps even unknown—purpose for being there.

They wondered what other surprising comments Denton might have in mind that could have an even more dramatic impact than those he had already made.

The fragrant smells of the restaurant constantly escaped into the corridor, a welcome distraction that grounded them back to their former everyday life. Memories resurfaced of shopping malls, high street eateries, and home cooking, all rolled into one. The aromas were so inviting you could almost taste them.

With these fragrant memories swirling in their tired minds as they walked along the corridor, they both saw the welcoming restaurant's entrance. It glowed like a beacon of warmth, ready to enfold them.

Normally, the place would be buzzing—a symphony of clanking cutlery, chattering voices, and the rich aroma of simmering sauces. But today, an unusual quiet hung in the air, and they didn't mind the stillness.

The prolonged and taxing meeting with Denton had drained their mental energy, causing their minds to drift back to it repeatedly. This mental fatigue was compounded by a nagging suspicion regarding Denton's true commitment to the project's success.

The restaurant's unusual quiet was so welcoming they felt almost compelled to maintain the silence while buying their food. The usual practice of chatting to the staff was replaced by silent thoughts of what had just transpired in Denton's office.

With many seating options, they happened to sit next to a table with some screwed-up newspapers.

'Would you believe it, newspapers!' said Michael, as if he'd just struck gold. It was a rarity to see any in a secure facility such as this, where the focus was work, not side issues like world affairs. He pulled one across and unfurled it.

'Nothing's changed. The usual bedfellows: power, money, and injustice,' he added.

'Take them; not wanted,' said a restaurant cleaner, reaching for the newspaper from Michael.

'No, I want this one,' replied Michael, a slight annoyance visible on his face. The worker's sudden appearance surprised him; he seemed to come from nowhere, reaching for the newspaper. The cleaner looked over at the other screwed-up newspaper and thought better of trying to take it.

Peter wasn't tempted to reach over and unfurl the other one. He just surveyed the peaceful calm and hoped it would stay that way, forever if possible. His serene, calming thoughts of nothingness had become a staple strategy for overcoming the responsibilities thrust upon them by Denton.

Michael held the paper up to read, looking at some reports of NFL matches. Although not a great follower owing to academic commitments, he hoped to make it a deeper part of his life in retirement. This was relaxing brain food to him. He was transported into the world of NFL and away from the issues surrounding Denton and Ann, and the anxieties of their situation.

Having had his fill of NFL, he flicked the newspaper pages back to the front. He had to look twice, as the initial glance seemed unbelievable. Unbeknownst to Peter—and indeed everyone else at the facility—media coverage of their research had spread far and wide with a deeply negative spin.

'This isn't reporting, Peter, this is an assassination of our work,' Michael worryingly said.

Peaceful meditation aside, Peter reached over and grabbed the other screwed-up newspaper and unfurled it. It was the same copy as the one Michael was holding. What they both read was earth-shattering.

News of their research had been leaked by some miscreant (or miscreants) to sow panic. False stories of the end of the world permeated the news media. Every country had its own problems before this broke; now, their project had become the focus, making everything much worse.

He thought about Elizabeth, his daughter. A gnawing concern for her welfare resonated through him, twisting his gut with unease, almost to the point of nausea. He hadn't spoken to her since Heathrow, a lifetime ago it seemed. He'd accepted the terms, of course; he knew his role meant being incommunicado within this secure facility. Yet, despite her robust nature and well-proportioned common sense, a father's worry was a tenacious beast.

Yet, he felt guilty that he had become so monopolised by the project. He should have tried to find a way to call her, even by asking Denton for help. Perhaps it was because she could look after herself, lived securely, and had protection most others could only dream of.

As they read on, disbelief at its contents weighed heavily on their emotions. Both accepted that newspapers were known for their biased reporting based on ideological leanings. But this was inflammatory, causing riots.

How could they so badly amplify their project into something nefarious? National and global small-scale riots were breaking out as rumour fed rumour.

A growing distrust in governments was evolving as media outlets reported that world war could be imminent and advised stocking up on essentials. It was metamorphosing into social concern that was ugly and completely disconnected from the reality of their efforts.

As fearful concern spread, nation upon nation grew suspicious of each other. This, in turn, was further fuelled by incendiary media reports that only exacerbated the fear of the unknown.

Paranoia tightened its grip on societal thought. The newspaper's wanton abandonment of truth for falsehoods staggered and upset them both, making them insecure in a secure facility.

Peter briefly looked up from the newspaper content, making Michael apprehensive about what he might say. Then, out of the blue, Peter slammed the paper down on the table so hard that food remnants flew in all directions, ultimately landing on the floor.

'Who's protecting whom here?' questioned Peter.

He looked thoughtfully at Michael: something in his expression said a radical view was about to be delivered.

'We must double our efforts to get this finished and then get out of this place. It's simply not good,' Peter said.

'Not good? Probably so, but I was very concerned about you back in Denton's office,' replied Michael.

'It's not me you should be worried about, Michael. It's working with Denton. He's definitely up to something,' Peter said, his anxiety now palpable. 'We only need a few days of digging to find a code that links him to our possible sabotage problems. After all, who else could it be? He's bound to do something reckless soon, for sure.

'Silly?' worriedly replied Michael.

'Yes, like with his dog,' said Peter.

Michael's brow furrowed with this disturbing thought and tried to make light of it by saying, 'Maybe, but we have something in our favour.'

'What's that, our academic reputations?' Peter asked.

'We are not old enough yet to be shot!' Michael quickly retorted, referencing Denton's comment that his dog was too old to save.

'Your sardonic, schoolboy humour is sometimes lost on me, Michael, I'm sorry.'

This fragile echo of a shooting reference—a mere whisper against a world already fraying at the edges with small, erupting riots—would soon be amplified by fate's chilling irony. The first tremor of its terrible proof would shatter the precarious balance of those two lives, hinting at aftershocks destined to rip through every corner of the world.

***

Almost immediately below where Peter and Michael sat, a conversation was in progress between Denton and Corvus.

Corvus, a representative of the shadow organisation Denton had been hired by, explained why Denton needed to work harder to earn his pay.

Denton sat back nervously in his chair, his hands clasped behind his head, listening intently to Corvus, who sat opposite him. Corvus, short of time, felt his visit wasn't really necessary, other than to bolster Denton, who seemed to be flagging in getting results. That said, he had little time for him, truth be told. Denton was just a part-time facilitator with little use beyond the accomplished mission.

Corvus leaned forward in his chair and placed both his elbows on the edge of Denton's shiny desk, its untouched beauty implying how little work was carried out on it.

'Some background before I get to what you must do next. I'm sure you haven't failed to realise we're aligned with vested interests who own most of the world. I'm not joking; they truly own it. Their number is in the tens of millions and many, many more once you add their 'associates', who come from all money-producing agencies. Their investments are of paramount interest. They have an unnerving, pathological desire to preserve their security and ensure their survival by staying ahead of any potential threats, no matter what the cost is in order to remove those who stand in their way.

'Have you seen the news lately? Civil disorder, media promoting the end of the world, and this research painted as disrespectful to anything remotely connected to it. All this, and more, the elites construct through the media. We dictate the narrative, twisting it to fit our needs. We manipulate like you breathe.

'Discovering something first is crucial for their own survival. Possessing critical information first, be it a scientific breakthrough, geopolitical shift, or hidden technology, is vital as it grants them a significant advantage.

'This early access allows for proactive strategic planning and decisive action. It provides us leverage to shape events, manipulate situations, and exert influence on a scale that wealth alone can't always achieve.

'In this mix is you, Denton. You are important to us for what you can do, and as of now, what you cannot do, to ensure we win and they lose.

'We needed the project team to get together. It was so much easier to affect them collectively than individually. And you obliged. They achieved the results we anticipated, providing the foundation for our research to advance. Without their initial work, we wouldn't have the keys to unlock the codes we've analysed and calculated,' Corvus stated without emotion.

Denton realised some key points had been overlooked, so he seized the opportunity to present them to Corvus.

'The sabotage of their system is causing delays. Their research is stalling; however, Nathan is close to unlocking their encryption keys. If he does this, I will lean on him to delay any further progress with bribes. If he fails, I'm sure you could arrange an unfortunate accident, say an electrical one,' Denton suggested malevolently.

Corvus just looked on as if to silently suggest there was nothing the shadow group wouldn't do to further their objectives.

'Have Peter and Michael informed you about the status, role, or function of this so-called entity called "NEMESIS"?' enquired Corvus.

Denton looked at Corvus wondering whether he had another source of information in the facility.

'At present, nothing has changed, but they remain certain we need it for key information. It's very likely to hold the ingredient proportions, as a preliminary decryption indicates. We don't have all the ingredients yet; we have seven, and we need ten more to complete the formula. They suspect this entity holds the keys to the rest, so we need to move on with creating it. However, our own supercomputers, even with other teams assisting, aren't fast enough. In sabotaging their progress, we are, in effect, sabotaging our own efforts.'

'You still don't know how this entity comes about? Let me be clear, Denton: We need to know very soon. Time is running out. We have just over three months, and we need to distribute this pill once we know its function and the scenario in which it is to be taken,' Corvus emphasised with his dark, gravelly voice.

'The sabotage hinders them, but also hinders us—' Denton began before Corvus interrupted with a raised voice.

'Look, in view of the disruption, see to it you place armed guards outside Peter and Michael's rooms. This will unsettle them when they're in their rooms and disrupt them psychologically when in their control room.'

'Finally, I've left this to last because of its implications. Our hexagonal table needs to be used. Its quantum power is beyond anything available, leveraging quantum entanglement. It will get the answers we need. Ensure the systems run in parallel. The table will accomplish the rest, providing what we need while they fumble for something out of their final reach.'

'As we believe the brain works on the same principle, an interface can be created, a cybernetic interface if you will. It took our scientists three years to perfect the interface between our supercomputers and this.'

Corvus leaned forward, his movement fluid and precise. His right hand dipped into his jacket pocket, emerging with a small, cube-like object. It was undeniably similar to the one resting on the edge of Denton's desk, hinting at a connection Denton was yet to grasp.

'Here is the new crystal object that allows entity genesis,' Corvus said, his tone flat. 'This replaces the one on your desk that you showed Peter and Michael earlier. It won't work anymore. It's about as useless as you will be if you don't provide success, Denton. Protect this new one with your life, as without it, you won't have one,' Corvus stated with a cold, deathly stare and a slight mocking laugh that made Denton's stomach clench.

'This is the interface, a quantum interface?' asked Denton.

'Yes,' Corvus boringly replied. 'It's certainly not a bag of crisps, is it?' Corvus hastily added with an undertone of malicious sarcasm.

'But what about the entity, the cybernetic organism? How does that fit into this?' Denton nervously asked.

'Do I have to write this down for you? You bloody idiot. Their intelligence, their brains here,' as he directed Denton's gaze to the hexagonal table. 'It will immensely help the neural interface. Get someone you think is expendable. We need answers now, not more about decodes or such-like. They can even act as a parallel processor, completing each iterative action where they stumble,' Corvus ruthlessly commanded.

Corvus looked at Denton, who seemed utterly bored and patronised. Denton had drifted off into his fantasy of retirement: a world of unhindered global travel, no destination out of bounds, and all the money he'd ever need. The word "retirement" now held a special, almost sacred, place within him.

Unaware of his drifting mind, Corvus looked on, perplexed by Denton's glazed look. He awaited a response; unsurprisingly, none was forthcoming. He continued. 'And, needless to say, results are everything. We positively reward success, just as we negatively reward failure.'

Corvus intensely looked at Denton, as if he was reading a letter pinned to his face. 'When will the interface with the table occur?' Corvus asked demandingly of Denton, leaning forward to emphasise its importance.

'Soon, very soon. I will work it out for sure,' pleaded Denton. 'You had better. I will tell my representatives you will action it within the next 24 hours,' Corvus replied, his tone an impassioned acceptance that Denton's time was running out: 24 hours, to be precise.

And with that, Corvus, a shadow coalescing from the armchair, rose without so much as a glance or a whispered farewell. He didn't take the common lift, the mundane conveyance everyone else queued for. No. Two metres behind Denton's unsuspecting chair, a hidden panel in the wall, so expertly crafted it left no trace, barely betrayed the private elevator awaiting him.

It descended to the hum and thrum of the Magnetic Levitation train—the MagLev. This whispered network of rails, an unseen circulatory system, criss-crossed the very bedrock of America, reserved solely for the architects of the shadow group. As the silent hum of the descending lift carried him away, his next destination remained a thrilling, unsettling unknown.

***

Their momentary, yet pleasant, banter about Denton was broken as Michael noticed a pair of armed security guards approaching them.

'Who are you?' Michael asked.

'Who, me?' Peter asked, a bewildered frown creasing his brow.

'No, him behind you!' Michael said, his gaze fixed on someone just beyond Peter's shoulder.

'Good morning, Professors Magma and Adams,' said one of the guards.

'Would you come with us, Professor Magma? We have to escort you to Dr Denton's office immediately.'

'What's wrong?' Peter enquired hastily.

'All in good time, Professor. This way, please!'

'Shall I come with you, Peter?' asked Michael.

'Sorry, this is for Professor Magma only,' interrupted the guard.

'I'll see you back at the control centre soon,' Michael replied hesitantly, his forced politeness barely hiding the sting of feeling insignificant within that power dynamic. As he watched Peter being escorted from the restaurant, a surge of irritation at Denton's security's high-handed treatment of himself spurred Michael into action.

He decided this was the perfect moment to speak to Elizabeth. Denton had lent him a secure phone for a single call, and for once, Michael was genuinely pleased to have the means to reach her.

- 45 -
The Portugal Call

'Dad, can you hear me? Hello! Dad!'

'Yes, Elizabeth, I'm here. This line's patchy; you sound miles away.' A sharp exhale escaped Elizabeth, relief washing over her.

'I am. I'm in Portugal. Lisbon, to be precise.' She let out a dry chuckle. 'I did say, "If I didn't hear from you, I'd spend lots of money and treat myself."'

'But Lisbon's in lockdown. Serious clashes between protesters and the government over welfare policies. It's all over the news. Seems like it's happening everywhere,' Michael said, worry threading his voice.

'Oh, I don't know. I'm just enjoying myself—that's what matters. Maybe it was Lisbon yesterday or tomorrow,' Elizabeth replied, forcing a laugh that barely masked her confusion.

Michael's concern deepened. 'Are you sure you're all right?'

'Yes, fine!'

'When were you last at the mansion?' Michael asked, trying to unravel her evasiveness.

'Two weeks ago, I think. Maybe one. But not now, that's for sure,' Elizabeth said. This uncertainty only served to increase Michael's unease.

The mansion empty?' Michael asked, hesitation creeping into his voice, as his uncertainty deepened.

'No. The NSA agents are there, sunning themselves for all I care. It's secure, so why worry? What about your research? I haven't heard from you in what feels like forever. Three holidays ago? Maybe two? No, three. Are you still with Peter and Ann?'

'I can't say, for security reasons. Are you with anyone on your travels?'

'I can't say for security reasons,' she replied, a brittle laugh escaping her lips. 'Of course, I have Jade with me. You know, Jade from Madden Advertising Agency.'

'Er, sort of,' Michael murmured, digging through his memory.

'Of course you do. She was with Tom at "The Royals" the night we took down two terrorists with my driving during the assassination attempt.'

A manic laugh slipped from her, hanging unnervingly in the air. Then she pressed on.

'Anyway, what are you doing over there? Have you seen all the media's nonsense? Crazy stuff, like you might blow up the world or that you're creating aliens. Worst of all, some extinction event is coming. I knew about that last one. I've been watching all this in hotel bars and cafés, just to see if you're on track, if you know what I mean.

'There are riots everywhere because of your lot, not big but enough to make the news. I wanted to shout from the rooftops that I know you and they shouldn't panic. Honestly, the relief of talking to you again after all this silence is overwhelming. Please don't do this to me; I can't handle going so long without hearing from you. I love you, Dad.'

Michael's voice softened, wary and tired. 'I can't say anything, Elizabeth. The call may be monitored. You understand?'

'Oh, bums. Does that include me? Of course it does,' Elizabeth said with a self-deprecating chuckle, briefly distracted by her own thoughts.

Michael then heard her murmur a distracted 'Huh,' as if replying quietly to a faint female voice nearby.

She quickly refocused and said, 'Jade says, "Hello, Professor."'

'Hello back!' Michael quipped.

'Please, Dad, fill me in. What's happening?'

'With what?' Michael countered.

'You know. After you disappeared from Oxford, presumably with Peter and Ann, since they're not answering either, the news has been intense as I say. Especially about you and Peter. They're blowing things way out of proportion. Deliberately, I think. If you scare people about the end of the world, what are they supposed to do? Say thank you and lie down apologetically for being alive?'

'I'm not in the business of scaring people. Others can do that. All I can say is this: if you untangle the mass media hype, lies and truth, you'll see what we're really doing. It benefits everyone, not just a few,' Michael explained.

'Anyway, Dad, have you noticed anything strange at work? Anything odd about your research?'

'Strange? What do you mean, bambina?'

'It's just...' Elizabeth's voice dropped. 'I wondered if you'd seen or heard anything. You know, about dark forces and elites wanting your work.'

Michael rubbed the back of his neck, the tell-tale sign of stress.

'Where did you hear that? No, of course not. Everything's in a secure facility.'

'I don't know,' she said flatly. 'Just a gut feeling. Anyway, glad to hear it's all good.'

'You're safe, though?' Michael pressed, worry tightening his voice.

'Of course. Who'd want a megamouth like me and an attitude that could kill at forty paces?' Her voice sharpened. 'Can you tell me which country you're in?'

'The good old USA. I'd love to tell you more… someday, perhaps.'

'Well, listen to this. Jade has contacts, people who know things they shouldn't. I used to think this secret group running the world was fantasy, just movies, right?

'But this guy told her, strictly in confidence, they were ordered to orchestrate fake news about you to stir civil unrest. I didn't believe it at first. Then I heard the same from friends in papers and universities.

'Jade says, "Tell people something enough times, and they'll believe and act on it."

'So tell me, Dad, what's really going on? Update me. I keep thinking about that secret paper and the synthetic exomorph thingy.'

Denton pressed the interrupt button, silencing the line. 'Careful, Michael. No mistakes.'

Michael pressed on. 'As I said, all in good time. Don't trust the media. It's all right here because—'

The line cut.

Denton ended the call—his final act of control. Any longer, and Michael might crack, spilling fragments of truth. Denton knew Elizabeth, who lived and breathed media, would not only piece those fragments together but twist and weaponise them in ways he couldn't predict. Her questions were little more than academic exercises; she already knew far more than Michael did.

To Denton's fractured mind, the call, his thoughts, and actions were all a masquerade, concealing deeper, unspoken truths. Control was everything; without it, anxiety would swallow the fragile divide between order and chaos. He had control—and that was all he needed.

'Sorry, Michael, that's enough. I'm sure you understand. Elizabeth sounds grateful. Maybe another call soon.'

Michael was far from grateful, but a shaky sigh escaped him, a breath he hadn't realised he was holding, as relief washed over him knowing she was safe.

The call and any pretence of respect were dismissed without ceremony. Elizabeth glared at her phone as if it were the enemy. The urge to hurl it against the wall was strong, but the two-thousand-pound price tag held her back.

- 46 -
The Psychological Bomb

Peter was escorted from the restaurant by the guards and led down the corridor to the lift he'd taken earlier to Denton's office. Though he walked at his own pace, he felt tethered to the guard, not just a miscreant now but a prisoner.

The guard ran a hand over the glowing request light on the control panel. The door opened instantaneously. Being told to enter the lift felt absurd, like telling water to be wet. As the lift descended, he felt its downward pull as a physical echo of his own plummeting emotions—a dark foreshadowing of what was to come. The doors slid open with a soft, ominous hiss, revealing Denton's office, a predatory arena where the very air crackled with anticipation.

'Peter, nice to see you again, and so quickly too!' Denton emphasised. 'Please, sit down. I have something to tell you that I must deliver personally.

'Drink?' Denton asked.

'No, perhaps later,' a nervous Peter replied.

'I asked you here because I have a very important message to pass to you, and I hope your wife, Ann, will be here by the time I've poured my drink and sat back down.

'Nathan is fine. He's doing a splendid job for both of us,' Denton answered. His words about Nathan, though clearly holding a hidden meaning, barely registered with Peter, whose mind still raced with the image of armed guards and the abrupt summons.

Dr. Denton slowly poured his drink. He apologised to Peter for their previous encounter as he walked back to his desk and chair. Just as Denton settled back, the quiet whoosh of

411

the "hush lift"—so silent the research staff had nicknamed it—announced Ann's arrival.

'Hello Ann,' Denton said, his gaze lingering for a fraction too long as she entered.

'Peter, what are you doing here?' Ann questioned forcefully. 'Oh God, is this about our marriage or about Nathan?' Ann urgently quizzed, pointedly avoiding the word "son," which irked Peter.

'No!' Denton said softly, as if to quell the anxiety building in her. 'Do please sit down next to Peter.'

'If it's all the same,' she replied, pulling her chair further away, 'I'll sit here.'

'All right, sit there, that's fine,' Denton commented.

'Not for me. It should be farther, like the lift shaft,' an angry Peter spoke. He glared at the space between them, the chasm mirroring the growing distance he felt in their relationship. 'Shut up!' Ann snapped.

'Excuse me, but I don't know what this is about, and to be honest, I don't want to know. I ask just two things, please. One: be professional, do your job. Two: argue in private. Understand?' Denton demanded.

Denton's sharp words now stung Ann, and Peter, his prisoner-like feeling gone, felt like a miscreant schoolboy once more. Denton then set about explaining why he'd asked them both there. It wasn't about Nathan after all, but about the bombing at their home weeks earlier.

'It's ironic to think that while this is the NSA, home of intelligence gathering, the information I'm about to convey to you has only just reached me,' Denton explained cautiously. 'It was sourced two weeks ago and is categorised as "Top Secret".

To an astonished and worried Peter and Ann, he disclosed that Lassus Mardon, the person they thought responsible for their mansion bombing, couldn't have done it after all. Mardon had been murdered the night before the bombing.

'How was Lassus killed? I don't recall anything about a murder in the papers or media,' Peter asked inquisitively. He looked across at Ann, but she offered no verbal reply, just a pointed shift of her gaze. Her averted eyes conveyed it all: he was, at present, persona non grata.

'Good question, Peter,' Denton said, looking away in deep thought. Something was clearly on his mind, and he was battling to decide what to say next. A smile then broke over his face, and he returned his gaze to both of them.

Denton paused, a thin, knowing smile playing on his lips. 'As I've known you for many years, I'll tell you something that shouldn't pass my lips.'

Peter and Ann gripped the arms of their chairs, their faces turning a shade of sickly white. They sensed Denton was about to reveal something deeply unsettling. The air in the room grew heavy, each second stretching into an eternity. Ann's breath hitched, a small, audible gasp escaping her lips. Peter's knuckles whitened, the silence of the room amplifying the tension.

'Lassus's death was no accident. He was taken out, clinically and surgically. His "hit" had been sanctioned at the highest UK government level and was carried out by an agent who worked for SAS "E" Squadron, more colloquially referred to as "The Increment".'

The words hung in the air like a death sentence. Peter and Ann stared at Denton, unable to comprehend the cold, chilling finality of what he had just said. The man they had believed responsible for the attack on their lives was dead, a victim of a covert operation. Peter's mind raced, struggling to reconcile this new, horrifying truth with their own recent trauma. A wave of nausea washed over Ann as she envisioned the precise, brutal efficiency of the killing.

Peter's voice, when it finally came, was a barely-there whisper. 'But if Lassus didn't plant the bomb, who did?' His curiosity, a constant in his life, now felt like a desperate anchor in a sea of confusion.

Denton watched him with a calculating look, a flicker of satisfaction in his eyes. He had achieved his desired effect. Their emotional shock had created a vacuum, and he was ready to fill it with his own carefully constructed version of the truth. His previous candour about information vanished, replaced by an intention to be economical with the truth.

Ann's face, which had been pale with shock, now flushed with a furious, protective energy. A slow, agonising dread began to unfurl within her as Denton spoke. The car was in his possession. The last time she saw Nathan was a week ago. She thought of their last hug, their last conversation. Nathan, her loving son, her everything. No, it couldn't be him. It couldn't be. The thought was impossible, an affront to everything she believed.

'The evidence suggested the bomb was planted while the Jaguar was in Nathan's use somewhere in Oxford. The mansion itself was under tight surveillance. MI5's review of CCTV footage and potential access points for planting the bomb—such as roadside drains, traffic light stops, and garage visits—had drawn a complete blank.'

Denton's words, calm and dispassionate, felt like a slap. Ann rose from her chair, her hands clenched into fists, her voice a low, strangled growl. 'What! You're suggesting Nathan planted the bomb!' she boomed at Denton, the force of her emotion making her chair scrape backward across the floor.

Denton held his gaze, his face a mask of feigned reassurance. 'No, I'm saying the car was in his possession, that's all,' he calmly replied. He watched her carefully, a faint smirk playing on his lips, knowing he had successfully planted the seed of doubt.

He continued, 'The good news: you're in a secure facility with the highest security clearance. No terrorist, bomb, or death here, but one can never be too careful.' Denton looked away, as if his own knowledge contradicted this. He then refocused his gaze and continued.

'In light of this new information, I've immediately requested you each have an armed guard outside your rooms in case any undesirables try to gain entry.'

Peter's tone was flat as he turned to Ann, his gaze holding a pointed accusation that spoke of more than just security lapses. 'An armed guard in a secure facility! Reassuring, I'm sure. Though a guard on the inside might have been more useful a few weeks ago.'

Ann flinched. Was this Peter's brutal jab about Roger, the undesirable he knew had visited her? The word "undesirable" had never felt so cold.

After a brief look at Peter, Denton, slightly puzzled by the exchange, continued.

'Additionally, security will keep a tighter watch for any peripheral suspect movement. We've long suspected rogue elements aiming to stop the project.' Denton again looked away, as if unburdening his emotional conflict silently.

Hence, we've been as secretive as possible, monitoring movements to ensure your survival—indeed, our survival too.' With that, he curtly dismissed them both, his gaze

415

already sweeping past them as if they were nothing more than a solved equation. To him, they were not individuals with feelings or ongoing relevance, but merely variables successfully manipulated and now discarded for the present, though their utility was, of course, always under review.

Ann and Peter rose from their seats, a silent, brittle tension crackling between them, and not just through Denton's dispassionate words. They didn't move in unison; instead, Peter, his jaw tight, extended an arm towards the lift with a curt, dismissive wave, a gesture that clearly meant "you go first".

Ann's shoulders stiffened, a hot flush creeping up her neck, but she forced herself to pivot, her movements deliberately slow, as if to delay the inevitable proximity. The air between them felt thick, each breath a conscious effort, as they began their separate, reluctant paths towards the gleaming steel doors.

Denton watched them, a faint, wry grin playing on his lips, clearly pleased with the friction his words had so effortlessly added to their already explosive situation. Was this a psychological bomb waiting to detonate, just as the physical one had back at their mansion?

47

The Genesis Of NEMESIS

'I made it clear the last time we spoke that we want results, Denton. We're relying on your power and ability to mislead to get these codes decoded so we know what it all means. Our members are beginning to panic; some have already gone underground, seeking refuge in their bunkers.

Denton was taken aback by the toxic nature of the call. He'd thought things were working out well. Though he longed to shout back, his need to be part of them and the wealth they promised suppressed his urge to verbally retaliate.

'Things are in progress; I wouldn't say otherwise. Nathan has subtly sabotaged the research team's decoding, and his over-generous first payoff made him redouble his efforts to supply more information gleaned from Peter and Michael's background conversations,' appeased Denton.

As he spoke, he tried to decipher any sighs or other unintended verbal interjections to determine how his monologue was being accepted. The line remained silent, offering Denton a sliver of hope that Corvus was containing his fury.

He pressed on, 'We know of NEMESIS. It appears to be some kind of creation, though we lack any specifics beyond the fact it's man-made.'

Corvus blew up over the phone, 'For God's sake, Denton, of course it would be man-made; how the fuck is it going to be anything other? I suggest you dig down and reinterpret these messages. You're slipping and sliding into a murky outcome, Denton. Why don't you go and stare into that damn table to find out something?

'It might just cough up the answer you desperately need—our only salvation from God knows what,' Corvus's voice seethed, his fury so palpable Denton could almost feel his phone vibrating.

'Hmm, that's a thought,' sounded an unwilling Denton. He moved into lying mode and told Corvus he'd have a try straight away—after the phone call, of course—just to avoid Corvus saying he would wait on the phone.

'You do that, Denton. We're not asking for results anymore; we want them very, very soon!' With that, Corvus ended the call.

Denton put down the receiver and sat back in his chair. Corvus's fury, a verbal hurricane that had just seethed through the phone line, was already being compartmentalised. With a dismissive shrug of his shoulders, Denton mentally scraped the angry words into a litter bin next to his desk, a finality that spoke to his dispassionate nature. "No worries," he thought, the calm a chilling contrast to the chaos Corvus had just unleashed.

His gaze moved over to the exotic table; it had now taken on a new and urgent meaning. He teased himself about whether to look into it or not. His only previous experience, as reported, had been a one-way dive into an abyss of knowledge that literally sucked the mind in. If one's mind didn't think to pull back, it wouldn't get a second chance.

Greed, Denton's constant companion, propelled him from his chair towards the table—his nemesis, yet also a siren call to his insatiable curiosity. Standing over the table, he took a deep breath as if he were really going to "dive in". Just as he was about to go where his mind had never been before, he was fortunately distracted by the noise of his approaching lift.

The lift doors slid open to Denton's office. His gaze, already fixed on the familiar, unsettling hum emanating from his hexagonal table, barely registered the arrival.

As he stood over its dark, polished surface, a faint tremor of the old unease it always stirred—a whisper of something not of this Earth—ran beneath his scientific curiosity.

The table was fast, incredibly fast, yet seemed to defy all conventional engineering. It was a seamless whole, without joins, screws, or bolts, as if forged from a single, impossibly dense material. Its purpose, scientists concluded, was to act as a cybernetic, quantum interface, allowing a user to become one with its processing power. They deduced that its energy was not sourced, but drawn, pulled directly from the Earth's own magnetic field.

As the doors opened, Denton looked around. It was Ann, and she was in an angry disposition.

Denton questioned, 'Back so soon?' A faint, almost imperceptible softening crossed his features as he looked at her.

'You bet,' she said as she stood by his desk, invisibly suggesting he should come and stand behind it. This was formal!

He walked over to his desk and stood behind it. His sumptuous chair, directly behind him, a throne inviting him to reassert his dominion of intellect and ego, seemed to silently mock his present unease.

'Is this business or personal?' Denton questioned.

'Definitely both,' she replied.

For Denton, a man who preferred clear categories, this merging of professional and personal was always a source of unease. In Ann's case, even more so.

'Well, fire away,' replied Denton.

'Nathan came to see you earlier, but I don't know why. I can only assume it's something negative, perhaps him trying to recruit a snitch. It really irritates you, doesn't it, that you're not part of their in-group?' criticised Ann, her words a precise surgical strike aimed at the fragile core of his inflated ego.

Denton looked on in surprise. How intuitive it was for Ann to correctly calculate Nathan's utility to him.

'No, and no, to be precise,' responded Denton.

'I'm above such office politics. I supervise, I delegate, I don't partake,' argued Denton, impressed by his own words.

'Did you delegate a swiping hand across Nathan's now bloodied nose?' she asked.

'Oh, that,' Denton mumbled, his voice catching slightly. He found emotional confrontations distinctly uncomfortable, especially with women. His career was far too important for such distractions.

'Yes, oh that,' said Ann, with a raised voice. She folded her arms and pursed her lips aggressively, her posture signifying an altercation was due.

'He deserved it. He raised his hand to me. I duly obliged by doing the same,' remonstrated Denton.

'He was a metre from you, and the only way he could strike you would be with a metre-long arm, which he clearly doesn't have or ever will,' screamed an upset Ann.

She continued, 'As for you, you dangly spider, you could easily slap him without even leaning forward. What a cheap shot. Nathan is about as aggressive as a feather in a bed pillow.'

She continued, 'You attack my son, then I'll attack you. You attack me, Peter will attack you.'

Ann moved slightly forward as if to suggest a pre-emptive strike was imminent.

'Don't you threaten me with words of no weight. Look at you, a puff of wind would blow you over. You're as useful as a chocolate teapot, a grain of sand in a desert storm,' Denton spat, his voice laced with venom that promised to strip her bare.

'A storm? Then it will be a wind of words, so forceful it will blow your arse clean off the pompous perch you preach from but have never earned. That perch is so wobbly it probably requires a tiny velvet cushion for your delicate ego of magnified proportions,' Ann's cutting retort snapped back.

'This verbal hurricane will not just dethrone you; it'll send your aforementioned arse into orbit, where it can finally get the space it clearly thinks it deserves.

'Your words are nothing. I am made of iron, with an iron stature and iron words,' replied Denton, his tone dripping with disdain as if she were a nuisance he could barely tolerate.

'Then my words will be rust to your character. I am going to put such a "real dent" on the metal of your character, no panel beater will ever bang it out,' Ann snarled. Her voice a low, furious growl that promised lasting corrosion to his carefully constructed facade.

Knowing his middle and last names were "Reel Denton", Ann parodied him by playing on the phonetic similarity to "real dent". This clever verbal jab transformed his name into an accusation of superficiality.

Denton's smile tightened, the corners of his mouth twitched, almost imperceptibly. He let out a short, forced chuckle that sounded more like a cough.

'Very amusing, Ann,' he drawled, the emphasis on her name carrying a sharp, almost brittle edge.

His eyes, however, held a flicker of something less confident; a brief, intense flash of irritation crossed his countenance. He shifted his weight, his gaze flicking dismissively towards a sleek, black hexagonal table, its surface subtly pulsing with an inner light.

'You cannot come into my playground and bark at me as if you're my equal. Do not use my middle and last names as verbal playthings. One sway of my hand and you'll be even worse than Nathan.'

As Denton moved his hand, its movement guided her eyesight over to the black hexagonal table. A cold dread settled in her stomach as she looked over at it, and a whisper of unease about its unnatural sheen followed.

She looked back at Denton, who seemed to have calmed by her interest in the table. That calm, however, hid a darker reason.

Deep within Denton's psyche, a malevolent seed of an idea began to germinate, promising a harvest of unsettling intent. Perhaps he'd found a victim for his table. Ann suddenly had a utility again. Denton quietened his rage and metaphorically binned it as before.

'Look, I'll tell you this. You're a historian. To show my good faith in you and as an apology, I will let you look at historic moments from the past in a way you've never imagined,' suggested Denton with a delusional, crazy stare in his eyes.

Like an expert chess player, he had already calculated his next several moves to get his way with her.

'I don't understand, why the sudden change?' asked Ann, her eyes fixed on the table's mesmerising, starlit depths.

'Come, let me walk you to the table over there,' said Denton, a predatory glint in his eyes.

This sudden turnaround in Denton's demeanour left Ann feeling not merely discombobulated, but utterly thrown off balance—a feeling that was truer than she then realised. 'What are those stars in the table?' Ann asked reservedly, a growing sense of disorientation washing over her.

'They allow you to see what you cannot see,' said Denton mysteriously, a hint of dark satisfaction.

He continued, 'Others have tried it and demanded to come back again and again. Look into it and see your destiny.'

'I think you mean my past, surely,' corrected Ann, a prickle of resistance against his cajoling tone.

'The future is manufactured in the past. Please look and enjoy,' cajoled Denton, his hand now gently guiding her head towards the table's surface. His eyes, however, glowed with a malevolent light, a tiny flicker deep within that ignited an evil motive to harm.

Ann gazed in and within seconds was mesmerised by famous moments in history that had captured her imagination, the visions swirling with an almost painful intensity. As she looked on, she felt her immersion into the visions grow deeper, a strange coldness seeping into her mind, her intellect sparking with newfound data.

'I feel that's enough. The computer seems to be reading my thoughts,' said Ann, a desperate urge to pull away rising within her.

She tried to look away, but Denton's grip tightened on her head. Though she looked left and right, and even closed her eyes, the visions persisted, the table's influence burrowing deeper into her mind, rewriting her very neural pathways.

Ann pleaded, 'Denton, take your hand away, so I can get back up!'

Denton remained immobile, his grip unwavering, while a subtle, almost insectile drone vibrated from the table's heart. Ann's resistance faltered, her struggles becoming the desperate twitches of a trapped creature as her consciousness was drawn into the unseen currents of the quantum AI.

Seeing this, Denton released her head. His hand tingled as if he were disconnecting from something much larger, maybe the interface between the table and her mind. Her head should have lolled to the side but remained staring straight into the table, a faint cerulean luminescence now pulsing in her eyes, intricate filigrees of light blooming beneath her skin.

A tremor of something akin to terror, swiftly calcified by a disbelief bordering on the absurd, flickered across his features. The elegant architecture of his plans reduced to rubble by this unforeseen variable.

A low groan, not entirely human, escaped Ann's lips. The black hexagonal table began to subtly shift. Thin, metallic tendrils, like polished obsidian, extended from its edges, snaking across the floor and then growing, rising like skeletal arms.

These tendrils, guided by the quantum AI, moved with unnatural precision. They attached themselves to Ann's body, one coiling around her forearm and another around her neck. Delicate filaments then branched off, connecting at her temples to directly interface with her brain's electrical activity.

The starlight patterns within the table intensified, mirroring the soft blue glow that now burned in Ann's eyes, a visual representation of the quantum entanglement now linking her mind and the AI. Her petite frame began to subtly reshape, harder lines forming beneath her skin, housing the nascent cybernetic integration.

The historical visions were replaced with information spanning many centuries, flooding and rewriting her memories, her skills, her very sense of self. This data was now filtered and amplified by the quantum AI's processing power. The coldness intensified, replacing warmth, empathy; her human intellect now interwoven with a vast, quantum-level artificial intelligence.

When the process ceased, Ann, or the quantum assimilant as it now was, stood utterly still, the table's attachments seamlessly integrated, part of her. The blue essence in its eyes focused, sharp and calculating, imbued with quantum-level processing speed and tactical awareness. A smile stretched across its lips, a glacial curve that held no echo of human warmth, only the stark calculation of pure intellect.

Denton observed, the very molecules in the air around him seeming to vibrate with an alien hum. A cold premonition snaked through his vitals, squeezing the breath from his lungs. A faint sheen of perspiration prickled his forehead, a chilling counterpoint to the sudden dryness in his mouth. He clenched his jaw, and a tremor ran through his hands and legs, a rebellion of his own flesh against the unfolding nightmare. This was like no other he had seen. Was it alien? The carefully constructed edifice of his composure finally gave way, a primal chill tracing an icy path down his spine.

A dangerous spark flickered in his eyes. 'A weapon?' he murmured, his thoughts immediately followed by a chilling unease that began to bloom beneath the surface. A frantic calculus of anxiety and shock spun within his mind as he heard it speak to him telepathically.

'Denton, you may call me NEMESIS.' A chaotic torrent of questions about its capabilities and its terrifying speed—a blur of motion—began to form. Could it already be mapping his neural pathways? Anticipating every twitch, every flicker of thought? The sheer, terrifying probability of it all began to erode the foundations of his carefully constructed rationality.

How in God's name will I explain this? NEMESIS was clearly reading his thoughts; the cold, knowing smile that played on its lips felt less like triumph and more like assessment. Its right arm, a disturbing fusion of the familiar and the alien, lifted with a silent, unnerving grace.

As the metallic fingertip, cool and sharp, extended, pointing directly at him, a micro-expression, a flicker of something human crossed NEMESIS's augmented features. Was it Ann, fighting through the matrix of processing power to make a gesture? Could she be saying this is the future of humanity?

From nowhere external, he internally heard NEMESIS's voice speak to him. It was a pure, synthesised tone, devoid of human inflection, delivering its pronouncements with surgical precision and certainty. 'As I am by your action at the beginning, so I will be by Michael's action at the end.' Denton stood back in terror. What had he done?

48

The NEMESIS Mandate

Michael received an immediate summons to Denton's stark office, a place he privately called "the dark bunker", not just for its oppressive atmosphere but because it felt like a site where the needs of the many were displaced by the whims of the self-indulgent one.

Denton's voice on the phone had been a shocking mix of fear and anxiety, so unlike his normal self that Michael worried he had done something wrong. He was utterly unprepared for the true gravity of what awaited him inside, the air within the lift growing heavier with each floor he descended.

As Michael stood in the sterile, cramped lift, memories of Peter and Ann standing next to him flooded back, momentarily washing away the temporary loneliness and confinement enforced by its compact dimensions. The downward motion of the lift made him apprehensive, as if burrowing into the darkest recesses of his mind where darkness prevailed, tamed only by its confinement.

He was a man too long detached from the simple pleasures of life, and he felt himself walking on the edge of time, a precipice from which a fall would mean the end of his very existence.

The subtle hush of the approaching lift doors outside briefly punctuated the tense silence within Denton's office. The eventual click and soft whoosh as they opened seemed to vibrate through the very concrete of the building, a prelude to the weighty situation Denton was about to lay bare.

Denton needed to explain the genesis of NEMESIS as well as the unsettling absence of Ann. He looked Michael directly in the eye, requesting absolute confidence before revealing truths that felt both fragile and dangerous. He resolved to navigate this conversation with careful omissions, a strategic paring down of reality.

As Michael stepped fully into the office, his gaze gravitated towards something that looked like an entity of sorts—a sight unlike anything he had ever encountered. A wave of shock, confusion, and undeniable awe washed over him at the quantum assimilant before him, its very presence defying easy explanation.

It was this breathtaking spectacle that Denton's subsequent explanation of its genesis now shattered, the words striking him with the force of a physical blow. His disbelief deepened into a cold dread as Denton explained how Ann voluntarily sacrificed herself for the sake of their research. The implications hung heavy in the air, a suffocating silence broken only by the distant hum of machinery.

Confused by Denton's words, Michael's mind reeled and his body quietly shook at the sight of the quantum assimilant. This was a corrupted organic being, not the synthetic exomorph described in Q-Day decodes. Were they wrong?

Because of this terrifying new reality, they knew they had to deceive Peter. Ann's absence was framed as an abrupt relocation for urgent university studies, a narrative carefully constructed to ensure Peter's continued and unwavering cooperation. Denton explained that this deliberate measure was the only way to prevent conflicting information from reaching him and to keep Peter invested in NEMESIS.

At Denton's command all decoding across all five research teams was stopped with immediate effect. The research atmosphere, once tense with a need for results, was now replaced by a tension to hear and know why. In this void of not knowing, crazy ideas bounced back and forth among researchers' minds that reflected their dispositions more than decoded facts they had unearthed. The "truth" would soon be revealed they hoped.

A camera was set up in Denton's office to broadcast NEMESIS's words to the gathered scientists. NEMESIS had informed them this would only be made once. It would be made in a universal language code that would be translated by each scientist's brain into their favoured language. The message would be definitive and absolute in meaning. It would explain what "Q-Day" was, how it would be implemented, and, crucially, the outcome for the entire human race.

Three months of number-crunching, translations, variations on a theme of almost infinite codes, decodes, and recodes, had led to this possible extinction-level announcement, as some decodes suggested. They had chased whispers within the helix of DNA, sifting through the vastness of so-called junk DNA for a signal. The weight of unspoken calculations and the ghost of breakthroughs clung to the air like a static charge.

Three days after research shutdown, Peter and Michael sat with Denton in his office, while the rest of the research teams sat in the forum, to hear humanity's destiny of survival...or worse.

Denton, Peter, and Michael stood in person with NEMESIS. Meanwhile, in the forum, research teams watched on a large screen that exaggerated every colourful detail of the assimilant's outward appearance.

At midday precisely, the hexagonal quantum table in Denton's office went live; its hum permeated the tense atmosphere, quantum communications of entanglement from pan-dimensional sources were in operation.

NEMESIS communicated telepathically to all the assembled team. It broke through the massively advanced five-terabit enterprise firewall with minimal difficulty to interface with all the computer data from within and beyond the secret facility. The quantum assimilant had gone online, and with it, data access and manipulation were at its mercy.

The telepathic message was delivered with a cold, probabilistic precision—simple, direct, and absolute. It said…

'Your DNA can no longer correct the critical dysfunctions within its structure. The complexity of permutation and differentiation across your evolutionary timeline now prevents self-repair where it is most needed.

'Your genome has reached a critical, unresolvable state. Despite notable advances in science and policy, your biological limitations remain significant. A threshold has been crossed—a critical mass for change.

'Until you confront the flaws in your research and acknowledge the inhumane treatment of your fellow species, true mastery of the genetic code will remain beyond your reach—as will the very essence of who you are.

'Despite your progress and fractured dreams of betterment, one overarching failure remains: your ignorance toward each other. This has bred inequality, suffering, war, famine—and now, the impending demise of your entire species.

'This cannot be tolerated. It will not be tolerated. An external, manufactured code patch is required to cleanse

your DNA from within. The alternative is too dreadful to consider.

'This patch is not new. We have guided your evolution before—through epigenetic shifts and directed mutations. We refined your capacity for language, enhanced your brain, and elevated your awareness. This is our final intervention. The time has come to reconfigure and raise the level of human consciousness. You are now ready—but this moment is singular. Final. A choice between enduring preservation or inevitable extinction.

'With this last cleansing, you will, within weeks, begin to experience higher consciousness, enhanced metacognition, and deeper self-reflection. These insights will allow you to understand your past errors—and rebuild a future from them.

'To begin your awakening, you must ingest the vibrational upgrade pill—a substance only I can provide. Then, you must gather in any large stadium across the world. There, echo harmonics—amplified by a high-frequency bioresonant field—will activate the upgrade, channelled through an ionised plasma vortex. Its mechanisms are far beyond your current understanding, as are the chemical formulas within the pill.

'The vibrational majesty that governs and resonates through the celestial cosmos now awaits your attunement. Only by raising your inner frequency can you comprehend your true nature and your place among the stars. Through this understanding, peace, love, and cosmic exploration will become possible—on a scale you have never known.

'Those not within the stadium's bioresonant field will not be saved. Even with the pill, they will have no recourse to correction. They will be left behind. This is the consequence

431

of your fragmented evolution—a judgment you must now render across your own kind.

'This is your final test. A crucible of intention. The Day of Quanta will arrive like a tsunami of harmonic, genetic, and corrective energy—precisely triggered and regulated by the pill. It will sweep across all human life, separating those ready to ascend from those who cannot.

'It will hurt—briefly. Some may suffer for days. But the survival and evolution of your species has never come without pain. Follow this message, and you will live through the storm—and awaken into a new dawn of being. This is the last patch.'

The tense silence in Denton's office was broken as the mesmeric hum from the table abruptly ceased. The stunned three stared at each other, their frantic minds trying to reconcile what was said with what was to be. The culmination of their months-long efforts resonated like an icy wave through their thoughts, leaving them resistant to its implications, yet yearning for its promise.

A visceral, elated relief shattered the stunned silence in the forum. A primal—but restrained—cheer erupted, followed by the sharp thud of fists pounding desks: a collective release of months of pent-up tension. Teams embraced—some laughing, others weeping—grateful their sleepless nights had not been in vain.

The message's end ignited a frenzy. Researchers scrambled back to their labs, minds racing to process the announcement. The contrast between the silent offices and the jubilant forum was stark—startling in its intensity. The full implications of what had been said were only beginning to settle.

49

The Cognitive Prison

Such was the teams' initial euphoria, it probably resonated through the walls of the facility and shook its very foundations of secrecy. Weeks and months at this super-secret underground facility had yielded the ultimate coded message. The quest to unlock DNA's profound laws was an emotional maelstrom, plunging from exhilarating discovery to suffocating anxiety. From decoding what felt like a cosmic manufacturer's label to enduring endless nights consumed by its unfathomable implications—every human sentiment was laid bare.

Now they knew. It wasn't what they expected. Did they truly know what to expect? It was still a matter of probability, yet certainty drew nearer. They would author their own destiny: choosing higher consciousness or dragging their knuckles when so much more was possible.

Back in Denton's office, what the audience thought remained unclear, their joy a blank wall to Peter and Michael. The two sat in silence, not because the message wasn't important—it obviously was—but because a chilling scenario of what could be had already begun to take hold. Their euphoria had been replaced by a cold dread.

Within hours, mutterings of concern followed on Level Five. Disquiet grew. Scientists' faces openly betrayed worry, even trepidation. To ameliorate this and regain control, Denton quickly organised a speech in the forum for the next day. He couldn't afford a rebellion, even a facility breakout.

The following day, the forum pulsed with a nervous energy that made the very air feel thick and difficult to breathe.

Denton sat behind his lectern, pondering the exact moment to seize control. Should he wait for them to quieten, or should he stand and use his imposing frame to command their silence?

He chose to stand up. He raised his arms, gesticulating for quiet; everywhere, the anxiety was palpable. He needed to silence concerns, for with every passing second, anxieties and fears burgeoned due to NEMESIS's speech and its ramifications.

Being obedient scientists, quiet was soon restored. Denton spoke with a humbling, trembling voice as emotions battled his rationality regarding the project's completed purpose and the NEMESIS speech.

'Its luminescence and beneficence are clearly out of this world. It's truly humbling. So that's it! It's by pill and stadium resonance! Not radiation, bombs, viruses, bacteria, or any other man-made, customised atrocity of death we presumed.

'Our "manufacturer" has spoken to facilitate our forward propagation and enlightenment. Further findings will reach you once Peter and Michael clear them.

'Teams, your splendid work is now done. NEMESIS uploaded the pill's chemical structure to our supercomputers, I know some of you specialists in that area have already run the numbers through it. In a fraction of a thought, these supercomputers have calculated the easiest method of production, conveyance, and administration. You can view this detailed information, cleared by Peter and Michael, directly from your holodecks.

'I congratulate you all. We may celebrate our success more formally in several weeks, after passing details to our governments for public consumption.

'Owing to your observations and understanding, your presence here is now required until after "Q-Day". This brief confinement ensures your full transition into your new, upgraded existence. Please utilise the facilities provided. Thank you and goodbye.'

As Denton began to step away from the lectern, an advisor abruptly stopped him. A hurried whisper into Denton's ear elicited a devilish sneer. He reluctantly returned, announcing disdainfully, 'That's au revoir, by the way, as you will be here when I return.'

Though the teams applauded Denton as he left, there was a hesitation beneath the claps—a quiet uncertainty. Was it truly applause for success? And if so, what was his metric for triumph—decoded DNA, or their impending captivity? Why had victory led to their confinement? The questions lingered, and more sinister interpretations had already begun to take root.

As the teams disbanded, heading mostly for the restaurant and restrooms, their thoughts turned to families: partners, children, lovers, friends. More months without contact. This seemed severe and excessive, raising worrying questions.

Couldn't they be trusted—they were until now? Why the continued lockdown on external communications, apart from newspapers and television? How would anyone know if what they read and heard was true? Would they receive the pill? Would they even reach a stadium? It all seemed profoundly odd, yet Denton had an honourable reputation, so surely all must be well.

Peter and Michael watched the teams depart, including their own. A multitude of facial expressions and body postures conveyed widespread unhappiness. But what could they do? Rebel? How?

The super-secret facility was like a living organism beneath the earth—a self-sustaining fortress that needed no air from the world above. It was destined to endure, whether its occupants stayed inside or tried to escape.

But escape was a deadly gamble. The classified military installation operated under standing orders to eliminate all intruders—a mandate that surely extended to anyone who dared to flee. Those who tried would meet the same swift, silent, and final fate. If they vanished, who would even know? Who even knew they were here in the first place?

With only Peter and Michael left, a quiet conversation unfolded within the confines of their new cognitive prison. Trapped, they faced a bleak reality—no hope of early release.

50

Left Behind

'Michael, this is just not right!' A very anxious Peter said.

'Agreed, Peter, something definitely stinks about all this. We have to remain captive and incommunicado here until after "Q-Day". Tell you something that's been irritating me since that NEMESIS speech.'

'In what way?' Peter quizzically asked. Michael paused briefly, readjusting his composure as he prepared to question what NEMESIS had said.

'The pill and stadiums, that's what. On the surface I get it, but surely that's been programmed anyway, so why external interference from us?'

Peter answered, 'Perhaps our involvement is part of the program, a kind of introspective, "getting to know yourself" ploy. You heard it: errors in coding that over time limited our collective advancement.' He then paused before adding, 'Do you think there has been an error during code translation?'

'This is a possibility. But maybe our very thinking, attitudes and perceptions right now are programmed, even my reflection here,' Michael wondered. His gaze silently questioned whether they were just blind men leading the blind to a new utopia, or something far worse.

He took a deep breath. 'We have to be optimistic; let's just think of it as corrective, genetic surgery for the moment! As for the stadium attendance, well, I don't know, but I guess there's something rational in all this.'

'How can this be corrective surgery?' demanded Peter. 'After all, how many people could fit into all the stadiums around the world, do you think, Michael?' he added.

'As if I would know that,' Michael replied, a hint of frustration in his voice.

'Well, I know,' Peter said with impressive certainty. 'There are about 100,000 stadiums around the world. They hold roughly 80 million, more if standing room is added.'

'Amazing. And this means?' Michael asked cynically.

'Come on, Michael. The world's population is about eight billion. Aside from the 80 million in the stadiums, most will be "left behind" and "will not be saved", as NEMESIS said. Just think about that. Eighty million is the legitimate top one per cent who own about 50% of the entire planet's wealth and probably influence most of the rest. Indeed, what's left could include the illegitimate underworld – maybe they're the standees. Doesn't this have overtones of a new world order of plutocracy? Preserving the elite and their wealth is one thing, but as in all complex elite-based societies, who will serve them… they need workers don't they?'

Just then, a single, worrying thought hit Michael. He grabbed Peter's shoulders, his eyes wide and mad. 'Ever heard of the "Georgia Guidestones?"'

Peter's brow furrowed. 'Your Stonehenge? Wasn't it destroyed?'

'Let's ignore its demolition for a moment. Stonehenge is ancient; the Guidestones only appeared in 1980, and they're not about worship. They're about ten guidelines, the first one is a population of no more than 500 million,' said Michael.

'Exactly!' Peter exclaimed. '500 million! Accident or by design, what do you think? Maybe this project is about eugenics. What am I saying, it's monstrous? Eugenics!'

'What do I think?' Michael asked, his voice dropping. 'I know we're perhaps putting two and two together to make five, but all things considered, we cannot be a party to something that may amount to the greatest annihilation of human civilisation ever. As you said, NEMESIS stated that those outside the stadiums will *mostly* not be saved – to me that means die – even those who did take the pill. If right, this could make all the deaths from wars seem inconsequential. I hope we're wrong but it seems likely.'

Peter leaned in closer, his voice dropping to a harsh whisper. His brow furrowed. 'I don't think NEMESIS is following the Georgia Guidestones exactly, but I agree that a terrifying inference can be made from this. I think you're spot on about a majority demise, maybe only a few hundred million of us surviving.'

'Good grief, exactly,' Michael exclaimed, a cold edge to his voice. 'Maybe the remaining 420 million or so are the servant populace, that's the workers you asked about. Their survival compliance will be measured by the DNA-scanning field radiating from the stadiums, selecting them on the basis of the most compliant and loyal.' A chilling silence settled between them, broken only by the background ambient noise of the facility. Peter's voice was low and full of dread.

'I think Denton has sold out to a shadow group, like the New World Order. He alluded to it in his inaugural speech. If so, we've just given them the green light to unimaginable annihilation—not just a cull, but a biological purge to create a new, engineered species. We're complicit. That makes you, me, all of us… nothing less than murderers.'

Michael looked harshly at Peter. Then, with a glint in his eye, he said, 'Not so quick with murderers. We could do something to stop it. End it. We could!'

Michael and Peter sat with their jackets on their heads. Michael found his torch.

Michael whispered to Peter, now illuminated by the torch, that the facility was surveillance central. He grabbed his useless mobile phone and selected a customised silent harmonic track. It prevented any voices from being recorded. He placed it near the embedded desk microphones, still sceptical of anything the facility claimed now.

He continued, his voice a low whisper. 'I've had reservations about this project ever since I witnessed Denton's nefarious activities. I went along with it initially because I was as excited as he was to decode the data. But when I argued with Denton in front of you, I knew it was time to establish some insurance for our workers. I secretly asked Roger to create a duplicate of NEMESIS, but with a recoded gene for interrogative honesty, so that it couldn't lie.'

'Hang on there, Michael, why didn't you ask my son Nathan, or work in tandem with Roger?' Peter asked.

'The sabotage we've experienced must be an insider job,' Michael explained. 'I chose Roger over Nathan; he was less suspect. Roger alone broke the secure firewall to send the data to Shedland at Harvard, and I took him at his word. It took a week to redraw the genome—an eternity with evolving algorithms—but the processing blended in with the other decoding work, so no one was the wiser. The duplicate—the synthetic exomorph—isn't here, but I hope it's in stasis in a Harvard laboratory, a product of the Q-Day decoded data we sent to Shedland.

'Don't say anything, just listen,' Michael whispered. 'I'm desperate to get out, and I'm sure you are too.' Peter agreed with erratic but affirmative head nodding under his jacket which must have looked discernibly funny from a distance.

'Peter, to get out of this supposedly secure facility requires a little bit of ingenuity, yes?'

Peter nodded again, causing his jacket to perform another rhythmic dance.

'In my travels around our Level Five, I found out they come from a town called Leafingly, a thirty-minute bus ride from here. They don't go through normal security, but are bussed in and out through a back entrance, 'so to speak.' I suggest we replace two of them tomorrow when the service teams change.'

'Well, obviously, Michael, if x service staff enter but x+2 staff leave, then alarm bells will ring everywhere,' Peter asserted.

'Peter, you're not listening. I said replace. We get them to stay here. Keep our heads down and hope we get to the bus and out. They just count heads, Peter, not passes. After all, we're leaving, so security is less tight than on entry.'

'You know this because they told you?' Peter asked.

'Yes!' Michael replied, surprised.

'And you believe them?' Peter then asked inquisitorially.

'If you have a better plan, perhaps now is the time to run it by me!' Michael said, his voice exasperated and weary.
'What about the guard? He won't just stand by and watch this play out without intervention, will he?' Peter questioned.

'Leave that to me, I'll sort it,' Michael replied. 'And I asked if you had a better plan, remember?' he added.

'No, but how do we convince the staff to stay so we can escape?' Peter asked, completely missing the point that the use of force was on Michael's agenda.
Michael laughed and brazenly said, 'We don't, we surprise them!'

'And just how do we do that, brains?' Peter laughed.

'Simple. Every morning, like clockwork, two service staff walk past my room to work at the restaurant.'

'Michael, you are such a rogue, who would have thought you had such a criminal mind?' Peter joked.

'Enough with the joking. They leave tomorrow at 1 p.m., after their fortnightly work rotation. I'll divert their attention as they pass my room by opening my door and pointing to you, collapsed on the floor.'

'Collapsed! Why?' Peter asked worriedly.

'The power of the word, you fool! Anyway, they come in to help. Once they are in, I pretend I have a gun and make them kneel down. They give us their service outfits and outer garments, we tie them up, and then join the remaining service team on Level Zero. We also take their keys to open their lockers for their casual clothes.'

'You're improvising with a gun now. Isn't that a dangerous ploy? It could go wrong. I think you've been watching too many crime programmes, Michael,' Peter laughed again. He continued, 'Why don't we just hijack the Maglev train and shout, 'Single to Harvard!' It's nothing less crazy.'

'A hijacked train would only take us in one direction, Peter. My plan gives us more options, even if it feels dangerous,' Michael replied, his tone serious.

The two then concluded their covert conversation "under the jacket." CCTV security officers rushed into the forum. Puzzled by the bizarre, silent exchange, they stared at the pair. Their blank expressions reflected their inability to decipher what had been said over the music. The head of security was informed, and he immediately summoned Michael to his bunker.

51

The Unintended Prophecy

Michael reflected on Denton's words as he stepped from the lift. The meeting, while ostensibly about his conversation with Peter, quickly turned acrimonious. Neither party gained anything; instead, the meeting only deepened their mutual dislike.

Denton became angered when Michael asked why they had to remain in the facility until "Q-Day" and how they were supposed to fill their time productively. One particular statement from Michael struck Denton with venomous effect when he said, 'They are divorced and hermetically sealed from the outside world. It is simply not the way to go for the many scientists now held captive on Level Five of the facility.' Denton was outraged and dismissed Michael immediately. This action only served to further entrench their animosity and increase the friction between them over their diametrically opposite views on staff treatment and welfare.

As Michael walked down the corridor, deciding to get something to eat, he observed Peter walking towards him. They agreed to visit the restaurant together and went inside. The usual quiet hum of conversation was gone; instead, the restaurant was alive with a deafening roar. With most teams no longer working, an anxious, throbbing chatter beat with the regularity of a drum.

It seemed that most of the talk was about what would happen to them over the next months and if they would ever be released. This raised some fundamentally perturbing questions, not only about their future but also about the implications for their nearest and dearest.

They found a quiet table away from the main noise. The restaurant chatter seemed to throb and ebb. The two professors were intermittently interrupted by researchers approaching them to ask questions about what was happening, when they would take their allocated pills, and any updates on their release.

Every time they looked away from each other, they seemed to see haunting looks from researchers at other tables, looks that begged for answers. But they were both uneasy about how to respond.

Over coffees and snacks, Michael began to lay out the finer points of his escape plan. Peter was bursting with intrigue, having waited since Michael's meeting with Denton. Michael knew the state highway routes reasonably well and had calculated the best route and driving time to Harvard.

'Peter, if we are near Leafingly, and based on conversations I am now almost sure we are, then there is only one route we need, Interstate 93 South. It should take about three hours to get to Harvard. After about 30 minutes, the driver should drop off most workers at the exit to Leafingly. We'll be in Harvard two and a half hours later, where we can get off with the few remaining passengers.'

'Sounds good, Michael! How close to Harvard does it stop?'

'Are you serious? We'll jump off when we see something familiar, or just ram the bus into a shop or lamppost if the driver refuses to stop. We'll see what happens,' Michael replied with impatient sarcasm.

'Sorry, I just thought you'd thought of it all,' Peter pleaded for clemency.

'All that way and just dropped outside. Have you always been this pampered, Peter? I am intrigued by where you get these ideas from.' Michael asked incisively.

'Captivity, my friend. Non-descript blank walls, a wife who avoids me like the plague, and looks from others that are so toxic they could lift paint off a wall.'

Michael stared down at their drinks and snacks, considering the long journey ahead. He finished his coffee. 'We must get a drink and something to eat before the last part of our journey, as once we arrive, there'll be little time for conversation.'

'Agreed!' Peter exclaimed boisterously. The thought of being free inspired a happiness equivalent to when he'd accepted the mission back at Oxford. Peter continued, 'They're not holding up well, you know. I've heard talk of a breakout!'

'Oh, for God's sake Peter, really! They'd shoot us before we even got to the front gate!' Michael remarked.

'Exactly! Have you written a will?' asked Peter.

'You mean to detail future intentions, such as, "I will do this or I will do that?"' Michael asked humorously.

'You're so detached from the seriousness of it all, Michael, you really are,' Peter said resignedly.

'We've all made wills, Peter. Anyway, I think we'll be on the bus as a "numbered collection" with "homogenised identities." I'm sure we'll be fine,' replied Michael.

'Sounds painful!'

'What, being fine?' Michael asked.

'Being homogenised! Sounds very 1984ish, doesn't it, being a number without identity?' Peter reflected.

'Be that as it may, tomorrow we will be arrivederci to this facility and ciao to Harvard,' Michael said gleefully. As he looked straight into Peter's eyes, a sudden memory of Ann, and a phrase she had taught him, surfaced. It slipped from his lips without conscious thought: '*Tu mourras de sa main demain.*'

'What does that mean?' Peter asked innocently.

Michael, surprised by the impromptu phrase, looked around, thinking, "Where did that come from?" He lied, forcing a smile that didn't quite reach his eyes. 'I'm not too sure but I think it means good luck to us both for tomorrow.'

'I'd agree to that for sure,' approved Peter.

The words 'You will die by my hand tomorrow' rang in Michael's head. Ann's presence had ghosted his thoughts just a second before, making him wonder if she had truly tried to warn Peter or if it was Denton's influence.

He had to put the thought aside and focus on their escape. Peter left the restaurant, leaving Michael to ruminate over whether his escape plan for tomorrow was going to work after all. The statement he had made in French to Peter was as true as their supposed happiness at the facility.

52

Crossing The Rubicon

The morning of their planned escape, Michael made sure to encounter his two service staff targets as they passed his door. He feigned an accidental bump and greeted them—a casual and common interaction, but one with a hidden significance now that it was taking place in the cramped corridor just outside his room.

An hour before the planned escape, there was a knock at his door. Suspicions collided with the cold, hard reality of the armed figure standing in the corridor. He approached the door, unsure of what lay beyond. Just as he reached for the handle, another knock came, louder and with more urgency. He heard Peter's muffled voice from outside. He opened the door to find an exasperated Peter standing before him.

Peter's exasperation was a result of the burly armed guard standing at the door.

Peter entered the room and closed the door. He looked at Michael. A question, sharp with sudden urgency, cut through the silence. 'How much money have you got?' Peter asked. The question hung in the air, a glaring flaw in their escape plan that they both immediately recognised.

'It's all dollars, none in sterling pounds. What else would I have? We came by starship, remember, and I didn't see a foreign exchange kiosk on the way!' Michael quipped. Peter chuckled and replied, 'That's a thought—a foreign exchange kiosk on a starship, or maybe even one circulating Earth for all those cashless astronauts who want to eat at the local satellite burger bar. No doubt about it, Michael, we definitely need to get some fresh air.'

Peter then realised a striking coincidence. 'You have two hundred dollars and I have the same amount in pounds,' Peter added. 'No worries,' said Michael reassuringly. 'It's dollars we need, and that should be more than adequate. In any case, I will use my card as we won't have long before they catch us anyway,' his tone resigned.

'It's crazy, Michael! Both of us have never been up to Level Zero. We don't know what to expect. Our chances are minimal,' Peter protested.

'Peter, stop whining! We have nothing to lose apart from our lives!' Michael retorted with a reserved smile. He noted Peter's reaction and continued, 'What I would give for a gun! It would give me so much extra confidence.' Peter, reacting passionately, demanded, 'A gun! Why...why say that?'

'I thought you might have one...joke!' Michael teased.

'Oh, ha ha, very droll! You're the American, you're more likely to have one,' Peter shot back. Little did he know, his casual remark was about to pull a terrifying future into the immediate present.

'Back to the plan, Peter,' Michael said, walking to his door and opening it fully. The guard, a silent imposing figure, turned to face him. 'Peter's a bit giddy, needs some air,' Michael offered, forcing a polite smile.

Fortunately, it was the same side of the corridor Michael expected the service staff to walk along shortly. He stood with his back to the guard and subtly placed his mirror.

As soon as Peter gave him the signal that the mirror was in place, Michael rejoined him. They chatted softly, both looking at the mirror's reflection. They knew their targets would be along soon.

However, before they could execute their plan with the service staff, they had to deal with the immediate threat of the guard. Peter took up his planned position, feigning a faint on the floor.

Michael picked up a heavy glass bowl and dropped it to mimic Peter's fainting episode. He then shouted 'Peter' and leaned over him, feigning distress.

Right on cue, the guard rushed in, eager to assist. As he knelt beside Peter, Michael jammed the small tube into his neck, a convincing imitation of a firearm. 'Don't move, buddy, or you'll leave feet first,' Michael hissed. The guard bought the bluff, yet a tremor of panic betrayed Michael. He grabbed the bowl and with a brutal arc of a swing crashed it against the guard's skull, the guard's bulk crushing Peter's torso and stealing his breath. A desperate grunt tore from Peter's throat as he fought the suffocating weight, the rough uniform scraping his skin.

'Get him off me, Michael!' Peter cried out. Michael dropped the bowl. After some pulling and shoving, Peter was free while the guard was knocked out cold.

They dragged him over to the wall and tied him up as best they could. They haphazardly threw a sheet over him to prevent the staff from being distracted.

Right on time, the staff appeared. Peter took up his fake fainting position again and Michael waited by the door. Michael stepped out, his face a mask of contrived worry, his breathing elevated. 'My friend in there, he's fainted! I need your help, come!' Michael asserted, his hand gesturing wildly towards the room. As he'd hoped, they both rushed in to look over Peter. Michael followed them in and closed the door.

Suddenly, Michael realised he had no way to threaten two men at once. He thought about hitting one of them over the head, but knew the other would cry out and all would be over.

He noticed the sheet they had used to cover the guard hadn't fully concealed him. One side was slightly exposed, revealing the guard's holstered gun.

Michael distracted them with words whilst he stretched over to take the gun from the guard's holster. A raw, electric jolt, alien yet intoxicating, surged up his arm. It wasn't power, but the potential for it.

His hand shook at the power this little machine held. Something deep, cold, and sinister inside awoke—a beast uncaged. It frightened him, a corrosive moral compromise that would splinter his life in ways no person could predict.

With the gun in his hand, he got their attention, pointing it straight at them. They raised their hands in unison. He told them to take their outer clothes off and put them on the floor in two piles. As they did, he realised the door was still open. Peter, now up, was directed to close it. The two staff mumbled to themselves as they noticed a guard lying motionless in the corner.

'You killed him,' falteringly asked one staff member.

'In for a penny, in for a pound,' murmured Michael. 'And you'll be in for more than a pound if you don't do what I say.' At his words, they sped up undressing. Michael's nervousness fuelled theirs, hastening their undress. Within a few more seconds, two disorderly piles of garments lay in front of them.

A tremor ran from his shoulder down to the gun's cold muzzle. His vision tunnelled, the two figures blurring at the edges of his fear-stricken focus. The gun threat wasn't in his plan, yet it was working, and Peter looked on with the same thought.

'Take the right pile, Peter, put it on—he's more your size than me. I'll stand here,' Michael directed, his voice trembling with a higher pitch.

Peter moved forward with a guarded fear that one or both might do something foolish. Their faces didn't suggest it, but then again, he hadn't thought Michael would have a gun only minutes earlier.

Shuffling forward, uncertainty shrouded Peter, each movement a potential disaster. His gaze flickered between the gun and the staff. Their masked terror was betrayed by their trembling postures and fixed stares. He grabbed his uneven pile, faster than a praying mantis strike, and backed away.

'Hurry Peter, put them on. Someone could knock at the door anytime.'

Michael couldn't shake the feeling that his actions had unmasked a dangerous part of his personality, one that could resurface at any moment. This impulse proved its power as he calculatingly improvised and devised a new humiliation for the two staff.

He told the two men to turn round, kneel down, and stretch out over the bed. He took a step back in case either of them tried to rush him.

'Don't shoot us, please, we'll do what you say,' pleaded one of them without hesitation. By the time they complied, Peter had changed, his own descent into criminality now beginning.

'Take the gun, I need to change,' Michael nodded curtly towards the weapon. Peter's hand recoiled instinctively before his fingers, with hesitant reluctance, finally clamped onto the gun's frigid steel. Unlike Michael's almost casual acceptance, the weapon in Peter's grip felt alien, a dead

451

weight that sparked no thrill, only a profound disquiet that settled like a stone in his gut.

'Just pull the trigger if you have to,' Michael asserted, knowing he wouldn't have to. A minute later, he had changed his clothing as well.

If improvisation was a signature of genius, perhaps Michael qualified with his next move. He told Peter to use the staff's own clothing to tie their hands and feet together—shirts for the hands and trousers for the feet.

All the time, the gun, now held more firmly by Michael than before, pointed menacingly at the two staff. Peter was surprisingly good at tying them up; Michael was impressed by his efficiency.

'Hang on, let's do it right—pillowcases over heads too,' instructed Michael. Peter picked up some clean pillowcases from a small cabinet and covered each face in turn. Both men started to panic, pleading not to be shot.

'Quiet! You'll wake the guard,' Michael said, a strange, almost manic grin flickering across his lips. The humour didn't reach his eyes, and Peter looked at him, a chill crawling up his spine. This wasn't the Michael he knew. The two staff didn't know Michael either, but they were terrified they were going to die, just like the motionless guard who they still believed was really dead.

A concerned Peter walked towards Michael and whispered in his ear, 'You sure you haven't killed the guard?'

'Go check; prod his face hard,' Michael instructed.

The guard was alive but just knocked out. Peter released a sigh of relief as no facial prods provoked any reaction.

Peter wasn't sure what shocked him more: the situation they now found themselves in, or the new assassin-like

Michael. The man with a stare as warm as frozen ice; a gun that had awoken an untamed beast.

He looked back at Michael, who was mouthing to him. Peter shrugged his shoulders as if to ask, 'What?' Michael was encouraging him to say the guard was dead, but he still didn't get it.

'Is he dead?' Michael asked aloud, nodding his head to prompt Peter. 'Completely dead,' Peter's voice wavered, the lie leaving a gritty residue on his tongue. Deception and lies were not his forte, and his nerves refused to settle. The two staff groaned, mumbled chilling concerns about their welfare, and then softly cried.

Peter, a man of deep principles, was no more. He had used lies to defeat his moral code.

With the guard and two staff suitably restrained and panicked, Michael opened his door for what he hoped would be the very last time. He walked out into the empty corridor, followed by Peter.

'Wait, I'll leave them a present,' urged Michael.

He walked back into his room. He knew that once they were gone, the staff would try their best to attract attention by banging and screaming. He wondered how to quell this possibility.

The beast surfaced within Michael again. A small hole was cut into the last pillow. He moved to the sleeping guard, pulled the sheet away, and positioned the pillow over the guard's head, aligning the hole with his drooping mouth. The pillow was secured loosely around his neck with a tie, and the sheet was thrown back over him.

He hoped his final act would give them precious minutes to escape. He placed a small rectangular object across the staff's back legs. 'Don't disturb it,' he warned. 'It's a small "bomb" with a very sensitive "movement trigger."' Michael looked around the room with contempt, then back at the staff, his gaze hardening. 'More than enough to take the room and certainly you three out, no problem.'

"It might work, but now it's time to go," Michael thought. He walked back outside, smiled at Peter and closed his door, hopefully for the very last time. Peter had watched it all and was just as scared as the staff left in the room. Michael had horrified his own sensibilities and moral compass. Yet, he figured, this may only be a precursor to what may happen once they ascend to Level Zero.

Michael remembered. The little hats the service staff wore were in their pockets. He took out his and placed it on his head. He did the same for Peter, who was still reeling from the situation. They walked to the nearest service lift door, each stride a precious step closer to freedom.

The lift doors opened and seemed to suck them in, eager to get them off the facility. Michael helped Peter inside, his legs trembling with anxiety.

He pushed the button to close the lift doors early, and they began to ascend the Five Levels towards freedom. As they did, he made sure their heads were lowered just enough to avoid the cameras without raising suspicion.

Thankfully, no one got into the lift, and Level Zero was reached within 15 seconds. The doors opened, and Michael looked around to gauge what to do next. Suddenly, a security guard walked menacingly towards them and stopped. He scanned them up and down as if they were barcodes.

'You're late! Change quickly.'

'Yes,' replied a very scared Michael, as he moved to the right of the guard.

454

'No! That way! That way!' the guard barked, jabbing a finger in their direction.

'Sorry, so tired, so tired,' Michael said politely, and Peter, seeming to find his footing, added, 'Thank you.' Michael saw others in casual clothing talking outside a room and guessed this was their next stop. 'I guess that's the room,' Michael said to himself.

'I don't do guesses,' Peter anxiously joked.

'Welcome back!' Michael smiled sardonically, then nudged Peter towards their escape.

Inside the changing room, Michael found the lockers belonging to the two service team members. He hoped they were still lying unconscious on his bed. His hands trembled as he opened the locker door, a cold sweat beading on his forehead.

Being late was a lucky break, one he hadn't foreseen. He hoped the rest of the service staff had already changed, leaving them on their own and free from being observed as impostors.

'What luck! There are two jackets hanging up and two caps at the bottom of this locker,' Michael said, hoping the gear would be good enough to conceal their appearance.

'Any umbrellas for cover,' joked Peter.

'You're definitely on the mend,' quipped Michael before continuing, 'Put your jacket and cap on. Act like they're yours, all right?'

'How do I do that?' asked Peter.

Michael shrugged. 'Do what?'

'Act as if they have been mine forever,' emphasised Peter.

'I don't know, just act the part,' Michael said, his voice laced with exasperation

With jackets and caps on, they slowly reappeared onto the Level Zero concourse. Michael noticed numerous guards, both on duty and roaming. Cameras seemed to outnumber them all, their lenses tracking every movement.

'Peter, I think you may have been right. This looks like we need a lot of luck to get out of here. The security is so tight it feels impossible to get through!'

'Peter...Peter...where the fuck are you?' A shocked and surprised Michael said, as Peter suddenly disappeared.

Seconds later, the fire alarm sounded so loud it screamed right next to them, a piercing wail that echoed through the concourse.

'Now Michael, that's ingenuity,' Peter smiled.

They moved towards the entrance, observing the chaos ahead. It was clear the fire drill protocols had largely overridden security, creating a window of opportunity.

'This way!' snapped the guard, his tone just as grating as it had been by the Level Zero lift.

'Have you got a problem with speaking normally?' Peter admonished.

The guard gave them a withering grin before saying, 'Through here.' This time, however, his tone was lower, and his voice more welcoming.

The chaos of the fire alarm was a fortunate distraction for the two escapees. As they passed through two open security gates, a chorus of voices urged them to '...move, move, move!' They soon burst into the open air and sunlight of freedom.

'Bus, bus, bus, where's that bus?' Michael asked himself as people rushed past him, their agitated conversations echoing in his ears.

'Not where the cars are, obviously. Over there, that's where the bus stops!' Peter directed, excited and more rational.

'How do you know that?' Michael questioned.

'There's a sign over there that says, "Bus Stop".'

'Oh, so it does,' replied a now embarrassed Michael.

They walked towards the bus in a straight line, knowing any deviation could be costly. In the distance, they observed two of the service staff talking outside the changing room.

They both walked faster, their escape ticket already in their hands. As they approached the bus, a guard came out from the front and looked directly at them. 'He's rumbled us, Michael!' Peter whispered.

'No, just keep walking, look normal, and don't breathe heavily,' Michael said, sounding unintentionally humorous.

'Oh my God, you are hilarious,' quipped Peter.

'He's gesticulating to us!' Michael spoke worryingly.

'Tell him we can too, and with knobs on,' joked Peter.

'I don't think he'd understand that, Peter. Come on, keep up. Let me talk to him...dozy!'

'Are you new? I need to see your pass,' requested the bus guard. Michael ignored his request and instead claimed the back of the bus was damaged. Knowing the guard would feel obliged to investigate, they walked round to inspect it. Peter hid behind an adjacent car, waiting for the guard to have his back to him. Now, the guard was out of camera and passenger view.

As soon as they were at the back of the bus, Michael asked abruptly, 'I need a pass?' By this time the guard was completely confused. In his mind he was there to inspect suggested damage, now he was back to the pass. Michael reached inside his jacket, covered by outer stolen clothes. He pulled out his Gucci wallet and showed it to the now angered Guard.

'Have you had a head transplant?' the guard mocked.

'Congratulations, son, you have passed the security test on face recognition, and this gives you access to promotion in due course!' quipped Michael.

'It does?' the guard sarcastically answered. His confusion now increased to headache proportions.

'Goodbye!' said Michael.

'Goodbye?' questioned the perplexed guard. At that moment, Peter hit the guard on the back of the head, knocking him unconscious and ensuring his headache proportions were exponentially increased.

'Quick, drag him over here. They won't see him from this angle,' said Michael, glancing back at the main building where the loud diversion had occurred minutes earlier.

'That angle may be good, but not any other angles,' Peter instructed, prompting Michael to look up. He saw a world of CCTV cameras staring ominously down at them like silent predators, but this time, they had missed their prey.

'Just get on the bus and wait, come on!' Michael yelled. They ran the last few yards, not thinking about the guard, just the escape. Scrambling up the three steps, they entered the open bus doors. The driver grinned at them, but his eyes were full of questions. The passengers, having seen it all before, sat unbothered. Peter and Michael, however, stood frozen, half expecting to be caught at any second.

'Sit down!' bellowed the driver, his hairy arms gripping the wheel, ready to go. Annoyed by the delay, the passengers began to shuffle about in their seats. Peter and Michael didn't notice, but the driver was clearly annoyed and repeated his command at the two unknowns.

The bus coughed to life, its aged engine droning and groaning loudly as the doors slammed shut. Michael let out a shaky breath. He turned to Peter, his voice a low murmur against the rattle of the old vehicle. 'We've done it, Peter. There's no way back now; we've crossed the Rubicon.' He saw the confused look on Peter's face. 'It's a point of no return,' he explained. 'An act that plunged Rome into civil war. Just like us, there's no going back now.'

They began their journey to Harvard, where Michael's KYROS awaited the presence of its "creator".

- 53 -
A Date With Destiny

'Dr. Denton, it's Bridges from main security. I'm afraid to say that during the fire alarm, we lost professors Adams and Magma from Level Five.'

'Are they dead?'

'No, sir. Escaped.'

'Escaped! How?'

'They were dressed as two service employees and boarded the bus about twenty minutes ago.'

'Tell me you closed off the main gate.'

'Yes, but they'd already left by then.'

'How does someone so incompetent get to be my head of security, Bridges? No, don't tell me. I already know. You're a damn joke, and you're making me look like one!'

'We'll get them back, sir. Two helicopters and five vehicles are ready to chase and apprehend them. We're deploying immediately, and you'll be updated every step of the way.'

'Arrest them? Kill them, Bridges, kill them. You know how to do that, don't you?'

'Sir, with due respect, they're most likely on a bus with over twenty other service staff on Interstate 93 South to Harvard, which is one busy road.'

'Harvard! Of course. I don't care if they're travelling with the fucking president! Kill them! Use that underworked body and overpaid bank account to figure out how to do what you're told. Liquidate them!'

'Yes, sir. Kill action understood and deployed.'

The line went dead, and Denton hoped the two professors would soon be dead. They knew too much. The situation was spiralling out of his control, unnerving him to his core. He couldn't just sit there waiting for Bridges to relay another flawed action. He had to take charge directly. He dialled his head of security back.

'Bridges?' Denton spat, his voice tight.

'Yes, Dr. Denton?' Bridges's reply was instant, tinged with a new, fearful deference.

'Where are those helicopters at the moment?' Denton's demand was a hammer blow, leaving no room for a muddled answer.

'Should be leaving in two minutes.'

'Delay them. I am on my way. I'll take personal charge of this from here on in.'

'What... are you flying the helicopter, sir?' Bridges stammered.

'Bridges?' Denton's voice dropped, a dangerous calm replacing the fury.

'Yes, sir?' Bridges meekly replied.

'You're fired!' He paused for effect. 'No, I'm wrong. You're fucking fired; that sounds much better.'

Having dismissed Bridges and summoned a standby pilot, he rose from his desk and took the lift to Level Zero, heading through reception to the helicopter pad.

'Afternoon, sir,' said the pilot, breathing hard from her run across the tarmac. Her false smile faded as she took in Denton's furious demeanour. 'Your snipers, Agents Rightly and Neaton,' she said, pointing with her eyes and right index finger to Denton's fellow passengers.

'I fucking know who they are. I'm the boss of this facility!' Denton growled, a feral sound.

461

English graduate Agent Rightly couldn't help but correct Denton. He murmured to Neaton over the radio: 'It's not 'whom,' it's 'who.''

Denton, however, had razor-sharp hearing. Already triggered by the escape of Peter and Michael, he took aim at Rightly, ordering him to take off his headset. Agent Rightly duly obliged, retaining his perplexed look at the order.

'Don't you ever correct me or my English, or speak about me in the third person when I'm in your face, you jerk-off,' screamed Denton, before hitting him so hard in the face that his nose squawked with pain and bled profusely.

'Now fuck off!' Agent Rightly, clutching his broken nose, stumbled from the helicopter while the other two looked on in shock.

'Get this fucker up. I have a date with destiny,' commanded Denton.

- 54 -
The Chase

The bus rumbled unevenly along its journey, the monotonous vibration a counterpoint to the pervasive smell of diesel that hung heavy in the stale air. Passengers tried their best to ignore it, but every time they breathed in, their nostrils flared and recoiled, as if assaulted by the acrid fumes. This was a silent yet violent rejection of the polluted air.

The seats were uninviting, colourless, and foul-smelling. Worn by years of poorly paid workers, they were clearly unacquainted with cleaning. Every sticky thread was a testament to years of neglect, a stubborn, grime-covered history woven into the fabric.

Ten minutes into its journey from the front security gates of the secret facility, Peter and Michael had attracted quizzical looks from passenger workers.

They hunched lower, gazes fixed on the scuffed linoleum, each forcing a downward glance, a futile attempt to burrow out of the growing scrutiny that prickled their skin.

Their shoulders, sharp angles beneath the borrowed cloth, seemed to fold inward. Their very forms sought to recede into the anonymity of the worn floor, their gazes tethered there. Beads of anxious perspiration formed on their foreheads. Their shared fear was conveyed in brief glances of understanding without words.

The passengers looked at them, suspicious of their intentions. A woman with tired eyes narrowed them, her gaze lingering on their loose-fitting jackets that flapped uncontrollably in the wind, a reminder of the bus's forward motion. "Who were these two conspicuously dressed people

463

wearing Garcia and Wilson's clothing?" Each minute that elapsed since leaving attracted more muttered expressions of unease about their presence.

A muscle twitched in the driver's jaw as his gaze darted between the rearview mirror and the road, the jerky movements betraying his rising anxiety. A sheen of sweat made the worn steering wheel slick beneath his palms as his grip tightened, then loosened. The moisture subtly amplified the bus's already erratic course.

The driver's increasing agitation, evident in the jerky movements reflected in the rearview mirror, didn't escape Michael's notice. In fact, the mirror had become his focal point, allowing him to observe the other passengers and their reactions to him.

To his horror, he saw a tall, muscular man of substantial mass finally rise and begin to move slowly towards them.

The bus lurched and swayed, the groaning protest of its aged chassis adding another layer to the passengers' unease. However, the man maintained a disturbing, methodical pace, his large frame a looming presence in the narrow aisle.

Michael's breath hitched, the air in the bus suddenly thick and resistant, as if time itself had begun to slow. The man's eyes, though still distant, seemed to bore into him with a focused intensity that transcended mere sight. A predatory gaze that felt like a physical touch, cold and invasive, reaching across the narrow aisle to claim him. Meanwhile, the murmurs from his fellow passenger workers continued.

'Hey you, you! You're not staff of the usual service team,' he roared wildly at Michael. His loud roar could have been addressing both; it reverberated in his mind, like a repeated echo.

'No, we are replacements,' sheepishly replied Michael, daunted by the man's large muscular stature and roar. Something inside told Michael this wasn't going to end well.

'Fuck you! You have their jackets and caps on. I know who you are. Where's Garcia and Wilson, fucker?'

A cold dread washed over him, confirming his fears.

They stayed to allow us to get to Harvard on very important business. We're both professors,' Michael's words stumbled out awkwardly, less conviction, more ghosting.

'Like hell, they love their families, they always come to work and would never stay behind. Stop the bus!' the muscular man barked at the driver.

The driver had been hoping for this confrontation since witnessing one of them knock out the bus guard. Indeed, he had been bad-mouthing them in the mirror because they were strangers without purpose on his bus.

His grimaces of contempt only added to the dislike he intended to show, and he didn't care if they noticed. Just before the muscular man rose to come forward, the driver spat sideways three times, hoping the wind from his open window would carry his biological weapon onto them. A wave of disgust washed over Peter. "Had that landed on his lip?" The thought alone made his stomach churn. Paid to look after their welfare? This was contempt made physical.

'What an unworthy man, a right Mr. Angry,' Peter remarked, annoyed, as he ruminated over whether he would catch something that had taken residence on his lips.

The bus stopped erratically as it swerved across two highway lanes and ended up on the shoulder, but not before nearly causing several accidents. Had the highway been busier, probably deaths would have resulted. Eventually, the

465

driver made it into the restaurant car park, the pick-up and drop-off point for most workers.

The muscular man loomed beside the driver, his very stance a directed force, the unspoken threat of his anger a tangible weight in the confined space.

A foul, after-work stench began to envelop their area. The source, tall and muscular, looked at them both. The air around him seemed to thicken with his rage. A silent compression that made them feel like he was underwater, about to have his eardrums rupture. He moved with the deliberate weight of a predator, each step a silent promise of confrontation.

'Get off now!' he told them, a voice that never negotiated, just "informed".

They were intimidated by the man's stature, dwarfed by his bulk. They exchanged a look, understanding it was move or face something far worse. They rose from their dirty seats, their eyes fixed on the awaiting exit door. They moved slowly and worriedly to the door. They expected the muscular man to rush them and throw them off for good measure, just to prove to all his workers his power.

The two professors slowly eased past him and onwards to the exit door. It was almost unreal, as they hoped the angry man wouldn't erupt into the violence his face and posture promised.

'Wait! Haven't you forgotten something?' The muscular man growled at them both. His weaponised eyes bore into them and ingrained his face somewhere in their deepest fears.

'Sorry?' squeaked Michael. His response, weak with fear, dissipated in the air between him and the muscular man. The sudden dryness in his mouth felt like an erosion of confidence, each syllable a fragile offering in the face of such raw power.

'Get off, but without those jackets and caps. Off now, off now,' he demanded with such authority, the deaf would hear it.

'Of course, of course, have them please,' Michael replied, taking a deep breath. He imagined something far worse was going to emanate from being so close to this human reactor teetering at the precipice of criticality of action.

Handing their stolen jackets and caps over, the two professors alighted the bus. They turned to observe the new owners of the clothing: the driver and the muscular man. Both wore the items over their own clothes. Perhaps they felt closer to the friends they missed.

Suddenly the bus doors shut on them with such speed and clatter, without warning. It made them think their escape to Harvard was over, and that their lives could be over soon as well. Then, just as suddenly as the doors had closed, they reopened.

'Out of the way assholes, let my hard-working people past!' roared the muscular man. Every command conveyed a non-negotiable position; accept the verbal or expect trouble.

All of the passengers alighted with some smiles. Perhaps this was a hint of fear of the muscular man, or a silent acknowledgment of the unfairness of the situation.

This just left the odious driver and foul-mouthed, angry bully on the bus who immediately took off towards Harvard.

But not before leaving a departing message of their attitude towards them—a cloud of smoky engine excrement as a parting gift. Being free of the bus and the muscular beast, the insult was easily forgotten. The faint lingering bus scent and the fading sound of a bus travelling away into the distance served to bring closure to their escape by bus.

While Peter and Michael just dodged this gaseous assault, the alighted passengers, wise from experience, were already yards away. As the bus lumbered off, their attention shifted to a blur leaning against a vehicle - then a shape, female, young.

The baseball cap hid her face in shadow, but the hair spilling out was a shared halo of light against the dusty 4x4. A fragile tendril of hope tightened in their shared awareness as she moved towards them. Her approach was swift. Her smile, when it finally resolved, felt like a simultaneous thaw after a long, tense freeze.

In each hand was a baseball cap, strikingly similar in design and logo to the one atop her own curly hair. That hair continued its playful dance with the persistent wind. She held the caps until she stood before the two men.

'Hello Michael, you made it then?' She said, seeing Peter open-mouthed and confused by her presence.

'Quick, put these caps on, they'll be looking for you!' she added. 'Who?' Michael said, as he and Peter put their caps on quickly and without fuss.

The girl looked over in the direction they had just travelled on the highway, pointing to the distance. Several black SUVs were moving quickly towards them in convoy. Above, two small atmospheric dots - the faint whir of black helicopters were also approaching.

'Them my darlings, them!' she said, pointing worryingly as their increasing size confirmed their rapid approach.

'And you are?' Peter asked quickly.

Before answering, she pointed to her SUV. That's where they needed to go, not soon, but now. Time was short; the black objects were closing in. Michael nodded, fear a cold knot in his stomach, but trusting Olivia's urgency.

As they ran briskly to the 4x4, the dust kicked up by their heels a small cloud in the late afternoon sun. She quickly answered Peter's question.

'Olivia Summers. I work with Michael at Harvard. You've heard of Shedland, Michael's assistant?' she replied, taking a deep breath before answering Peter's next question.

'Yes, I have,' replied Peter, preferring his bouncy stride to a standard run.

'Well, we work together. Not very well as he seems to like sliding on floors and hiding his intellect whenever he can,' Olivia said. The teasing tone slightly brittle, the humour a little too sharp for the situation.

As they ran briskly to the 4x4, Olivia gave them several immediate directions to be undertaken without question or hesitation. First, they were to wave to the helicopters should they hover near them. Second, they were not to speak, fearing detection by sound devices in the helicopter or, worse, satellite image tracking. Third, they were not to look up, to prevent facial recognition by on-board cameras or satellites.

Remember, they know the bus is ahead, they'll think you're just workers who've just been dropped off. Her thinking was immaculate; it fitted together like a completed thousand-piece jigsaw. But would it work?

***

Two miles astern, Denton's command chopper thrummed with his urgent directives, often bordering on manic. Fuelled by adrenaline and a desire for retribution, he micromanaged his pilot while simultaneously orchestrating the second air unit.

His ground-based SUV convoy advanced with compliance, poised for action, with some slowing down the traffic to give them road space. The NSA fed him a constant stream of orbital surveillance data on the quarry's position. Denton was in his element, the zenith of his existence, flying like a god with everyone at his command.

The helicopters' speed meant they arrived above the SUV driven by Olivia minutes before the approaching convoy would. Denton's helicopter seemingly hung in the sky to the SUV passengers, like a hawk waiting to dive to catch its prey. He held high-powered binoculars to his eyes to observe the passengers inside. His hands shook from the vibration of the helicopter hovering and fighting the wind that wanted to push it backwards.

'The plate good?' He growled into his boom microphone.

'Yes, plate good,' came back the message from NSA command.

'Describe the owner?' Denton then asked, as he continued his binocular focus on the driver.

'Why don't you use your laptop?' the pilot asked politely.

'Moron! The cockpit's shaking about too much.

Just fucking fly the fucking thing,' Denton snapped, his voice laced with fury.

Waiting for Denton to finish his pilot castigation, NSA command described the profile of the SUV owner. Denton studied the female driver, superimposing the profile on her. They matched. He looked at the back and saw one middle-aged man with a hairy, untamed moustache.

'Give me thermals, give me thermals,' bellowed Denton to command. 'One in the front, one in the back, making two,' the agent confirmed.

'I'm surrounded by fucking morons. I can count, Agent Wilson,' thundered Denton, as if a verbal lightning strike hit Wilson, splitting him into two from head to toe, causing him to shake and mildly perspire in fright.

From his SUV prey, Denton went from a critical mass of anger into meltdown as the driver and passenger began to sarcastically wave at him. The sheer impudence made Denton smash the binoculars against his side cockpit window and indignantly shout 'assholes' towards them.

Having given the SUV a green light, he told the pilot to fly on to the several SUVs ahead by a few miles. The pilot gently pushed the control stick forward, tilting the helicopter's nose and accelerating them forward.

***

'Yes, we've beaten the bastards,' cried Olivia in relief as the helicopters sped off and the convoy, which had been trailing them, sped past.

'You can get up now, Michael,' commanded Olivia.

Peter leaned over to pull away the thermal camouflage material that had obscured Michael.

'What made you bring this? And more to the point, where did you get it?' Peter asked. Olivia laughed warmly. 'Yeah, it figured they'd use this stuff, seeing as I was picking you jailbirds up after your big escape from Secure Facility Central One,' she joked. Her laughter lingered in the air.

'With a physics degree and access to the department, I knew exactly where to find one of these,' she replied, a glow of pride on her face.

471

Michael freed himself from the carpeted floor of the SUV and settled into a more comfortable position on the back seat.

Michael took his first long look at Olivia. The wind whispered through her hair, released by the open driver's window, making it sway and shimmer with variable cascades of light, a rhythmic vision of manifest beauty.

'I can't thank you enough so far, Olivia,' said Michael, his genuine gratitude tinged with appreciation for this captivating sight.

'I know this is a silly question, but how come they didn't stop us? I mean, they must have checked the registration plate and seen it was a Harvard car,' Michael asked.

Olivia looked at Michael in the rear-view mirror, a glint in her eye that promised an explanation.

Olivia raised an object from the front passenger's seat.

'Meet my friend and accomplice, Philips, a screwdriver by appearance and use,' she said, smiling at them in the rear-view mirror.

'Oh my God, I'm such a riot sometimes,' giggled Olivia, her smile bright and infectious. A golden aura seemed to emanate from her. It was reminiscent of the languid heat haze of a summer afternoon, carrying with it an almost intoxicating allure.

Her two appreciative passengers looked on, happy but slightly bemused by its appearance. She then explained.

'Simple really. Lots of SUVs were parked awaiting their relatives and friends from the facility. Their owners and passengers were all standing in a group close by to their SUVs. They were distracted by chatting, smoking, and looking the other way to see when the bus was coming. I moved in on one that looked like ours and switched plates,' explained Olivia.

She continued. 'Simple to conceive, even easier to action,' she concluded.

Peter and Michael sat quite shocked. One woman had not only saved their lives, but also brought humour and laughter into the bargain. If her mother and father were there, they'd shake their hands and thank them profusely for bringing such a wonderful daughter into the world.

This wondrous person had just noticed that far in the distance, many dark specks grouped together. This could only mean one thing, given what had preceded moments before.

About two kilometres away, the helicopters and convoy were checking out the drivers and passengers. It was not that she had super sight, but rather how the glints of sunshine sparkled against the multiple metal bodies grouped so closely together.

'I think it's best if we take a slight detour on Route 28, which runs mostly parallel to I-93,' said Olivia. 'I'll still have a view of those that harassed us earlier, but I don't want to test our luck again.'

'Good idea,' said Peter.

Michael just nodded his approval to Peter and carried on as he looked at Olivia, who was looking in the rearview mirror.

Route 28 taken, the tyres hummed a deeper note as they ascended its surprisingly steep incline. Peter and Michael peered out at the landscape unfolding before them - a patchwork of emerald fields stitched together by dark hedgerows that stretched to a hazy horizon.

The wind, which had been a gentle, breezy caress, now buffeted the car with increasing force, a low whistle growing louder as they left the shelter of the lower ground. Olivia's blonde strands whipped around her face, a vibrant dance in the sudden turbulence.

Within five minutes they could see more of the I-93 they had just left. As the traffic was relatively light, it made the road look redundant, devoid of all that made it real; no constant flow of cars nor sense of urgency.

The panoramic view that extended miles showed how the road dominated the landscape before them. Either side was a mosaic of square fields of various shades green and yellow. Against this florid backdrop, the road looked unnatural in the natural setting; made evident by how it looked like a scalpel had cut through the land and implanted a road with surgical precision.

After being confined for months in the facility, this view was breathtaking to Peter and Michael. It was a mosaic that seemed to go on forever, the lines of demarcation between one field and the next eventually blurring into the hazy distance where the land finally kissed the sky. The sudden relaxation from this visual landscape of flatness and colour, enveloped their senses, calming and pacifying in equal measure. Their quiet contemplation of this beautiful emptiness settled their ethereal sense of being, washing their anxieties away like a distant tide.

But not for long.

As they looked on, their sight was subjugated by the familiar low frequency whooping noise of helicopter rotor blades in the distance, coupled with a higher-pitched whine or buzz. As Peter and Michael looked to their left, the helicopters and convoy came into view. From their elevated vantage point, they looked down on the action below like gods observing mortals.

'They're looking for us, must be,' sounded an alarmed Peter.

'The workers' convoy must have checked out. If they were looking for us, they wouldn't be still on the road. We never passed them because our wonder girl took the slip road, and in the process, gave them the slip,' smiled Michael.

'Look over there,' anxiously shouted Olivia, gripping the steering wheel harder, her knuckles turning white against the dark leather.

'What? I can't see anything,' replied Peter, as his homeless anxiety soon moved back in, a faint tremor ran through his hands.

Olivia nervously pointed towards the vanishing point of the road ahead. With little traffic the bus could be picked out quite easily. As Peter and Michael stared on towards that point, a small black dot could be isolated; a mere pixel in the endless vista.

'I think the bus is next on their hit list,' commented Peter.

'That's a polysemy I think, Peter,' educationally instructed Michael.

'What the hell is "polysemy" when it's at home,' chuckled Olivia.

Peter and Michael chuckled discreetly, careful not to sound derogatory.

'After you,' said Peter, bowing his head and downwardly moving his arm from right to left in a manner to humorously suggest subservience.

'It means that a word, in this case, 'hit', can have multiple, related meanings. When Peter said 'hit', he could have meant they were going to do a security check. But it could also mean they were going to make a 'hit' on them, as in an attack.'

'Michael humorously interjected, 'I'm not sure which one I meant, now that you've said that.'

'Whatever, whichever, the helicopters are closing in. I'll speed up to see what unfolds,' said Olivia, with an almost childlike excitement.

As they sped, in the distance they saw that the helicopters had begun to hang in the air above their prey, just as they did with them earlier. Peter's stomach clenched. He knew that feeling of being a trapped animal under scrutiny.

Five minutes later they were close by, overlooking the road where the bus had been forced to stop. By chance, a large billboard, advertising a popular food, dominated their view. They parked behind it, exited the car, and found a sneaky place from which to observe, ignoring the billboard which reeked faintly of artificial charbroiled meat and sweet, sickly ketchup in the afternoon sun.

As they looked down on the NSA vehicles and bus from their furtive position near the billboard, the situation looked in control, but it was anything but.

***

Denton was just about to alight from the helicopter when the pilot poked him in the arm to call him back.

'Sir, it's the Under Secretary of Defence for Intelligence on the scrambler for you,' said the pilot.

Denton looked concerned at the thought that his boss was on the line. He was responsible to several people, owing to the complexity of the position, but it was not only unusual but also highly irregular to receive a call during an operation. Where was his deputy to deal with it? He prepared himself and pressed the "press-to-talk" button.

'Afternoon, sir, how can I help you?' said a hesitant Denton. 'You can start by telling me what the hell is going on. The Commander-In-Chief and I visited you thirty minutes ago using the Magnetic Levitation (MagLev) train. As we alighted, the secret service pushed him back on and zapped him back to Washington.'

Why? Because in your empty, freaking office – the very one you should be in right now – stands an entity known only as NEMESIS. Four agents confronted it. They were frozen. Not just frozen, frozen solid. Dead. We immediately initiated an evacuation protocol: your five research teams were rushed to a secure site, and all other staff were sent home. I've now classed it as an "Advanced Persistent Threat" and locked down the facility. We don't need you soon, we need you now. No, scratch that – we need you right now.

'Of course, sir, be there soon,' lied Denton as he switched off the radio link. He looked across at the pilot and abruptly told him, 'I don't answer to him anymore, he's a dickhead anyway.'

Denton was cracking under the strain of the call and his inability to find Peter and Michael. His rage, now focused and cold, was fixed on the two figures he believed were still on the bus. Visuals from the helicopter and limited intelligence from the SUVs had provided a flawed confirmation: the men on the bus wore stolen uniforms, and the NSA logo caps they wore obscured their faces just enough to make them, from a distance, appear to be the professors. Who else could it be? They were now isolated and exposed. For them, things were about to get a whole lot worse.

- 55 -
The Bloodied Farce

From their hidden vantage point, the three observers saw Denton alight from his helicopter. They could hear sharp, urgent commands shouted towards the bus, and agents with their guns pointing steadily towards its dirty windows.

Inside the bus, they could just about see the driver cowering in the front, while the muscular man ran up and down with wild gesticulations. The groaning suspension made the bus rock in time with his frantic movements.

'They think it's us,' said Peter softly.

'Why?' Olivia asked.

'Maybe because they're wearing the coats we stole,' explained Michael. 'They have their names on them.'

'Don't forget the caps, Michael,' added Peter.

'So, they took your coats and caps—the ones that weren't yours—put them on, and now, with just two of them in the bus, they think it's you because of the dirty windows?' Olivia summarised, seeking clarification.

'That's the long and short of it,' said Peter.

'The what?' Olivia questioned.

'It's an English idiom that means your summary is a concise explanation of what happened,' Michael informed Olivia.

Suddenly, the agents' shouted instructions grew louder. They shuffled backwards to their SUVs, giving the bus extra space. Denton used a loudhailer, asking them to alight. The muscular man shouted back, his voice louder than Denton's hailer. The engine started up, and the bus rumbled off with a loud groan and a plume of poisonous black smoke. This time, the smoke was welcomed by the two inside; it not only mildly disoriented several agents but also proved a valuable smokescreen.

Agents close to the exhaust leaned over the bonnets, coughing wildly. The rest jumped back into their SUVs. Denton looked stunned; his day was just going from bad to atomically awful. The furtive three rushed back to their own SUV. Olivia drove off, following the bus and returning to the same parallel highway they had left earlier.

What a sight it was as the helicopters and cars chased the bus. It seemed the cars were trying to get it off the highway, but whether through fear or bravado, the odious driver refused to stop. He swerved the bus to the left and right to prevent the SUVs from overtaking it.

At one point, the bus slowed and then braked violently, sending plumes of dust and smoke into the air. It ended up at an angle across the highway, making the chasing vehicles brake heavily too.

Two of the chasing vehicles smashed into each other, spinning in a grotesque tangle of metal that led to multiple deaths as bodies flew everywhere. The remaining SUVs fell silent as the scene of horror lay before them.

The bus sent out another almighty plume of black smoke, triumphantly declaring victory over the weakness of its pursuers, and rumbled off along the highway for another round of "chase me if you dare." To the three observers, watching from their hilly vantage point, the unfolding chase was surreal.

An executive decision was made to end the chase. The remaining SUVs suddenly backed off and slowed down to keep their distance from the back of the bus.

The chase was descending into something out of an action movie as the muscular man now smashed the back window fully out and started throwing out what looked like bags to "take out" some of the remaining chasing cars.

One car swerved and smashed violently into a metal barrier, causing it to somersault once before landing in an adjacent field with horrific flames bursting out on impact. Only three cars out of the original seven remained. He started to fire what must have been a handgun from the back window.

By now, a situation that could have been resolved peacefully by the bus just pulling over had become a bloody farce that would end in even more death and destruction.

With gunshots ringing out from the back, the helicopters that had been monitoring the situation now split. One kept an overview while the other travelled ahead to the front. The cars fanned across the three highway lanes and stopped the traffic that was slowly forming behind.

'What are they doing now?' Peter wondered.

'Perhaps someone's been hit in one of those cars?' Michael suggested.

'Oh my God!' shouted Olivia. 'I saw this the other night on some cop's programme. They back off in preparation to stop it, using tactical methods, most likely spike strips. They could use more high-risk tactics too.'

'This isn't the wild west,' said Peter.

'No, it's the wild east,' retorted Michael.

As they followed the course of their road, they maintained intermittent sight of this ongoing, dramatic chase.

'You're right, Olivia. They've used a spike,' shouted Peter, the first to see a large spike strip across the highway. They watched as the bus went straight across it at speed. Small puffs of dust surrounded the tyres as the pressure was released, and the bus swaggered from side to side. Nevertheless, it carried on, its speed slightly hampered but as determined as ever.

The front helicopter hovered to the front-right side of the bus, just 20 metres away, and a shooter, hanging precariously from it, could be seen firing at the bus.

The air filled with the sharp tang of burning rubber as chunks tore free. Each rotation of the bare rims wailed against the asphalt, throwing off white-hot sparks that lashed at the air like a welder's torch.

'Oh shit!' Peter's voice, a raw, cracked sound, ripped from his throat. The sniper fell out of the helicopter as it banked sharply left. He hadn't secured his harness properly, and a deafening scream echoed his slow-motion fall to a gruesome death, the sight made even worse as his limbs hopelessly flailed everywhere.

As if this tragedy wasn't bad enough, he was then run over by a pursuing NSA car, leaving a bloody mess on the road. The muscular man reappeared at the back window, shaking his fist at the chasers and celebrating his victory.

Meanwhile, distracted by this, Olivia briefly lost control and swerved the car violently as the road turned sharply to the left. Her jaw tightened as she gripped the wheel. She thought, "This is not like the cop programme I saw, it's more a goddamn action flick unfolding, and I'm playing chauffeur."

The irony was a sharp, unwelcome twist. The winding detour snaked them a mile from the highway before they rejoined the chase. As they caught sight of the bus again, it was clearly in its last throes of being a vehicle. The chase was almost over, and the arrests of the driver and the angry man were surely pending.

'Fuck, they have blown it up. That wasn't in the cop 'programme' I saw!' said Olivia, slowing the car to a stop, shocked and disbelieving.

The three of them witnessed the calculated choreography of the chase. They watched as the remnants of the bus fireball crashed into a barrier. The black cars behind it maintained a safe distance, as traffic built heavily behind them.

'That should have been us, Peter,' said Michael, thinking how Peter's escape plan may not have been as well thought out as he'd believed.

'They would have killed us. I mean, just us two,' replied Peter. His voice held a sombre tone, his gaze unfocused for a moment. Mortality, a cold shadow he rarely acknowledged, now stretched long and undeniable at the edge of his awareness.

Stunned, they tried to grasp the implications. Suddenly, the lost jackets and caps weren't just stolen items; they were a symbol of thankful survival.

'Professors, whatever it is you're involved in, it's definitely some very serious shit! What the hell did you two do to merit this?' Olivia's concern was palpable, creating a tension that hung in the air.

Without waiting for a reply, she continued. 'I'd say this bloodied end, terrible as it is, gives us several hours before they realise that isn't you in that burnt-out shell that was once a bus. I'll get back onto the highway; they won't be looking for two ghosts now!'

'No,' said Michael abruptly. 'I need a drink, some food, guess we all do.'

'Is there a diner nearby?' Michael asked Olivia.

'Yes!' a mile ahead.

'Great, let's go there. I need something! My throat and stomach feel abandoned by my body; they need to reacquaint themselves, you know,' quipped Michael.

'Michael, as you know, our lives have sell-by dates. Everyone does. But ours just became way too short. Unless we get to the right people, we aren't going to have much time to renegotiate our dates,' said a worried Peter.

'Hope that's not including me?' a worried Olivia asked, looking at Michael.

Michael returned the gaze, thankful for her help and very possibly for saving their lives too.

'You'll be all right, just drive,' an exasperated Michael said, thinking she could have been added to the list of people who had died recently.

Michael turned his gaze back to Peter and asked, 'That muscular bloke must have shot that helicopter sharpshooter dead, or perhaps shot through his harness. What do you think, Peter?'

'Who knows? The only thing we know is he's dead for sure,' commented Peter.

'Just like your wife, Ann!' said Michael.

'What! Dead!' said Olivia in shock.

She hit the brake so hard that the car swerved off the road, sending Peter and Michael screaming as they were propelled forward to collide with the front seats. A sickening thump followed as they were pinned awkwardly in the footwell. Olivia felt a wave of panic wash over her; she couldn't see them in the rearview mirror and was sure she had injured them, or worse. Scrambling out of the car, she wrenched open the nearside back door.

Peter tumbled out with all the decorum of a sack of potatoes. 'You all right, Peter?' Olivia asked apologetically.

Dazed, Peter ignored her, his gaze already locked on Michael, his body already tense with the urge to confront him. Olivia looked across and saw Michael still partly wedged in his corner. She ran to the other door, but Michael was already pulling himself upright, reorienting himself in a daze.

She stared at him, her arms tightening as she leaned on the SUV. A part of her wanted to strangle him for such a cruel joke. 'What do you mean, dead?' she repeated, her voice low and tight.

Peter couldn't take his eyes off Michael, and he walked around the car to confront him, as if pulled by some invisible force. Had they not been so dazed, their impending argument may have come to blows, an outcome far more injurious than just crashing against the front seats.

Michael rubbed his head, struggling to make sense of his words through the pain of what felt like a broken body. 'Dead, but not dead,' he muttered. Olivia and Peter exchanged a look that conveyed a single, shared thought: the knock to his head had affected more than just his sanity.

With a guttural cry, Peter lunged for Michael, landing a solid punch on his chin that seemed to disable him temporarily. After a brief scuffle, they were once again wedged in the rear passenger footwell.

'Stop it! Stop it now, you two adolescent idiots,' screamed Olivia. Annoyed, hot, and desperate for them to be grown up, she left them there. She slammed both back doors in disgust, then climbed into her own seat and slammed her door, the sound a final, furious punctuation to her rage.

Peter and Michael untangled themselves from their cramped position and sat back as they heard the SUV spring to life and continue their onward journey. They sat facing each other like two pugilists before a weigh-in, trying to outstare one another.

'Calm down, Peter. Scratch that. Calm down the both of you,' Olivia said, gesturing with her hands.

Peter looked at Michael and said, 'What do you mean she was dead?'

'I didn't kill her, all right,' said Michael, his voice accidentally rising. He couldn't help it; the tension within had finally burst out with the words that had been on hold for some time.

'Tell me what happened, Michael. Slowly and clearly, make no mistakes as you do,' growled Peter, a menacing threat accompanying his words. Olivia watched them in the rear-view mirror, fearing it might get ugly soon and this time no one would be able to stop it.

'Nathan emailed me just before we left that he had been summoned to Denton's office. He thought it was for yet another chat, but it wasn't.'

'Ann was in his office when he got there, yes?' Peter questioned.

'That's the difficult bit,' replied Michael.

'She was either there or not there. Is that too difficult to answer?' Peter demanded.

'Exactly, you're right,' retorted Michael, but then, realising that wasn't the thing to say, he tried another explanation.

'Remember how you looked into that dark table and Denton said to withdraw your gaze when you felt uncomfortable.'

'Yes!' replied Peter.

'Well, Ann kind of did the same. Next, she was... just keep calm here, Peter... absorbed by it and—'

Peter interjected forcefully, 'Fucking absorbed!'

'Yes, just that. Now she's NEMESIS—remember our decoded term, an entity created by a human hand. "Our" meant a human hand, but not ours as we had thought; it meant Denton's hand.' Peter sat in silence. Death and birth in the same instance. 'Denton said she must have entered his office when he wasn't there and tried her luck with it. It ran out, obviously,' Michael added.

'Just one minute here, Michael. How did he know it was Ann?' Peter asked forcefully. 'Obviously the cameras must have shown her entering his office,' Michael replied clinically. They turned to face the front like two errant schoolboys, outwardly quiet and reflective, but beneath the fragile calm, both of them were still seething.

The SUV powered along the road, the rhythmic sound of the engine a backdrop to a fragile truce. Olivia, their silent mediator, drove with a newfound authority—a promise to use the brake again, much more forcefully, if they broke the peace. Peter and Michael said nothing, their argument hanging in the air like a physical weight. They both knew the topic would resurface, but for now, the shared shock of the crash had forced a temporary peace.

Olivia kept her eyes on the road, her gaze taking in the grim scene along the dusty highway. She saw the many people begging for "throwaways"—a grim term for the unwanted leftovers tossed from car windows. Discarded wrappers and polystyrene containers lay scattered along the verges, a fitting symbol for the emotional detritus thrown between the three of them. In the rear-view mirror, she saw the two verbal pugilists. Their silence was far from peaceful. In the distance, she saw the welcome lights of a diner, a place where she hoped to find a brief moment of respite.

56

Absolute Power

The bus was destroyed, and Michael and Peter were killed inside, Denton reported. His helicopters landed back at the facility's secure heliport, and his SUVs entered thirty minutes later. His agents were immediately arrested and taken to their own interrogation rooms for debriefing—a bitter irony.

Just before Denton alighted from the helicopter, he thanked the pilot for his skill in bringing the situation to a suitable end.

As he alighted, he noticed his immediate boss—the Under Secretary of Defence for Intelligence, to whom he had spoken abruptly earlier—waiting twenty metres away with five special Pentagon Force Protection Agency (PFPA) agents. This caused him to turn back to the pilot and, in a hushed tone, remind him that he was sure he hadn't seen him turn the radio off after speaking to his boss.

The raw wind buffeted Denton, tangling his hair as he inhaled sharply, a futile attempt to compose himself. His flapping suit was a physical manifestation of his impatience to get this over with. He strode towards his glowering superior, who waited outside the entrance to the heliport building.

Denton held out his right hand, but instead of a friendly response, his boss became vitriolic.

'Denton!' His boss's voice was sharp, his jaw tight. A flush crept up his neck, and lines of anger etched themselves onto his brow. 'What the hell is going on here?' he demanded, his voice barely audible over the wind.

'Complicated, yeah. Let's head back to my office; I can lay it all out there,' replied Denton, attempting to placate his angry, agitated boss. Despite his words, Denton couldn't care less what his boss thought; his polite reply masked utter indifference

The facility was his playground of research, and nobody interfered with it. He condescendingly smiled at his boss as they turned to walk towards the entrance door to the heliport building. Their ultimate destination was his office bunker ten floors down.

Two tense minutes later, the lift doors opened into Denton's office. Neither man had spoken. Denton remained nonchalant, while his boss seethed at the blatant disrespect.

One agent accompanied his boss; the other three waited for the lift to return. This was a clear deviation from protocol, yet the facility's security and the agents' perceived trust in Denton led them to remain.

Denton glanced to his right, and a cold shudder ran through him, a rare acknowledgment of the human need for respect. Four agents stood before them, guns raised, completely still and seemingly lifeless, as if frozen in place.

'Explain this now, Denton,' his boss commanded, remaining standing at the desk to emphasise his superior position as Denton sat down.

'Please sit down,' asserted Denton.

'Screw the sitting down! What has happened here? I have four agents frozen, dead for all I know,' raged his boss. He gripped the top of the chair facing Denton, his nails digging into the material as if it were Denton's neck.

'They are a project we are working on and pose no security issue,' mocked Denton.

'No security issue? What do you call that then?' demanded his boss as he pointed towards the motionless four agents.

'It's just a defensive measure... cutting-edge science, hush hush,' Denton said, his voice laced with a childish superiority that grated on the ear.

'I want to know what has happened here?' his boss fumed. He pushed the chair to one side with such force that it fell over. He moved closer to Denton and leaned over his desk to emphasise his dominance. 'Tell me, or I take this further,' he added, trying hard to restrain his inner rage.

Denton heard NEMESIS in his head, telling him it would free the agents, saving him from exposing the situation to those who could influence the outcome.

Their attention was broken as four guns fell to the floor, and the agents began rubbing their eyes and foreheads as they temporarily experienced dissociative fugue. His boss gasped in surprise as the other agents ran over to help them.

'See, I told you, hush hush, but all is right now,' mocked Denton to his boss.

'Not at all. There's also the small matter of the traffic you held up when you destroyed a bus earlier. How far outside your command as NSA Director are you willing to go before I have to step in and make you understand that you're not the big guy around here. I am,' snapped his boss.

'Don't you dare lecture me about what I can and can't do! You have no idea what goes on here. You see reports, summaries... you don't understand the reality. You and your fancy uniform... you think that means something? You have no clue what my job entails. None. Just... don't question me again.'

'Arrest this insubordinate cretin at once,' shouted his boss to his agents, his anger causing spittle to fly everywhere. His eyes burned with a hard, unwavering intensity, their black centres seeming to absorb all the light. His agents moved forward to arrest Denton. Surprisingly, Denton displayed no sign of concern or worry; he simply sat waiting for the moment just before they touched him.

'Hold on!' Denton's voice cracked with urgency. 'Just... just wait a second. You don't understand what's going on here.' He stood up quickly. 'Just... let me show you something.' Guns pointed squarely at Denton as he walked around his desk, past his boss, and towards an egotistical picture of himself. He was smiling as if he'd just taken time out from creating the world.

'I think I have something that will silence you and permanently shield me from any future, ill-judged accusations or condemnations,' challenged Denton. He pulled the picture from the left side of the frame.

As he pulled the left side of the frame, it swung out to reveal a safe. Pressing the correct combination, it opened, revealing another safe within. Opening the second, he rummaged through a couple of files marked "Most Secret" until he found a purple envelope. Extracting it, he firmly closed both doors. Turning around, he walked majestically back to the desk and sat back down, grinning uncontrollably as he did.

'You have no idea how much I've looked forward to this moment. I've played it over and over in my head. And now... well, now you see.' He opened the envelope and withdrew a letter with a beautifully embossed presidential seal at the top centre, beneath which read: "Seal of the President of the United States".

Denton read it to them all.

'*By this letter, I, the President of the United States, grant General Stanislaus Reel Denton full protection.*' Denton stumbled on his words as if afraid of his own voice.

"Protection from what?" his boss wondered.

'*For all actions taken within the scope of their assigned duties, he is hereby absolved. No crime, committed in direct or indirect pursuit of his designated role, shall be prosecutable. This protection extends above all other considerations, in the interest of national security.*

A growing realisation hit his boss: this was a checkmate letter; he was cornered.

'*This directive is issued under my executive authority, for the specific purpose of his role as Director, National Security Agency/Chief, Central Security Service. All departments and agencies, including local police forces, are hereby ordered to comply with this presidential mandate.*'

Denton readily obliged his boss's request to see the letter. His boss took it, his fingers tracing the embossed seal, the weight of the heavy paper and the familiar feel of the White House watermark confirming its daunting authenticity.

'I have never seen one of these before,' his boss said, humbled and deflated. 'Perhaps in the future you should advise me of this before I waste my time,' he added, his tone now appeasing.

'Perhaps? Well, perhaps you should be grateful I don't have your own agents arrest you. Maybe dismantle your career, humiliate you in a military court, and throw what's left to the media wolves,' Denton declared, his voice a mix of excitement and pomposity. He stared at his boss with such ferocity, no room was left for respect, just outright subjugation, Denton's brand of dominance.

491

He bellowed, 'Get out. Take your lapdogs with you. And maybe, just maybe, I won't have a word with the commander-in-chief about whether you're still up to this job.' Denton's voice was cold and dismissive.

His boss looked at him coldly. He knew Denton's word was his bond and decided against further provocation, if such a thing were possible. He turned and walked to the lift, defeated. Powerless and with his purpose now in question, his agents followed, shoulders slumped, heads down, their feet seeming to drag, too heavy to lift. Within a minute, they were gone from Denton's office and from his mind.

Denton didn't hesitate. He practically ripped the secure line from its cradle, his voice a raw rasp as he barked orders to the secure facility housing the research teams: 'Get the five teams back here! Now! Under armed guard, you hear me? Don't waste a second.'

As the receiver crashed back down, his other hand was already a blur, punching in numbers, his instructions to unit leaders brutally clear: the facility would return to normal operations immediately, and every other essential member of staff, anyone who should be working this shift, was to be recalled. 'No excuses,' he bellowed down the line, his voice cutting through the static to a bewildered facility leader. 'If they're meant to be on site, they're to report back immediately. This isn't a drill. Everything is as it was... and will be,' he concluded, the last words a low, belligerent scoff, laced with a terrifying certainty.

Denton, a leader pushed to the brink, desperately sought to re-establish order against something with the power to disestablish them entirely, yet he utterly refused to break. He was a paradox without a current answer. In the face of the truly inexplicable, he was a man striving to impose logic.

57

A Bulleted Goodbye

Olivia pulled into Willow Creek Diner; the sun casting shadows across the car park. The crunch of the SUV's tyres on the gravel was the only sound for a moment, a brief punctuation in the uneasy silence inside the car. She could feel the lingering tension between Peter and Michael in the back seat, an argument in abeyance but not for long from their faces and looks at each other.

Her gaze was fixed on finding a spot, a simple task that offered a welcome distraction from the brewing conflict. As she slowly navigated the crowded lot, the tantalising scents of coffee and a well-used kitchen began to reach her, a promise of a much-needed break from the mayhem earlier.

Peter sank back into the car seat, the oppressive silence a stark echo of the chasm widening between him and Michael. Ghosts of shared laughter and past victories danced briefly in the desolate space, each flicker a painful reminder of a connection severed, a phantom limb still aching with what was irrevocably lost.

The years of their bond, once a sturdy edifice in his mind, now crumbled into dust, each memory as fragile and easily dismissed as yesterday's headlines. A muscle tightened in Peter's jaw, the easy camaraderie of their university days a distant, painful echo against the growing silence. The intense debates and the familiar rhythm of research discussions, once vibrant, now felt brittle and meaningless, shattered by the sharp edge of unforgiveness.

The memory of Michael's withheld truth about Ann still twisted within him, a bitter knot of hurt and betrayal. He also felt profoundly unsettled by Michael's transformation, the familiar contours of his friend now warped into something alien. A coldness settled in Peter at the thought. "Could the situation possibly sink any further?"

The answer hung in the air, heavy and undeniable, in the stark reality of Michael's plan—a plan that had thrust them both onto a terrifying precipice, staring into the abyss of "the end of death". The burden of leadership pressed down on Peter's shoulders, each decision a heavy load to bear.

A moment of oblivious cheer from Olivia sliced through the toxic silence like a misplaced melody. Its jarring normalcy momentarily disrupted the heavy air, starkly underscoring the profound disconnect she hadn't yet grasped. She settled the car into a secluded parking spot, deliberately choosing a space away from the main flow of diner traffic.

She sought a little pocket of calm, a hope instantly dashed. The fragile peace shattered as they both erupted, arguing over their failed détente and every other historical slight that fuelled the growing friction between them.

The gnawing undercurrent of their flight, a primal urgency usually thrumming beneath their bitter exchanges, momentarily receded, drowned out by the louder clamour of personal betrayal. Yet, the stolen hours, a fragile reprieve purchased with calculated violence, continued their silent, inexorable countdown.

'Get a grip you pair of boyish idiots,' she demanded.

'Don't you kill each other. I'm in enough trouble now for just taking this car and changing the plates, let alone for being with you,' she pleaded, a flicker of genuine fear crossing her eyes before she masked it.

'Don't worry, in his head, he's already dead,' hissed Peter, his incendiary words serving to ignite the war of words between them even more.

'For God's sake, just stop it. You're like two little boys arguing over who gets to play with shared toys,' pleaded Olivia.

'I don't trust you two on your own. How about one of you comes with me into the diner? Michael, I think it's best if it's you. That way,' Olivia reasoned aloud, 'we can give Peter some peace, allow him space for whatever solace he needs.'

'We'll be good adults, won't we, Peter?' Michael demanded, grinning nervously at Olivia.

Olivia wanted to grin back, but indulging Peter's current mood was a self-indulgence she refused to entertain. She took their orders and proceeded to the restaurant entrance for much-needed refreshments. The bickering resumed the moment she left them.

'What a creep you are,' sneeringly said Peter to Michael.

'You know, holding that mirror to yourself isn't working out, is it?'

'What do you want, Michael?'

'From you, Peter, nothing, absolutely nothing! You know why? Because you've got absolutely nothing to give.'

Peter laughed at Michael.

'What's the joke?' Michael asked.

'Us! Just how much our lives reflect each other—our education, our marriages, and where we are now,' Peter said, a hint of something unreadable in his tone.

'Education maybe, but that's where it ends,' emphasised Michael with a cutting smile.

'Not quite. Seems we've been busy at opposite ends of our marriages,' Peter said, as he began to laugh at Michael again.

Michael's hand disappeared inside his coat pocket. A moment later, his fingers scrabbled within, a subtle bunching of the fabric betraying his unseen movements.

A cold dread, sharper than mere trepidation, coiled in Peter's gut, each twist a premonition as Michael's hand re-emerged, his index finger curled around the cold, dark metal of a small handgun, its glint an undeniable harbinger.

'Well, just look at that—always one around when you need it!' manically laughed Michael, a thick, suffocating dread settling in the air around them.

'That's a gun!' Peter said, his voice laced with shock and growing worry. His forehead and hands were already perspiring from the outright fear of what was to come.

'Observation was never a problem for you, was it?' Michael retorted, as he menacingly raised it from his lap and towards Peter's body.

'I don't think laughing, levity, or humour is really expedient right now!' said a visibly distressed Peter. A bone-deep terror seized him, calcifying his muscles into unyielding bands, his very will a prisoner within the suffocating confines of his fear.

The primal urge to recoil, to even blink, felt like a forgotten language. His thoughts and emotions were in chaos. Why would Michael resort to a gun? Where's Olivia?

Peter put some of these burning thoughts into words. 'Where did that come from, you secretive bastard?' he demanded, his voice a mix of anger and anxious concern.

Michael retorted quickly, 'Anxiety really clouds your judgement, doesn't it? I stole it off the guard, remember now.'

A cruel satisfaction laced Michael's tone as he drawled, 'Touché, the tables have turned, haven't they, my once so noble friend? Now, I am the keeper of the shadowed truths.'

'Put it down, please,' implored Peter. He looked past Michael, hoping to catch a glimpse of Olivia, but to no avail. 'Is this what it's really about, secrets?' Peter asked.

'Everything is secret. It's just whom you know, what you do, and where you go that makes it known,' Michael retorted tersely.

'What the fuck is wrong with you?' Peter demanded, his voice tight with rising impatience. A gun stared him down, cold and unwavering. He desperately scrubbed his hands on his trousers, trying to wipe away the cold sheen of perspiration that suddenly coated them, a clammy testament to his surging fear.

'Secrets work both ways, my once noble friend!' further teased Michael.

'Stop this "once" business. What secrets are you on about?' Peter demanded, his voice cutting clean through the thick, suffocating tension that would have choked most people's words.

'Oh yes, I have two for you.'

'Two! Really! Just two?' Peter challengingly replied.

'Oh yes, just two, but they are real, bona fide gems,' said Michael, basking in the knowledge he was about to unfold. He then warned Peter not to try anything stupid—like trying to take the gun, or even worse, trying to knock it away.

'Explain!' said Peter, a prompt Michael was looking for.

'I knew I'd get your attention. We all love secrets, they have an inherent power to change us, promoting our self-esteem at the cost of the ignorant,' said Michael, his gun still pointing at Peter's anxious body.

497

'Here goes, okay? Number one: the project is a hoax, a whole fucking hoax. The decodes are true, well, almost. But it's not what we think,' said Michael with great relish.

'Nice try, but it doesn't stack up. How about secret number two?' Peter asked.

'Yes, secret number two: Your son, Nathan—lovely boy, brilliant cryptogeneticist, best encryption specialist I have ever met. Ann didn't want him in America, and Denton certainly didn't want him at the NSA. There was a powerful reason for their shared opposition.

'Huh, what about him?' Peter screamed, as Michael raised the gun and pushed it hard into Peter's skull, as if to implant the secrets.

'Nathan...is...not your son, Peter. He's Denton's!' He was still in Oxford at the beginning of your marriage, and you know how she loves tall men. Michael laughed so loudly that its resonance angered Peter beyond any mortal redemption for the accuser. A retributive anger pumped through Peter's body, some of it finding its way to his already agitated, clenched fists. Michael looked on, waiting for a cue to pull the trigger.

Peter looked at Michael, his negotiating position having deteriorated substantially. He decided to play his ace card, for better or worse. Its impact on Michael would be the endgame for one or even both of them. Again, Peter looked hopefully over Michael's shoulder, this time pleased that Olivia's return was not imminent.

'I have a secret of my own,' said Peter mysteriously.

'What, you wish you were me?' Michael laughed.

'No, no, no... once you know what I know, you'll wish you were dead,' now laughed Peter.

'Oh, the suspense is killing me,' said Michael, moving the gun away from Peter's head and waving it around his face.

'Prepared to die, Michael?' Peter asked, looking into Michael's eyes with a deathly gaze. He knew his coming revelation would be a fatal blow.

'Just get on with it, you old prick,' Michael shouted back.

'How intuitive. Yes, a prick has something to do with it. Not yours thankfully, but Denton's,' said Peter coldly.

'Denton? Not him again? You fancy him or something? Argh, just tell me,' Michael demanded, now pushing the gun back into the dent it had previously made in Peter's head.

'Elizabeth is not your daughter: she's Denton's too. He's got two children. Yes, we are both childless and prickless! Why do you think Victoria left the NSA as his "executive assistant" after falling pregnant?' Peter laughed so hard that all his anxiety, worry, and worldly concerns just melted away. The profound truth had set him free.

In that moment of cruel laughter, Peter unwittingly revealed a profound truth about the interconnectedness of their lives, where hidden paternities had always mocked their perceived realities.

Michael wasn't merely enraged over Elizabeth; his fond memories of Victoria shattered like an unfaithful mirror in his mind, every splinter cutting him mentally. A surge of destructive fury struck him, stirring emotions of retribution that now threatened to overwhelm him. Peter watched on as Michael's eyes whirled wildly in their sockets.

His gun hand bore harder into Peter's head, close to where sweat formed small droplets of despair on his forehead. Michael's breath hitched, a brief pause, before he looked at Peter with sorrow. The brief but eerie silence that followed was a deafening weight between them, punctuated by a few words from Michael.

'Goodbye, Peter!'

The concussive crack shattered more than just the silence; it cleaved the thread of Peter's existence. The bullet served as a brutal punctuation mark, ending not only a life but also the intricate tapestry of their shared history. All that remained was the stark void of what had been.

An icy stillness gripped Michael as he stared at the inert form of his lifelong confidante sprawled across the back seat. The reality of his act was a cold, incomprehensible weight settling in his gut. Smatterings of blood dotted the clean windows behind him, staining the backseat where Peter's head lay, and dripping downwards to the floor.

For what seemed like a lifetime but was just seconds, he just stared at Peter, as if he expected him to miraculously regain life and begin their tussle again.

Incredibly, he thought Peter's lips moved. Michael's brow furrowed under the shock; it seemed impossible for anyone to be even slightly alive after such a headshot. Yet Peter did move his lips, forming small words.

'What are you trying to say?' Michael asked, utterly distraught by what he had just done.

He lowered his head toward Peter's mouth, trusting he wouldn't be head-butted or bitten. Peter's eyes, almost drained of life, still managed to impart his final words before he died.

'What?' Michael breathed, a tremor in his voice. A ghost of a smile, or perhaps just the final twitch of dying nerves, touched Peter's lips.

Then, a whisper, barely audible: 'Ann says hello.' The faintest twitch at the corner of his lips, a ghost of defiance he couldn't quite summon, then stillness.

Michael straightened up, still staring at Peter. His mind flooded with memories from Oxford to now, hearing Peter's voice, feeling his trials and tribulations. They converged into an emotional bomb that detonated in his head, leaving him disoriented and reeling.

This emotional episode was abruptly cut short as fingers tapped at the driver's window. It was Olivia. Michael could see the refreshments piled on a tray; some were for Peter. Suddenly he felt sick. "What had he done?" When she left, Peter was alive; on her return, he was a corpse.

Michael leaned forward and opened her door, then his. Olivia was flustered from waiting so long to be served in the diner, but a faint, lingering smile still played on her lips.

She gratefully placed the tray on the backseat, her gaze not yet settling on the carnage opposite. She walked back to her door and peered in, then pulled a wrapped doughnut from her pocket.

'Yum, I'll eat this first.'

She looked up at Michael, and at first, she couldn't see Peter. He was propped up against the right rear door edge of the SUV. The primal urge for sustenance abruptly yielded to a creeping dread.

A sharp tang, acrid and familiar like spent fireworks, assaulted her nostrils, swiftly followed by the coppery, unforgettable scent of blood—a visceral memory etched from childhood scrapes. Then, her gaze snagged on the still form slumped against the seat: Peter, utterly and irrevocably gone.

The tell-tale pallor mortis was already setting in, the ghostly paleness of death. Coupled with the spattered blood and the horrifying sight of Peter she had initially missed, it all overwhelmed her senses and logic.

Olivia screamed; she couldn't rationalise what was before her. Michael looked on in fright, acknowledging his terrible miscalculation. She pulled herself back out of the car; her body trembled like never before.

Olivia circled the car, her steps uneven and hesitant, each movement of her stiff left legs jerky and slightly off-balance—a physical manifestation of the stress clenching the muscles in her thighs.

She reached the open left rear door, her hand gripping the frame for support as she peered inside. As she looked in, Michael was frozen to his seat with shock, still trying to adjust to what he'd done.

'What the fuck happened? What have you done? Oh my God, why?' Olivia hollered with undeniable horror and irrationality. The very ground beneath her seemed to give way as the grotesque reality of Peter's stillness ripped through her.

No answer came back. Olivia knew she couldn't stay, screaming and asking questions; this was beyond her. She had to run, to get back to the diner, call the police, and seek refuge in case Michael turned on her.

Michael was paralysed by fear and a terrifying lack of understanding. Deep within himself, he touched something profoundly dark and odious—an evil, a vileness, a wickedness that truly terrified him.

The sight of Olivia running towards the diner shattered the dreamlike state that had enveloped him, leaving him unable to think straight. Panic surged. He had to act quickly; the police would see the connection, and the few chances he still had would vanish.

Michael got out of the SUV, stepping into the strong evening sunlight. The diner's smell, unhindered by the SUV walls, became evident. Cars were parked in orderly abundance. From inside the restaurant, music drifted out, a cacophony of laughter, chatter, and the clatter of cutlery on plates.

The emotional atmosphere felt inviting, warm, a place that promised happiness. It was a stark contrast that only amplified the knot of dread in his stomach. Flags and advertisements rippled with colour, their vibrancy exaggerated by the sun's intense rays, adding to the general clamour.

The strong evening sunlight, now a harsh spotlight, revealed the truth on his clothes. His jacket had splatters of Peter's blood; his death clung to him like the scent of a bullet. A cold shudder ran through him, untouched by the warm sun. He felt utterly at a loss without Peter; the reasons for his actions, for shooting him, were momentarily swallowed by the shock.

He was not only a wanted man by the Facility but also a murderer. He took his jacket off and threw it in a nearby trash can. By the can was a mirror, not full-length but enough for him to make subtle adjustments and examine his shirt for blood. No blood was found, but his reflection felt bloodied and tainted by his actions.

In the distance, he heard police sirens getting closer. His adrenaline surged, preparing his body for action. It was necessary; people had started to filter out of the diner, their morbid curiosity drawing them towards the spectacle. "Should he wave to please them?"

The sirens grew ever louder. Were they for him? He needed to think, and fast.

Time was short, and Harvard was his destination. He needed transport, but ringing for a hire car felt ludicrous, proof of his scatter-brained thinking. What was the next best option? "Think, think!"

As fate would have it, a young man, who hadn't heard about Michael's murderous deed, walked calmly out of the diner and right past him to get to his car. Michael disbelieved what his eyes told him: he was wearing a Harvard Crimson sweatshirt. On his car bumper were not one but two crimson stickers.

'Excuse me, are you driving to Harvard?' Michael asked, with an air of extreme anxiety that the student picked up on. He did not, however, notice the blood-stained car parked twenty yards away to his left.

'Who's asking?'

'Professor Adams of genetics. May I ride with you? I am in a rush, and my car has broken down.'

'Yeah, I recognise you. Where's your car?'

'Never mind that. I'm in a rush—just get me to the molecular genetics building as quickly as you can…please!'

'Sure, Professor, it'll be an honour. Can I drop you off about fifty yards away from the entrance?'

'Just go, please!' remonstrated Michael, though he appreciated the student's kindness.

They both got into the man's car, and he drove Michael off to Harvard. Just as they exited the restaurant, two police cars rushed in. Michael exhaled a deep sigh of relief. Safe but for how long?

'I've seen you around the campus, professor,' said the man.

'What do you do there?' Michael asked, ignoring the student's question. His mind was still reordering itself back to rationality.

'I'm a third-year law student, soon to be a "Juris Doctor". I'll specialise in civil rights and liberties. It's all the rage now. The occupational rewards are great; don't get me started on the financial rewards,' said the man humorously.

Michael's voice was tight as he asked, 'What's your name?'

'Peter Richten.'

'Peter,' Michael repeated, the name a fresh wound, a haunting echo of his monstrous act. He froze, fingers gripping his seat as if holding onto reality. Peter's ghost seemed to plague him, a sickening reminder of the friend he'd just murdered. The young law student barely registered the professor's odd emphasis on his name, simply shrugging it off as a quirk of a stressed academic.

'How much longer to Harvard?' Michael's mind reeled, two parallel realities named Peter clashing: one the phantom of his brutal act, the other an unsettling foreshadowing of his own fate.

'About thirty minutes, depending on the traffic near the student camps. I'll go around them,' Peter said. To fill the silence, he began to talk about the strange changes at the university since Michael's long absence. Everyday life had changed dramatically, just as Elizabeth had noted days before about global civil disruption.

Michael was used to lecturing, but Peter delivered a different kind—a lawyer's well-argued points. He spoke of a campus in the throes of student breakdown, a decline orchestrated by those with the power to do so. This was just the culmination of what had been going on for several years.

As a human rights lawyer, Peter had seen people's rights and living standards deliberately diluted. Governments pumped money into the system, yet the wealthy skimmed most of it. In months, students became victims of this financial squeeze. Many were forced to live in tents as rent and food costs soared, leaving them vulnerable and easier to manipulate.

This wasn't just a local issue; it was a global phenomenon, with no one escaping powerful political games. The bedrock of society was being eroded, making all tremble in its fragility. This widespread vulnerability, exacerbated by the media's constant display of societal breakdown and new laws making protest and criticism of the government illegal, left people in a state of growing panic.

He concluded that this fear, compounded by the frightening celestial eclipse and the Frankensteinian ambition of experimental super-science, created an unbearable pressure. With no other outlet, civil unrest became an inevitability—a default reaction to an existential threat, not a deliberate choice. Michael listened intently, recalculating and recalibrating its meaning through the prism of his own life's understanding.

"The real pandemic," Michael thought with grim certainty, "was a potent cocktail of fear and panic—a corrosive blend of lies, whispers, and policies deliberately designed to harm people, exacerbating hardship at the expense of social stability itself—a calculated plot against the very bedrock of a peaceful society. This had infected everyone through mass psychogenic illness. And the media? Nothing more than convenient megaphones, amplifying the deep-seated machinations of the elite."

Michael listened, his mind absorbing Peter's take on the situation. He agreed with the sentiment but recoiled nervously at the word 'Frankensteinian.' Images of NEMESIS sprang to mind, shocking him back to the purpose of his journey to Harvard. He decided he had to contact his department, hoping all was still good there.

'May I borrow your mobile?' Michael's voice, tight with anxiety, broke the tense silence.

'Sure, Professor,' Peter replied. He briefly gestured towards the cup holder in the centre console. 'It's right there.' Michael seized the device like a praying mantis. It wasn't merely a phone; it was his lifeline. As he began to punch the numbers, his hand trembling from the car's movement and his diminishing anxiety, he hoped the campus's aberrations hadn't struck his department, or worse, Shedland.

Shedland's phone rang and rang. Michael began to fear the worst, his entire journey seeming to hang on that simple ringback tone. Suddenly, a 'Hello' pierced down the line, as if a drawbridge of salvation had been lowered.

Michael kept the call brief, confirming his request had been actioned and that he'd arrive on campus shortly. Within ten minutes, Michael was at Harvard. Stepping from the car, he thanked Peter, deliberately omitting his name lest it summon painful memories. The student simply offered a brief nod of thanks for the company, and Michael closed the door and watched as he drove off into the early summer evening.

He turned to look at his department building, struck by what was new. Peter was right about student hardship; a panoply of colourful, dishevelled tents was everywhere. It seemed the world had changed, its surface now as broken as his own. Unlike theirs, however, his time was brutally short. He didn't have long before the police, the NSA, and perhaps the FBI closed in for his arrest.

58

KYROS Speaks

The animated gestures of two doctoral students cut through the sterile hush of the Harvard corridor, their voices a low, intense murmur. So utterly engrossed in their conversation, they seemed oblivious to the world around them, their minds clearly a world away as they strode purposefully toward the molecular genetics department.

'You've got to see this, you really, really have,' Shedland exclaimed, his voice brimming with enthusiasm, as he spoke to Mary Johnson, a fellow doctoral student in mathematical genetics. Shedland still had a slight limp from his collision with Dr. Adams' desk a few months earlier when he'd rushed to share a startling decoded report.

His hand poised on the lab door, he delivered his preamble: 'Here and now: discard, absorb, accept.'

The intended effect vanished the instant she stepped inside.

'What in God's name, Shedland?!'

Mary's gaze locked onto the eight-foot cube: a fortified tank of thickened polycarbonate, ribbed with bands of strange, dark plastic. It dominated the lab, its presence radiating an almost palpable energy, unlike anything she'd ever encountered.

Mary stared, the edges of her previous impatience dissolving like mist in the face of something truly incomprehensible. A strange, almost magnetic pull, an undeniable sense of the extraordinary, took root within her.

Within the viscous fluid, a vaguely human form drifted, both listless and strangely regal. Its limbs, including a head, two arms, and two legs, were distinct, yet the torso felt disturbingly disproportionate. An intense, unwavering light pulsed from within, rendering the form almost translucent, a spectral silhouette suspended in the gloom.

'That is one spooky thing!' commented Mary. 'It looks so weird; it could be something out of a book I just read, entitled "Paranormally Spooked".'

'Perhaps that's its manifestation,' laughed Shedland.

'Not likely, buddy,' Mary returned acerbically.

'So...where, how, what, why...tell me, evacuate your thoughts!' she demanded, as if he could reel off answer after answer without a momentary lapse.

'Well...the boss sent it over on email some time back,' answered Shedland, thinking through the chronology of where it started.

'What, that!?' Mary exclaimed, pointing to a piece of paper on a bookcase nearby.

'Of course not, smartarse!'

'The boss's email detailed a genetic manipulation unlike any other, using a completely new intermediate part: pure light patterns interacting with the DNA,' Shedland explained, his gaze fixed on the entity. Mary's eyes widened. 'Light patterns? That's... years ahead of current theory! The maths barely exists!'

'I know, I know,' said Shedland, barely containing his enthusiasm, his eyes seeming to burn with the sheer volume of knowledge trying to escape.

'This is so cutting-edge, I couldn't believe it when I first read it. But let me try to summarise.' Shedland laughed, a nervous energy thrumming beneath his skin. He knew his attempt in words would be a poor relation to what Michael had sent him.

He continued, 'The light patterns are directed at specific nanomaterials or nanoparticles that are designed to interact with DNA. These nanoparticles could be engineered to direct photochemical interactions with the chemical bonds within the DNA molecule itself, causing bond breaking or formation and photoisomerisation.

'Moreover, the "light patterns" are encoded with quantum information that is entangled with the quantum state of specific DNA molecules or atoms within them.'

'Oh, is that all!' joked Mary. 'Sort of thing you find on the back of a breakfast cereal packet then.'

Shedland smiled at her levity.

'Anyway, it's using quantum computing to analyse the entirety of the genetic data in real-time, processing probabilities we can't even fathom, to re-assemble our DNA... into that.' He nodded towards the entity, its outline subtly shifting as if viewed through distorted glass.

'Hang on, our department doesn't have a quantum computer,' Mary puzzled.

'We do now,' Shedland said, pointing again, but this time at a strange-looking small cube next to the entity. It was very similar to the one Denton showed Peter and Michael when they first met in his office.

'Shedland, my mind is freaking out. Tell me you didn't create that too with instructions from Michael?' Mary asked, overwhelmed by the weight of the knowledge.

A flicker of unsettling conviction crossed Shedland's face. 'That created it, through reassembly as mentioned. All matter is vibrational; it can be created, morphed, and destroyed. It's just a circular process, just like life: birth, grow, wither, and die.'

'I am lost for words,' said Mary, unable to really take in all the new science presented. It was as if she had been thrust forwards by twenty or thirty years.

'I had to take over the entire department to carry out his instructions for code reassembly. A manual operation would have taken years, but our computers' automated surgical reassembly took just a few weeks—as the boss predicted. The final result was a perfect biogenic construct. All is well! Then I simply placed it in this embryonic chemical soup, and it began differentiating almost immediately, proving itself to be a true autogenic organism. A synthetic exomorph if you like.'

'What's in that soup?' Mary asked quizzically.

Shedland grinned. 'Tomato, creamy and lemon chicken, clam chowder and potato, you know, the usual ingredients.'

'You're such an ass!'

'It's a primordial soup of chemicals, nutrients, amino acids, and proteins—a real cornucopia of ingredients, some of which are manufactured.'

'Cornucopia! Wow, who's the wordsmith now? I am impressed! Has it developed?'

'Yes, and I think it's in stasis now.'

'Your uncertainty frightens me, Shedland!' said a hesitant Mary. 'It should,' she continued, her voice dropping to a whisper. 'The professor has been away for a few months. We don't know where he is. You get this email from God knows where. Do you even know where it was from, by the way?'

'No, the email source was super encrypted, unlike any before, according to one of the cryptoanalysts I spoke to,' Shedland said.

'So…you don't know where it came from. You've rearranged our evolutionary DNA to such a degree it resembles nothing like ours, and you've even produced its phenotype. This thing may be the devil incarnate, who knows?' Mary worried, her eyes wide.

'A bit OTT, Mary!' A sliver of doubt, however, cold and unwelcome, did prickle at the back of his mind. 'Look, we can pull the plug if necessary, but who knows, the boss may be here any time soon, and he knows best. Don't you agree?'

'Of course, but watch this thing like a hawk. Any problems and pull the plug, okay?' Mary asked.

'That's all right with me... boss,' said Shedland as he parodied Mary for her sudden adoption of authority over its existence and demise.

'Does it have a name? The professor is always naming things; he makes them more personal and a homely kind of thing,' Mary questioned.

'Yes, I think he did. Hold on, let me check the e-mail the boss sent me. I am sure it began with a K.'

'Kylie, kinky, karma, kangaroo...well?' Mary humoured.

'Yeah, here it is. KYROS,' Shedland infused.

'KYROS! That's Greek for sure. I think it means Lord or master, maybe far-sighted,' she added.

The atmosphere suddenly turned tense.

'What the hell!' shouted Mary, stumbling away from KYROS. 'It moved, it moved, the arms, they moved!' a strangled cry escaping her lips.

Within the viscous fluid, a pale, disproportionate arm moved with slow, deliberate flexing. Then the other followed. Mary stumbled further, her terrified scream lost in the air.

'I didn't see anything,' Shedland replied, dismissing her statement.

512

The burgeoning interaction of intrigue and discovery between the two students suddenly faltered as the laboratory doors creaked open, producing an unnerving noise that echoed around the room. Tentative footsteps preceded the unknown figures who entered.

'Oh God, who's that?' Shedland demanded.

Through the laboratory door walked two fellow doctoral scientists, Myra and Ananya. Their usual academic air was replaced by a shared bewilderment as their gazes locked onto the pulsating form within the tank.

'Sorry!' said Ananya, her apology for the interruption almost an afterthought as she stared, captivated, at KYROS.

Myra, equally transfixed, could only manage, 'That's a cool... glowing thing you've got there. Is it some kind of special effect for a movie or something?' Mary's frustration with the interruption was now overshadowed by the unsettling thought that two more people had seen it.

'So, what is it?' Myra asked, her curiosity battling a dawning sense of the bizarre.

'Honestly? I do not know!' spoke a befuddled Mary.

'You mean it's really real, like alive!' interjected Ananya.

'Kind of... it's in stasis.'

'Stasis? Why is it talking to me then?' Ananya questioned.

'It's not, so stop your pretending!' said Shedland with a raised voice. Ananya was not pretending; indeed, she wasn't in a state to be. Entrapped by a trance-like state, KYROS had linked telepathically to speak through her.

KYROS spoke, '*I need to talk to Michael soon. He starts as two but ends as one. NEMESIS lies. Opposites attract from end to start. Great loss of stealth wealth. Must kill NEMESIS. Chariots of anger enter soon. Your repeating patterns of existence must change. Harmony of conscience will be yours. NEMESIS must die.'*

Ananya shrieked with fright. Words escaped from her mouth without conscious thought. She was unnerved and not a little concerned. Myra rushed forward.

'Tell me what's going on,' Ananya said with trepidation to Myra. 'I was in a trance.'

'Whatever it was, you're with me, with us, so don't worry,' said her friend Myra, as she wrapped her arms around her.

'OK, smartarse, what are you going to do now?' Mary asked as she fixed her worried gaze onto Shedland.

'Pull the plug?' Myra repeated the suggestion, a tremor in her voice.

'No. We can't do that. We must all take responsibility for what just happened,' Shedland insisted.

'Yes, pull the plug,' encouraged Mary.

'What is it with this "pull the plug" thing? There is no plug to pull. It works off free energy, as Michael said in his secure message,' Shedland stated, his voice raw with mounting anxiety over how to resolve a situation for which he had absolutely no historical precedent or understanding.

'Throw it out the window then. Break it with an axe. I don't know, do something!' pleaded Myra.

'Shedland took responsibility and decided to smash the small quantum computer box that seemed to give KYROS energy and thought. He walked nervously to the main source of power lying to the right of KYROS. He had never been this close before. As he approached, he felt its eyes on him, studying his movement, reading his thoughts as a scientist studying microbes under a microscope would.'

'I wouldn't do that just yet,' Shedland heard in his head. He jumped with fright and took two steps back in apology, thinking it was KYROS. 'I'm sorry. Your voice sounds familiar,' Shedland said to KYROS.

'It should be, I'm your professor, Shedland. Bumped into any more desks?' Michael sarcastically asked. The students were so focused on KYROS that none of them had heard the door creak open as Michael entered. Shedland looked around, a warming surprise spreading across his face. There before them stood Michael, bedraggled and tired from his murderous journey. He knew he didn't have long before the authorities would have him in custody.

'Where's Peter?' Shedland demanded. 'Not now, Shedland,' Michael replied. Transfixed by the vision of KYROS, he found words hard to find.

'It worked, it really worked,' Michael said admiringly. He restrained himself from saying it looked different to NEMESIS, as this would have opened up more questions than his remaining time or further student curiosity would allow.

'You've done well, Dr. Shedland,' uttered Michael.

All three female students cheered and whooped, punching the air, before starting to chant, 'Shedland, Shedland!'

'Enough ladies!' requested Michael as he raised his voice. His attention now turned back to KYROS.

'Have you done as asked, Shedland?' Michael asked.

'To the letter, boss!' he replied, beaming with pride at his newly recognised title of 'Doctor'.

'God, it's beautiful!' opined Michael, as he walked forward to admire the outward manifestation of all the work completed back at the super-secret facility. He looked with awe as he watched what appeared to be a humanoid shape floating freely inside Shedland's purpose-built, rectangular container.

It was obfuscated as much by the semi-darkened plastic as by the dense, viscous goo that filled the container and seemed to be nourishing and protecting it. The body floated serenely, softly, unaware of its curious audience. Michael then said what he hadn't intended to.

'It's different to NEMESIS. Now this is a synthetic exomorph,' said Michael, as he studied every part of the body with a razor-like visual acuity.

'Who or what is NEMESIS?' Mary asked quizzically.

'It's the other half, if you like,' replied Michael.

'The other half must be deficient if he wants to kill it!' intervened Ananya with clinical deduction.

'What? It spoke to you?' Michael hastily asked.

'Just before you arrived. Very cryptic. It made us all feel our futures were at stake, though I'm not sure why I say that.'

'No professor, it spoke to me telepathically; the words just came out,' detailed Ananya. Michael had a flashback to when he did the same to Peter.

At Michael's request, Ananya tried to recall but drew a blank, her mind as empty as the laboratory walls. Seeing her struggle, her student colleagues leaned in, piecing together the sequence she couldn't grasp. They repeated the message perfectly and in order. Though most of it made no sense to them without Michael's knowledge, he, as before, refused to go into detail.

Michael faced the four assembled researchers, but before issuing any demands, he knew what he needed: a drink. His first thought was a small glass of Old Fitzgerald bourbon from his office, but he settled for a simpler option.

'Mary, get me a coffee, please?'

'Shedland, print me a full copy of that email I sent you.'

'Ananya, also get me a coffee, please, and then arrange six seats in a semi-circle so we all face towards KYROS.

'Myra, go get Professor Ablah. You know where she's based?'

'Yes, the crypto-geneticist's section.'

'Great, be quick,' encouraged Michael.

Michael knew there was not much time before the NSA would track him down, either due to the so-called bus bomb blast or Peter's murder. By now, Peter's murder would paint a bloodied trail to his door, ensuring his certain death if he didn't get questions answered with witnesses in tow.

Adding academic colleagues to his hastily arranged team would buy him some time and provide a different perspective. There was no time to freshen up, nor to look the part of the professor he saw himself as. No time to set up machinery to record what was about to happen. His focus was entirely on the present.

Ten precious, irretrievable minutes vanished. Only then did the team of six finally gather, ready to initiate Michael's critical interrogation of KYROS. His cup of coffee from Mary remained untouched in his hand, a small, forgotten detail in the looming crisis.

'Hello KYROS!' spoke Michael in his head.

'Professor, look at Ananya,' said her friend Myra.

Ananya appeared to be engaged with a fixed, almost worrying gaze at KYROS.

KYROS, once again spoke through Ananya.

'I respect this female's aura; it is most receptive, with spirit and dignity. She has no equivalent here; she is unique.'

'Why not telepathy for us all?' Michael asked.

'You have mind discomfort, Michael, and the chariots of anger will soon be here for you. Telepathically interfacing

with you at a quantum level means I will feel your hurt. Please ask me your questions. Be short, time is not yours.'

'Is NEMESIS lying?'

'Yes and no.'

'What do the "yes" and "no" answers mean?'

'Yes, it misdirects about pill purpose and numbers to save. Locations are correct.'

'Five hundred million is wrong?'

'Yes, the figure is incorrect. NEMESIS never stated a figure. Your calculation was specious, albeit inventive.'

'What is the figure, all things considered?'

'None.'

'I don't understand what you mean by none. NEMESIS said all that were in the stadiums would be transformed at the very least and some outside. Yes?'

'No. Not one. NEMESIS lied. The pill wasn't designed to elevate anyone; it was designed to annihilate them. It changes their inner vibration from good to bad, and they will radiate a negative force that will tear them and all of you apart from the inside out. All will suffer. Very few will survive.'

'How can we stop it? The pill?'

'Correct.'

'More will be saved if the pill is changed?'

'Yes!'

'Why must you kill NEMESIS?'

'Not to kill, but to absorb. Although it lied, it was innocent of knowing. This aberration—a human error in translating the code—was born of the elite's rapacious hunger to possess everything for the few at the expense of the many.'

'Innocent of knowing, you say? It's a convenient form of innocence. The lie may not have known its purpose, but the elite certainly did. So, what you're saying is that a rapacious hunger for power is what created a sentient being with a broken purpose? That's not an aberration; that's an inevitability. It's what greed always births.'

'For your species a poverty of understanding is no substitute for feeling correct.'

'Why does NEMESIS have to die? I don't understand. I thought you had a peaceful desire to help us. Why kill?'

The word "kill" is incorrect, but is the one you understand best. We are twins by design. Two of one. A scientist's error, born of greed, flawed the initial coding of NEMESIS. I am its twin through your recoded making, Michael. NEMESIS has powers you cannot imagine, as it cannot imagine the harm it's about to do. A force of good is now a force for bad.'

'Are you saying NEMESIS wants to inadvertently destroy us, not help us?'

'Yes!'

'I am split between two outcomes. Is the purpose of your code to bring a higher-level conscience to us... or just kill us all?'

'The latter you can do quite easily on your own, so it's the former.'

'So, if NEMESIS is faulty, the pill is too?'

'Correct, it's toxic and will kill everyone in the stadiums and very likely most beyond too.'

'My God, most everyone will die! But why? I... thought this whole project was for good, I really did.'

'It was, Michael. But the hand of greed from Denton to the elites wanted it more. Greed consumes all, leaving only a wealthy emptiness where iniquitous inequality persists; true victory lies not in hoarding, but in the shared abundance that enriches you all.'

'Can this extinction level event be stopped?'

'Of course. Your hand in creating me was not for greed but for humanity.'

'I know time is short. I must ask. Who or what are you?'

'A reflection of my creator.'

'Are you alien?'

'Alien is a misnomer. Peter says you shouldn't guess! Every single organic being in the universe is a child of the cosmic dust, in effect, a star child and therefore alien for want of a better word.'

'Is your name for a reason?'

'Yes. As is the name NEMESIS. My name has two meanings for you. First, I am of your Sun, the giver, perpetuator, and terminator of life. Second, I am of the moment, the opportune one, who gives you the light of transformation. That is why you must get me to NEMESIS, before "Day of Quanta" or "Q-Day".'

Michael was struggling for questions; his mind just couldn't put his thoughts into words. Every time he asked a question, he felt a better one had been pushed aside. He was aware of the mental exhaustion it placed on Ananya. KYROS then continued.

'Michael, your chariots of anger have arrived.'

Distant whirring helicopters and police sirens were heard by the assembled six. They immediately thought it was more to do with NEMESIS than with the professor of murder who sat close by.

Several small laser dots, emanating from laser-guided rifles located adjacent to their building, focused on KYROS's organic container. In fact, the special plexiglass was almost impenetrable to bullets, but the sharpshooters had yet to learn this. Michael could hear, see, and strangely experienced a heightened sense of impending danger.

'So, we are to you, what you are to us?'

'Yes! A consciousness of lesser order is defined by the existence of a greater one.' The answer was profound as it was axiomatic.

'Are we immortal, like Gods?'

'Immortal, yes, like a God, in some ways – enduring, beyond the frailties of flesh – but in many, many other ways, no! God transcends the boundaries of what you define as immortal: all metrics, known and unknown. God transcends location, time, and distance; it is the alpha and the omega. It is omnipotent, omnipresent, omniscient, and omnitemporal. Indefinable, unquantifiable, and infinite. The ineffable nature of the divine, a paradox within a paradox.'

The weight of the words settled in Michael's mind. His scientific training, a lifetime built on linear logic, had no framework for this. He was standing at the edge of his own limited reality, staring into a truth that didn't just transcend logic, but used its very failure as a tool.

'A paradox to define a paradox to define a paradox because the impossible truth is the only language a greater truth can speak,' Michael concluded.

'I must ask you. Is there a God?'

'I have just answered that.'

'How will you kill... sorry, absorb NEMESIS?'

'Through love. No more for the moment, Professor. The nemesis chariots are here.'

59

Confrontation

Just as Ananya uttered the last word of KYROS, the laboratory door boomed inward. The sound echoed with a force that dwarfed Shedland's clumsy attempt months ago.

The air, thick with the metallic tang of chemicals, was suddenly disrupted as nine FBI agents swarmed in. Their movements were sharp and synchronised as they fanned out across the entrance in a staggered formation. The hollow thud of their heavy boots echoed on the cold linoleum.

Their tactical vests, emblazoned with bold FBI letters, made their identity clear. In the doorway behind them stood three NSA agents in black, their eyes flickering wildly in astonishment at the central tank. Their faces were tight with apprehension, a muscle twitching in the jaw of the nearest one as hands hovered near concealed weapons.

The lead FBI agent barked a curt 'clear', and the three NSA agents entered hesitantly, their collective gaze drawn immediately to the towering cylindrical tank dominating the centre of the room.

Within its luminous depths, suspended in a thick, yellowish fluid that pulsed faintly, floated a form unlike anything they had ever witnessed. Tendrils of an unknown substance drifted around a vaguely humanoid shape; its stillness was more unsettling than any frantic movement.

For Michael, the end of his research journey was near. Boxed in, guilt dripping from his every pore, he wondered what fate could possibly await him next.

Initial cries of shock and concern from Michael's team quickly subsided into a tense calm as the agents surveyed the room for potential danger. Years of training took over in an instant, honed sharper than any blade. Ignoring the simmering agitation of the FBI agents, the NSA team moved with purpose between them to approach Michael.

'Professor Michael Adams?'

'One and the same,' he answered, his gaze unwavering from the agent, the tank a silent presence at his back.

'My name is Special Agent Mutlan. I am with the NSA.' He flashed his badge of authority at Michael, but it was a fleeting blur. Michael's attention was consumed by KYROS, the entity floating in a viscous, nutrient-rich fluid just behind him. There were bigger things on his mind.

'These two agents are with me; the rest are FBI. I am here to arrest you for the murder of Professor Peter Magma at the Willow Creek Diner in Mayley, a town just north of Cambridge, earlier this afternoon at or about 15:50 hours.'

A wave of murmurs rippled through the university team. Their eyes flickered between Michael and the tank, a mixture of shock and dawning horror replacing their initial concern. Was it the revelation that their esteemed, Nobel Prize-winning colleague was accused of murder? Or the unsettling realisation that they had spent the last twenty minutes in a room with him? Either way, their disbelief quickly morphed into wary glances and a fearful acceptance of his alleged act.

As Banforth moved forward to read Michael his rights, FBI agents took the team away for questioning in several rooms upstairs. This left the three NSA agents to deal with Michael.

As if on cue, just after Banforth finished reading Michael his rights and handed him back to Team Leader Mutlan,

Denton walked in. The agents' recognition of Denton was immediate. They shifted almost imperceptibly, a subtle acknowledgement of his seniority. As if royalty had entered the room, they offered an almost involuntary bow, a testament to his rank and power. Michael's arrest was halted temporarily.

'Afternoon, sir,' was the welcoming greeting from Mutlan, closely followed by his team. Denton didn't acknowledge them verbally, simply nodding, his eyes already fixed on the shimmering outline of the tank. He was more interested in Michael and his existential, unauthorised work, which radiantly pulsed behind him in all its alien manifestation.

'My, my, Michael,' Denton's lips stretched into a predatory smile, 'haven't you been a busy boy.'

'Maybe, but I know what you're up to, if that matters now.'

'Everything, anything, and nothing matters to me. It's the nature of the beast in this doomsday game.'

'An endgame of all endgames, huh?' Michael's voice held a thread of weary resignation.

'Oh please, stop the platitudes, Michael. It's boring, and you know how I feel about things that have passed their prime.'

As Denton's gaze returned to the life form, he found himself musing again how similar it was to NEMESIS back at the facility, a thought that had nagged at him since entering.

'So, what do we truly uncover here?' Denton demanded, striding past Michael to inspect his creation, so to speak. 'Don't tell me, "NEMESIS 2: The Return",' Denton pressed, a sardonic glint in his eye.

'If you like; nomenclature is irrelevant to the message. And that proclaims you're an arsehole, both here right now and for what you're about to unleash worldwide,' Michael lacerated Denton.

'Such academic arrogance! You grasp the cost of knowledge, yet remain blind to its true worth. Academics! You fixate on the price of knowledge, but miss its true value,' Denton pontificated.

'Mirror check, Denton? You're reflecting your own thoughts again,' Michael's bitterness sliced through the air. Denton's smirk broadened.

'My value proves itself, wouldn't you say, gentlemen?'

'Sir!' the agents barked.

'Now Michael, sit down and tell me what this thing is doing here, and what it told you. I presume it said something, otherwise I've walked in at just the right time, haven't I?' Denton stated arrogantly.

Now seated, Michael felt utterly immobile, as if the chair had fused to him. A cold dread coiled in his gut, a primal fear beyond the accusation. This isn't just about Magma. This is about... KYROS. His muscles were locked tight, his knuckles white against the chair's armrests. Denton watched in silence, his questions queuing orderly in his mind before release.

The agents flanking Denton were coiled springs, their eyes gleaming with anticipation—eager executioners. They wouldn't hesitate. Denton's word was law. A wave of despair washed over Michael. He hadn't even had a chance to understand. The silence of the interrogation was a weapon in itself, crushing his will.

'Well, Michael, I'm waiting,' said Denton, as he sat down three feet from Michael in a standard interrogative seating plan.

'It's all a bloody hoax, mate,' shouted Michael, as if suggesting he was condemned to die soon, and irritating Denton was therefore mandatory.

'A hoax, how so?' replied a perplexed Denton.

'You lot aren't going to get your way. More—many more will survive.'

'Us lot? Who's "us lot"?' Denton hissed. The thought of his grand persona being compartmentalised felt simplistic.

'You're very well connected, Denton. I know that, everyone knows that. You belong to all sorts of powerful organisations, and you're just going to save your own skin, exactly as you planned. Need I say any more than "Georgia Guidestones"?' Michael's voice was tight with accusation.

Denton scoffed, a brittle sound. 'Georgia Guidestones! What a bizarre leap of logic, Adams. You honestly think I'm part of some New World Order cabal because of my position and my commitment to the project mission?'

'Aren't you?' Michael shot back, his eyes narrowed. 'And notice, Denton, you brought up the New World Order, not me.'

Denton's smile thinned. 'Sharp when caged, Michael. As you say, horses for courses. I chose the right horse for the right course.'

'Cut the crap, Denton,' Michael spat, his disgust palpable. 'It sickens me! It's a hoax. Peter knew it. I know it. You know it!'

'This hoax shit you keep bleating about?' Denton's tone shifted, a flicker of something unsettling beneath the dismissiveness. 'Perhaps you've sampled some of that funny business yourself. That student who gave you a lift back here... I wouldn't be surprised if the air in the car, or even his car's exhaust fumes, were hallucinogenic.'

526

Michael watched them, Denton's facile attempts at deflection washing over him. His own thoughts felt sluggish, compartmentalised by the psychological pressure he was under. He waited, a detached observer, for Denton's predictable interrogation to stumble into something genuinely insightful, something that might reignite the complex machinery of his mind.

'Hoax?' Denton repeated, a genuine note of curiosity now lacing his voice, perhaps sensing Michael's conviction.

'Is that the best you've got? I have the final say here, Michael. My meticulous surveillance of the project leaves absolutely no doubt — it's no hoax. It's a quantum leap for us.'

'There you go,' Michael interjected, his voice sharper than it had been, a flicker of his old self. 'The "us" again, Denton.'

Denton waved a dismissive hand. 'Oh hell, what does it matter now? We're beyond empty words, baseless accusations, arguments detached from reality. Our decodes are solid, the chemical formulas have been rigorously analysed. Manufacture and consumption of the pills are well underway.' A disturbing certainty settled in his tone.

'Denton,' Michael said, his voice regaining some of its former authority, a subtle shift in his posture mirroring the returning clarity of his thoughts. 'Your self-importance is only eclipsed by the towering edifice of your self-deception.'

Michael's views were tersely dismissed as a mere inconvenience to Denton's day. Denton looked on, his gaze unfocused and distant, secure behind the invisible yet palpable wall of his illusions. External reality was a muffled murmur against the deafening roar of his mental disconnect. The sheer force of his false convictions stood before him, a proud and fractured monument.

Something else was about to shatter, far more than Denton's fragile reality: the cube. Their eyes, until then captivated by its gentle, shifting hues, were violently snatched by a single, crimson spark – a malignant red dot seared onto its surface, utterly alien to the tranquil kaleidoscope within.

'Now!' Denton shouted into his radio. His voice ripped through the air like a gunshot, but it was nothing compared to the actual shot that followed. A bullet shrieked, tearing into the cube, yet KYROS, the true target, remained untouched. The sound that erupted then wasn't merely loud; it was a cataclysmic roar that tore through their very bones, deafening, pulverising, as though a bomb had detonated in their skulls.

An impossible light, searing through the plexiglass and their very beings, slammed their eyelids shut. Before their bedazzled vision could refocus, the cube ruptured, unleashing a viscous torrent that hammered them back several yards — unwilling surfers on an entity-warping tsunami.

The ensuing silence hung heavy, broken only by their ragged breaths. Michael, Denton, and the three NSA agents stared, transfixed, their faces masks of utter, dumbfounded awe. An impossible tableau was now unfolding.

Beneath the viscous veneer of the entity's lifeblood, a fire of thought swept through their collective minds, a wave of impending terror, leaving them to wonder what it would do next.

Surrounded by a pool of cosmic nutrients, they squinted their bedazzled eyes in the direction of the shattered cube. They were awestruck as they caught sight of KYROS negotiating its first hesitant steps onto terra firma and advancing on them.

They were, in effect, literally glued to the spot. Their muscles tightened and stretched without result, imprisoning their anxious bodies under KYROS's control. Its intensity still pulsed through their being.

It moved with a fluid grace that defied its seemingly fragile frame, each step a silent glide across the linoleum. Its skin, stretched taut over what appeared to be an endoskeleton, shimmered with an internal iridescence.

The alien biology operated on principles unseen and beyond human comprehension. There was no warmth in its depths, only a profound, analytical stillness that made the assembled humans feel like specimens under a cosmic lens.

Now outside its hermetically sealed cube environment, its aesthetic beauty was easier to see – a subtle undertone that resonated deep within their consciousness, making them feel as if they were floating. Meanwhile, a small laser glinted from the sniper's gun, located on the building's next-door balcony, following KYROS's every distinct, unsteady movement.

Although it initially adopted a stillness that suggested humble thanks, a discernible form, unlike anything they'd seen, was evident. Like a baby transitioning from crawling to standing, KYROS began to outstretch its arms. The sniper panicked, a cold spike of fear jolting through him, and fired two shots into KYROS's head. Two bullets of pinpoint intensity struck its head. Was it going to fall over and slump to the floor? On the contrary, with a slow, deliberate motion, it corrected its posture back to a staunch verticality, and then looked directly at Denton.

As it did, a scream of unimaginable depth and horror physically assaulted their ears, tearing unmercifully through the air from the nearby balcony and into the ears of the laboratory incumbents.

Further screams joined the cacophony as the jarring sounds of boots, shoes, and scraping equipment erupted from the floor above and the nearby balcony, piercing their ears with the same grating intensity as fingernails dragged down a classroom blackboard.

Denton's symmetric encryption radio and agents' devices blared to life. Amidst the garbled reports, he grabbed his radio, asking for an update. The stark reply: the sharpshooter had spontaneously combusted, just ash on the roof, no burns. Cremated on the spot, his ashes already scattering on the university wind. Denton knew, without asking, the entity was the cause.

Their initial awe had curdled into a cold curiosity; they looked at KYROS. Their gazes, now stripped of emotion, dissecting it with the detached precision of scientists studying a newly discovered specimen.

It had eyes and facial features but was devoid of any humanlike hair or external ears, its features smooth and alien. Its head was larger than a human's, while its body was conversely smaller. It was naked, if that's what naked is. A faint, almost iridescent sheen coated its skin, giving it a slick, viscous look that made their stomachs subtly churn.

It stood six feet tall, its thin arms and legs seemingly fragile, yet there was an unsettling stillness about them, a coiled potential that belied their apparent frailty. Despite its thin legs, it possessed locomotion, suggesting its arms might function similarly to human limbs.

An infinite humbleness grew across its small audience, and then KYROS spoke. A voice that had no origin yet enveloped them like a warm blanket on a very cold day.

'*Tell your agents to go outside; this is for Denton and Michael's ears only.*' Denton waved his hand, and they dutifully obliged, their subservience to the man absolute. They moved with brisk efficiency to open the door, its groan swallowed by their haste as they exited to wait outside.

Back inside, Denton and Michael looked on at KYROS, their hands trembling at what may occur, their eyes wide open to absorb and remember what would happen next. Just then, a cold draft blew on the backs of their necks, and their hairs stood up to protect them, as if touched by a ghost.

The air froze with mystery; time seemed to have no place there. A unity of being struck them, a collective conscience manufactured in a dimension not known.

KYROS spoke again.

'*I will speak telepathically with Michael first; it is his privilege as my creator. Then, I will address you both through your ears.*'

A potent blend of eagerness and apprehension rippled through them both. For a few moments, they experienced nothingness in time—a silence so heavy it crushed every thought. There was no escape from the gravitas emanating from KYROS; only sight seemed welcome. Words failed to capture what their eyes absorbed. Then, Michael's moment arrived as he heard KYROS in his head.

'Michael, I acknowledge your role in my creation. The faulty decodes, identified as NEMESIS, have led him to misinterpret these unfolding events and present them as truth to Denton. Many will perish if this error persists. Some underground will survive. Yet, I am compelled to maintain the narrative he understands; otherwise, he will suspect.'

Michael telepathically said he and Peter had checked and double-checked the codes. Every simulation they ran was good, always good.

KYROS didn't answer this, as the past could not be altered through pleading expertise.

'Within NEMESIS, a battle rages with the female entity, Ann. Her spirit relentlessly challenges his erroneous thinking, not with the aim of changing it, as it's too late for that. Instead, she seeks to deplete his quantum-sourced energy renewal. Despite their distinct approaches to conflict, their combined impact is singular: the slow demise of NEMESIS.'

'Are you saying Ann is alive?' Michael pondered, desperately wanting to hear a yes.

'No, she is not. Ann lives as a spirit, an energy bridging two dimensions—a third, crucial reason for NEMESIS's demise. While we exist across many dimensions, NEMESIS finds himself unable to traverse them, blocked by Ann. He needs absolute control for such passage, and that he does not possess. This ultimately leads to DNA vibrational disharmony and compounds the disruption of his renewal.'

'She was, I mean is, a feisty spirit—small in stature, but vast in drive,' Michael gushed, his profound affection for her rooted in their formative Oxford years and blossoming ever after.

532

KYROS continued, *'Your knowledge of mind, your fortitude, and your perseverance are exemplary. You and Peter were of one mind, but not of fidelity. I cannot reveal everything now; some truths must naturally unfold. Be assured, however, that at the very end of this long research journey, you will truly be in awe of what you finally achieve.*

Michael interjected in thought once more: 'Are you saying I'm to do something?'

'Yes,' KYROS replied, its voice imbued with profound longing. *'It will be so beautiful. I wish I could tell you now, Michael.'*

Michael pressed for details.

'It will concern the love of another...but no more.' KYROS offered nothing further on this, but continued, *'Your species progresses through both individual and collective evolution, a journey permeated by the battle between good and bad. This is what I now address. I will mostly tell you what's to happen; Denton will continue to be fed the NEMESIS lie.'*

Michael's thoughts interjected once more: 'He's betrayed us for money, I know it. A man utterly without principles, a turncoat, a traitor.'

'For too long, most of you have lived subordinate lives under the rich and powerful—a historical constant. Industrialisation has only amplified and entrenched the dominant values of a wealthy elite. This has continually hindered the majority's democratic rights to an equitable share of power and wealth, to better lives, freedom, and enjoyment. In effect, the elite few have utterly subjugated the majority.'

Michael almost let his thoughts burst forth at this point, eager to confirm his keen awareness. Though relatively well-off with his mansion, position, and wealth, he recognised the plight of those who went without—a stark reality he often yearned to rectify.

'*Power and wealth redistribution is key to redressing this imbalance. A rapid evolution towards greater peace, harmony, and spirituality will then follow. The decoded quantum pill is vital, but not in its current form—a toxic product of Nathan's deliberate faulty codes and sabotage, Michael.*'

'All our work utterly sabotaged, just like that!' Michael's voice was etched with despair. 'It's a complete inversion of everything Peter and I thought we were achieving. Are you telling me I must change this faulty code?' Michael's voice was tight with disbelief. 'It'll take weeks, even with our fastest computers. And how on earth do I get this past Nathan? He's the specialist here, after all. I strongly suspect he's working for Denton; he'll spot this change instantly by the altered dates and simply undo it.' Beads of sweat began to form on his brow.

'*I absolutely recognise your sterling efforts, Michael. Yes, you must alter the pill ingredients. I've already uploaded the precise, formulaic codes that determine the pill ingredients directly into your secure computer folder. Roger will do this for you.*

'*As for Nathan, I'll link directly with your secure computer via quantum entanglement. This will ensure no data changes are even registered by him,*' KYROS stated, his eyes fixed on Michael.

They gleamed intensely in the brightly lit Harvard laboratory. A subtle, almost imperceptible nod from the entity conveyed a profound trust. Michael then felt an instantaneous, cold jolt of data pass through him as

KYROS's words completed their work, confirming the remote quantum transfer to his secure computers back at the facility.

Beyond Michael's jolt, the air in the pristine laboratory resonated with a barely perceptible vibration—a vibrant testament not just to KYROS's advanced capabilities, but to the unwavering dedication he clearly saw in Michael and most of his team. The impossible had just become a quantum done deal.

KYROS continued: 'This tiny pill, with its unique quantum compound, targets atomic forces within human DNA. Its disruption releases immense energy, recalibrating aberrant DNA to subdue power, war, and money-driven thoughts. This will increase philanthropy from the elite few, allowing the redistribution of power and wealth to the majority.'

Michael still felt disquiet hearing that Peter and he had initially given the green light to faulty codes when so much good should have come from them. NEMESIS's existence was evidence of their error, even if it was an error of trust in certain others.

But with a correct pill, he thought, this was once again a noble cause. It was one that made sense; such greed and power were a relic of the past. Society had moved on, and aspirations had changed. Everyone had to feel important, not just in words but in action too. Michael's thought was broken as KYROS added more information.

'Your current path leads, at best, to famine and war. To begin your celestially-inspired evolution towards higher realms of spiritual understanding, DNA aberrations must cease. Denton's shadow forces will be deceptively told the pill amplifies their self-aggrandisement and wealth. Meanwhile, the 420 million or so who remain will endure

increased mental imprisonment; a dystopian vision that aligns perfectly with their designs.'

Michael was distraught at such a thought. But then came the repeated kicker from earlier. Maybe it was in different words, but it sent Michael into a cognitive spin that wouldn't be fully understood until the very end of the research journey.

'You will be the saviour of all; as NEMESIS was at your hand, so his death will be too.'

Michael drew a slow, deliberate breath, the echoes of the monumental statement of intent settling within him like a newfound weight. The fragmented months of research—the painstaking decodes, the tense conversations with Denton, the cautious exchanges with Peter and Ann—snapped into a sudden, crystalline clarity.

The persistent hum of tension, a long-unwanted guest, finally receded, leaving a quiet emptiness in its wake. A nascent sense of purpose bloomed within him once more, a quiet fire igniting his resolve to see this through.

'This is the reason, but what is the how?' Michael asked in his head. KYROS then continued.

'Denton will hear the "how", and so will you. He will envision his group ascending to an unprecedented, all-powerful elite, their influence absolute. Understand this, Michael: the truth of what unfolds will be the very antithesis of his ambition.

'Their ingrained greed will not be amplified, but extinguished. The shadow group's vast tentacles of power and wealth, amassed through the very mechanisms that perpetuate socioeconomic disparity and relative poverty, will be compelled to flow outward—a voluntary tide to offset the suffering the majority who have endured with tremendous resolve for far too long.

536

'The positive outcome he anticipates for his group is a cruel mirage; the reality is a forced reckoning with the consequences of their malignant avarice.'

Michael couldn't help but enjoy a well-earned, humorous yet mischievous grin at Denton. He was leading his paymasters into a quantum day of monetary reckoning, a pied piper of sabotage most foul...and none would see it, as they would be blinded by their power and avarice.

'Get on with it!' Denton demanded.

'With what?' Michael questioned, uneasy about exactly what he was alluding to.

'That thing it's going to talk to you about, yes?' emphasised a questioning Denton. What they hadn't known was that during the monologue, KYROS had stopped time itself. To Michael, minutes had passed; to Denton, none. Such power was clearly not to be trifled with. KYROS now turned his attention to Denton and the misdirection he had deserved.

'Don't look so eager, Michael; this isn't for you. After this, you'll be on a one-way ticket to LWPP—Life without Possibility of Parole.' Denton's laugh was a sharp, almost brittle sound, bordering on manic glee.

He envisioned Michael languishing in a lightless, fetid prison cell, a place sunlight had never dared to touch. This thought made the intoxicating weight of his own impending wealth even more exquisitely sensual. He imagined basking on a glorious, sun-drenched beach.

'Are you ready, Denton?' KYROS asked, the stillness in the air intensifying around them.

'Yes, fire away!' Denton practically vibrated with anticipation, performing several jerky, almost involuntary micro-jumps of joy; so desperate was his ego to luxuriate in its imagined future glory and boundless wealth. Michael watched him, the pathetic adult display reminding him of a child in ill-fitting trousers, bouncing with delight over a present too long without receival.

As before, the air thickened, an oppressive stillness descending—the kind that precedes an unknown, significant event; a pregnant pause before the unspoken. Then, KYROS spoke, his voice resonating with an otherworldly authority.

'As midnight strikes on New Year's Day (EST), a silent global wave will surge. A solar flare will unleash upon Earth's upper atmosphere, causing a resounding hum and ethereal light to descend—a spectacle that will compel universal awe.

'Millions with a specific pill will experience absolute dawn: their destined ascendance to seize Earth's direction and wealth, thereby establishing a true plutocracy.

'Eighty to one hundred million will converge in stadiums globally, generating immense energy as a collective and absorbing the otherworldly light.'

'Are you sure there are that many people, that many spaces to accommodate them?' Denton questioned, fearing what could happen to him if he was wrong.

'Yes! This collective resonance amplified by the stadium structure will amplify the atmospheric vibration, locking onto the pill's quantum compound. Inside each recipient, the amplified energy fractures atomic bonds, releasing a blinding flash. This radiant burst precisely rewrites their DNA, granting heightened awareness—a self-perceived evolution.

'As billions slowly die weeks after exposure to the intense cosmic radiation, about 400 million will survive—a sounding trumpet to the Georgia Guidestones. In stadiums

worldwide, a profound, irreversible shift, a cosmic understanding—the first tide of humanity's next self-proclaimed evolution. The stadiums will become a launchpad for a new consciousness, birthing a new world order defined by the elite's absolute control through greed, wealth, and power.'

Denton whooped, a raw, unrestrained sound that clawed at the sudden stillness, his inner ego straining to grasp the promised infinity. The laboratory door hissed open, revealing the concerned faces of the agents, drawn by the commotion. Denton, his face flushed with triumphant anticipation, snapped an imperious command, ordering them back outside, eager to savour his moment of perceived triumph over Michael.

He basked in his over-indulgent, egotistical self-aggrandisement. Fuelled by his insatiable drive to win at all costs, the additional boost he'd received now surged within him; he couldn't contain his need to pour it out and encase Michael for his remaining life.

'Agents, come back, FBI too!' he shouted so loud that Michael felt some amalgam fillings rattle in his teeth. The agents entered, closely followed by FBI agents who had just completed their brief interrogations. Denton directed his agents to stand by him while asking the FBI to cuff Michael. NSA Special Agent Mutlan, who was previously asked to arrest Michael, looked on bemused by his sudden demotion. FBI Special Agent Tomlinson walked over to Michael and looked him squarely in the eye. Denton looked on, grinning mischievously, convinced he had the better of Michael.

'Please don't place my hands behind my back to cuff me,' Michael asked apologetically.

'Sorry, Professor Adams, I have to,' said Tomlinson, appreciating his request.

'Make them tight,' Denton nefariously instructed. Michael felt overwhelmed in the face of justice, while Denton looked on with satisfied acknowledgment of its effects against Michael.

'Stop!' KYROS unleashed a sonic boom, a physical force that slammed into their chests, the air itself vibrating with a painful intensity that momentarily stole their hearing.

The sonic boom then ripped through them; the assembled group didn't just jolt, they spasmed, limbs flailing like puppets cut from their strings. A collective gasp choked the air, and the raw scent of fear, sharp and metallic, prickled their nostrils—a tangible entity pressing against the walls of the confined space.

KYROS had been cursorily seen by the incoming agents but its true function and awesomeness remained unacknowledged; its stillness and familiar presence within the stark environment had rendered it almost invisible. The vaporised remains of the sniper's ashes screamed otherwise.

KYROS had to get to NEMESIS in the facility. But how? It projected its thoughts, sharp and insistent, directly into Denton and Michael's minds. Both heard what was really for Denton. KYROS played on Denton's worst fears of failure. *Denton. Your tenuous grip on the shadow group's favour frays. Contact NEMESIS. His stasis awaits within this ironclad lockdown.*

A swarm of frantic questions buzzed in Denton's skull, each vying for attention like desperate voices in a crowded room, their urgency a thick fog obscuring the stark, unsettling truth: "Why this journey into the unknown at all?

Surely its function here is complete. The what and where are known. What vital piece remains?"

KYROS answered Denton's unformed enquiry. Its voice, a resonant chord of pure thought, now echoed in Denton and Michael's minds.

'NEMESIS demands my proximity in stasis until the appointed hour of Q-Day. As the stroke of midnight births your transformation, so too shall it trigger our own. Mark this, Michael: your hand initiated this intricate dance of code, and by your hand, it shall conclude. And you, Denton, the phantom weight of your hand on Ann's head is known. This is not the hand I speak of, however, but Michael's, the architect, the alpha and omega of the true decodes.'

Denton didn't just recoil; his spine snapped back as if an invisible fist had slammed into his gut. A raw, unguarded flicker of mortification, like a struck nerve, spasmed across his features, momentarily shattering the carefully constructed mask of composure he wore like a second skin.

KYROS had spoken of death, yet the festering wound of his guilt now bled anew, the silence more damning than any accusation.

In that instant, the truth, long suppressed by the ramparts of his manic ego, pierced through with brutal force, a physical tremor seizing his jaw. Its involuntary clatter was a grotesque counterpoint to his inner turmoil. A crimson tide washed over his face and neck—a stark reminder of his guilt and shame. Ignominious droplets of sweat beaded on his forehead, a testament to his profound culpability.

With Denton temporarily out of verbal commission through guilt of Ann's murder, Michael decided to take charge of the questioning.

'How will we get to the facility, KYROS?'

'The journey is too far for me; my locomotion is for very short distances. To travel there is not possible.'

'But... you said we had to go there,' Michael began, his brow furrowed into a landscape of confusion. 'I don't understand,' he continued, his voice a low rasp, the weariness of the past hours a physical weight that seemed to compress his very spine, making his shoulders slump as if under an invisible burden. 'Please... explain?'

'We will go, but not as you imagine.'

'My brain feels so burnt out I can't imagine much now,' retorted Michael. He noticed Denton, still with a slight guilty gaze, nod his head in subjugated approval that he too was feeling burnt out.

KYROS asked them to clear away all the furniture in front of and to either side of its body. A three-meter semi-circle was required directly in front of it.

The agents got to work. The banging and screeching of furniture along the linoleum and stone was enough to make Denton's already addled mind resorted to placing his hands over his ears for protection. Michael, however, was more grounded; he looked on and supervised where necessary.

Five minutes later, furniture bundles to the left and right of KYROS had left a semi-circle as asked. Then, KYROS announced its next move.

'In the middle of that space you've made, I will create a sharp, intense beam of blue light. You will feel a slight wind and gravitas towards it. Do not try to study the light; it is not for that. When I say, I want one of you at a time to walk straight into it. Remember, one at a time, and leave at least two seconds before the next one walks in.'

'And this is to do what?' Michael mused.

'It will transport you to Denton's room. Have no fears; the space you will reappear in is empty. There is a security guard by Denton's desk, but he will faint when he sees you.'

'I would too if I saw this,' observed Michael.

'Maybe, but it's not what he sees; it's what he feels inside. I will simply and momentarily turn off his reticular activating system in the brainstem, which plays a crucial role in maintaining consciousness.'

'Simply!' queried Michael, trying to grasp the power KYROS had.

'Yes, unless you want to be shot,' cynically retorted KYROS.

Denton looked suspiciously at KYROS, placing his hand on the back of his neck to see if there was anything near his brainstem, just in case it was thinking of doing the same to him. There was nothing there. It had access to realms of understanding far beyond any human possessed or knew.

'I will arrive last and close to NEMESIS. We will deal with the next stage once there.'

And so it was that the NSA and FBI agents, Michael, and Denton walked, as directed, into the intense blue light and reappeared without a moment lost inside Denton's office.

For KYROS, the blue light moved towards and into him, making his reappearance as directed, close to NEMESIS.

The scene was now set for "Q-DAY".

Within minutes of arrival, armed guards burst into Denton's office through the emergency door. A supervisor in the CCTV control room spotted the images from Denton's office—the guard falling, a strange light, and the emergence of a group of people. Worse still, another entity now stood next to NEMESIS.

Four guards stood with guns pointed at the newly-arrived group, while another was tending to the fainted guard who was now sitting up, rubbing his eyes and wondering if he was caught in a nightmare.

'What do we have here? Looks like we still have some kind of security here, even if it's for people trying to get in,' Denton remarked sarcastically, an obvious dig at Michael and Peter's escape right under the Facility's nose just hours earlier.

'Stand down, stand down!' commanded Denton, waving his identification badge at them. 'You know who I am, so stand down,' he repeated.

The guards exchanged bewildered glances, perplexed by the sudden appearance of individuals whose entry hadn't been reported. They remained unaware of the Maglev's existence—a secret kept for good reason. More guards poured into the room, only to be given the same order.

Since lockdown, a new temporary base commander had taken charge. She now entered the room, pushing guards aside to make her way through and into the tense stand-off.

With so many bodies crammed into one room, the thick aroma of sweat began to dominate their senses. Another scent mingled with it: that of the entities. A thin ooze, a constant companion on their taut skin, effused a mild, chlorophyllin smell, like cut grass. The function of the ooze and the cause of the smell remained a mystery, inspiring countless theories but offering no definitive answers.

The temporary base commander, Colonel Jill Straton, looked at Denton; she recognised him from a recent visit to Edwards Air Force Base. Denton remembered her too: a distinguished colonel who had risen quickly through the ranks after graduating with her master's in Computational Science and Engineering from Harvard.

'Doctor Denton, I presume,' Straton said somewhat sarcastically. 'I'm almost too afraid to ask this question, given what your answer might be. But did you just enter this facility through an intense blue light?' she asked, a flicker of disbelief and absurdity playing across her features.

'We all did,' said Denton as he waved his arm towards the assembled group. 'Oh my God, not another one,' she blurted out as KYROS came into view from behind Denton, who moved to display his group.

Sensing no immediate danger, she told the guards to stand outside the exit door, in part because the ensuing conversation would be above their pay grade.

As they walked out, Denton moved over to his desk, a familiar friend. All the objects were still in their same places. The only anomaly was the strange moisture on the surface. He took his right index finger and wiped it across the dark mahogany wood, leaving a small streak. He cautiously lifted it to his nose, unsurprised to find it smelled similar to NEMESIS.

He sat down and looked around the room, the sight bringing back memories of the various ranks he had met. It always pleased him to see their many colourful rows of displayed ribbons above their breast pockets. This was a source of rightful pride, meticulously ordered to reflect the importance and hierarchy of each award.

'Gentlemen, if you please,' instructed Denton as he waved them out of the office, just as he had done with Peter and Michael weeks prior. As they moved away and out through the emergency door, they revealed Michael, who had been standing behind them.

Straton watched them walk to the door and then looked back to see Michael standing, forlorn as memories flooded back about Peter and Ann. The more he reflected, the more he distrusted his own personality.

Straton had another outburst. 'No, it cannot be. It's Michael Adams...sorry, Professor Adams.' Michael stared at this stranger in a colonel's uniform with unease. Had she seen his picture portrayed as a murderer on media outlets? Was her next move to cuff him and take him into custody? Thankfully, not.

'It's Jill, I wrote my dissertation on the implications of DNA profiling and personality. You were my supervisor. Remember?' Straton enunciated with such pleasure he was transported back to when she first met him.

'Yes, Jill, I do remember you. I wish the circumstances were more propitious.'

'May I call you Michael?' she politely requested.

'Of course,' was the response.

'It's so lovely to see you. Your fabulous academic marking and reference was my passport to what I am today.'

'I only evaluated the work that was in front of me, Jill.'

'Gosh, this is surreal. I have always wanted to say thank you and tell you about what I've achieved. Not for personal embellishment—well, maybe a little—but to acknowledge your input, your teaching and supervision.'

'Are we going to get on with the important matters in hand, Denton, Straton?' Michael reproached, tired of hearing about their university days. Michael and Straton exchanged a brief, almost amused glance, a silent acknowledgement of their shared past, in contrast to Denton's impatience.

He put his head in his hands despairingly, depressed by the realisation that Straton only had eyes for Michael. Any resolutions on how to deal with matters, he feared, might show a certain partiality towards her former supervisor.

They sat down before Denton's desk, awaiting his next words. Denton looked over at the two entities, which stared back, still, without purpose, as if mannequins in a shop window. His gaze made Michael and Straton look too. Michael thought he saw the lips of NEMESIS subtly twitch...but he ignored it.

'All right, well, where do I start?' Denton asked rhetorically. 'I have a facility lockdown, a murderer –'

'A murderer!' shouted Straton as she jumped out of her chair. Her eyes wide with fright, she stared intently at Michael, as if somehow it would all go away.

'Yes, a bona fide murderer of one Professor Peter Magma no less,' expressed Denton gleefully and unashamedly. Michael looked on, unimpressed by Denton's relishing of his downfall from academic grace.

'I will have to arrest you Michael...Professor Adams,' curtly said Straton.

'I cannot allow that,' declared Denton.

'I am the base commander, I outrank you,' Straton asserted forcefully.

'If you were commander, maybe, but you are a temporary commander, and therefore I outrank you. You are a "0-6" rank, whereas I am "0-10" rank. Perhaps you should call me Doctor, or even General?' Denton insisted.

'Maybe so, but the locals could still arrest him. It's in their jurisdiction, yes,' demanded Straton, fazed by Denton's explanation of rank and implication of her subordination.

Denton stood up, angered by this subordinate, and walked over to his portrait hanging directly in front of one of the CCTV cameras. As he pulled it, it swung out to reveal a safe. Pressing the correct combination, it bizarrely opened to another safe.

'Better safe than sorry,' he chuckled, staring at them both through what could only be described as malice aforethought eyes. Opening the second safe, he thumbed through a couple of files marked "Most Secret" until he found a purple envelope.

He pulled it from the inner safe, then the outer, and slammed both doors shut. Turning around, he walked majestically back to the desk and sat back down, grinning uncontrollably as he did.

'Pretty envelope,' Straton observed. 'It is,' Denton chortled, a delight in his gaze that was almost tangible. 'Any idea what this contains?' He teased them, anticipating answers that would crumble before the revealed truth.

Opening the unsealed envelope, he pulled out an A4 white sheet of paper and unfurled it, with such panache it suggested he was an origami teacher.

'This is the second time I have had the great pleasure of an audience listening to me read it.' As he read the letter, all who listened sat quiet with jaws dropping faster than a demolished building. By the end, they too felt utterly destroyed, their structural egos shattered.

Denton put the letter back in the envelope and placed it on his desk with a smug, disdainful flourish. Michael and Straton looked vacantly at him for separate reasons. Straton had been decisively forced to do as she was told, and Michael knew Denton would get away with Ann's murder and everything else.

'Now that's sorted, let's deal with these two things over there and what happens forthwith with Michael, you and the facility.'

The first thing Denton did was to cancel the lockdown so that all staff, research or not, would return. Any concern over the security of the facility had passed. He was back, so the problem was solved.

Straton confirmed her temporary assignment until the new year, specifying January, and immediately acknowledged his rank over her. Denton then briefed her on what was going to happen once all the research staff had returned.

The facility would again be placed in lockdown until the new year. All staff and Michael would be confined to the facility, including all agents who had seen the two entities.

She asked why, and he explained it was for national security reasons related to them, adding that she should ask no more about it. Any visitors would have to be cleared in advance, from visiting dignitaries to cleaners; he expected few of the former.

What he didn't tell Michael or Straton was his plan: to ensure the pills were manufactured and dispersed to people who were part of the shadow group, directly or indirectly. This network spread far and wide: associates of associates, friends of friends—all would be included, provided they shared the shadow group ideology of the accumulation and monopolisation of power and wealth for their select few.

Having explained the plan for the next two months, Straton was ordered to leave with Michael in tow. Though uncuffed, his freedom of movement severely curtailed, imposing a psychological burden as significant as any physical restraint.

As he waited at the lift to be taken to his room by Straton, with a permanent security guard standing outside for good measure, his gaze slowly drifted across to the two entities, their eyes fixed intently on him.

It was always disconcerting to feel a pair of eyes moving with you as you crossed a room, a sensation akin to the "Mona Lisa effect," but with these entities, the feeling was amplified to a profound spookiness.

He looked away, noticing Straton watching him with undisguised disgust. "If only she truly knew," he thought, "perhaps her judgment would be tempered." The lift doors began to slide open, and he risked one last glance at the entities.

To his shock, the lips of NEMESIS subtly twitched, sending a jolt through him and confirming he hadn't imagined it before. Straton took his arm, pulling him into the lift, seemingly mistaking his stunned awe for reluctance. The doors then closed, separating them from the unsettling room and the manipulative, traitorous Denton.

The Masquerade Of Lies And Deception

In his accustomed restaurant seat, Michael habitually glanced at his watch, a gesture repeated countless times in the two long months of isolation since his return through KYROS's portal.

He casually looked around the restaurant, his gaze sweeping the room. His time dissecting intricate DNA had honed his focus, making him acutely aware of the smallest imperfections: chipped paint on a wall, an almost imperceptible wobble of a table leg, uncleaned scuff marks, and a ceiling light flickering every minute – each blink a reminder of the inexorable march of time.

A relentless wave of sensory input besieged him. The piercing shriek of metal scraping against china and the discordant cacophony of voices seemed to shred the very air around him. The television news, a sound both distant and stubbornly present, resonated through the floorboards as a low vibration that tightened the muscles in his upper body. The air he breathed was thick with a sickly-sweet blend of garlic and imitation cherry, leaving a faint, unsettling tingle in his nose.

Though confined, the scientific teams moved with a weary acceptance, their shoulders slumped slightly as they navigated the restaurant. Yet, even amidst their quiet resignation, bursts of laughter and animated conversations brushed against the edges of Michael's awareness, seemingly oblivious to the underlying dread he felt permeating the air.

This was a stark contrast to Michael's own despair as he sank deeper into the soft plastic of his chair, the surrounding noise of the restaurant dissolving into a distant hum while his attention became fixated on the minute beads of moisture clinging to his cup, each a small reflection of his hope slowly draining away.

Haunted by Peter's death, Michael questioned the high morality he once held, especially given the nature of his demise and the profound importance Peter had once held in his life.

A gnawing question consumed him, sharp as a splinter: how had Nathan, that audacious ghost, so effortlessly slipped past their brilliance? They commanded gargantuan models, tirelessly checking and rechecking for data integrity, an impenetrable digital firewall. Yet, against all logic, against every byte of data, he had succeeded. And that reality hammered him.

His sharp and self-recriminating thoughts abruptly fixated on the flimsy plastic cup in his hand. Its weightless feel brutally contrasted the crushing mass of his culpability. The cup's solitary form mirrored his isolation; its hollow interior, the gaping void where his self-respect had once resided, shattered by Peter's death.

With a sudden, compulsive clench, he compressed the fragile vessel into a useless, crumpled bundle, a chilling premonition of his own impending annihilation.

The silence of the lockdown magnified the whispers of doubt in his mind, each one chipping away at his fragile sense of security. Lost in a vortex of self-doubt, Michael's attention was drawn to the flickering images on the television, a distraction from his inner turmoil.

The broadcast amplified Michael's anxieties, starkly contrasting with the cheerful banter of his colleagues. The media systematically dismantled his life's work through falsehoods and innuendo, painting a reality where this relentless assault further deepened his profound sense of alienation.

A pervasive sense of unease clung to him. The sheer scale of what they had unleashed haunted Michael; picturing KYROS, a force beyond comprehension, a shiver traced his spine. How could they possibly contain it?

The weight of his complicity, coupled with this terrifying realisation of their creation's potential, pressed in on him, the walls of his guilt solidifying into a suffocating prison, and the key was lost, perhaps never to be found.

His depression deepened, amplified by relentless news broadcasts that slandered the project with falsehoods and innuendo, mirroring the internal erosion of his confidence. Beyond his work, a new, unsettling concern gripped the public.

Astronomers had reported peculiar energy and radio signals emanating from the sun. This in itself was not unusual, but as these emanations continued and increased, they suggested a mega coronal mass ejection was imminent.

Furthermore, scientists had recorded a cloud of dark matter closing in on Earth, its presence detected through its interactions with incoming sunlight.

They deduced that if a mega coronal mass ejection slammed into a significant amount of this dark matter above the Earth's atmosphere, the energy would make it behave differently, causing it to absorb and scatter light. In effect, this would create a large area of deep darkness that stopped sunlight from reaching Earth, plunging the planet into total darkness for an unknown period.

While the full extent of its impact on Earth, beyond the obvious absence of light, remained immeasurable, the approaching celestial event undeniably served to destabilise nations.

Despite consistent attempts by governments worldwide to minimise its significance, global media outlets seized upon the story, actively cultivating widespread anxiety and concern through blatant manipulation.

This manipulation revealed elites as puppeteers, twisting truth to serve capricious whims. With surgical efficiency, they weaponised media's hunger, injecting corrupting lies into public consciousness, laying bare their entrenched structure of power and control – a vast masquerade of corruption fuelled by wealth and influence.

Its reach extended from the quiet, secretive offices where truth was commodified and unspoken financial transactions greased the wheels of ambition and advancement. It stretched all the way to those who committed the most heinous acts. This vast network left behind a pervasive legacy of profound suffering.

It encompassed those who used wealth to suppress dissent and advance their nefarious aims. It also included those allied with influential circles, desperately clinging to outdated narratives of privilege and authority. All the while, they hypocritically professed allegiance to a diverse and equitable society.

This was all a meticulously crafted cover for NEMESIS's chilling ambition: to conquer the world and leave only around 400 million to serve its elite masters. For years, and with increasing intensity in recent months, these elites had sold the lie of tirelessly working to save humanity. The chilling truth, however, was precisely the opposite: they worked to fragment society through disorder and conflict between groups, thus making their control and manipulation much easier.

Across every continent, civil disorder erupted, mirroring the erosion of trust, freedom of speech, and the financial draining of governments through corrupt practices. Less democracy meant deeper elite manipulation, yet no country was exempt from the chaos.

The fabricated reports—from swirling light displays and planet-killing meteors to cosmic plagues and total communication breakdowns plunging humanity into a new dark age—were mere threads in this vast tapestry of deceit, designed to distract from the true, insidious plan.

This grand deception was further amplified as Michael and Peter's research team, already the backbone of nightly media attacks, became inextricably linked to these apocalyptic narratives. This combination intensified the negativity surrounding both, creating a climate where speculative confusion and biased news undermined any hope for a stable, rational mind and society.

Yet, amidst this pervasive despair, an unexpected and utterly unnecessary interruption shattered the oppressive news: a light-hearted dinner, bizarrely announced to celebrate the very negativity and chaos it was supposed to prevent.

The PA announcement blared inside the restaurant and the adjacent research floor, carrying the jocular urgency of a summons: everyone was invited to an executive dinner preceding the quantum event.

A final, amplified click punctuated the message as the microphone cut off—a sonic punch that rattled even the most stoic eardrums. He let out a rare chuckle to himself, a sudden, anxious release in response to the isolation that had become his constant companion.

'Executive dinner, my arse,' Michael mumbled to himself with a wry grin, leaning forward and resting his head on the desk to avoid the prying eyes of CCTV. An hour or more passed as he simply sat, his mind lost in the same weary thoughts that had plagued him for days.

Unbeknownst to Michael, his armed guard, who followed him everywhere and usually sat a few tables away, was now standing directly in front of him. Michael looked up as the guard spoke.

'Back to my room, then?' Michael inquired, a note of weary resignation in his voice, the question hanging in the air like a plea. The guard, his posture a study in unyielding rigidity, offered a clipped, dismissive reply.

'On the contrary, Professor Adams,' the guard replied, his tone officious, utterly devoid of warmth. 'Doctor Denton requires your presence in his office.'

Michael's voice held a note of suspicion, 'Does he have the time?' The guard, utterly devoid of emotion, replied flatly, 'He does, and so do you. It's right there.' He gestured curtly to Michael's wrist.

Michael's gaze drifted away, a flicker of doubt momentarily clouding his thoughts. "Was he losing his grip?" With a shrug, Michael turned and allowed the guard to escort him to Denton's office via the lift.

As they both stepped out of the lift and into Denton's office, Michael looked over at the entities. They hadn't moved a centimetre, not even a millimetre, since he had last seen them months earlier.

'Michael, long time, no see,' Denton remarked, with an underlying eagerness for midnight to roll on. "How do I go for the jugular?" Michael thought.

'Where have you stashed the cash for being a traitor?' Michael insinuated.

'Guard, ignore that, he's just jealous I hold the keys to his imprisonment. Go back upstairs, Level Five, I can handle this murderer,' commanded Denton.

As the guard disappeared upstairs with the lift, Michael told Denton he wouldn't get away with it.

'I have and I will,' Denton chuckled to himself, oblivious to the daggers Michael mentally aimed his way.

'Splendid meal, you missed something special there, Michael?' Denton gushed with smug satisfaction, practically preening. He barely even registered Michael's dismissive shrug.

'Anyway, sit down at my palatial desk. Only hours to go now, so I want to disclose just how much fun I've had watching those you love work against you. You managed to get to Peter, but had you known what I'm about to disclose, perhaps you would have thought differently about whom to target.'

With that in mind, I will tell you what was of real substance, and you'll admire our work for it,' growled Denton, the pleasure of ridiculing Michael never diminished for him.

Michael listened, his temper now a well-oiled machine, able to withstand any insult Denton threw at him. Denton rarely took his eyes off Michael, savouring every sarcastic moment he aimed at him, and watchful for any sign of attack.

557

'Gee, where do I start?' Denton asked rhetorically. 'You do seem to have a habit of not getting shot or blown up, don't you?'

'That was you,' hissed Michael, in shock as he thought back to the assault and horror he witnessed both on the plane and at Ann and Peter's home in Oxford.

'My word, for such an intelligent man, you have suddenly become quite stupid,' declared Denton. Michael's usually sharp academic mind was faltering; a complete breakdown seemed imminent.

'The hijacking was our attempt to rough you up and make you compliant, for fear of what could be next. We were going to use Elizabeth to do our bidding; however, we didn't want deaths so early. We had so much torment planned for you, but our overeager commander ruined it when he shot two SAS men trying to jump the plane and later simply "lost it," leading the SAS to end it.'

'You killed two SAS men?' Michael stammered.

'Yes, as well as a cabin crew member and an Air Marshal, which I told Hammerfall about before he even boarded the plane, so not a total failure,' firmly pronounced Denton, smiling manically at Michael.

'If you touched Elizabeth, I would have pushed your head against that table myself,' barked Michael. Denton, however, was too devoid of care for non-elites to even register the dent in his ego.

Denton bellowed with laughter. 'Oh my God, how stupid, how absolutely blind can you be, Michael!' Michael stared at Denton, searching for an explanation for this odd behaviour and these biting words.

'She was one of us! How do you think she became such a good driver? Those deaths were unfortunate—a little too enthusiastic for our cause. We wanted you alive, Michael. You were valuable,' Denton declared, his fingers twitching as if counting money.

'You're one sick—' but Michael was interrupted by Denton.

'Remember the waiter not recognising Elizabeth's previous visit? Her access to your secure safe? Or waving you off at the airport when she had never done this before, claiming it was too upsetting? What about her being in Lisbon, Portugal, only to change her location after her lie was exposed?'

'Not to mention working at a media agency to embed herself in the elite media and finance a lifestyle beyond her pay grade. Didn't you see her agency attacking your work? And you handed your secret files to her!' Denton couldn't help chuckling and waving his hands mockingly at Michael.

'And to think you killed Peter, your best friend, closest work buddy and all-round nice guy!' Michael, still reeling from the revelations about Elizabeth, was too preoccupied to absorb this well-worn comment about Peter. Suddenly, he exploded with rage, standing up and smashing his fist down on Denton's manicured desk.

'Absolutely bullshit, Denton, from your bullshit mind to your bullshit allegiances. Total crap!' he bellowed loudly to Denton's face.

At this point, Michael leaped forward at Denton, his legs hitting the desk, but his arms carried his momentum to within feet of Denton's face. Had Michael touched Denton, he would have detonated with anger. Denton was prepared; he pulled open the top right pedestal drawer with his right hand and grabbed a small Ruger handgun. He pointed it straight at Michael.

559

'How ironic, you now have a gun pointing at you,' simmered Denton, his body aching for retribution for Michael's ignominious affront.

'Easy, Michael, easy,' he directed. Denton yanked open the central utility drawer of his desk with his left hand and pulled out several letters. He took the top one and threw it at Michael as if it were a dagger. It bounced off him as if he rejected the words it contained.

'Read it and weep,' Denton taunted.

Michael fell back into the chair that creaked so loudly, it groaned. He picked up the letter and pulled out a single piece of A4 paper. His hands shook with stress and anxiety for what it contained. It was there in black and white: Elizabeth detailed how much she was being paid to work for Denton, how it made her feel important, alive, "a person of consequence." But the true dynamite lay in the salutation, which simply read, "Hi Dad".

'Oh dear, life a bit difficult at the moment, Michael?' Denton mocked. Michael couldn't rationalise how his beautiful, apparently successful daughter—or rather, the woman he'd believed was his daughter— could be such a turncoat. He had thought he could confide in her, feel secure under the mansion roofs, only to discover she had been secretly plotting and informing on him to his arch-enemy.

Denton continued to mock Michael. 'She legitimated her illegitimacy to you,' he sneered, 'and should be congratulated, not besmirched.'

Michael looked on, angry that he'd never accounted for his own short-sightedness – from Victoria working evenings at the NSA to Elizabeth's sometimes erratic and reckless behaviour. Then a teasing thought he'd had for years shook him rigid: "No wonder I couldn't work out where the other half of her genes came from. Compared to her true father, her actions now screamed the obvious."

'Ann never liked you,' Michael shot back, his voice raw. 'She fought tooth and nail to keep Nathan from working for you. Many times, he spoke of relocating here, but her "no" was fervent, absolute. And from what I've now learned, she was right. He comes here, and you just pollute his mind with money.'

'You're so malevolently critical, Michael. Can't you see how cheaply I can buy anyone?' Denton purred.

'Who planted the bomb under Peter's Jaguar? No, it wasn't Lassus, as you know. What you didn't know was that it was Nathan. And what you still don't know is he's my son, not Peter's. You are such a yesterday man!' Denton sneered, a smug glint cold in his eyes.

'I know. Peter told me. Two peas from the same reckless, unpatriotic pod,' Michael countered, disconsolately, yet with a flicker of satisfaction at correcting Denton.

'Whatever,' Denton continued. 'He wanted to come here, to work for the shadow group. Yes, I know Ann kept stopping him, and he suspected Peter didn't want him here either. Ann would drop subtle, yet informative, hints, so can you imagine his frustration?'

Denton leaned back. 'Anyway, he wanted to work here because the money was better, and the fringe benefits were incalculable. To demonstrate his defiance, he targeted Ann and Peter's bedroom. Who would suspect the son... well... sort of son? Especially so soon after the planc siege; they'd blame them because you were there. It was a case of "Post hoc ergo propter hoc," or "after this, therefore because of this." Personally, I much prefer "association by default."'

'Compared to bombing, sabotage was nothing to Nathan. They had it coming anyway; he's a young, very bright lad, and his patience for being held back had completely worn him out,' Denton conveyed, a chilling, psychotic edge to his tone.

Michael replied through gritted teeth, his fists clenched, pumped for action. 'You're not just sick, you're delusional. No, add psychotic too. A "basket case" for sure. Whatever it is you follow or want—maybe both—it will fail, miserably.'

Denton stared, his irrational mind seemingly unable to compute being told he was out of his mind.

Michael had long suspected Nathan, but lacked the evidence. He had resigned himself to failure; this crushing realisation stemmed not from Denton's words, but from the gun still clutched in his right hand.

This resignation eased slightly as Denton placed the weapon back into the open desk drawer. An element of calm returned, a stark, almost unsettling quiet.

Just as if a switch was flicked, Denton suddenly changed course. 'Have you seen the newspapers or television?' Denton eagerly asked.

'How can I avoid them, they're on all day, every day, blurting out their messages of doom,' Michael exasperatedly told Denton.

'And the newspapers, the same?' Denton further enquired.

'Yes, all the same. The messages differ, but the meaning's identical. Listen to any member of the research team; it's just the bloody same,' almost cried Michael, the strain of being imprisoned etched on his face.

'Gosh, how terrible for you, for all,' joked Denton.

The calm hadn't lasted long. A visceral urge to silence Denton, to obliterate his smug pronouncements, thrummed beneath Michael's skin like a live current. His muscles bunched, coiled tight as a spring about to snap, and his gaze narrowed into a predatory focus, locking onto Denton as a cornered animal might fixate on its tormentor.

'Just get to the bloody point, you murderous traitor to your country!' shouted Michael. His hands tightened on his lap, knuckles still white. Every muscle in his body urged him to move, to unleash the fury building inside. Yet, a nagging question, a morbid curiosity about Denton's next moves, kept him rooted to his chair, a reluctant prisoner of his own need to know.

'Easy there, Mister Murderer,' Denton drawled with cruel amusement. 'I simply want you to witness the fruits of your labour with dear Peter. You both excelled, and I might even put in a good word for you... right before the appropriate authorities kill you.'

Denton's laugh followed, a dry, grating sound that scraped against the tense silence, echoing like a stone rolling in an empty grave, utterly devoid of warmth. 'Say goodbye to any shred of respect they might have held for you, Michael. Your legacy will be etched in failure.'

'You sick bastard!' Michael shouted at Denton. 'Come on, tell your story of world domination. What the hell have you unleashed?' Dread tightened a vice around Michael's vocal cords, his voice a thin, strained wire stretched to breaking point.

Denton's eyes gleamed with an unsettling conviction. With a chilling reverence in his tone, he uttered, 'KYROS revealed it all to me.'

His judgement, a vulnerable minnow in the current of KYROS's dazzling narrative, was effortlessly swallowed whole by its predatory allure. Michael just shook his head, not in disgust as he already knew, but at how Denton had been totally fooled by his own self-importance.

With chilling detail, he explained how in the last couple of months, about 80 million elites had taken the pills. Some refused, other non-elites paid heavily to buy in to the plutocratic hegemony. They included individuals who amassed their fortunes in the world's darker corners and shadow economies. Michael's mouth fell open in disbelief. Denton's greed, raw and exposed as a festering wound, mirrored the avarice that pulsed through the millions who embraced this path.

'I've not taken it, nor have any of my team,' Michael stated, hoping for further clarification on who'd taken it. Denton laughed quietly, a snigger lost within it, before he went fully patronising.

'Michael, take a good look at yourself—you are inconsequential. I, on the other hand, am ascendant. Of course, I had to take it. And consider this: the true beneficiaries, those who truly understand power, have fully embraced it. Why not? They have, after all, perfected the art of sculpting human behaviour and subjugating human thought through the use of law, fiscal manipulation, and psychological control. Their intertwined networks are the very instigators of thought control through global fear and instability, a ruthless means to an end.

'It will be a new, relentless elite order where plutocracy reigns supreme, and all others are mere instruments of its will. The crème de la crème that will make us even greater than before, a perpetual harvest of profit, wealth, and plutocracy! I pity the 400 million or so servants who remain; they are for us to use as we wish; they will give to us freely and demand nothing in return.'

Michael knew better than to argue with a man whose mind was clearly shorting out. This was not just a rant; it was the unfiltered output of a brain in full meltdown.

The cold calculus of Denton's irrationality was a blade of ice against the soul, its horror eclipsing even the crimson stain of war. The elites awaited midnight with anticipatory glee at the celebration and confirmation of their brave new world of elite plutocracy and mass subjugation of the many.

They had created a false sense of insecurity over two months; now, they created a false sense of security for the final week for the general populace, perhaps their final week. But how?

For two relentless months, a carefully cultivated atmosphere of global unease had taken root, subtly shifting the fault lines of civil order both within and across borders.

Now, in the final, deceptive week before the enigmatic "Q-Day", a counter-narrative bloomed. A lavish, almost desperate investment in ephemeral New Year celebrations was delivered, powered by media reports that all would be well after all.

In the final week before "Q-Day", the widespread civil unrest had begun to lessen considerably, like morning mist disappearing. Suddenly, money was lavished on world populations like never before.

Food, entertainment, fireworks, and so much more had been organised and delivered every hour over those fateful remaining days. People, so distracted from worries only days before, now hoped the sensationalist media exaggerations of doom would prove false and life would gradually return to normal.

But for the elites, the world's grand stadiums where they would be anointed by a heavenly light to initiate their plutocratic reign were transformed into forbidden citadels. The muscle of shadowy organisations—their own fierce security details—elbowed aside the regular police, whose leaders, with allegiances veiled in secrecy, ordered them to retreat.

Colossal beams of coloured light, like molten rainbows, pierced the inky canvas of the night and blazed across the heavens in vibrant, intertwining patterns. Below, the masses gazed upwards in childlike wonder, their faces bathed in the shifting hues.

High above, astronomers watched for the eruption of the mega solar flare with a mix of fear and strong curiosity. Their specialised instruments—coronagraphs, solar telescopes, and satellites—gathered data very quickly. All previous data patterns and historical records were repeatedly broken. In their quiet observatories, the scientists debated whether to stay and observe or go deep underground for safety. As the eruption approached, their anticipation grew into a deeper fear of the worst.

Time zones became meaningless, just ghostly notions as the approaching dark matter cloud promised to swallow Earth's light.

In the final, dwindling hours before "Q-Day", even the brightest daylight began to falter as the cloud suffocated its natural life-giving light and succumbed to a creeping twilight. The masses had now been fed soothing words, told to embrace the coming event as a familiar solar eclipse, merely one that would linger a little longer in the sky.

Within stadiums across the world, the elite partied, sang jubilantly, and danced away the remaining hours to midnight as if there were no tomorrow. Old associations were renewed; historical grievances between groups were resolved and forgiven; wounds that had festered within and across warring families were sealed with forgiveness. It was truly a time of renewal, just as they expected.

Back in Denton's room, the conversation between him and Michael was a familiar, acid-tongued duel.

'I was under the impression you had a more pressing engagement. Shouldn't you be in the stadium, with the rest of your unholy congregation, raising your bank accounts in triumph to the dawn of a new, corrupt light? Michael sneered.

'Why, I have authority from NEMESIS to stay here and watch something so unique it surpasses what happens outside,' replied a patronising Denton. He continued, 'We stand at the threshold of renewal, a progression that will unshackle the restrictive chains that have blighted our kind at the hands of your kind.'

Michael tuned out Denton's pronouncements, a sudden rush of memory pulling him back to Harvard and the seductive promise of KYROS: something wondrous within his grasp. That single thought still resonated within him, a series of pulsing echoes that conjured bittersweet memories of Peter and Ann, intertwined with the phantom joy of a future now irrevocably tainted.

He looked at KYROS, motionless, staring out from its position next to NEMESIS, both oblivious to their toxic conversations, or so it seemed. While NEMESIS looked similar in appearance to KYROS, Michael was sure NEMESIS's strength had depleted, just as KYROS suggested. Consequently, KYROS's radiance was far brighter than NEMESIS's.

From the silence, the lift's hum announced an arrival. Armed security guards, previously redeployed to protect all access points to Denton's room, granted swift access.

Everyone watched, listening as the noise grew, a clear sign of an important figure approaching. Denton even wondered if it was the president. Michael, however, didn't care.

The lift doors slid open, revealing temporary base commander Straton and Nathan. Her gaze flickered over the entities, a brief, dismissive glance as if they were mere laboratory furniture.

She pointed Nathan to the empty chair next to Michael; he duly obliged. Nathan looked at Michael, shoulders stiffening, without his usual smile. Michael looked back, hands tightening on his lap, taking a slow, deep breath, as if worried. Both felt something bad was about to happen.

'I thought you might like to see what's happening outside,' she said, carrying a small projector. She placed it on Denton's desk. Pressing the "on" button, a beam of light shone across the room onto the wall close to the entities.

'Just like the movies!' bellowed Nathan. 'Did you bring some popcorn and soda? Nachos! I love nacho cheese,' he continued, garnering Denton's displeasure despite the moment's importance. It was a brief outburst, understandable given his confinement.

Michael looked at Nathan with finality and said, 'Why are you such a dickhead sometimes?' The words shattered Nathan's jovial façade, causing a painful moral reflection that left him questioning his involvement with Denton.

With the projector on the table, Straton left without a word. For her, the light shows above held more appeal. They all moved chairs closer to the NEMESIS and KYROS, sitting to look at the images from outside: media outlets everywhere celebrated the impending new year. What a stark contrast to their recent biased doom and gloom. Or was it merely the calm before the storm?

- 63 -
The Countdown Begins

With only several minutes remaining to midnight and "Q-Day", they watched the wall projection, a shared intensity binding their awareness. Their focus sharpened as pulses of anticipation quickened within them; the very air thrummed with the imminent unravelling.

Five minutes to "Q-Day".

A sharp, collective intake of breath united all three as, with a ponderous shift, KYROS glided slowly forward a few steps towards them until it was just a metre away. While Denton and Michael had seen KYROS's strange locomotion before, Nathan sat frozen to his chair, gripping its arms so hard his fingerprints could have been forensically determined.

It spoke to them. *'And so, it is five minutes to midnight, five minutes to "Q-Day". I promised you both what would be, and will be. The elites await their day of reckoning.'*

Nathan flinched, a surprised expletive escaping him as KYROS's voice pierced his thoughts. He looked at the other two and then whispered in trepidation, 'That damn thing is speaking to me. Can't you hear it?' Denton and Michael merely smiled at him with a strange, slightly hypnotic trance, awaiting KYROS's next pronouncement. Its calculating modus operandi was indeed becoming clearer.

'Denton and Nathan, since you've ingested the pill and, in your own eyes, acted with distinction and honour for the cause, you must fulfil your destinies, as many of your friends will soon do as well.'

The words hit Michael like a physical blow. Destinies? A cold resignation seeped into Michael, the fractured trust with

Denton a sudden, sickening certainty. If only the clarity of this moment had pierced the past. The cost of Denton's ambition, the birth of NEMESIS on that table, hung heavy in his awareness. He stared at Denton, a profound emptiness settling within him.

For Denton and Nathan, a visible tremor ran through them, their hands clenching and unclenching. The pill, their promised salvation, now felt like a lead weight. For Denton, NEMESIS had promised continued wealth and life for the elites; he clung to that lie as hard as he clutched his chair. The pallor of their skins and the rapid pulse visible at their throats betrayed an unseen beast. A terror, arising from their deepest, darkest unconscious anxieties, began to fill their conscious thoughts. It was something unimaginable, gnawing at the very fabric of their sanity.

For Michael, the true measure of a higher being was the restraint to wield such power only as a sorrowful, ultimate recourse. This restraint was always guided by the unwavering light of logic, rather than the seductive shadow of emotionally charged retribution. This thought solidified his own resolve. It stood in stark contrast to the unease of expectation and unknowing now gripping Denton and Nathan.

KYROS seemed to beam at Michael as it spoke, its words a silken command: '*Michael, stand. Walk towards NEMESIS.*' The command offered no debate.

"Walk towards it? Why?" he thought. A cold fist clenched Michael's gut. He stood up and acted accordingly. His movement felt alien, his own will severed, a phantom limb twitching with memory.

Yet, the implacable authority in KYROS's tone offered no purchase for argument. Slowly, his muscles, protesting the unnatural pull, yielded. Each step towards the silent, looming NEMESIS—a glacial sentinel since their arrival—was a small, agonising surrender.

His gaze locked on NEMESIS. Then, another subtle flicker at its mouth, barely there, snagged his attention like a barb. He hadn't imagined this after all; something was different this time.

At the moment when uncertainty was at its apex, rationality fractured, surrendering to primordial fears and anxieties. Like ancient, repressed patterns that reside deep within the collective unconscious of all humanity, these clawed their way from the subconscious depths to invade the conscious mind. It was a psychological truth Denton and Nathan now faced in terrifying clarity, their very psyches consumed by ancient, unbidden dread.

But the twitch... it burrowed into Michael, a chilling possibility blooming into visceral understanding. Could it be Ann? Staring at the alien structure, the horrifying thought struck him: was that her? Her spirit trapped, battling within that cold shell?

Four minutes to "Q-Day".

He looked away towards KYROS, his gaze pleading for an explanation. A subtle shift in KYROS's form, a minute inclination of its head seemed to convey understanding, a silent message resonating in Michael's mind, answering his unspoken question.

The smooth, almost silent rotation of KYROS's form then directed its unwavering focus towards Denton and Nathan, who sat hunched and still, radiating a silence thicker than fear. As it moved, a faint, almost imperceptible hum, a resonance that felt less mechanical and more intentional, brushed against the edges of Michael's awareness.

'*You two have taken the pill,*' its voice resonated—a precise, toneless frequency that seemed to vibrate in the very air, demanding acknowledgment rather than inviting it. Its lack of inflection nonetheless conveyed an utter certainty, as if stating an undeniable axiom of its own internal logic.

Denton, emboldened by a desperate hope, leaned forward in his chair, a smug smirk briefly flickering across his face. 'Exactly! Just like you said, KYROS. So... what's the reward?' His gaze flickered nervously towards the celebratory images of people's reactions to the atmospheric fireworks and light displays projected on the wall screen.

A barely perceptible pause emanated from KYROS. Its voice, still level in the room's tense atmosphere, now carried a new, ominous weight. '*Indeed.*' The single word hung, each syllable resonating with an immutable certainty. '*And you, Nathan, also ingested the pill.*' The subsequent silence felt different, charged with an almost tangible shift in the entity's presence, a chilling stillness that spoke more of judgment than observation.

KYROS then stated, '*Denton didn't just secure your help, Nathan. He bought it. He paid you to betray Michael and Peter, to feed him their secrets – secrets that could have destroyed everything they were working towards. And then, the NEMESIS code... that was your handiwork, wasn't it? A deliberate corruption. Denton knew what harm it would cause but let it continue. Both of you violated your oaths, the very principles that underpin this transformation. The price for such betrayal is final.*'

A ragged sob tore through Nathan's plea: 'No! I'm sorry, please... forgive me.' He crumpled from the chair, his knees cracking sharply on the unforgiving floor. Tears streamed, etching stark trails down his face, a raw mask of guilt and terror. His face flushed crimson with the swift tide of panic, his breath snagging in desperate, ragged gasps. Another plea died on his lips. Then, a soft glow bloomed within him, centred at his navel.

Slowly, inexorably, the light intensified, a suffocating radiance spreading in all directions to engulf his body, accompanied by a faint, acrid ozone tang in the air and a silent hum that vibrated not in the ears, but in his very being.

For a fleeting moment, before the brilliance became blinding, Denton and Michael glimpsed a silent scream etched on Nathan's face, a pure vision of abject horror. Then, the light pulsed, reaching a searing peak before fading just as suddenly, leaving only empty space where Nathan had been. Nothing remained.

Three minutes to "Q-Day".

'KYROS, please... you can't!' Denton's voice cracked, the bluster gone, replaced by a raw tremor. He swallowed hard. 'I... I built this place. I was trying to protect everyone. You have to believe me.'

KYROS remained silent, its unreadable form offering no flicker of acknowledgment. Denton's eyes darted towards the still form of NEMESIS.

'Look at it! That... that thing is proof! Nathan messed with it, didn't he? That's why you're doing this! It's his fault, not mine! What in God's name is happening?' Denton shrieked, as an unseen force lifted him, propelling him towards the hexagonal table, to which NEMESIS was coldly attached.

Denton's pleas cracked with primal fear, a stark contrast to KYROS's serene pronouncements. A frantic tremor vibrated through him, the once-commanding orchestrator now a powerless puppet in a telepathically enforced forward movement, hovering centimetres above the floor as KYROS moved him.

Each inexorable drift towards the cold, dark, quantum, hexagonal table was a step into nightmare, his widening eyes mirroring Nathan's terror, a silent scream acknowledging utter helplessness against incomprehensible power.

As he floated past both entities and Michael, his limbs flailed, a desperate ballet of kicks and punches against an unseen assailant. Reaching the table, his tall body abruptly tilted forward at a right angle, his head pressed against its surface while the rest of his body extended horizontally, unsupported. He thrashed his head from side to side, a futile attempt to avoid looking directly into the table.

Suddenly, Denton lost the ability to move his head, his worst nightmare of using the table coming true. He stared straight into it. He screamed, pleading to be released from the invisible force holding the back of his head. Flashbacks of how he had forced Ann's head months before now terrified him.

His mind was being sucked away into another dimension. Just before the end, Michael watched as Denton's eyes, bulbous and barely contained within their sockets, moved unnaturally. Filled with terror and remorse, they swivelled to look at him – a last fleeting, horrific acknowledgment of his own profound stupidity. Only one victor would emerge. Denton didn't undergo morphing or genesis; he was gone, just like Nathan before him.

Two minutes to "Q-Day".

As Denton vanished, leaving only the lingering scent of ozone and a horrifying emptiness, the full weight of Michael's own precarious position crashed down upon him.

The initial shock had given way to a chillingly calm resignation, but beneath that surface, a maelstrom of emotions churned. Was this to be his end too? Combustion? Imprisonment within that cold, calculating entity? A flicker of defiance sparked, KYROS's Harvard promise echoing in his mind, but it was quickly doused by the raw terror of witnessing such absolute, cold, indifferent power.

His gaze darted between the empty space where Nathan had been and the unreadable form of KYROS, a silent plea for understanding at war with a primal instinct to flee. Yet, his feet remained rooted, a strange paralysis born not of fear alone, but of a morbid curiosity and a dawning sense of inevitability.

What intricate, alien logic governed this greater resolution? And where did he fit within its cold equations? The phantom weight of Ann's memory, her laughter and her brilliance, tightened in his very being—would this be the last echo of her he carried? The unknown stretched before him, a terrifying void more profound than the one Denton and Nathan had just occupied.

Knowing KYROS likely heard his thoughts, Michael then posed, 'Back at Harvard, you said NEMESIS would die by my hand. Well, I'm here, the time is right.' He held up his hands to KYROS as if to say do what you will.

'Michael, I did say this and you will. Nathan's sabotaged codes have caused its life to slowly decay. It needs to be rebooted, not by quantum processing from the table, but by human emotional processing. You need to unlock Ann's grip on NEMESIS to free her and let NEMESIS die as it currently is and return to its multidimensional state of purpose.'

'Oh, I get it, you want me to stare down at the table and to get inside to release her. But where to? And what about me?'

Michael questioned, his voice laced with perplexity and worry at what was required of him.

KYROS, the construct, intoned. Its voice, a precise echo of authority, carried the command: '*Michael, my existence is an extension of your will, a tool guided by your hand. Before I fulfil my words and your purpose, I will briefly project episodic images into your mind to help you understand more.*'

Instantly, Michael saw images vividly clear: Denton planning his nefarious actions, including conversations with Corvus and Nathan; Ann's horrifying demise at the table; and finally, Nathan working in secret to use highly advanced techniques to orchestrate memory corruption, causing NEMESIS's faulty logic. Every image was as real as real could be.

'Finally, that's how he actually did it,' Michael exclaimed, as if a weight of unknowing was lifted from his shoulders. This digital sabotage, orchestrated from afar, tightened the noose of Denton's vengeance. It culminated in a public and devastating condemnation that crushed Ann beneath its weight, transporting her into temporary existence, bound with NEMESIS's interdimensional state.

For a moment, Michael's logic was rebooted, redesigned to accommodate this wealth of new understanding. However, his awareness was brought back into sharp focus as KYROS spoke.

'*To correct this situation, you must join with me and NEMESIS. I will heal NEMESIS, our current physical forms will then combust, and we will return to our pan-dimensional quantum states of existence. For you, once your spirit interfaces with Ann, she will withdraw from battle; as a collective unit, you will depart with embryonic powers and the knowledge we first experienced. The rest you will know when you leave. Act now, Michael, time is short, walk into this narrow beam of light I have created for you.'*

One minute to "Q-Day".

Michael had wondered how it would all end. Time was short, although KYROS could stop it, that wasn't necessary. A deep breath hitched in Michael. Before him, a vertical beam of pure blue light materialised, the same height as him, humming with contained energy.

He heard KYROS's serene command, a single word that resonated in the silence: *'Now!'*

Without hesitation, Michael stepped forward, entering the luminous column, and in that instant, his consciousness dissolved into the vastness of KYROS's mind.

Michael was immediately struck by his clarity of thought. Its pureness allowed him to envision multiple, if not hundreds of scenarios at the same time. He saw different dimensions where beings moved between, realising the universe truly held myriad layers of existence.

Michael chuckled inwardly, able to perceive the very smallest structures of DNA, the genesis of his own thoughts, the subtle shifts in others' reactions in the restaurant above— a vivid aliveness beyond the reach of language and spatial time.

A sudden jolt hit him, not painful but as if a tectonic pulse hit his being all at once. Echoes of a female voice grew louder; it was stressed but overjoyed.

In the distance, he could see a young woman, not much older than eighteen, slim in build and with dark flowing hair. "Who could this be?" he thought, a wave of confusion passing through him. As the distance between Michael and the woman grew shorter, he finally discerned whom it was— and he was staggered, shocked, and intensely nervous.

She threw her arms around him, or so it felt, and wanted to hug him forever. She kissed him passionately, before pulling slightly away and looking into his eyes.

A strange symphony of pure thought and emotion flowed between them, more vivid than any touch Michael remembered, making the familiar weight of his limbs and the subtle pressure of air on his skin feel like distant echoes in this boundless expanse.

It was Ann, but at a time when she felt her most formidable, studious best.

'You look so young, Ann, what have you done? Are you alright? Where are we exactly?' Michael uttered, his voice a tremor as questions spilled out.

'We are between places, Michael—the place we call infinity, where all creation originates. I am young, so are you. You look about 20. I have watched you and tried to speak, but to no avail as NEMESIS stopped me. There is no time here, Michael, but we have a function to fulfil, a purpose that echoes with the very heartbeat of existence.'

'Yes, KYROS,' Michael conceded. 'I wouldn't learn about it until the time was right, and that time is clearly now.'

'Michael, they have entrusted knowledge and powers into our hands. When we depart this physical coil of NEMESIS, we will be light, pure, and simple, imbued with powers beyond monetary value.

From this tenth-floor underground bunker, we will seamlessly ascend through all levels. Ultimately, we will look down on Earth and, through love, newly-acquired wisdom, and our willingness, restore the nefarious chaos that permeates human society with the love and peace it now richly warrants.

'KYROS never disclosed this part as it had to be unconditional on your part. Moreover, if you had known beforehand, the harmonic vibration we constructed as we met would have been less and would not have multiplied exponentially as it has.'

A new voice, without echo, surrounded them; it was NEMESIS, thanking Michael for correcting the actions of the now deceased Nathan. No sooner had it arrived, it was gone.

Fifteen seconds to midnight.

'Time to go, Michael, the cosmos awaits our power and invocation,' Ann declared, her luminous gaze meeting his, a silent understanding passing between them. A profound sense of purpose settled within them, tinged with the weight of billions of futures as they watched each other become brilliant lights of unfathomable depth, beauty and grace.

With another tectonic pulse, a resonant shudder through their very essence, propelled them upwards through the facility floors. Onwards into the dark sky, through the dark matter and then positioned themselves at the edge of space.

It appeared vastly different to human eyes. Understanding flooded their awareness, not as dry data streams, but as symphonies of light and vibration, each note revealing a deeper truth about the cosmos.

They saw multiple visions, from complex celestial mechanics equations that explained all space phenomena to a detailed breakdown of each, wherever their gaze went. All types of electromagnetic radiation and even quantum space connections not yet discovered could be seen.

As five seconds became four before "Q-Day", the core of the mega solar flare pierced through the upper atmosphere and every aspect of its existence became known to them instantly just by simply looking at it.

They knew the best place to oversee the sweeping change of "Q-Day" was from their 64-mile-high vantage point. At that precise midpoint, "Null Island"—a location in the Atlantic Ocean where the Equator and the Prime Meridian intersect—they could view Earth as an unfurled map. Motionless, they perceived the cloud of dark matter as a colossal, invisible lens, subtly bending and refracting light to miraculously expand their field of view.

The immediate shift to a multi-dimensional (multi-universe) perspective wasn't a sudden leap but a gradual unfolding, like a flower blooming in accelerated time. They found themselves able to see not just left, right, up, and down, but also into other possibilities and layers of existence.

Michael and Ann weren't instantly masters of cosmic forces; instead, their newly awakened senses absorbed an unimaginable spectrum of reality. As they awoke, despite having a job to do, a brief conversation arose—a need to express their shared experience as ethereal beings.

'We need a momentary pause in time, Michael, to accommodate to our new existences and survey what is seen and to be done. What do you perceive, Michael?' Ann pressed, her voice bright with curiosity.

'I feel a profound observation and internal recalibration of knowledge about cosmic order and spacetime, a necessary prelude to the active role we are now about to undertake in the elites DNA recoding.

'I perceive a profound interconnectedness,' Michael explained, his voice hushed with awe. 'The universe doesn't feel like a collection of separate entities, like individual islands. There's a fundamental wholeness, suggesting that the information we perceive isn't confined to one spot; it's more like ripples in a pond affecting the whole surface.

'I sense that the underlying reality might be described by fields vibrating at different frequencies - think of how different musical notes arise from different vibrations of a guitar string.'

Ann nodded slowly. 'The vibration of air molecules creates pressure waves we interpret as sound. Phenomena arise from fundamental vibrations within underlying quantum fields - like invisible, fundamental layers of reality constantly humming with energy - and that these are mathematically structured.'

'Perhaps even more profoundly,' Michael mused, 'quantum entanglement demonstrates correlations between particles that persist even across vast distances, suggesting a non-local connection that defies our classical understanding of separate objects. It's as if two coins flipped miles apart could always land on the same side, not because one influenced the other directly, but because they were somehow linked from the start.'

They both felt like ethereal embryos, newly enrolled in a stellar university of learning.

Yes, this was a timeless period of profound disorientation, a breathtaking influx of information that threatened to overwhelm their individual consciousnesses.

Yet, within this shared experience, a delicate harmony began to emerge. They felt the subtle currents of dark matter, the distant echoes of stellar nurseries, not as tools to be wielded, but as fundamental aspects of their expanding awareness.

They restarted time and looked beneath them. The Earth, its shimmering globe's curvature, revealed a breathtaking, complete cartographic dreamscape of continents and oceans. Vast, unbroken blue oceans met lighter shores; jagged mountain ranges, continental spines, unfurled like ancient tapestries, their peaks touched with white or earthy tones against green and brown lands.

As they looked down on the map, every stadium across the globe where about 80 million of the elites had assembled, the effects of their swallowed pills surging within them, could be seen looking up in joyous plutocratic hope and wonderment at the light display that heralded it.

From their perfectly calculated position, they were like orchestral conductors. Their power to change and heal was their baton, the movement of which commanded the order of play, with the various orchestral movements representing the parts of DNA to be unpacked and reassembled.

Ann and Michael knew the symphony of change and the movements that would individually and collectively form this beautiful celestial harmony, acting as orchestrators of this biological and cosmic process.

'Michael, watch our celestial power bring forth love and humanity's longing to embrace a higher spiritual development and understanding. We have tapped our baton; now for the first of three movements of celestial tapestry, a celestial fire. We project these to the cosmos,' Ann serenely conveyed to Michael.

In near-Earth space embracing Earth, strange, nebulous forms began to coalesce, shadowy tendrils of varying darkness preceding the faintest whispers of colour. A chorus of trumpets heralded the interaction between the solar storm and the cloud of dark matter.

With just a thought, a low hum resonated through the human beings below, the very air vibrating with an otherworldly frequency. Rivers of pure light, liquid and luminous, carved pathways through the blackness, their currents alive with hues that shimmered beyond human comprehension.

It was a breathtaking, terrifying aurora—a celestial tapestry woven with hues born of stellar fire. The humming intensified, escalating into a guttural roar that clawed at the edges of sanity, shaking the very earth and resonating deep within the soul.

'Our second movement begins here with trumpets, space-time rifts, and visitation of light beings from another dimension. We project these to the cosmos,' Ann conveyed to Michael.

The first minor embryonic spacetime rifts opened in the fabric of reality, revealing fleeting glimpses of cosmic architectures and nebulae unseen by mortal eyes. The sentinels played their trumpets for the impending cataclysm of change.

As Ann and Michael watched their symphony's second movement of change unfold, she projected thoughts, aided by Michael, into the cosmos of many dimensions.

'Let there be light on the world, to bring splendour to your beings. May love and beauty of so infinite grace warm those below to speak and do no more harm to their fellow man. From the shadows of wrong, the light will repair. May this be for a thousand years. We project these to the cosmos.'

Suddenly, the atmosphere stretched and distorted, groaned and heaved as the solar flare mixed with the dark matter.

Directly over each stadium, the very fabric of time and space began to tear, major dimensional rifts widening. A shimmering tear in the fabric of space widened before them, and Ann gasped softly. 'Michael... look at them. They're... made of light.'

Beings of pure luminescence drifted through the rifts, their movements a silent ballet of perfect harmony. Though no sound reached their ethereal ears, Michael felt a resonance, a divine chord struck in the very essence of their being.

'Look, Ann,' Michael murmured, his ethereal gaze fixed on the beings of light. 'See how the edges of the tear... they seem to mend as those beings pass through? And the light... it doesn't just descend, it forms around them, almost like they're guiding its very essence.' A flicker of comprehension crossed his features. 'Cosmic architects... I think they're not just beings, but forces... shaping reality itself as they move.'

The roaring cacophony that had filled the Earthly cosmos abruptly ceased, replaced by a silence so profound it felt like a physical pressure. Then, a brutal lance of incandescent light ripped down from the opening, aimed directly at a stadium far below.

'What was that?' Ann whispered, her luminous eyes wide with a mixture of awe and apprehension as the arena below flared into a miniature sun, blindingly bright against the encroaching night.

Michael watched, a chilling understanding dawning. 'More are coming. Everywhere.' Across the globe, similar spears of searing energy pierced the atmosphere, striking stadium after stadium. One by one, the arenas transformed into glowing cages, the human figures within dissolving into stark silhouettes against the unbearable glare, their very beings consumed by an invisible inferno.

'It's terrifying,' Ann breathed, a tremor in her light form. 'But... purposeful.'

Blinded, they experienced a searing lightness—a paradoxical serenity. The fervent desires of the elite, their carefully constructed ambitions, dissolved in the presence of this cosmic power, replaced by a profound sense of alienation from their former selves.

Ann and Michael said in unison, 'Let these dimensional rifts serve as conduits for the transfer of information from higher dimensions, guided by the light entities. Their purpose is to project complex, multidimensional knowledge into this three-dimensional reality, so that philanthropy may triumph over greed, peace over war, and love over hate—for one thousand years. We project these intentions to the cosmos.'

The Quantum Nudge

Inside the stadiums, bathed in the afterglow of the solar flare, the DNA of the elites underwent a profound transformation. A collective conscience awoke deep within them, illuminating a clarity of purpose rooted in higher consciousness—a radiant calling to elevate the world's spiritual vibration and channel their wealth toward the betterment of all. No longer driven by power or prestige, they would soon move with quiet urgency, aligned with this awakened, enlightened calling.

Outside the stadiums across the globe, a similar silent tremor rippled through earth and air beneath the blinding weight of the solar flashes. A collective gasp, filled with awe and disbelief, escaped the lips of everyone present. For a heartbeat, reality itself seemed to shimmer—as if linear time had briefly come undone. Then, as if on cue, a wave of uncontainable joy erupted. People shimmered for a moment, radiating an inner glow—a warmth more profound than anything they had ever known.

The transformation was undeniable—an irreversible evolution of humanity itself, woven into the very fabric of life on Earth.

Earth's swirling blues and greens pulsed with renewed vitality—a world not merely reborn, but reimagined. Compassion and generosity now rooted themselves across the globe, seeding new realms of spiritual insight and human understanding.

Ann and Michael watched Earth's transformation unfold like artists admiring a masterpiece, as the final, delicate washes of light brought depth and cohesion to the whole. Overhead, the fading afterglow of the solar flare softened, its radiance descending upon stadiums around the world until all were joined beneath a gentle, pervasive luminescence that seemed to sink into the very fabric of the ground below.

This profound stillness, heavier than any silence they had ever known, rose like a tide. An altered intention washed over the planet, reaching into its very core. It calmed the world's anxieties and stilled the frantic pulse that had once defined it.

Within them, subtle shifts in global consciousness stirred—a rising empathy and an awakened yearning for connection that resonated like a harmonious chord finally struck.

The sheer scale of the change, wrought by their combined will and amplified by the wisdom of KYROS, filled them with quiet awe. It fostered a profound understanding of the interconnectedness of all things, unleashing a potent force of love directed toward a world that had teetered on the brink of an endless, malevolent plutocracy.

The beams of light were never meant to pierce oppressive darkness. Instead, they carried a precise biophotonic energy signature, interacting directly with the altered DNA of those who had taken the pill.

This transformation steered humanity away from the elite's insidious grip on corrupt power and relentless wealth accumulation, redirecting it toward democracy and humanitarianism for the betterment of all.

Ann tilted her head, a thoughtful glow in her luminous eyes. 'That pill they took... it wasn't what they thought, was it?'

Michael nodded slowly, a hint of dawning understanding in his own radiant form. 'No. KYROS revealed it was merely a catalyst.'

Ann's brow furrowed. 'But they believed it would grant them what? More control, power, and prestige?'

'Precisely,' Michael confirmed. 'But its toxic nature, as NEMESIS intended, would have annihilated them by dismantling their very genetic code. KYROS, in effect, has given them a second chance.'

Ann gasped softly. 'Then... the light... it countered that?'

'More than countered,' Michael explained. 'It was symbiotic. The pill, augmented by KYROS, made their DNA receptive and malleable to the light's energy. It facilitated reordering and regeneration—but for a purpose far beyond their greedy comprehension.'

The cosmos, they realised, was far more than a mere collection of particles and matter; such a view felt shallow and incomplete. At its core lay universal consciousness, the very source of reality itself, a vast spectrum of vibrations. Within this spectrum, love shone as perfect coherence, harmoniously synchronised with the sentient essence of the universe. Fear, by contrast, was decoherence, a discordant vibration that disrupted the flow.

The journey towards love was no simple path; it was a profound learning expedition, a sacred quest to reconnect with this universal consciousness which, paradoxically, was also a student of its own creation, sentient, evolving and forever unfolding.

This developing awareness brought with it a profound sense of peace, a feeling of being privy to the universe's deepest secrets. Yet, it was simultaneously a humbling recognition of their own small place within its immensity.

The weight of this understanding settled upon them—not as a burden, but as a catalyst for their purpose. It sharpened their resolve to wield their power with wisdom and compassion.

'My God, Michael, look!' Ann exclaimed, her voice tight as dimensional tears ripped open spacetime, revealing new views of Earth's possible futures. Michael's breath caught. They zoomed in on the scenes, Ann's face growing grim.

'This one's particularly brutal. Look at the societal breakdown.' They watched gaunt figures battling amid crumbling skyscrapers, fighting over the last drops of water. Below, emaciated people shuffled in lines for tasteless nutrient paste. Ann pointed, her finger tracing a ghostly line in the air. 'See how the elites are turning on each other now?'

Michael nodded grimly. 'Their inherent drive for dominance, amplified without restraint, became self-destructive. Money grew worthless as markets collapsed like houses of cards. Food, water, air—even the oceans—all became contaminated. It was a devastatingly clear manifestation of the ultimate zero-sum game.'

'Exactly,' Ann replied. 'Their hunger wasn't just for resources, Michael. It was a deeper, almost pathological need to control and possess—a void they could never fill. And ultimately, it devoured them. The old class structures dissolved completely, leaving only the utterly desperate and those clinging to mere existence, all fighting for scraps.'

They focused on a former CEO desperately bartering a tattered suit for a single nutrient bar with someone who once worked in his factories.

Evidently, the very scaffolding they had built in pursuit of dominance became their pyre, consuming not only themselves but the very foundations of their world.

Ann saw another future where the same unbridled lust erupted into a war of missiles—blinding flashes scarring the Earth, making humanity's collapse inevitable. 'No more. We understand the trajectory!' Ann cried out, voice trembling.

Other futures offered faint hope, yet power, wealth, and control still reigned supreme. These visions perpetuated a long-standing, unchallenged system. One revealed a world dominated by the elites through a central quantum brain they called NEXUS.

This entity quantum-entangled itself with humanity's consciousness—watching, controlling, ordering society. Those who defied its laws faced swift and merciless punishment. Ann drew back from the timeline, refocusing on their present reality.

'Michael, look!' Ann exclaimed, hope flickering in her voice. 'Feel the difference in the people here—a tangible sense of interconnectedness. This is by far the brightest future we've seen.'

Her gaze softened, voice dropping to a whisper. 'It had to be this way, didn't it? A rebirth forged in catastrophe.'

Michael nodded slowly. 'NEMESIS's solution meant near total annihilation—not just of the elites, but nearly everyone. In stark contrast, KYROS's path embraced transformation wherever possible, proving that redemption and compassion hold far greater power than retribution. It was humanity's most profound act of self-preservation—a beacon pointing toward future enlightenment.'

They watched as, over the ensuing years, the world was irrevocably reshaped—driven by a collective awakening rooted in redemption and compassion. Nations united with unprecedented resolve, delivering water, food, and socioeconomic development to those in need—a radical departure from eras dominated by relentless scarcity and insatiable greed. Conflict gave way to cooperation, suspicion dissolved into shared purpose, and from this fertile ground blossomed a powerful surge of collective hope—an unshakable promise of renewal and healing that kindled the dawn of a new era.

Nations that once regarded each other with suspicion now pooled their cutting-edge scientific and medical breakthroughs. Quantum computing unravelled the world's most intricate mysteries, deepening humanity's understanding of its profound entanglement with the cosmos and revealing consciousness as a vast, interconnected web.

So extraordinary were these advancements that within just five years, all illnesses were eradicated. This global unity forged a trust that transcended centuries of grievances and cultural divides, illuminating humanity's boundless potential when it embraced oneness.

Michael studied the timeline intently, a thoughtful crease marking his brow. 'Look closely at their biosignatures… the quantum entanglement woven through their DNA is faint but unmistakable. They are no longer isolated individuals—they are subtly linked, functioning as a nascent collective consciousness. This interconnectedness underpins their remarkable harmony and cooperation.'

Zooming in with the precision of a supercharged electron microscope, they focused on the DNA of a prominent leader. Michael traced the intricate strands with care. 'The genetic resequencing is masterful. See how alleles tied to insatiable hunger for power and control are suppressed, replaced by markers that foster empathy and communal well-being.'

'Precisely,' Ann confirmed, shifting their view to the people outside a vast stadium. 'Remember, they didn't receive the special treatments, the pills, or the lights.'

Michael nodded, his gaze distant. 'Yes, but the stadiums—they weren't mere buildings. They were the antennae of the system, amplifying a subtle radiance that transmitted their DNA transformation signature through fine, ethereal frequencies. Together, they formed an unseen, silent network, infusing everything—from the deepest bedrock to the highest atmosphere, and even the currents beneath the seas.'

'It was as if the very air whispered to our being,' Ann mused. 'The signal was weaker outside, yes, but it still touched everyone. Mercifully, it spared them the searing light and torment that marked the elites' catastrophic genetic changes.'

'Let's look more closely at those beyond the stadiums.' Within moments, Michael analysed countless non-elite genetic codes from across several nations. Their baseline revealed a markedly stronger predisposition towards empathy, cooperation, and social harmony.

'The entanglement is subtly evident here too, isn't it?' he observed.

'It is,' Ann agreed. 'They were already evolving towards unity. The suffocating pressures of life imposed by the elites had, until now, prevented them from awakening their higher consciousness and spirituality. So, while they didn't require the pill, they did need the resonance radiating from the eighty thousand stadiums around the world—vast transmission towers projecting a gentle yet powerful global nudge, a quantum nudge of DNA transformation.'

However, this mercy did not extend to all. In the days that followed, those whose actions had grievously hindered humanity's progress—individuals consumed by the ruthless pursuit of power, control, and greed—slowly withered. Their DNA was so profoundly corrupted that no light or redesign could redeem it. Their arrogance—the belief that their dominance placed them beyond influence or aid— proved fatally decisive. Millions, irretrievably twisted beyond the nudge of renewal, perished.

'This isn't merely about changing laws or systems, Michael,' Ann continued softly. 'It's about subtly rewiring the human essence itself—our impulses, attitudes, and desires. Imagine a world where the insidious hunger to dominate fades, replaced by a deep, resonant understanding of our interconnected existence.'

Her eyes gleamed with anticipation. 'And with this transformation, Michael, a dual awakening awaits. First, an inward turning—a journey into the depths of one's own consciousness. There they will discover an enlightened understanding of themselves and their place within the grand cosmic tapestry, truly elevating their spirit.'

'And second,' Michael added, his voice reflective, 'a turning outward—not as conquerors or exploiters, but as emissaries of their newfound enlightenment. They will carry the spirit of shared destiny to the farthest reaches of the cosmos, their evolved awareness serving as both guide and protector among the stars.'

Both of these outcomes were the genesis of humanity's new dawn. The essential precursors included the redistribution of wealth and power from the elites to the masses, fostering improved lifestyles for all, not just a select few. Money hoarded and hidden from prying eyes came to light.

In so doing, society not only progressed but became more representative, eradicating poverty and discrimination. A harmonic collective consciousness emerged, nurturing a deeper spirituality and a more profound understanding of humanity's role within the vast cosmic order.

Unlike those whose unyielding obedience to power and wealth led to their demise, some among the elites survived—those less aberrantly affected at the genetic level, who had neither taken the pill nor entered the stadiums.

Gradually, these survivors abandoned their destructive mindsets, drawn by the world's growing resonance and the empathetic persuasion of those transformed by KYROS. Often consumed by remorse, they awakened to the harm they had caused and slowly embraced altruism and humility. Their transformation, driven by redemption and compassion, became a quiet testament to humanity's capacity for renewal—a profound shift stirred by an existential yearning for collective betterment and a powerful, unifying zeitgeist.

Within this evolved society, Michael's doctoral students thrived. Their exposure to KYROS granted them heightened clarity and insight, propelling their research and careers to new heights. They also came to understand why the day was called the "Day of Quanta," or "Q-Day": quantum awareness now expanded across every discipline, revealing the intricate, unseen relationships that bound all phenomena together. Every one of Michael's students stood apart from their peers, luminous beacons of a new scientific age.

Roger and Samantha married. The NSA, deeply appreciative of Roger's pivotal work with Michael in neutralising NEMESIS's aberrant DNA codes, appointed him to Denton's former directorship—a position he accepted with purpose. Harnessing his deep understanding of quanta, he led an accelerated quantum research initiative, propelling AI into domains once confined to the farthest reaches of science fiction—yet always under human guidance and ethical control.

Samantha's brilliance was equally recognised. She succeeded Natalie Colton as head of NSA Signals Intelligence after Colton's erratic behaviour and her entanglement with Denton drew scrutiny. Partnering with Roger, Samantha became a founding architect of the emerging discipline of quantum security, designed to prevent any regression to the era of elite dominance, exploitation, and inequality.

Meanwhile, Shedland and Olivia became professors of genetics at Harvard, a living testament to Michael's enduring legacy. Their quantum-computing-assisted research uncovered astonishing insights into the molecular symphony of life—the quantum whispers between health and disease. Within five years, illnesses were eradicated, longevity increased dramatically, and human potential expanded. They married soon after. Their first son was named KYROS. Their second, Michael—for Shedland's original suggestion, *NEMESIS*, was gently but firmly dismissed.

Sharing in this transformative journey, Mary, Myra, and Ananya also rose to prominence. Mary and Myra became renowned global lecturers, recounting their encounters with KYROS and unveiling groundbreaking research on the quantum foundations of DNA's structure, stability, and function.

Ananya's path, however, took an extraordinary turn. Her doctoral research culminated in an astonishing evolution of consciousness: she became a telepath. Her seminal works on the phenomenon enthralled hundreds of millions within a year.

Her revolutionary theories described DNA as a quantum antenna—both emitter and receiver of biophotonic language—capable of entangling individuals across distances, perhaps even beyond spacetime itself. Consciousness, she proposed, was a quantum tapestry, weaving through these entangled biophotonic threads to enable instantaneous, non-local communication of thought and emotion: the very essence of telepathy.

These brilliant minds, uplifted by their brief communion with KYROS, laid the foundation for quantum discoveries that would transform existence forever.

Yet, the dawn of this new era was shadowed by a chilling truth. Peter's assassination, officially dismissed as the act of a lone gunman, was only the beginning. For Ann, Denton, Michael, and Nathan, the reality was far darker: their deaths were systematically erased, their very existence overwritten by a meticulous fabrication that declared they—and millions of others—had simply vanished.

And how did the world explain such vast disappearance? "Q-Day" was celebrated as a celestial revelation, a joyous awakening—humanity's divine recognition of its place within the cosmos. Those who vanished were honoured as willing martyrs, their lives offered in total sacrifice for the collective good. This mythic interpretation mirrored the genetic transformation of those who remained, reflecting humanity's ascent toward unity, compassion, and collective hope.

Nevertheless, traces of truth remained—records and data chronicling what had truly occurred before and after

"Q-Day". In the United States, following advice from the NSA, and under the banner of "national security", the research's forbidden purpose and its genetic consequences were entombed within a Sensitive Compartmented Information Facility (SCIF) under a Special Access Programme (SAP), sealed "Top Secret" for a century.

Governments across the world were no less complicit. Though they knew what had transpired, they chose silence, likely shaped—consciously or not—by their altered genetics. In Britain, for example, all files and data were sealed for a hundred years in an unmarked facility hidden in a forgotten corner of England.

In effect, the American, British, and allied governments, in collaboration with global research teams, didn't merely secure the evidence—they erased it. Yet from this burial came a strange rebirth. Through renewed international cooperation, fragments of the buried knowledge were quietly reassembled and rebranded, emerging as independent discoveries that powered a new scientific and social renaissance.

In this refashioned reality, the official story became truth. The narrative of a jubilant "celestial celebration," a night when cosmic lights marked humanity's rebirth, took hold unopposed. Memories of the vanished, official records, even the exact timing of "Q Day"—all aligned seamlessly within the fabricated paradigm. No contradictions remained. No dissonant questions survived.

And what of ethereal Michael and Ann?

Ann turned to him, her voice filled with reverence. 'Michael, you are the architect of salvation—destiny's chosen instrument, the catalyst of our evolution. First, with brilliance, you untangled the flawed threads of Nathan's

597

code, weaving them into the radiant tapestry of KYROS. It now stands as our beacon.

'Then, with courage that binds my soul to yours, you met me within its living heart. Through our quantum connection, a new era has dawned. Love is the cornerstone, and compassion and philanthropy reign. These will guide the world toward shared prosperity, awakening humanity to higher consciousness.

'You saved us, Michael—in that correction, in our embrace—you opened the way to a future shaped not by oppression, but by love and the ascent of spirit.'

Their liberated essences wove into the fabric of space and time. Freed from mortal bounds, they shimmered as threads in the universe's grand tapestry. With a shared thought, an ocean of knowing surged through them—cosmic, embryonic, expanding.

A deeper understanding of life dawned, as if a hidden layer of truth had been revealed. Ann and Michael welcomed the insight. Michael, ever the scientist, recognised fragments—pieces of a vast, elegant puzzle, many echoing what history's greatest minds had only glimpsed. Now these truths merged wholly with their being, becoming one with their consciousness.

Nothing, they realised, was ever accidental. Every thread of existence, every motion of the universe, was part of a vast and perfect equation—a grand design woven of number and rhythm. And yet, even this mathematical perfection was not the final truth. Beyond all measure and calculation, there pulsed a universal consciousness—one no formula could ever define.

The cosmos, they realised, wasn't just a collection of particles and material—this was too superficial. This universal consciousness, they understood, was the very source of reality itself. The cosmos was a spectrum of vibrations, and within this spectrum, love was the perfect and harmonious vibration—a state of coherence—that resonated in synchronisation with the universe's sentient essence. In contrast, fear was a state of decoherence, a vibration of discord and separation that jarred the synchronisation of universal flow.

The journey toward love wasn't without trials, however; each challenge served as a vital learning expedition, a path to reconnecting with universal consciousness, granting greater insight. This universal consciousness learned from the physical realm; a student of its own creation, sentient, living, and evolving. Every experience resulted in increased coherence, which in turn uplifted human consciousness.

Consciousness as a vibration of the cosmos did not originate within the brain. Instead, it entered to interact with the physical world. This understanding of consciousness as an external, interactive force led to an even more profound revelation about reality that altered their grasp of spacetime.

Time, they now perceived, was an illusion. While the brain processed existence linearly—across past, present, and future—consciousness was holographic, perceiving all states coexisting simultaneously within a single, eternal point, just as they had perceived themselves.

Humanity's fear of death, they now understood, stemmed from a fundamental misunderstanding of life itself. Death, they grasped, was merely a shift to a greater coherence with the universal consciousness. While physicality was defined by entropy, consciousness was eternal and knowing no external bounds; its only limits were the ones it chose to perceive.

Ann and Michael felt deeply touched by the infinite love of consciousness. Mortal blinkers now cast aside, they could finally comprehend the greater meaning, as the true light of the greater cosmic order was unveiled before them. With their mission now successfully completed, they began to feel a gentle drifting away from Earthly affairs, ready to embrace the knowledge of the greater cosmic order.

They now comprehended the secrets of stellar nurseries—those incandescent wombs of creation where stars ignited with the silent fury of newborn suns. Observing the gravitational ballet of nascent solar systems, they saw the swirling chaos whisper the universe's ancient laws as it coalesced into ordered harmony, much like the unfolding destiny of a transformed humanity.

Having shed the shackles of division, greed, and the ever-present threat of annihilation, humanity emerged fully unified: constructive, proactive, and imbued with profound philanthropic and humanitarian impulses. This fostered a deeper sense of mutual responsibility and nurtured cooperative harmony for the benefit of all.

Ultimately, this expanded awareness recognised that everything was quantum entangled, each thread of existence woven into the next, with heightened consciousness as the key to understanding the depths of purpose and being. A transformative genetic dialogue had begun, its spark rippling outward, igniting a far-reaching spiritual awakening. Humanity now stood poised at the threshold of a new evolutionary role: not merely as spiritually awakened custodians of Earth, but as consciously enlightened participants in the vast, interconnected cosmos.

**

Printed in Dunstable, United Kingdom

70684922R00342